Paddington
Treasury

Paddington Treasury

MICHAEL BOND

With illustrations by **Peggy Fortnum**
Hand-colored by Caroline Nuttall-Smith

HOUGHTON MIFFLIN COMPANY
BOSTON

Paddington Treasury

to Brenda

Contents

Paddington on the Move

A Bite to Eat

A Special Day Comes Undone

Introduction
by *Michael Bond*

I suppose the two questions writers are most frequently asked about their work are: "Where do you get the idea?" and "How long did it take you to write it?"

In the case of Paddington, the first question is easy. In fact, it has been posed so many times over the years I can hear a kind of glaze come over my voice as I repeat the answer. On the other hand, I suppose the time to worry is when people stop asking!

It was Christmas Eve 1956: cold and wet. I was doing last-minute shopping in London's Oxford Street and having missed a bus, I went inside the Selfridges department store to shelter from the sleet. It was almost closing time, and wandering through the almost deserted toy section, I came across a small bear all alone on a shelf. Acting on impulse, I bought it as a stocking filler for my wife, Brenda, and because we were living near Paddington railway station at the time, that's what we called him.

The following spring, I was sitting at my typewriter one morning staring at a blank sheet of paper, and in order to get my mind working I tapped out the words: "Mr. and Mrs. Brown first met Paddington on a railway platform, which is how he came to have such an unusual name for a bear, because Paddington was the name of the station . . ."

It certainly did the trick, because although I hadn't set out with any intention of writing a children's book, or indeed any kind of book, at the time I was deeply into adult short stories and radio plays, ideas suddenly began to flow, and in the space of a normal working morning I found myself with what turned out to be the first chapter of a book. Ten days later, at the rate of a chapter a day, plus two days for "dotting the i's" and "crossing the t's," I had a book on my hands, or rather my agent did.

Which, I suppose, answers the second question.

Except, of course, it doesn't. In the case of a series, the first book is always the easiest; you go wherever your fancy takes you, the world is your oyster. *But*, and it is a big *but*, you also set parameters for all the ones that follow.

It's like making a cake. If all the right ingredients are assembled in the correct proportions, and if they are mixed together in the right order, then baked for just the right amount of time, the result can be rewarding. Repeating the success, recapturing the freshness of the original, is something else again and can often take much, much longer. In short, how long is one piece of string? One of the truest things ever said is that "Writing is one per cent inspiration, ninety-nine per cent perspiration."

Writing is a lonely occupation, and in the end I suppose all you can do is write to please yourself and hope that others enjoy it too. Most people have a small voice inside which says whether something is right or wrong, and you ignore that at your peril.

Luckily, another factor often takes over. Once your character is firmly established in your mind, things start to happen of their own accord. For example, I never sit down and try to plot out a Paddington story, or indeed with any of my characters. I simply put them in a situation and see what happens. Luckily, in Paddington's case something almost always does; he's that kind of bear. On good days he takes over in unexpected ways and I sometimes find myself laughing out loud. I couldn't resist laughing, for instance, at the self-confidence of a bear who simply, by donning a false beard and dark glasses from a disguise outfit he was given for Christmas, takes it for granted that no one will recognize him and is very upset when they do.

Someone once wrote me saying he was so used to Paddington being the name of a bear he now thought it was a funny name for a railway station. I know just what he means!

So, to answer yet another question. Do I believe in Paddington? Of course I do. If a writer doesn't believe in his own characters, then how can he or she expect others to? But it's very rewarding when they do.

Here, in one bumper book, are some of the best of Paddington's many adventures. I hope you enjoy them.

Part One

In the
Beginning

Chapter 1

Please Look After This Bear

M r. and Mrs. Brown first met Paddington on a railway platform. In fact, that was how he came to have such an unusual name for a bear, for Paddington was the name of the station.

The Browns were there to meet their daughter, Judy, who was coming home from school for the holidays. It was a warm summer day and the station was crowded with people on their way to the seaside. Trains were humming, loudspeakers blaring, porters rushing about shouting at one another, and altogether there was so much noise that Mr. Brown, who saw him first, had to tell his wife several times before she understood.

"A *bear*? On Paddington Station?" Mrs. Brown looked at her husband in amazement. "Don't be silly, Henry. There can't be!"

Mr. Brown adjusted his glasses. "But there is," he insisted. "I distinctly saw it. Over there—near the bicycle rack. It was wearing a funny kind of hat."

Without waiting for a reply, he caught hold of his wife's arm and pushed her through the crowd, round a cart laden with chocolate and cups of tea, past a bookstall, and through a gap in a pile of suitcases towards the Lost Property Office.

"There you are," he announced triumphantly, pointing towards a dark corner. "I told you so!"

Mrs. Brown followed the direction of his arm and dimly made out a small, furry object in the shadows. It seemed to be sitting on some kind of suitcase, and round its neck was a label with some writing on it. The suitcase was old and battered, and on the side, in large letters, were the words WANTED ON VOYAGE.

Mrs. Brown clutched at her husband. "Why, Henry!" she exclaimed. "I believe you were right after all. It *is* a bear!"

She peered at it more closely. It seemed a very unusual kind of bear. It was brown in color, a rather dirty brown, and it was wearing a most odd-looking hat, with a wide brim, just as Mr. Brown had said. From beneath the brim two large round eyes stared back at her.

Seeing that something was expected of it, the bear stood up and politely raised its hat, revealing two black ears. "Good afternoon," it said in a small, clear voice.

"Er . . . good afternoon," replied Mr. Brown doubtfully. There was a moment of silence.

The bear looked at them inquiringly. "Can I help you?"

Mr. Brown looked rather embarrassed. "Well . . . no. Er . . . as a matter of fact, we were wondering if we could help *you*."

Mrs. Brown bent down. "You're a very small bear," she said.

The bear puffed out its chest. "I'm a very rare sort of bear," it replied importantly. "There aren't many of us left where I come from."

"And where is that?" asked Mrs. Brown.

The bear looked round carefully before replying.

"Darkest Peru. I'm not really supposed to be here at all. I'm a stowaway!"

"A stowaway?" Mr. Brown lowered his voice and looked anxiously over his shoulder. He almost expected to see a policeman standing behind him with a notebook and pencil, taking everything down.

"Yes," said the bear. "I emigrated, you know." A sad expression came into its eyes. "I used to live with my Aunt Lucy in Peru, but she had to go into a home for retired bears."

"You don't mean to say you've come all the way from South America by yourself?" exclaimed Mrs. Brown.

The bear nodded. "Aunt Lucy always said she wanted me to emigrate when I was old enough. That's why she taught me to speak English."

"But whatever did you do for food?" asked Mr. Brown. "You must be starving."

Bending down, the bear unlocked the suitcase with a small key, which it also had round its neck, and brought out an almost empty glass jar. "I ate marmalade," it said rather proudly. "Bears like marmalade. And I lived in a lifeboat."

"But what are you going to do now?" said Mr. Brown. "You can't just sit on Paddington Station waiting for something to happen."

"Oh, I shall be all right . . . I expect." The bear bent down to do up its case again. As it did so, Mrs. Brown caught a glimpse of the writing on the label. It said simply, PLEASE LOOK AFTER THIS BEAR. THANK YOU.

She turned appealingly to her husband. "Oh, Henry, what *shall* we do? We can't just leave him here. There's no knowing what might happen to him. London's such a big place when you've nowhere to go. Can't he come and stay with us for a few days?"

Mr. Brown hesitated. "But Mary, dear, we can't take him . . . not just like that. After all . . ."

"After all, *what*?" Mrs. Brown's voice had a firm note to it. She looked down at the bear. "He is rather sweet. And he'd be such company for Jonathan and Judy. Even if it's only for a little while. They'd never forgive you if they knew you'd left him here."

"It all seems highly irregular," said Mr. Brown doubtfully. "I'm sure there's a law about it." He bent down. "Would you like to come and stay with us?" he asked. "That is," he added hastily, not wishing to offend the bear, "if you've nothing else planned."

The bear jumped, and his hat nearly fell off in his excitement. "Oooh, yes, please. I should like that very much. I've nowhere to go, and everyone seems in such a hurry."

"Well, that's settled then," said Mrs. Brown, before her husband could change his mind. "And you can have marmalade for breakfast every morning, and . . ." She tried hard to think of something else that bears might like.

"*Every* morning?" The bear looked as if he could hardly believe his ears. "I only had it on special occasions at home. Marmalade's very expensive in Darkest Peru."

"Then you shall have it every morning, starting tomorrow," continued Mrs. Brown. "And honey on Sunday."

A worried expression came over the bear's face. "Will it cost very much?" he asked. "You see, I haven't very much money."

"Of course not. We wouldn't dream of charging you anything at all. We shall expect you to become one of the family, shan't we, Henry?" Mrs. Brown looked at her husband for support.

"Of course," said Mr. Brown. "By the way," he added, "if you *are* coming home with us, you'd better know our names. This is Mrs. Brown and I'm Mr. Brown."

The bear raised his hat politely—twice. "I haven't really got a name," he said. "Only a Peruvian one which no one can understand."

"Then we'd better give you an English one," said Mrs. Brown. "It'll make things much easier." She looked round the station for inspiration. "It ought to be something special," she said thoughtfully. As she spoke, an engine standing at one of the platforms gave a loud wail and a train began to move. "I know what!" she exclaimed. "We found you on Paddington Station, so we'll call you Paddington!"

"Paddington!" The bear repeated it several times to make sure. "It seems a very long name."

"Quite distinguished," said Mr. Brown. "Yes, I like Paddington as a name. Paddington it shall be."

Mrs. Brown stood up. "Good. Now, Paddington, I have to meet our little daughter, Judy, off the train. She's coming home from school. I'm sure you must be thirsty after your long journey, so you go along to the café with Mr. Brown and he'll buy you a nice cup of tea."

Paddington licked his lips. "I'm *very* thirsty," he said. "Sea-water makes you thirsty." He picked up his suitcase, pulled his hat down firmly over his head, and waved a paw politely in the direction of the café. "After you, Mr. Brown."

"Er . . . thank you, Paddington," said Mr. Brown.

"Now, Henry, look after him," Mrs. Brown called after them. "And for goodness' sake, when you get a moment, take that label off his neck. It makes him look like a parcel. I'm sure he'll get put in a luggage van or something if a porter sees him."

The café was crowded when they entered, but Mr. Brown managed to find a table for two in a corner. By standing on a chair, Paddington could just rest his paws comfortably on the glass top. He looked round with interest while Mr. Brown went to fetch the tea. The sight of everyone eating reminded him of how hungry he felt. There was a half-eaten bun on the table, but just as he reached out his paw a waitress came up and swept it into a pan.

"You don't want that, dearie," she said, giving him a friendly pat. "You don't know where it's been."

Paddington felt so empty he didn't really care where it had been, but he was much too polite to say anything.

"Well, Paddington," said Mr. Brown as he placed two steaming cups of tea and a plate piled high with pastries on the table, "how will that do?"

Paddington's eyes glistened. "It's very nice, thank you," he exclaimed, eyeing the tea doubtfully. "But it's rather hard drinking out of a cup. I usually get my head stuck, or else my hat falls in and makes it taste nasty."

Mr. Brown hesitated. "Then you'd better give your hat to me. I'll pour the tea into a saucer for you. It's not really done in the best circles, but I'm sure no one will mind just this once."

Paddington removed his hat and laid it carefully on the table while Mr. Brown poured out the tea. He looked hungrily at the pastries, in particular at a large cream-and-jam one, which Mr. Brown placed on a plate in front of him.

"There you are, Paddington," he said. "I'm sorry they haven't any marmalade ones, but these were the best I could get."

"I'm glad I emigrated," said Paddington as he reached out a paw and pulled the plate nearer. "Do you think anyone would mind if I stood on the table to eat?"

Before Mr. Brown could answer, he had climbed up and placed his right paw firmly on the bun. It was a very large bun, the biggest and stickiest Mr. Brown had been able to find, and in a matter of moments most of the inside found its way onto

Paddington's whiskers. People started to nudge each other and began staring in their direction. Mr. Brown wished he had chosen a plain, ordinary bun, but he wasn't very experienced in the ways of bears. He stirred his tea and looked out the window, pretending he had tea with a bear on Paddington Station every day of his life.

"Henry!" The sound of his wife's voice brought him back to earth with a start. "Henry, whatever are you doing to that poor bear? Look at him! He's covered all over with cream and jam."

Mr. Brown jumped up in confusion. "He seemed rather hungry," he answered lamely.

Mrs. Brown turned to her daughter. "This is what happens when I leave your father alone for five minutes."

Judy clapped her hands excitedly. "Oh, Daddy, is he really going to stay with us?"

"If he does," said Mrs. Brown, "I can see someone other than your father will have to look after him. Just look at the mess he's in!"

Paddington, who all this time had been too interested in his bun to worry about what was going on, suddenly became aware that people were talking about him. He looked up to see that Mrs. Brown had been joined by a little girl with laughing blue eyes and long fair hair. He jumped up, meaning to raise his hat, and in his haste slipped on a patch of strawberry jam that somehow or other had found its way onto the glass tabletop. For a brief moment he had a dizzy impression of everything and everyone being upside down. He waved his paws wildly in the air, and then, before anyone could catch him, he somersaulted backwards and landed with a splash in his saucer of tea. He jumped up even quicker than he had sat down, because the tea was still very hot, and promptly stepped into Mr. Brown's cup.

Judy threw back her head and laughed until the tears rolled down her face. "Oh, Mummy, isn't he funny!" she cried.

Paddington, who didn't think it at all funny, stood for a moment with one foot on the table and the other in Mr. Brown's tea. There were large patches of white cream all over his face, and on his left ear was a lump of strawberry jam.

"You wouldn't think," said Mrs. Brown, "that anyone could get in such a state with just one bun."

Mr. Brown coughed. He had just caught the stern eye of a waitress on the other side of the counter. "Perhaps," he said, "we'd better go. I'll see if I can find a taxi." He picked up Judy's belongings and hurried outside.

Paddington stepped gingerly off the table and, with a last look at the sticky remains of his bun, climbed down onto the floor.

Judy took one of his paws. "Come along, Paddington. We'll take you home and you can have a nice hot bath. Then you can tell me all about South America. I'm sure you must have had lots of wonderful adventures."

"I have," said Paddington earnestly. "Lots. Things are always happening to me. I'm that sort of bear."

When they came out of the café Mr. Brown had already found a taxi, and he waved them across. The driver looked hard at Paddington and then at the inside of his nice clean taxi.

"Bears is extra," he said gruffly. "Sticky bears is twice as much again!"

"He can't help being sticky, driver," said Mr. Brown. "He's just had a nasty accident."

The driver hesitated. "All right, 'op in. But mind none of it comes off on me interior. I only cleaned it out this morning."

The Browns trooped obediently into the back of the taxi. Mr. and Mrs. Brown and Judy sat in the back, while Paddington stood on a tip-up seat behind the driver so that he could see out of the window.

The sun was shining as they drove out of the station, and after the gloom and the noise everything seemed bright and cheerful. They swept past a group of people at a bus stop and Paddington waved. Several people stared and one man raised his hat in return. It was all very friendly. After weeks of sitting alone in a lifeboat there was so much to see. There were people and cars and big red buses everywhere—it wasn't a bit like Darkest Peru.

Paddington kept one eye on the window so he wouldn't miss anything. With his other eye he carefully examined Mr. and Mrs. Brown and Judy. Mr. Brown was fat and jolly, with a mustache and glasses, while Mrs. Brown, who was also rather plump, looked like a larger edition of Judy. Paddington had just decided he was going to like staying with the Browns when the glass window behind the driver shot back and a gruff voice said, "Where did you say you wanted to go?"

Mr. Brown leaned forward. "Number thirty-two Windsor Gardens."

The driver cupped his ear with one hand. "Can't 'ear you," he shouted.

Paddington tapped him on the shoulder. "Number thirty-two Windsor Gardens," he repeated.

The taxi driver jumped at the sound of Paddington's voice and narrowly missed hitting a bus. He looked down at his shoulder and glared. "Cream!" he said bitterly. "All over me new coat!"

Judy giggled and Mr. and Mrs. Brown exchanged glances. Mr. Brown peered at the meter. He half expected to see a sign go up saying they had to pay another fifty pence.

"I beg your pardon," said Paddington. He bent forward and tried to rub the stain off with his other paw. Several bun crumbs and a smear of jam added themselves mysteriously to the taxi driver's coat. The driver gave Paddington a long, hard look. Paddington raised his hat, and the driver slammed the window shut again.

"Oh dear," said Mrs. Brown. "We really shall have to give him a bath as soon as we get indoors. It's getting everywhere."

Paddington looked thoughtful. It wasn't so much that he didn't like baths; he really didn't mind being covered with jam and cream. It seemed a pity to wash it all off quite so soon. But before he had time to consider the matter the taxi stopped and the Browns began to climb out. Paddington picked up his suitcase and followed Judy up a flight of white steps to a big green door.

"Now you're going to meet Mrs. Bird," said Judy. "She looks after us. She's a bit fierce sometimes and she grumbles a lot, but she doesn't really mean it. I'm sure you'll like her."

Paddington felt his knees begin to tremble. He looked round for Mr. and Mrs.

Brown, but they appeared to be having some sort of argument with the taxi driver. Behind the door he could hear footsteps approaching.

"I'm sure I shall like her, if you say so," he said, catching sight of his reflection on the brightly polished letterbox. "But will she like me?"

Chapter 2

A Bear in Hot Water

Paddington wasn't quite sure what to expect when Mrs. Bird opened the door. He was pleasantly surprised when they were greeted by a stout, motherly lady with gray hair and a kindly twinkle in her eyes. When she saw Judy, she raised her hands above her head. "Goodness gracious, you've arrived already," she said in horror. "And me hardly finished washing up the dishes. I suppose you'll be wanting tea?"

"Hello, Mrs. Bird," said Judy. "It's nice to see you again. How's the rheumatism?"

"Worse than it's ever been," began Mrs. Bird. Then she stopped speaking and stared at Paddington. "Whatever have you got there?" she asked. "What is it?"

"It's not a *what*," said Judy. "It's a bear. His name's Paddington."

Paddington raised his hat.

"A *bear*," said Mrs. Bird doubtfully. "Well, he has good manners, I'll say that for him."

"He's going to stay with us," announced Judy. "He's emigrated from South America and he's all alone with nowhere to go."

"Going to *stay* with us?" Mrs. Bird raised her arms again. "How long for?"

Judy looked round mysteriously before replying. "I don't know," she said. "It depends on *things*."

"Mercy me!" exclaimed Mrs. Bird. "I wish you'd told me. I haven't put clean sheets in the spare room or anything." She looked down at Paddington. "Though judging by the state he's in perhaps that's just as well!"

"It's all right, Mrs. Bird," said Paddington. "I think I'm going to have a bath. I had an accident with a bun."

"Oh!" Mrs. Bird held the door open. "Oh, well in that case you'd best come on in. Only mind the carpet. It's just been done."

Judy took hold of Paddington's paw and squeezed. "She doesn't mind really," she whispered. "I think she rather likes you."

Paddington watched the retreating figure of Mrs. Bird. "She seems a bit fierce," he said.

Mrs. Bird turned. "What was that you said?"

Paddington jumped. "I . . . I . . ." he began.

"Where was it you said you'd come from? Peru?"

"That's right," said Paddington. "Darkest Peru."

"Humph!" Mrs. Bird looked thoughtful for a moment. "Then I expect you like marmalade. I'd better get some more from the grocer."

"There you are! What did I tell you?" cried Judy as the door shut behind Mrs. Bird. "She *does* like you."

"Fancy her knowing I like marmalade," said Paddington.

"Mrs. Bird knows everything about everything," said Judy. "Now, you'd better come upstairs with me and I'll show you your room. It used to be mine when I was small and it has lots of pictures of bears round the wall, so I expect you'll feel at home." She led the way up a long flight of stairs, chattering all the time. Paddington followed closely behind, keeping carefully to the side so that he didn't have to tread on the carpet.

"That's the bathroom," said Judy. "And that's my room. And that's Jonathan's—he's my brother, and you'll meet him soon. And that's Mummy and Daddy's." She opened a door. "And this is going to be yours!"

Paddington nearly fell over with surprise when he followed her into the room. He'd never seen such a big one. There was a large bed with white sheets against one wall and several big boxes, one with a mirror on it. Judy pulled open a drawer in one of the boxes. "This is called a chest of drawers," she said. "You'll be able to keep all your things in here."

Paddington looked at the drawer and then at his suitcase. "I don't seem to have very much. That's the trouble with being small—no one ever expects you to want things."

"Then we shall have to see what we can do," said Judy mysteriously. "I'll try and get Mummy to take you on one of her shopping expeditions." She knelt down beside him. "Let me help you to unpack."

"It's very kind of you." Paddington fumbled with the lock. "But I don't think there's much to help me with. There's a jar of marmalade—only there's hardly any left now and what there is tastes of seaweed. And my scrapbook. And some centavos—they're a sort of South American penny."

"Gosh!" said Judy. "I've never seen any of those before. Aren't they bright!"

"Oh, I keep them polished," said Paddington. "I don't *spend* them." He pulled out a tattered photograph. "And that's a picture of my Aunt Lucy. She had it taken just before she went into the Home for Retired Bears in Lima."

"She looks very nice," said Judy. "And very wise." Seeing that Paddington had a sad, faraway look in his eyes, she added hastily, "Well, I'm going to leave you now, so that you can have your bath and come down nice and clean. You'll find two taps, one marked hot and one marked cold. There's plenty of soap and a clean towel. Oh, and a brush so that you can scrub your back."

"It sounds very complicated," said Paddington. "Can't I just sit in a puddle or something?"

Judy laughed. "Somehow I don't think Mrs. Bird would approve of that! And don't forget to wash your ears. They look awfully black."

"They're meant to be black," Paddington called indignantly as Judy shut the door.

He climbed up onto a stool by the window and looked out. There was a large, interesting garden below, with a small pond and several trees that looked good for climbing. Beyond the trees he could see some more houses stretching away into the distance. He decided it must be wonderful living in a house like this all the time. He stayed where he was, thinking about it, until the window became steamed up and he couldn't see out anymore. Then he tried writing his name on the cloudy part with his paws. He began to wish it wasn't quite so long, as he soon ran out of cloud and it was rather difficult to spell.

"All the same"—he climbed onto the dressing table and looked at himself in the mirror—"it's a very important name. I don't expect there are many bears in the world called Paddington!"

If he'd only known, Judy was saying exactly the same thing to Mr. Brown at that very moment. The Browns were holding a council of war in the dining room, and Mr. Brown was fighting a losing battle. It had been Judy's idea in the first place to keep Paddington. In this she had not only Jonathan on her side but also her mother. Jonathan had yet to meet Paddington, but the idea of having a bear in the family appealed to him. It sounded very important.

"After all, Henry," argued Mrs. Brown, "you can't turn him out now. It wouldn't be right."

Mr. Brown sighed. He knew when he was beaten. It wasn't that he didn't like the idea of keeping Paddington. Secretly he was just as keen as anyone. But as head of the Brown household he felt he ought to consider the matter from every angle.

"I'm sure we ought to report the matter to someone first," he said.

"I don't see why, Dad," cried Jonathan. "Besides, he might get arrested for being a stowaway if we do that."

Mrs. Brown put down her knitting. "Jonathan's right, Henry. We can't let that happen. It's not as if he's done anything wrong. I'm sure he didn't harm anyone traveling in a lifeboat like that."

"Then there's the question of pocket money," said Mr. Brown, weakening. "I'm not sure how much pocket money to give a bear."

"He can have a pound a week, the same as the children," replied Mrs. Brown.

Mr. Brown lit his pipe carefully before replying. "Well," he said, "we'll have to see what Mrs. Bird has to say about it first, of course."

There was a triumphant chorus from the rest of the family.

"You'd better ask her then," said Mrs. Brown when the noise had died down. "It was your idea."

Mr. Brown coughed. He was a little bit afraid of Mrs. Bird, and he wasn't at all sure how she would take it. He was about to suggest they left it for a little while when the door opened and Mrs. Bird came in with the tea things. She paused for a moment and looked round at the sea of expectant faces.

"I suppose," she said, "you want to tell me you've decided to keep that young Paddington."

"May we, Mrs. Bird?" pleaded Judy. "Please! I'm sure he'll be very good."

"Humph!" Mrs. Bird put the tray down on the table. "That remains to be seen. Different people have different ideas about being good. All the same . . ." She hesitated at the door. "He looks the sort of bear that means well."

"Then you don't mind, Mrs. Bird?" Mr. Brown asked her.

Mrs. Bird thought for a moment. "No. No, I don't mind at all. I've always had a soft spot for bears myself. It'll be nice to have one about the house."

"Well," gasped Mrs. Brown as the door closed behind Mrs. Bird. "Whoever would have thought it of her!"

"I expect it was because he raised his hat," said Judy. "It made a good impression. Mrs. Bird likes polite people."

Mrs. Brown picked up her knitting again. "I suppose someone ought to write and tell his Aunt Lucy. I'm sure she'd like to know he's safe." She turned to Judy. "Perhaps it would be a nice thought if you and Jonathan wrote."

"By the way," said Mr. Brown, "come to think of it, where is Paddington? He's not still up in his room, is he?"

Judy looked up from the writing desk, where she was searching for some notepaper. "Oh, he's all right. He's just having a bath."

"A *bath*!" Mrs. Brown's face took on a worried expression. "He's rather small to be having a bath all by himself."

"Don't fuss so, Mary," grumbled Mr. Brown, settling himself down in the armchair with a newspaper. "He's probably having the time of his life."

Mr. Brown was fairly near the truth when he said Paddington was probably having the time of his life. Unfortunately, it wasn't in quite the way he meant it. Blissfully unaware that his fate was being decided, Paddington was sitting in the middle of the bathroom floor drawing a map of South America with a tube of Mr. Brown's shaving cream.

Paddington liked geography. At least, he liked *his* sort of geography, which meant seeing strange places and new people. Before he left South America on his long journey to England, his Aunt Lucy, who was a very wise old bear, had done her best to teach him all she knew. She had told him all about the places he would see on the way and she had spent many long hours reading to him about the people he would meet.

It had been a long journey, halfway round the world, and so Paddington's map occupied most of the bathroom floor and also used up most of Mr. Brown's shaving cream. With the little that was left he tried writing his new name again. He made several attempts and finally decided on PADINGTUN. It looked most important.

It wasn't until a trickle of warm water landed on his nose that he realized the bath was full and was beginning to run over the side. With a sigh he climbed up onto the side of the bath, closed his eyes, held his nose with one paw, and jumped. The water was hot and soapy and much deeper than he had expected. In fact, he

had to stand on tiptoe even to keep his nose above the surface.

It was then that he had a nasty shock. It's one thing getting into a bath. It's quite another matter getting out, especially when the water comes up to your nose and the sides are slippery and your eyes are full of soap. He couldn't even see to turn the taps off.

He tried calling out "Help," first in quite a quiet voice, then very loudly: "HELP! HELP!"

He waited for a few moments, but no one came. Suddenly he had an idea. What a good thing he was still wearing his hat! He took it off and began bailing out the water.

There were several holes in the hat because it was a very old one that had once belonged to his uncle, but if the water didn't get much less, at least it didn't get any more.

"That's funny," said Mr. Brown, jumping up from his armchair and rubbing his forehead. "I could have sworn I felt a spot of water!"

"Don't be silly, dear. How could you?" Mrs. Brown, busy with her knitting, didn't even bother to look up.

Mr. Brown grunted and returned to his newspaper. He knew he had felt something, but there was no point in arguing. He looked suspiciously at the children, but Judy and Jonathan were busy writing their letter.

"How much does it cost to send a letter to Lima?" asked Jonathan.

Judy was about to reply when another drop of water fell down from the ceiling, this time right onto the table.

"Oh, gosh!" She jumped to her feet, pulling Jonathan after her. There was an ominous wet patch right over their heads *and* right underneath the bathroom!

"Where are you going now, dear?" asked Mrs. Brown.

"Oh, just upstairs to see how Paddington's getting on." Judy pushed Jonathan through the door and shut it quickly behind them.

"What's up?" said Jonathan.

"It's Paddington," cried Judy over her shoulder as she rushed up the stairs. "I think he's in trouble!"

She ran along the landing and banged loudly on the bathroom door. "Are you all right, Paddington?" she shouted. "May we come in?"

"HELP! HELP!" shouted Paddington. "Please come in. I think I'm going to drown!"

"Oh, Paddington." Judy leaned over the side of the bath and helped Jonathan lift a dripping and very frightened Paddington onto the floor. "Oh, Paddington! Thank goodness you're all right!"

Paddington lay on his back in a pool of water. "What a good thing I had my hat," he panted. "Aunt Lucy told me never to be without it."

"But why on earth didn't you pull the plug out, you silly?" said Judy.

"Oh!" Paddington looked crestfallen. "I . . . I never thought of that."

Jonathan looked admiringly at Paddington. "Wow," he said. "Imagine you making all this mess. Even I've never made as much mess as this!"

Paddington sat up and looked round. The whole of the bathroom floor was covered in a sort of white foam where the hot water had landed on his map of South America. "It *is* a bit untidy," he admitted. "I don't really know how it got like that."

"Untidy!" Judy lifted him to his feet and wrapped a towel round him. "Paddington, we've all got a lot of work to do before we go downstairs again. If Mrs. Bird sees this, I don't know what she'll say."

"I do," exclaimed Jonathan. "She says it to me sometimes."

Judy began wiping the floor with a cloth. "Now just you dry yourself quickly so you don't catch cold."

Paddington began rubbing himself meekly with the towel. "I must say," he remarked, looking at himself in the mirror, "I *am* a lot cleaner than I was. It doesn't look like me at all!"

Paddington did look much cleaner than when he had first arrived at the Browns'. His fur, which was really quite light in color and not dark brown as it had been, was standing out like a new brush, except that it was soft and silky. His nose gleamed and his ears had lost all traces of the jam and cream. He was so much cleaner that when he arrived downstairs and entered the dining room some time later, everyone pretended not to recognize him.

"The tradesmen's entrance is at the side," said Mr. Brown from behind his paper.

Mrs. Brown put down her knitting and stared at him. "I think you must have come to the wrong house," she said. "This is number thirty-two, not thirty-four!"

Even Jonathan and Judy agreed there must be some mistake. Paddington began to get quite worried until they all burst out laughing and said how nice he looked now that he was brushed and combed and respectable.

They made room for him in a small armchair by the fire and Mrs. Bird came in with another pot of tea and a plate of hot buttered toast.

"Now, Paddington," said Mr. Brown when they were all settled. "Suppose you tell us all about yourself and how you came to Britain."

Paddington settled back in his armchair, wiped a smear of butter carefully from his whiskers, put his paws behind his head, and stretched out his toes towards the fire. He liked an audience, especially when he was warm and the world seemed such a nice place.

"I was brought up in Darkest Peru," he began. "By my Aunt Lucy. She's the one who lives in the Home for Retired Bears in Lima." He closed his eyes thoughtfully.

A hush fell over the room, and everyone waited expectantly. After a while, when nothing happened, they began to get restless. Mr. Brown coughed loudly. "It doesn't seem a very exciting story," he said impatiently.

He reached across and poked Paddington with his pipe. "Well, I never," he said. "I do believe he's fallen asleep!"

Chapter 3

A Shopping Expedition

The man in the gentlemen's outfitting department at Barkridges held Paddington's hat at arm's length between thumb and forefinger. He looked at it distastefully.

"I take it the young . . . er, gentleman will not be requiring this anymore, Modom?" he said.

"Oh yes, I shall," said Paddington firmly. "I've always had that hat—ever since I was small."

"But wouldn't you like a nice new one, Paddington?" said Mrs. Brown, adding hastily, "For *best*?"

Paddington thought for a moment. "I'll have one for *worst* if you like," he said. "*That's* my best one!"

The salesman shuddered slightly and, averting his gaze, placed the offending article on the far end of the counter.

"Albert!" He beckoned to a youth who was hovering in the background. "See what we have in size 4⅞." Albert began to rummage under the counter.

"And now, while we're about it," said Mrs. Brown, "we'd like a nice warm coat for the winter. Something like a duffle coat with toggles so that he can do it up easily, I thought. And we'd also like a plastic raincoat for the summer."

The salesman looked at her haughtily. He wasn't very fond of bears, and this one especially had been giving him funny looks ever since he'd mentioned his wretched hat. "Has Modom tried the bargain basement?" he began. "Something in Government Surplus . . ."

"No, I haven't," said Mrs. Brown hotly. "Government Surplus indeed! I've never heard of such a thing—have you, Paddington?"

"No," said Paddington, who had no idea what Government Surplus was. "*Never!*" He stared hard at the man, who looked away uneasily. Paddington had a very persistent stare when he cared to use it. It was a very powerful stare. One that his Aunt Lucy had taught him and that he kept for special occasions.

Mrs. Brown pointed to a smart blue duffle coat with a red lining. "That looks the very thing," she said.

The man gulped. "Yes, Modom. Certainly, Modom." He beckoned to Paddington. "Come this way, sir."

Paddington followed the assistant, keeping about two feet behind him and staring very hard. The back of the man's neck seemed to go a dull red and he fingered his collar nervously. As they passed the hat counter, Albert, who lived in constant fear of his superior and who had been watching events with an open mouth, gave Paddington the thumbs-up sign. Paddington waved a paw. He was beginning to enjoy himself.

He allowed the salesman to help him on with the coat and then stood admiring himself in the mirror. It was the first coat he had ever possessed. In Peru it had been very hot, and though his Aunt Lucy had made him wear a hat to prevent sunstroke, it had always been much too warm for a coat of any sort. He looked at himself in the mirror and was surprised to see not one, but a long line of bears stretching away as far as the eye could see. In fact, everywhere he looked there were bears, and they were all looking extremely smart.

"Isn't the hood a trifle large?" asked Mrs. Brown anxiously.

"Hoods are being worn large this year, Modom," said the salesman. "It's the latest fashion." He was about to add that Paddington seemed to have quite a large head anyway but he changed his mind. Bears were rather unpredictable. You never quite knew what they were thinking and this one in particular seemed to have a mind of his own.

"Do *you* like it, Paddington?" asked Mrs. Brown.

Paddington gave up counting bears in the mirror and turned round to look at the back view. "I think it's the nicest coat I've ever seen," he said, after a moment's thought. Mrs. Brown and the salesman heaved a sigh of relief.

"Good," said Mrs. Brown. "That's settled, then. Now there's just the question of a hat and a plastic mackintosh."

She walked over to the hat counter, where Albert, who could still hardly take his admiring eyes off Paddington, had arranged a huge pile of hats. There were bowler hats, sun hats, trilby hats, berets, and even a very small top hat. Mrs. Brown eyed them doubtfully. "It's difficult," she said, looking at Paddington. "It's largely a question of his ears. They stick out rather."

"You could cut some holes for them," said Albert.

The salesman froze him with a glance. "Cut a hole in a *Barkridges'* hat!" he exclaimed. "I've never heard of such a thing."

Paddington turned and stared at him. "I . . . er . . ." The salesman's voice trailed off. "I'll go and fetch my scissors," he said in a quiet voice.

"I don't think that will be necessary at all," said Mrs. Brown hurriedly. "It's not as if he had to go to work in the City, so he doesn't want anything too smart. I think this woolen beret is very nice. The one with the pompom on top. The green will go well with his new coat and it'll stretch so that he can pull it down over his ears when it gets cold."

Everyone agreed that Paddington looked very smart, and while Mrs. Brown looked for a plastic mackintosh, he trotted off to have another look at himself in the mirror. He found the beret was a little difficult to raise, as his ears kept the bottom half firmly in place. But by pulling on the pompom he could make it stretch quite a long way, which was almost as good. It meant, too, that he could be polite without getting his ears cold.

The salesman wanted to wrap up the duffle coat for him, but after a lot of fuss it was agreed that, even though it was a warm day, he should wear it. Paddington felt very proud of himself and he was anxious to see if other people noticed.

After shaking hands with Albert, Paddington gave the salesman one more long, hard stare and the unfortunate man collapsed into a chair and began mopping his brow as Mrs. Brown led the way out through the door.

Barkridges was a large store, and it even had its own escalator as well as several elevators. Mrs. Brown hesitated at the door and then took Paddington's paw firmly in her hand and led him towards the elevator. They had already tried an escalator on the way to Barkridges, and she felt once was enough.

But to Paddington everything was new, or almost everything, and he liked trying strange things. After a few seconds he decided quite definitely that he preferred riding on an escalator. They were nice and smooth. But elevators! To start with, it was full of people carrying parcels and all so busy they had no time to notice a small bear—one woman even rested her shopping bag on his head and seemed quite surprised when Paddington pushed it off. Then suddenly half of him seemed to fall away while the other half stayed where it was. Just as he had got used to that feeling the second half of him caught up again and even overtook the first half before the doors opened. It did that four times on the way down and Paddington was glad when they reached the ground floor and Mrs. Brown led him out.

She looked at him closely. "Oh dear, Paddington, you look quite pale," she said. "Are you all right?"

"I feel sick," said Paddington. "I don't like elevators. And I wish I hadn't had such a big breakfast!"

"Oh dear!" Mrs. Brown looked round. Judy, who had gone off to do some shopping of her own, was nowhere to be seen. "Will you be all right sitting here for a few minutes while I go off to find Judy?" she asked.

Paddington sank down onto his case looking very mournful. Even the pompom on his hat seemed limp.

"I don't know whether I shall be all right," he said. "But I'll do my best."

"I'll be as quick as I can," said Mrs. Brown. "Then we can take a taxi home for lunch."

Paddington groaned.

"Poor Paddington," said Mrs. Brown, "you must be feeling bad if you don't want any lunch."

As he heard the word *lunch* again, Paddington closed his eyes and gave an even louder groan. Mrs. Brown tiptoed away.

Paddington kept his eyes closed for several minutes and then, as he began to feel better, he gradually became aware that every now and then a nice cool draft of air blew over his face. He opened one eye carefully to see where it was coming from and noticed for the first time that he was sitting near the main entrance to the store. He opened his other eye and decided to investigate. If he stayed just outside the glass door he could still see Mrs. Brown and Judy when they came.

And then, as he bent down to pick up his suitcase, everything suddenly went black. "Oh dear," thought Paddington, "now all the lights have gone out."

He began groping his way with outstretched paws towards the door. He gave a push where he thought it ought to be but nothing happened. He tried moving along the wall a little way and gave another push. This time it did move. The door seemed to have a strong spring on it and he had to push hard to make it open, but eventually there was a gap big enough for him to squeeze through. It clanged shut behind him and Paddington was disappointed to find it was just as dark outside as it had been in the store. He began to wish he'd stayed where he was. He turned round and tried to find the door but it seemed to have disappeared.

He decided it might be easier if he got down on his paws and crawled. He went a little way like this and then his head came up against something hard. He tried to push it to one side with his paw and it moved slightly, so he pushed again.

Suddenly there was a noise like thunder, and before he knew where he was, a whole mountain of things began to fall on him. It felt as if the whole sky had fallen in. Everything went quiet and he lay where he was for a few minutes with his eyes tightly shut, hardly daring to breathe. From a long way away he could hear voices and once or twice it sounded as if someone was banging on a window. He opened one eye carefully and was surprised to find the lights had come on again. At least . . . Sheepishly, he pushed the hood of his duffle coat up over his head. They hadn't gone out at all! His hood must have fallen over his head when he bent down inside the store to pick up his case.

Paddington sat up and looked round to see where he was. He felt much better now. Somewhat to his astonishment, he found he was sitting in a small room in the middle of which was a great pile of tins and basins and bowls. He rubbed his eyes and stared, round-eyed, at the sight.

Behind him was a wall with a door in it, and in front of him was a large window. On the other side of the window a large crowd of people were pushing one another and pointing in his direction. Paddington decided with pleasure that they must be pointing at him. He stood up with difficulty, because it was hard standing up straight on top of a lot of tins, and pulled the pompom on his hat as high as it would go. A cheer went up from the crowd. Paddington gave a bow, waved several times, and then started to examine the damage all around him.

For a moment he wasn't quite sure where he was, and then it came to him. In-

stead of going out into the street, he must have opened a door leading to one of the store windows!

Paddington was an observant bear, and since he had arrived in London he'd noticed lots of these windows. They were very interesting. They always had so many things inside them to look at. Once, he'd seen a man working in one, piling tin cans and boxes on top of each other to make a pyramid. He remembered deciding at the time what a nice job it must be.

He looked round thoughtfully. "Oh dear," he said to the world in general, "I'm in trouble again." If he'd knocked all these things down, as he supposed he must have done, someone was going to be cross. In fact, lots of people were going to be cross. People weren't very good at having things explained to them and it was going to be difficult explaining how his duffle coat hood had fallen over his head.

He bent down and began to pick up the things. There were some glass shelves lying on the floor where they had fallen. It was getting warm inside the window so he took off his duffle coat and hung it carefully on a nail. Then he picked up a glass shelf and tried balancing it on top of some tins. It seemed to work, so he put some more tins and a bowl on top of that. It was rather wobbly, but . . . He stood back and examined it. Yes, it looked quite nice. There was an encouraging round of applause from outside. Paddington waved a paw at the crowd and picked up another shelf.

Inside the shop, Mrs. Brown was having an earnest conversation with the store detective.

"You say you left him here, Madam?" the detective was saying.

"That's right," said Mrs. Brown. "He was feeling ill and I *told* him not to go away. His name's Paddington."

"Paddington." The detective wrote it carefully in his notebook. "What sort of bear is he?"

"Oh, he's sort of golden," said Mrs. Brown. "He was wearing a blue duffle coat and carrying a suitcase."

"And he has black ears," said Judy. "You can't mistake him."

"Black ears," the detective repeated, licking his pencil.

"I don't expect that'll help much," said Mrs. Brown. "He was wearing his beret."

The detective cupped his hand over his ear. "His *what*?" he shouted. There really was a terrible noise coming from somewhere. It seemed to be getting worse every minute. Every now and then there was a round of applause and several times he distinctly heard the sound of people cheering.

"His *beret*," shouted Mrs. Brown in return. "A green woolen one that came down over his ears. With a pompom."

The detective shut his notebook with a snap. The noise outside was definitely getting worse. "Pardon me," he said sternly. "There's something strange going on that needs investigating."

Mrs. Brown and Judy exchanged glances. The same thought was running through both their minds. They both said "Paddington!" and rushed after the detective. Mrs. Brown clung to the detective's coat and Judy clung to Mrs. Brown's as they forced their way through the crowd on the pavement. Just as they reached the window a tremendous cheer went up.

"I might have known," said Mrs. Brown.

"Paddington!" exclaimed Judy.

Paddington had just reached the top of his pyramid. At least, it had started off as a pyramid, but it wasn't really. It wasn't any particular shape at all and it was very rickety. Having placed the last tin on the top, Paddington was in trouble. He wanted to get down but he couldn't. He reached out a paw and the mountain began to wobble. Paddington clung helplessly to the tins, swaying to and fro, watched by a fascinated audience. And then, without any warning, the whole lot collapsed again, only this time Paddington was on top and not underneath. A groan of disappointment went up from the crowd.

"Best thing I've seen in years," said a man in the crowd to Mrs. Brown. "Blessed if I know how they think these things up."

"Will he do it again, Mummy?" asked a small boy.

"I don't think so, dear," said his mother. "I think he's finished for the day." She pointed to the window where the detective was removing a sorry-looking Paddington. Mrs. Brown hurried back to the entrance followed by Judy.

Inside the store the detective looked at Paddington and then at his notebook. "Blue duffle coat," he said. "Green woolen beret!" He pulled the beret off. "Black ears! I know who you are," he said grimly. "You're Paddington!"

Paddington nearly fell over backwards with astonishment.

"However did you know that?" he said.

"I'm a detective," said the man. "It's my job to know these things. We're always on the lookout for criminals."

"But I'm not a criminal," said Paddington hotly. "I'm a bear! Besides, I was only tidying up the window . . ."

"Tidying up the window," the detective spluttered. "I don't know what Mr. Perkins will have to say. He only dressed it this morning."

Paddington looked round uneasily. He could see Mrs. Brown and Judy hurrying towards him. In fact, there were several people coming his way, including an important-looking man in a black coat and striped trousers. They all reached him at the same time and all began talking together.

Paddington sat down on his case and watched them. There were times when it was much better to keep quiet, and this was one of them. In the end it was the important-looking man who won, because he had the loudest voice and kept on talking when everyone else had finished.

To Paddington's surprise, he reached down, took hold of his paw, and started to shake it so hard he thought it was going to drop off.

"Delighted to know you, bear," he boomed. "Delighted to know you. And congratulations."

"That's all right," said Paddington doubtfully. He didn't know why, but the man seemed very pleased.

The man turned to Mrs. Brown. "You say his name's Paddington?"

"That's right," said Mrs. Brown. "And I'm sure he didn't mean any harm."

"Harm?" The man looked at Mrs. Brown in amazement. "Did you say *harm*? My dear lady, through the action of this bear we've had the biggest crowd in years. Our telephone hasn't stopped ringing." He waved towards the entrance to the store. "And still they come!"

He placed his hand on Paddington's head. "Barkridges," he said, "Barkridges is grateful!" He waved his other hand for silence. "We should like to show our gratitude. If there is anything—anything in the store you would like . . . ?"

Paddington's eyes gleamed. He knew just what he wanted. He'd seen it on their way up to the men's department. It had been standing all by itself on a counter in the food store. The biggest one he'd ever seen. Almost as big as himself.

"Please," he said, "I'd like one of those jars of marmalade. One of the big ones."

If the manager of Barkridges felt surprised he didn't show it. He stood respectfully to one side, by the entrance to the elevator.

"Marmalade it shall be," he said, pressing the button.

"I think," said Paddington, "if you don't mind, I'd rather use the stairs."

Chapter 4

A Disappearing Trick

"Oooh," said Paddington, "is it really for me?" He stared hungrily at the cake. It really was a wonderful cake. One of Mrs. Bird's best. It was covered with icing and it had a cream and marmalade filling. On the top was one candle and the words TO PADDINGTON. WITH BEST WISHES FOR A HAPPY BIRTHDAY—FROM EVERYONE.

It had been Mrs. Bird's idea to have a birthday party. Paddington had been with them for two months. No one, not even Paddington, knew quite how old he was, so they decided to start again and call him one. Paddington thought this was a good idea, especially when he was told that bears had two birthdays every year, one in the summer and one in the winter.

"Just like the Queen," said Mrs. Bird. "So you ought to consider yourself very important."

Paddington did. In fact, he went round to his friend Mr. Gruber straightaway and told him the good news. Mr. Gruber looked impressed and was pleased when Paddington invited him to the party.

"It's not often anyone invites me out, Mr. Brown," he said. "I don't know when I went out last, and I shall look forward to it very much indeed."

He didn't say any more at the time, but the next morning a van drew up outside the Browns' house and delivered a mysterious-looking parcel from all the shopkeepers in the Portobello Market.

"Aren't you a lucky bear!" exclaimed Mrs. Brown when they opened the parcel and saw what was inside. It was a nice new shopping basket on wheels, with a bell on the side that Paddington could ring to let people know he was coming.

Paddington scratched his head. "It's a job to know what to do first," he said as he carefully placed the basket with his other presents. "I shall have a lot of thank-you letters to write."

"Perhaps you'd better leave them until tomorrow," said Mrs. Brown hastily. Whenever Paddington wrote any letters he generally managed to get more ink on himself than on the paper, and he was looking so unusually smart, having had a bath the night before, that it seemed a pity to spoil it.

Paddington looked disappointed. He liked writing letters. "Perhaps I can help Mrs. Bird in the kitchen," he said hopefully.

"I'm glad to say," said Mrs. Bird, as she emerged from the kitchen, "that I've just finished. But you can lick the spoon if you like." She had bitter memories of other occasions when Paddington had "helped" in the kitchen. "But not too much," she warned, "or you won't have room for this."

It was then that Paddington saw his cake for the first time. His eyes, usually large and round, became so much larger and rounder that even Mrs. Bird blushed with pride. "Special occasions demand special things," she said, and hurried off in the direction of the dining room.

Paddington spent the rest of the day being rushed from one part of the house to another as preparations were made for his party. Mrs. Brown was busy tidying up. Mrs. Bird was busy in the kitchen. Jonathan and Judy were busy with the decorations. Everyone had a job except Paddington.

"I thought it was supposed to be my birthday," he grumbled as he was sent into the drawing room for the fifth time after upsetting a box of marbles all over the kitchen floor.

"So it is, dear," said a flustered Mrs. Brown. "But your time comes later." She was beginning to regret telling him that bears had two birthdays every year, for already he was worrying about when the next one was due.

"Now just you watch out of the window for the postman," she said, lifting him up onto the windowsill. But Paddington didn't seem very keen on this. "Or else," she said, "practice doing some of your magic tricks, ready for this evening."

Among Paddington's many presents was a magic set from Mr. and Mrs. Brown.

It was a very expensive one from Barkridges. It had a special magic table, a large mystery box that made things disappear if you followed the instructions properly, a magic wand and several packs of cards. Paddington emptied them all over the floor and settled down in the middle to read the book of instructions.

He sat there for a long time, studying the pictures and diagrams and reading everything twice to make sure. Every now and then he absent-mindedly dipped a paw into his marmalade jar, and then, remembering that it was his birthday and there was a big tea to come, he reached up and stood the jar on the magic table before returning to his studies.

The first chapter was called "Spells." It showed how to wave the magic wand and the correct way to say "abracadabra." Paddington stood up clutching the book in one paw, and waved the wand several times through the air. He also tried saying "abracadabra." He looked round. Nothing seemed to have changed, and he was about to try again when his eyes nearly popped out of his head. The jar of marmalade he'd placed on the magic table only a few minutes before had disappeared!

He searched hurriedly through the book. There was nothing about making marmalade disappear. Worse still, there was nothing about making it come back again, either. Paddington decided it must be a very powerful spell to make a whole jar vanish into thin air.

He was about to rush outside and tell the others when he thought better of it. It might be a good trick to do in the evening, especially if he could persuade Mrs. Bird to give him another jar. He went out into the kitchen and waved his wand a few times in Mrs. Bird's direction, just to make sure.

"I'll give you abracadabra," said Mrs. Bird, pushing him out again. "And be careful with that stick, or you'll have someone's eye out."

Paddington returned to the drawing room and tried saying his spell backwards. Nothing happened, so he started reading the next chapter of the instruction book, which was called "The Mystery of the Disappearing Egg."

"I shouldn't have thought you needed any book to tell you that," said Mrs. Bird at lunchtime, as Paddington told them all about it. "The way you gobble your food is nobody's business."

"Well," said Mr. Brown, "so long as you don't try sawing anyone in half this evening, I don't mind. I was only joking," he added hurriedly, as Paddington turned an inquiring gaze on him. Nevertheless, as soon as lunch was over, Mr. Brown hurried into the garden and locked up his tools. With Paddington there was no sense in taking chances.

As it happened he had no cause to worry, for Paddington had far too many things on his mind, what with one thing and another. The whole family was there for tea as well as Mr. Gruber. Several other people came along too, including the Browns' next-door neighbor, Mr. Curry. He was a most unwelcome visitor. "Just because there's a free meal," said Mrs. Bird. "I think it's disgusting, taking the crumbs off a young bear's plate like that. He's not even been invited!"

"He'll have to be quick to get any crumbs off Paddington's plate," said Mr. Brown. "All the same it is a bit much, after all the things he's said in the past. And not even bothering to wish Paddington many happy returns."

Mr. Curry had a reputation in the neighborhood for meanness and for poking his nose into other people's business. He was very bad-tempered and was always complaining about the least little thing that met with his disapproval. In the past that had often included Paddington, which was why the Browns had not invited him to the party.

But even Mr. Curry had no cause to complain about the tea. From the huge birthday cake down to the last marmalade sandwich, everyone agreed that it was the best meal they had ever had. Paddington himself was so full he had great difficulty in mustering enough breath to blow out the candle. But at last he managed it without singeing his whiskers, and everyone, including Mr. Curry, applauded and wished him a happy birthday.

"And now," said Mr. Brown when the noise had died down, "if you'll all move your seats back, I think Paddington has a surprise for us."

While everyone was busy moving their seats to one side of the room, Paddington disappeared into the drawing room and returned carrying his conjuring outfit. There was a short delay while he erected his magic table and adjusted the mystery box, but soon all was ready. The lights were turned off except for a standard lamp and Paddington waved his wand for quiet.

"Ladies and gentlemen," he began, consulting his instruction book, "my next trick is impossible!"

"But you haven't done one yet," grumbled Mr. Curry.

Ignoring the remark, Paddington turned over the page. "For this trick," he said, "I shall require an egg."

"Oh dear," said Mrs. Bird as she hurried out to the kitchen, "I know something dreadful is going to happen."

Paddington placed the egg in the center of his magic table and covered it with a handkerchief. He muttered "abracadabra" several times and then hit the handkerchief with his wand.

Mr. and Mrs. Brown looked at each other with great dismay. They were both thinking of their carpet.

"Hey presto!" said Paddington, and pulled the handkerchief away. To everyone's surprise, the egg had completely disappeared.

"Of course," said Mr. Curry knowledgeably, above the applause, "it's all done by sleight of paw. But very good though, for a bear. Very good indeed. Now make it come back again!"

Feeling very pleased with himself, Paddington took his bow and then felt in the secret compartment behind the table. To his surprise he found something much larger than an egg. In fact . . . it was a jar of marmalade. It was the one that had disappeared that very morning! He displayed it in his paw; the applause for this trick was even louder.

"Excellent," said Mr. Curry, slapping his knee. "Making people think he was going to find an egg, and it was a jar of marmalade all the time. Very good indeed!"

Paddington turned over a page. "And now," he announced, flushed with success, "the disappearing trick!" He took a bowl of Mrs. Brown's best flowers and placed them on the dining table alongside his mystery box. He wasn't very happy about this trick, as he hadn't had time to practice it, and he wasn't at all sure how the mystery box worked or even where you put the flowers to make them disappear.

He opened the door in the back of the box and then poked his head round the side. "I shan't be a minute," he said, and then disappeared from view again.

The audience sat in silence. "Rather a slow trick, this one," said Mr. Curry after a while.

"I hope he's all right," said Mrs. Brown. "He seems very quiet."

"Well, he can't have gone far," said Mr. Curry. "Let's try knocking." He got up, knocked loudly on the box and then put his ear to it. "I can hear someone calling," he said. "It sounds like Paddington. I'll try again." He shook the box and there was an answering thump from inside.

"I think he's shut himself in," said Mr. Gruber. He too knocked on the box and called out, "Are you all right, Mr. Brown?"

"No!" said a small and muffled voice. "It's all dark and I can't read my instruction book."

"Quite a good trick," said Mr. Curry, some while later after they had pried open Paddington's mystery box with a penknife. He helped himself to some biscuits. "The disappearing bear. Very unusual! But I still don't see what the flowers were for."

Paddington looked at him suspiciously, but Mr. Curry was far too busy with the biscuits.

"For my next trick," said Paddington, "I would like a watch."

"Are you sure?" asked Mrs. Brown anxiously. "Wouldn't anything else do?"

Paddington consulted his instruction book. "It says a watch," he said firmly.

Mr. Brown hurriedly pulled his sleeve down over his left wrist. Unfortunately, Mr. Curry, who was in an unusually good mood after his free tea, stood up and offered his. Paddington took it gratefully and placed it on the table. "This is a jolly good trick," he said, reaching down into his box and pulling out a small hammer.

He covered the watch with a handkerchief and then hit it several times. Mr. Curry's expression froze. "I hope you know what you're doing, young bear," he said.

Paddington looked rather worried. Having turned the page, he'd just read the ominous words, "It is necessary to have a second watch for this trick." Gingerly he lifted up a corner of the handkerchief. Several cogs and some pieces of glass rolled across the table. Mr. Curry let out a roar of wrath.

"I think I forgot to say 'abracadabra,'" faltered Paddington.

"Abracadabra!" shouted Mr. Curry, beside himself with rage. "Abracadabra!" He held up the remains of his watch. "Twenty years I've had this watch, and now look at it! This will cost someone a pretty penny!"

Mr. Gruber took out an eyeglass and examined the watch carefully. "Nonsense," he said, coming to Paddington's rescue. "It's one you bought from me for next to nothing six months ago! You ought to be ashamed of yourself, telling lies in front of a young bear!"

"Rubbish!" spluttered Mr. Curry. He sat down heavily on Paddington's chair. "Rubbish! I'll give you . . ." His voice trailed away, and a peculiar expression came over his face. "I'm sitting on something," he said. "Something wet and sticky!"

"Oh dear," said Paddington. "I expect it's my disappearing egg. It must have reappeared!"

Mr. Curry grew purple in the face. "I've never been so insulted in my life," he said. "Never!" He turned at the door and waved an accusing finger at the company. "It's the last time I shall ever come to one of your birthday parties!"

"Henry," said Mrs. Brown as the door closed behind Mr. Curry, "you really oughtn't to laugh."

Mr. Brown tried hard to keep a straight face. "It's no good," he said, bursting out. "I can't help it."

"Did you see his face when all the cogs rolled out?" said Mr. Gruber, his face wet with tears.

"All the same," said Mr. Brown when the laughter had died down, "I think perhaps you ought to try something a little less dangerous next time, Paddington."

"How about that card trick you were telling me about, Mr. Brown?" asked Mr. Gruber. "The one where you tear up a card and make it come out of someone's ear."

"Yes, that sounds a nice quiet one," said Mrs. Brown. "Let's see that."

"You wouldn't like another disappearing trick?" asked Paddington hopefully.

"Quite sure, dear," said Mrs. Brown.

"Well," said Paddington, rummaging in his box, "it's not very easy doing card tricks when you've only got paws, but I don't mind trying."

He offered a pack of cards to Mr. Gruber, who solemnly took one from the middle and then memorized it before replacing it. Paddington waved his wand over the pack several times and then withdrew a card. He held up the seven of spades. "Was this it?" he said to Mr. Gruber.

Mr. Gruber polished his glasses and stared. "You know," he said, "I do believe it was!"

"I bet all the cards are the same," whispered Mr. Brown to his wife.

"*Ssh!*" said Mrs. Brown. "I thought he did it very well."

"This is the difficult bit," said Paddington, tearing it up. "I'm not very sure about this part." He put the pieces under his handkerchief and tapped them several times with the wand.

"Oh!" said Mr. Gruber, rubbing the side of his head. "I felt something go pop in my ear just then. Something cold and hard." He felt in his ear. "Why, I do believe . . ." He held up a shining round object to the audience. "It's a pound! My birthday present for young Mr. Brown! Now I wonder how it got in there?"

"Oooh!" said Paddington as he proudly examined it. "I didn't expect that. Thank you very much, Mr. Gruber."

"Well," said Mr. Gruber. "It's only a small present I'm afraid, Mr. Brown. But I've enjoyed the little chats we've had in the mornings. I look forward to them very much and, er"—he cleared his throat and looked round—"I'm sure we all hope you have many more birthdays!"

When the chorus of agreement had died down, Mr. Brown rose and looked at the clock. "And now," he said, "it's long past all our bedtimes, most of all yours, Paddington, so I suggest we all do a disappearing trick now."

"I wish . . ." said Paddington, as he stood at the door waving everyone good-bye, "I wish my Aunt Lucy could see me now. She'd feel very pleased."

"You'll have to write and tell her all about it, Paddington," said Mrs. Brown as she took his paw. "But in the morning," she added hastily. "You've got clean sheets, remember."

"Yes," said Paddington. "In the morning. I expect if I did it now I'd get ink on the sheets or something. Things are always happening to me."

"You know, Henry," said Mrs. Brown as they watched Paddington go up the stairs to bed, looking rather sticky and more than a little sleepy, "it's nice having a bear about the house."

Chapter 5

A Picnic on the River

Paddington sat up in bed with a puzzled expression on his face. Happenings at number thirty-two Windsor Gardens, particularly breakfast, always followed a strict timetable, and it was most unusual for anything to waken him quite so early.

He took a careful look round his room, but everything seemed to be in its place.

The photograph of his Aunt Lucy, taken shortly before she entered the Home for Retired Bears in Lima, was on the table beside the bed, along with his jar of special marmalade and several other items.

His old hat and duffle coat were both hanging on the door peg, and his Peruvian centavos were under the pillow.

Most important of all, when he lifted the bedclothes and peered underneath, his small leather suitcase with its secret compartment containing his scrapbook and a number of important papers was still at the bottom of the bed.

Paddington heaved a sigh of relief. Although he had lived with the Browns for some time, he had never quite got used to having a room of his own, and he wasn't the sort of bear who believed in taking chances.

It was at that point, just as he was absent-mindedly dipping his paw into the marmalade jar before going back to sleep, that Paddington pricked up his ears and listened.

There were voices—quite a number of voices—coming from the garden. Several times he heard a door bang, and then, in the distance, he heard a noise remarkably like that of clinking plates, followed by the sound of Mr. Brown shouting orders.

Paddington scrambled out of bed and hurried across the room to the window. It sounded most interesting and he didn't like to think he might be missing anything. As he peered through the glass, he nearly fell over backwards with astonishment at the sight which met his eyes. He breathed heavily on the windowpane and rubbed it with his paw to make sure he wasn't dreaming the whole thing.

For there, on the lawn outside, all the Brown family—Mr. and Mrs. Brown and Jonathan and Judy—were gathered round a large wicker basket. Not only that, but as he watched, Mrs. Bird, their housekeeper, came out of the kitchen carrying a huge plate piled high with sandwiches.

Paddington climbed off the windowsill and hurried downstairs. It was all very mysterious and it definitely needed investigating.

"Trust Paddington!" said everyone as he came through the kitchen door just as they were shutting the lid of the hamper.

"That bear can smell out a marmalade sandwich a mile away," grumbled Mrs. Bird.

"Honestly," said Judy, waving her finger at him. "It was meant to be a surprise. We got up specially early."

Paddington looked from one to the other with growing astonishment.

"It's all right, Paddington," laughed Mrs. Brown. "There's no need to be alarmed. We're only going for a picnic on the river."

"And we're having a competition," cried Jonathan, waving a fishing net in the air. "Dad's promised a prize to whoever makes the first catch."

Paddington's eyes grew rounder and rounder. "A picnic?" he exclaimed. "I don't think I've ever been for a picnic on the river before."

"That's good," said Mr. Brown, twirling his mustache briskly. "Because you're going on one now. So hurry up and eat your breakfast. It's a lovely day and we may as well make the most of it."

Paddington needed no second bidding, and while the Browns were busy packing the rest of the picnic gear into the car he hurried back indoors, where his breakfast was waiting. He liked doing new things, and he was looking forward to the day's outing. One of the nicest things about living with the Browns was the number of surprises he had.

"I hope I've never ever done everything, Mrs. Bird," he said as she came into the dining room to see if he'd finished his toast and marmalade. "I shouldn't have any surprises left then!"

"*Hmm,*" replied Mrs. Bird sternly as she bundled him out of the room. "You'll be getting a surprise if you don't wash those bacon-and-egg stains off your whiskers before we go out. I've never known such a bear for getting in a mess."

Paddington put on his injured expression as he disappeared into the hall. "I was only trying to be quick, Mrs. Bird," he explained.

Nevertheless, he hurried upstairs to the bathroom. There were several important things to be done before he went out for the day. First of all there was his suitcase to be packed, and then he had to consult his atlas. Paddington was very keen on geography, and he was interested in the thought of having a picnic on the river. It sounded most unusual.

◆ ◆ ◆

"I don't know why it is," said Mrs. Bird as she adjusted her hat for what seemed like the fortieth time, "but whenever this family goes anywhere it always takes enough to keep a regiment for a month."

The Browns were packed into the car heading along the road towards the river. Besides the Browns, Mrs. Bird and Paddington, there was the hamper, a cassette player, a pile of cassettes, a number of parcels and some fishing nets—not to mention several sunshades, a tent and a pile of cushions.

Mrs. Brown shifted uncomfortably as she agreed with Mrs. Bird. Paddington's leather suitcase was sticking in her back and his old hat, which he insisted on wearing in case of sunstroke, kept tickling the side of her face.

"Is it much farther?" she asked.

Paddington, who was sitting beside her on the front seat, consulted his map. "I think it's the next turn on the right," he announced, following the route with his paw.

"I do hope so," said Mrs. Brown. They had already taken one wrong turn that morning when Paddington had followed a piece of dried marmalade peel on his map by mistake.

"Fancy turning right at a piece of dried marmalade peel," grumbled Mr. Brown. "That policeman didn't like it at all."

Anxious to make amends, Paddington stuck his head out of the window and sniffed.

"I think we must be getting near, Mr. Brown," he called. "I can smell something unusual."

"That's the gas works," said Mr. Brown, following the direction of Paddington's paw. "The river's on *this* side."

Just as he spoke they swept round a corner and there, straight in front of them, was a broad expanse of water.

Paddington's eyes lit up as they all clambered out of the car, and while the others were unloading the supplies he stood at the water's edge and surveyed the scene. He was most impressed.

The towpath was crowded with people and there were boats everywhere. Rowboats, canoes, punts and sailboats with their white sails billowing in the wind. As he watched, an excursion boat packed with more people swept by, sending a large wave shooting across the water and causing all the smaller boats to rock. Everyone on board seemed very cheerful and happy and several of them pointed towards Paddington and waved.

Paddington raised his hat in reply and then turned to the others. "I think I'm going to like the river," he announced.

"I do hope so, dear," said Mrs. Brown uneasily. "It *is* your treat."

She looked at the row of boats moored by the landing. The day before it had seemed a very good idea of Mr. Brown's to have a picnic on the river. But now they were actually here she had a nasty feeling in the back of her mind and she knew Mrs. Bird was feeling the same way. Close up, the boats looked awfully small.

"Are you sure they're safe, Henry?" she asked, looking at them nervously.

"Safe?" echoed Mr. Brown as he led the way onto the dock. "Of course they're safe, Mary. You just leave everything to me.

"I'll put you in charge of all the ropes and things, Paddington," he called. "That means you can steer."

"Thank you very much, Mr. Brown," said Paddington, feeling most important. His eyes gleamed with excitement as he climbed into the boat and carefully examined everything with his paws.

"The boatman's rather busy," said Mr. Brown as he helped the others in. "So I said we would shove off by ourselves."

"Paddington!" exclaimed Mrs. Brown as she picked Mrs. Bird's best sun hat off the floor of the boat. "*Do* mind what you're doing with that fishing net. You'll have someone's head off."

"I'm sorry, Mrs. Bird," said Paddington. "I was only testing it."

"All right," said Mr. Brown as he settled himself on his seat and took a firm grip on the oars. "Here we go. Stand by at the helm, Paddington."

"Do *what*, Mr. Brown?" cried Paddington.

"Pull on the ropes," shouted Mr. Brown. "Come on—left paw down."

"Oh dear," said Mrs. Bird nervously as she clutched the side of the boat with one hand and gripped her sunshade with the other. Out of the corner of her eye she could already see a number of people staring in their direction.

In the back of the boat Paddington pulled hard on the two ropes tied to the rudder. He wasn't quite sure whether Mr. Brown had meant *his*, Mr. Brown's left or his own left, so he pulled both just to make certain. Everyone waited expectantly while Mr. Brown strained on the oars.

"I should have thought, Henry," said Mrs. Brown, after a few moments had gone by, "it would have been much easier if you'd untied the boat from the dock first."

"What!" exclaimed Mr. Brown. He mopped his brow and looked crossly over his shoulder. "Hasn't anyone done that yet?"

"I'll do it, Mr. Brown," called Paddington importantly, as he clambered along the side of the boat. "I'm in charge of ropes."

The Browns waited patiently while Paddington examined the rope. He wasn't very good at knots because they were rather difficult with paws, but eventually he announced that all was ready.

"Right!" shouted Mr. Brown, as he braced himself once more. "Here we go. Cast off, Paddington. Hold on everyone!"

"Do what, Mr. Brown?" cried Paddington, above the splashing of the water. Having a picnic on the river was much more complicated than he had expected. There were so many ropes to pull he was getting a bit confused. First of all Mr. Brown had told him to untie the rope. Now he had shouted to everyone to hold on.

Paddington closed his eyes and held on to the rope with both paws as tightly as he could.

He wasn't quite sure what happened next. One moment he was standing on the boat—the next moment it wasn't there anymore.

"Henry!" shouted Mrs. Brown, as there was a loud splash. "For goodness' sake! Paddington's fallen in the water!"

"Bear overboard!" cried Jonathan, as the boat shot away from the bank.

"Hold on, Paddington!" called Judy. "We're coming."

"But I *did* hold on," cried Paddington, as he came up spluttering for air. "That's how I fell in."

Mrs. Brown lunged into the water with her sunshade. "Do hurry, Henry," she cried.

"I'm sure Paddington can't swim," said Judy.

"What did you say?" called Paddington.

"She said you can't swim," yelled Mr. Brown.

When he heard what Mr. Brown said Paddington began waving his paws wildly in the air and there was a gurgle as he promptly sank.

"There now, Henry," exclaimed Mrs. Brown. "Now look what you've done. He was all right until you spoke."

"I like that!" said Mr. Brown, giving his wife an expressive look.

"It's all right," shouted Jonathan. "Someone's thrown him a lifebelt!"

By the time the Browns reached the dock, Paddington had already been rescued and was lying on his back surrounded by a large crowd. Everyone was staring down at him making suggestions while the man in charge of the boats pulled his paws back and forth, giving him artificial respiration.

"Thank goodness he's safe," exclaimed Mrs. Brown thankfully.

"Don't see why 'e shouldn't be," said the man. "If 'e'd layed 'isself down, it'd only 'ave come up to 'is whiskers. The water's only about nine inches deep just 'ere. Probably a lot less now—judging by the amount 'e's swallowed. Kept 'is mouth open when 'e went under I daresay."

Judy bent down and looked at Paddington. "I think he's trying to say something," she said.

"*Grrrr,*" said Paddington as he sat up.

"Now just you lie still for a moment, young feller-me-bear," said the boatman, pushing Paddington back down again.

"*Grrr,*" said Paddington. "ITHINKI'VELOSTMYHAT."

"ITHINKI'VELOSTMYHAT," repeated the man, looking at Paddington with renewed interest. "Are you one of them foreign bears? We get a rare lot of overseas visitors at this time of year," he said, turning to the Browns.

"I *come* from Peru," spluttered Paddington as he got his breath back. "But I *live* at number thirty-two Windsor Gardens in London, and I think I've lost my hat."

"Oh dear," said Mrs. Brown, clutching her husband's arm. "Did you hear that, Henry? Paddington's lost his hat!"

The Brown family stared at each other in dismay. They often grumbled about Paddington's hat—usually when he wasn't listening—because it was so old. People had a habit of pointing at it when they were out and it made them feel embarrassed. But all the same, they couldn't even begin to picture Paddington without it.

"I had it on when I fell in the water," cried Paddington, feeling on top of his head. "And now it isn't there anymore."

"Gosh," said Jonathan. "It had so many holes in it too! Perhaps it's sunk."

"Sunk!" cried Paddington in dismay. He ran to the edge of the dock and peered at the muddy water. "But it can't have *sunk*!"

"He's always worn it," explained Mrs. Brown to the boatman. "Ever since we've known him. It was given to him by his uncle in Peru."

"*Darkest* Peru," said Paddington.

"Darkest Peru," repeated the boatman, looking most impressed. "You'll be wanting the Thames Conservancy, sir."

"No, I don't," said Paddington firmly. "I want my hat."

"He means they look after the river, dear," explained Mrs. Brown. "They may have found it for you."

"It's the current, sir," explained the boatman. "Once you get away from the bank it's very strong and your hat may have got swept over the waterfall." He pointed along the river towards a row of buildings in the distance.

"Got swept over the waterfall?" repeated Paddington slowly.

The boatman nodded. "If it ain't already been sucked into a whirlpool."

Paddington gave the man a hard stare. "My hat!" he exclaimed, hardly able to believe his ears. "Got sucked into a whirlpool?"

"Come along," said Mr. Brown hastily. "If we hurry we may be just in time to see it go over."

Closely followed by Mr. and Mrs. Brown, Mrs. Bird, Jonathan, Judy, the boatman and a crowd of interested sightseers, Paddington hurried along the towpath with a grim expression on his face, leaving a trail of water behind him.

By the time they reached the waterfall the news had already spread and several men in peaked caps were peering anxiously into the water.

"I hear you've lost a very valuable Persian cat," said the lockkeeper to Mr. Brown.

"Not a *cat*," said Mr. Brown. "A *hat*. And it's from Peru."

"It belongs to this young bear gentleman, Fred," explained the boatman as he joined them. "It's a family heirloom."

"A family heirloom?" repeated the lockkeeper, scratching his head as he looked at Paddington. "I've never heard of a hat being a family heirloom before. Especially a bear's heirloom."

"Mine is," said Paddington firmly. "It's a very rare sort of hat, and it's got a marmalade sandwich inside. I put it in there in case of an emergency."

"A marmalade sandwich?" said the lockkeeper, looking more and more surprised. "Wait a minute—it wouldn't be that thing we fished out just now, would it? All sort of shapeless . . . like a . . . like a . . ." He tried hard to think of words to describe it.

"That *sounds* like it," said Mrs. Bird.

"Herbert!" called the man to a boy who was standing nearby watching the proceedings with an open mouth. "See if we've still got that wassname in the shed.

"It might well be an heirloom," he continued, turning to the Browns. "It looks as if it's been handed down a lot."

Everyone waited anxiously while Herbert disappeared into a small hut by the side of the lock. He returned after a few moments carrying a bucket.

"We put it in here," said the lockkeeper apologetically, "because we'd never seen anything like it before. We were going to send it to the museum."

Paddington peered into the bucket. "That's not a wassname," he exclaimed thankfully. "That's my hat."

Everyone breathed a sigh of relief. "Thank goodness," said Mrs. Bird, echoing all their thoughts.

"There's a fish inside it as well," said the lockkeeper.

"What!" exclaimed Paddington. "A fish? Inside my hat?"

"That's right," said the man. "It must have been after your marmalade sandwich. Probably got in through one of the holes."

"Wow!" exclaimed Jonathan admiringly as the Browns gathered round the bucket. "So there is!"

"That means Paddington's won the prize for catching the first fish," said Judy. "Congratulations!"

"Well, if it's some kind of competition," said the lockkeeper, "I'd better get you a jam jar to put the fish in, sir."

"I suppose," he said, looking rather doubtfully at the hat, "you'll be wanting to wear it again?"

As Paddington gave him a hard stare he backed away and hurried off in search of a jam jar. "There you are," he said when he returned. "With the compliments of the Thames Conservancy."

"Thank you very much," said Paddington gratefully, offering the man his paw.

"Not at all," said the man, as he stood on the side of the lock to wave them goodbye. "It's a pleasure. After all, it's not every day we have the opportunity of saving a bear's heirloom from going over the waterfall. I shall remember today for a long time to come."

"And so shall I remember it," said Mr. Brown as he stopped rowing some while later and let the boat drift lazily downstream in the current. "It may not have been the quietest day we've ever spent on the river, but it's certainly the nicest."

And the Brown family, as they lay back in the boat watching the shimmering water and listening to the music from the cassette player, had to agree.

Paddington, as he held on tightly to his hat with one paw while he dipped the other into a jar of his favorite marmalade, agreed most of all. Now that he had got his hat back and everything had been restored to normal, he felt it was quite the nicest day he'd had for a long time.

Part Two

Paddington Lends a Paw

Chapter 6

A Spot of Decorating

Paddington gave a deep sigh and pulled his hat down over his ears in an effort to keep out the noise. There was such a hullabaloo going on, it was difficult to write up the notes in his scrapbook.

The excitement had all started when Mr. and Mrs. Brown and Mrs. Bird received an unexpected invitation to a wedding. Luckily both Jonathan and Judy were out for the day, or things might have been far worse. Paddington hadn't been included in the invitation, but he didn't really mind. He didn't like weddings very much, apart from the free cake, and he'd been promised a piece of that whether he went or not.

All the same, he was beginning to wish everyone would hurry up and go. He had a special reason for wanting to be alone that day.

He sighed again, wiped the pen carefully on the back of his paw and then mopped up some inkblots which somehow or other had found their way onto the table. He was only just in time, for at that moment the door burst open and Mrs. Brown rushed in.

"Ah, there you are, Paddington!" She stopped short in the middle of the room and stared at him. "Why on earth are you wearing your hat indoors?" she asked. "And why is your tongue all blue?"

Paddington stuck out his tongue as far as he could. "It *is* a funny color," he admitted, squinting down at it with interest. "Perhaps I'm sick with something!"

"You'll be sick all right if you don't clear up this mess," grumbled Mrs. Bird as she entered. "Just look at it. Bottles of ink. Glue. Bits of paper. My best sewing scissors. Marmalade all over the table runner, and goodness knows what else."

Paddington looked round. It *was* a bit of a mess.

"I've almost finished," he announced. "I've just got to make a few more lines and things. I've been writing my memories."

Paddington took his scrapbook very seriously and spent many long hours carefully pasting in pictures and writing up his adventures. Since he'd been at the Browns, so much had happened it was now more than half full.

"Well, make sure you *do* clear everything up," said Mrs. Brown, "or we won't bring you back any cake. Now do take care of yourself. And don't forget—when the baker comes, we want two loaves." With that she waved goodbye and followed Mrs. Bird out of the room.

"You know," said Mrs. Bird as she stepped into the car, "I have a feeling that bear has something up his paw. He seemed most anxious for us to leave."

"Oh, I don't know," said Mrs. Brown. "I don't see what he *can* do. We won't be away all that long."

"Ah!" replied Mrs. Bird darkly. "That may be. But he's been hanging about on the landing upstairs half the morning. I'm sure he's up to something."

Mr. Brown, who didn't like weddings much either and was secretly wishing he could stay at home with Paddington, looked over his shoulder as he let in the clutch. "Perhaps I ought to stay as well," he said. "Then I could get on with decorating his new room."

"Now, Henry," said Mrs. Brown firmly. "You're coming to the wedding and that's that. Paddington will be quite all right by himself. He's a very capable bear. And as for your wanting to get on with decorating his new room . . . you haven't done a thing about it for over a fortnight, so I'm sure it can wait another day."

Paddington's new room had become a sore point in the Brown household. It was over two weeks since Mr. Brown had first thought of doing it. So far he had stripped all the old wallpaper from the walls, removed the picture rails, the wood round the doors, the door handle, and everything else that was loose, or that he had made loose, and bought a lot of bright new wallpaper and some paint. That's where he had stopped.

In the back of the car, Mrs. Bird pretended she hadn't heard a thing. An idea

had suddenly come into her mind, and she was hoping it hadn't entered Paddington's as well; but Mrs. Bird knew the workings of Paddington's mind better than most and she feared the worst. Had she but known, her fears were being realized at that very moment. Paddington was busy scratching out the words "AT A LEWSE END" in his scrapbook and was adding, in large capital letters, the ominous ones "DECKERATING MY NEW ROOM!"

It was while he'd been writing "AT A LEWSE END" in his scrapbook earlier in the day that the idea had come to him. Paddington had noticed in the past that he often got his best ideas when he was at a loose end.

For a long while all his belongings had been packed away ready for the big move to his new room, and he was beginning to get impatient. Every time he wanted anything special, he had to undo yards of string and brown paper.

Having underlined the words in red, Paddington cleared everything up, locked his scrapbook carefully in his suitcase and hurried upstairs. He had several times offered to lend a paw with the decorating, but for some reason or other Mr. Brown had put his foot down on the idea and hadn't even allowed him in the room while work was in progress. Paddington couldn't quite understand why. He was sure he would be very good at it.

The room in question was an old spare room which had not been used for a number of years, and when he entered it, Paddington found it was even more interesting than he had expected.

He closed the door carefully behind him and sniffed. There was an exciting smell of paint and whitewash in the air. Not only that, but there were some ladders, a worktable, several brushes, a number of rolls of wallpaper and a big pail of whitewash.

The room had a lovely echo as well, and he spent a long time sitting in the middle of the floor while he was stirring the paint, just listening to his new voice.

There were so many different and interesting things round that it was a job to know what to do first. Eventually Paddington decided on the painting. Choosing one of Mr. Brown's best brushes, he dipped it into the can of paint and then looked round the room for something to dab it on.

It wasn't until he had been working on the window frame for several minutes that he began to wish he had started on something else. The brush made his arm ache, and when he tried dipping his paw in the paint can instead and rubbing it on, more paint seemed to go onto the glass than onto the wooden part, so that the room became quite dark.

"Perhaps," said Paddington, waving the brush in the air and addressing the room in general, "perhaps if I do the ceiling first with the whitewash I can cover all the drips on the wall with the wallpaper."

But when Paddington started work on the whitewashing, he found it was almost as hard as painting. Even by standing on tiptoe at the very top of the ladder, he had a job to reach the ceiling. The bucket of whitewash was much too heavy for him to lift, so that he had to come down the steps every time in order to dip the brush in. And when he carried the brush up again, the whitewash ran down his paw and made his fur all matted.

Looking round him, Paddington began to wish he was still at a loose end.

Things were beginning to get in rather a mess again. He felt sure Mrs. Bird would have something to say when she saw it.

It was then that he had a brain wave. Paddington was a resourceful bear, and he didn't like being beaten by things. Recently he had become interested in a house that was being built nearby. He had first seen it from the window of his bedroom, and since then he'd spent many hours talking to the men and watching while they hoisted their tools and cement up to the top floor by means of a rope and pulley. Once Mr. Briggs, the foreman, had even taken him up in the bucket too, and had let him lay several bricks.

Now the Browns' house was an old one, and in the middle of the ceiling there was a large hook where a big lamp had once hung. Not only that, but in one corner of the room there was a thin coil of rope as well.

Paddington set to work quickly. First he tied one end of the rope to the handle of the bucket. Then he climbed up the ladder and passed the other end through the hook in the ceiling. But even so, when he had climbed down again, it still took him a long time to pull the bucket anywhere near the top of the steps. It was full to the brim and very heavy, so that he had to stop every few seconds and tie the other end of the rope to the ladder for safety.

It was when he undid the rope for the last time that things started to go wrong. As Paddington closed his eyes and leaned back for the final pull, he suddenly felt, to his surprise, as if he were floating on air. It was a most strange feeling. He reached out one foot and waved it round. There was definitely nothing there. He opened one eye and then nearly let go of the rope in astonishment as he saw the bucket of whitewash going past him on its way down.

Suddenly everything seemed to happen at once. Before he could even reach out a paw or shout for help, his head hit the ceiling and there was a clang as the bucket hit the floor.

For a few seconds Paddington clung there, kicking the air and not knowing what to do. Then there was a gurgling sound from below. Looking down, he saw to his horror that all the whitewash was running out of the bucket. He felt the rope begin to move again as the bucket got lighter, and then it shot past him again as he descended to land with a bump in the middle of a sea of whitewash.

Even then his troubles weren't over. As he tried to regain his balance on the slippery floor, he let go of the rope, and with a rushing noise the bucket shot downwards again and landed on top of his head, completely covering him.

Paddington lay on his back for several minutes, trying to get his breath back and wondering what had hit him. When he did sit up and take the bucket off his head, he quickly put it back on again. There was whitewash all over the floor, the paint cans had been upset, making little rivers of brown and green, and Mr. Brown's work hat was floating in one corner of the room. When Paddington saw it he felt very glad he'd left *his* hat downstairs.

One thing was certain—he was going to have a lot of explaining to do. And that was going to be even more difficult than usual, because he couldn't even explain to himself quite what had gone wrong.

It was some while later, when he was sitting on the upturned bucket thinking about things, that the idea of doing the wallpapering came to him. Paddington had a hopeful nature, and he believed in looking on the bright side. If he did the wallpapering really well, the others might not even notice the mess he'd made.

Paddington was fairly confident about the wallpapering. Unknown to Mr. Brown, he had often watched him in the past through a crack in the door, and it looked quite simple. All you had to do was to brush some sticky stuff on the back of the paper and then put it on the wall. The high parts weren't too difficult, even for a bear, because you could fold the paper in two and put a broom in the middle where the fold was. Then you simply pushed the broom up and down the wall in case there were any nasty wrinkles.

Paddington felt much more cheerful once he'd thought of the wallpapering. He found some paste already mixed in another bucket, which he put on top of the table while he unrolled the paper. It was a little difficult at first, because every time he tried to unroll the paper he had to crawl along the table pushing it with his paws and the other end rolled up again and followed behind him. But eventually he managed to get one piece completely covered in paste.

He climbed down off the table, carefully avoiding the worst of the whitewash, which by now was beginning to dry in large lumps, and lifted the sheet of wallpaper onto a broom. It was a long sheet of paper, much longer than it had seemed when he was putting the paste on, and somehow or other, as Paddington waved the broom about over his head, it began to wrap itself round him. After a struggle he managed to push his way out and head in the general direction of a piece of wall.

He stood back and surveyed the result. The paper was torn in several places, and there seemed to be a lot of paste on the outside, but Paddington felt quite pleased with himself. He decided to try another piece, then another, running backwards and forwards between the table and the walls as fast as his legs could carry him in an effort to get it all finished before the Browns returned.

Some of the pieces didn't quite join, others overlapped, and on most of them there were some very odd-looking patches of paste and whitewash. None of the pieces were as straight as he would have liked, but when he put his head on one side and squinted, Paddington felt the overall effect was quite nice.

It was as he was taking a final look round the room at his handiwork that he noticed something very strange. There was a window, and there was also a fireplace. But there was no longer any sign of a door. Paddington stopped squinting and his eyes grew rounder and rounder. He distinctly remembered there *had* been a door, because he had come through it. He blinked at all four walls. It was difficult to see properly because the paint on the window glass had started to dry and hardly any light was coming through, but there most definitely wasn't a door!

◆ ◆ ◆

"I can't understand it," said Mr. Brown as he entered the dining room. "I've looked everywhere and there's no sign of Paddington. I told you I should have stayed at home with him."

Mrs. Brown looked worried. "Oh dear, I hope nothing's happened to him. It's so unlike him to go out without leaving a note."

"He's not in his room," said Judy.

"Mr. Gruber hasn't seen him either," added Jonathan. "I've just been down to the market and he says he hasn't seen him since they had cocoa together this morning."

"Have *you* seen Paddington anywhere?" asked Mrs. Brown as Mrs. Bird entered, carrying a tray of supper things.

"I don't know about Paddington," said Mrs. Bird. "I've been having enough trouble with the water pipes without missing bears. I think they've got an air lock or something. They've been banging away ever since we came in."

Mr. Brown listened for a moment. "It *does* sound like water pipes," he said. "And yet . . . it isn't regular enough, somehow." He went outside into the hall. "It's a sort of thumping noise. . . ."

"Gosh!" shouted Jonathan. "Listen—it's someone sending an S.O.S."

Everyone exchanged glances and then in one voice cried, "Paddington!"

"Mercy me," said Mrs. Bird as they burst through the papered-up door. "There must have been an earthquake or something. And either that's Paddington or it's his ghost!" She pointed towards a small white figure as it rose from an upturned bucket to greet them.

"I couldn't find the door," said Paddington plaintively. "I think I must have papered it over when I did the decorating. It was there when I came in. I remember seeing it. So I banged on the floor with a broom handle."

"Gosh!" said Jonathan admiringly. "What a mess!"

"You . . . papered . . . it . . . over . . . when . . . you . . . did . . . the . . . decorating," repeated Mr. Brown. He was a bit slow to grasp things sometimes.

"That's right," said Paddington. "I did it as a surprise." He waved a paw round the room. "I'm afraid it's in a bit of a mess, but it isn't dry yet."

While the idea was slowly sinking into Mr. Brown's mind, Mrs. Bird came to Paddington's rescue. "Now it's not a bit of good holding an inquest," she said. "What's done is done. And if you ask me, it's a good thing, too. Now perhaps we shall get some proper decorators in to do the job." With that she took hold of Paddington's paw and led him out of the room.

"As for you, young bear, you're going straight into a hot bath before all that plaster and stuff sets hard!"

Mr. Brown looked after the retreating figures of Mrs. Bird and Paddington and then at the long trail of white footprints and pawmarks. "Bears!" he said bitterly.

Paddington hung about in his room for a long time after his bath and waited until the last possible minute before going downstairs to supper. He had a nasty feeling he was in disgrace. But surprisingly the word "decorating" wasn't mentioned at all that evening.

Even more surprisingly, while he was sitting up in bed drinking his cocoa, several people came to see him, and each of them gave him ten pence. It was all very mysterious, but Paddington didn't like to ask why in case they changed their minds.

It was Judy who solved the problem for him when she came in to say good night.

"I suppose Mummy and Mrs. Bird gave you ten pence because they don't want Daddy to do any more decorating," she explained. "He always starts things and never finishes them. And I suppose Daddy gave you some because he didn't want to finish it anyway. Now they're getting a proper decorator in, so everyone's happy!"

Paddington sipped his cocoa thoughtfully. "Perhaps if I did another room, I'd get another thirty pence," he said.

"Oh no, you don't," said Judy sternly. "You've done quite enough for one day. If I were you I shouldn't mention the word 'decorating' for a long time to come."

"Perhaps you're right," said Paddington sleepily as he stretched out his paws. "But I *was* at a loose end."

◆ ◆ ◆

Chapter 7

Paddington Makes a Clean Sweep

Paddington stood in the middle of the Browns' dining room and gazed round with interest.

When Mrs. Bird had brought him his breakfast in bed that morning he'd had his suspicions that something unusual was going on. Breakfast in bed on a weekday was a sure sign that Mrs. Bird wanted him out of the way. But not even the distant bumping noises, which had been going on from quite an early hour, had in any way prepared him for the sight which met his eyes.

Normally the Browns' house was tidier than most, but on this particular morning the dining room looked very much as if a hurricane had recently passed through. The furniture had all been moved to one end. The carpet had been rolled up and was standing against one of the walls. There were no curtains at any of the windows and the pictures had all been taken down. Even the grate was cold and empty and the only heat came from an electric fire at one end of the room.

"I didn't know you were cleaning your springs, Mrs. Bird," he exclaimed, looking most surprised.

"Not cleaning our springs," repeated Mrs. Bird. "*Spring cleaning*—that's quite a different matter."

"It means cleaning the whole house from top to bottom," explained Mrs. Brown. "It'll be your room next. We can't leave it a moment longer."

"And talking of not leaving things a moment longer," said Mrs. Bird as she hurried out of the room, "if we don't get a move on and buy that curtain material we shan't have any dinner tonight."

"Do you think we ought to take him with us?" asked Mrs. Brown, as she followed Mrs. Bird into the hall, leaving Paddington to investigate the unusual state of affairs in the dining room by himself. "He's got a very good eye for a bargain."

"No," said Mrs. Bird firmly. "Definitely not. It's bad enough shopping when the spring sales are on at the best of times, but if that bear comes with us there's no knowing what we shall end up with. Bargain or no bargain, he can stay and mind the house."

Mrs. Brown cast a doubtful look after her housekeeper as she disappeared up the stairs. Although from past experience she agreed with Mrs. Bird on the subject of Paddington accompanying them on shopping expeditions, the thought of him being left in charge of the house when they were in the middle of spring cleaning raised even more serious doubts in her mind.

"I can see it's going to be one of those days," she called as the sound of hammering came from somewhere overhead. "What with the chimney, and spring cleaning into the bargain, anything can happen."

"And probably will," said Mrs. Bird as she came back down the stairs adjusting her hat. "But worrying about it won't alter things. Where's that bear? I haven't given him his instructions yet."

"Here I am, Mrs. Bird," called Paddington, hurrying into the hall.

Mrs. Bird looked at him suspiciously. There was a gleam in his eyes which she didn't like the look of at all, but fortunately for Paddington she was in too much of a hurry to look deeply into the matter.

"I've left you some salad on a tray," she said. "And there's a stew ready on the stove—only mind you don't singe your whiskers when you light the gas. And don't let it boil dry. I don't want to find any nasty smells when I get home."

"Thank you very much, Mrs. Bird," said Paddington. "Perhaps I could do some tidying up while you're out," he added hopefully, as he followed the others towards the front door. "I've never done any spring cleaning before."

Mrs. Brown and Mrs. Bird exchanged glances. "You may do some dusting if you like," said Mrs. Brown. "But I shouldn't do too much tidying up. It's all rather heavy and you might strain yourself. I'm afraid we shall have to eat in the kitchen for a day or two—at least until Mr. Brown has cleaned the chimney. Though goodness knows when that'll be."

Mrs. Brown gave Paddington one last look as she hurried after Mrs. Bird. "I do hope he'll be all right," she said.

"Willing paws make light work," replied Mrs. Bird. "And if it keeps him out of mischief there won't be any great harm done."

Mrs. Brown gave a sigh, but luckily for her peace of mind every step down Windsor Gardens took her farther and farther away from number thirty-two, for if she had been able to see inside her house at that moment she might have felt even less happy about leaving Paddington to his own devices.

After he closed the front door Paddington hurried back down the hall with an excited gleam in his eyes. There was an idea stirring in the back of his mind to do with a large interesting-looking box with a Barkridges label tied to the outside which he'd seen standing by the dining room fireplace.

For some days the word "chimney" had cropped up a number of times in the Brown household. It had all started when Mrs. Bird opened the dining room door one morning and found the room full of smoke.

Shortly afterwards Mr. Brown spent some time on the telephone only to announce that all the local chimney sweeps had so much work on their hands they were booked up for weeks to come.

At the time Paddington hadn't given the matter much thought. It seemed rather a lot of fuss to make over a little bit of smoke, and after peering up the chimney once or twice he'd decided there wasn't much to see anyway. Even when Mr. Brown dropped a chance remark at breakfast one morning about doing it himself he hadn't paid a great deal of attention.

But the news that operations were about to commence, together with the arrival of the mysterious-looking box, had aroused his interest at last.

The outside of the box exceeded his wildest dreams. Even the label was exciting. It was made up of a number of brightly colored pictures called EASY STAGES, and across the top in large capital letters were the words SWEEP-IT-KLEEN. THE ALL-BRITISH DO-IT-YOURSELF CHIMNEY SWEEP OUTFIT.

Underneath, in smaller print, the label went on to say that even a child of ten could make the dirtiest chimney spotless in a matter of moments. To show how easy it all was the first picture had a small boy fitting the various bits and pieces together as he prepared to sweep his father's chimney.

Paddington felt a slight pang of guilt as he lifted the lid of the box and peered inside, but he soon lost it as he settled down in an armchair, dipping his paw into a jar of marmalade every now and then as he examined the contents.

Although none of the pictures on the label mentioned anything about bears being able to sweep their chimneys, it made everything look so clear and simple he began to wonder why anyone ever bothered to hire a real chimney sweep at all.

One picture even showed a large bag labeled SOOT standing next to a pile of silver coins and followed it with the inscription MAKE MONEY IN YOUR SPARE TIME BY SELLING SOOT TO YOUR NEIGHBORS FOR THEIR GARDEN.

Paddington couldn't quite picture Mr. Curry actually paying for someone else's soot but all the same he began to feel that Mr. Brown's outfit was very good value indeed.

Inside the box there was a large round brush together with a number of long rods with metal ends which screwed together to form one long pole. Underneath the rods was yet another compartment containing a sack for the soot and a sheet with two armholes so that the person sweeping the chimney could fix it to the mantelpiece and work without getting the rest of the room dirty.

Paddington tried putting his paws through the sheet, and after screwing the brush onto one of the rods, he spent several enjoyable minutes while he hurried round the room poking it into various nooks and crannies.

It was when he decided to test it up the chimney itself that a thoughtful expression gradually came over his face. The brush went up and down remarkably easily, and even with only one rod the grate was full of soot in no time at all.

Paddington grew more and more thoughtful as he shoveled the soot into the sack and then tried fixing a second rod to the first. Although Mrs. Brown hadn't actually mentioned anything about sweeping the chimney he felt sure it could quite easily come under the heading of dusting.

Number thirty-two Windsor Gardens was a tall house, and as the bundle of rods by Paddington's side got smaller and smaller, so the pile of soot in the grate grew larger and deeper.

Several times he had to stop and clear it away to make room for his paws as first the sack and then several of Mrs. Bird's old grocery boxes became full to the brim. He was beginning to give up hope of ever reaching the top when suddenly, without any warning, the brush freed itself and he nearly fell over into the grate as he clung to the last of the rods.

Paddington sat in the fireplace for a while mopping his brow with a corner of the sheet and then, after disappearing upstairs for a few moments, he hurried outside carrying his binoculars.

According to a note on the box lid the exciting part about sweeping a chimney was always the moment when the brush popped out of the chimney pot and he was particularly anxious to see it for himself.

Carefully adjusting the glasses he climbed the ladder which Mr. Briggs, the builder, had left standing against the side of the house and peered up at the roof with a pleased expression on his face. The view through the binoculars of the brush poking out of Mr. Brown's chimney pot almost exactly matched the picture on the box.

Paddington spent some time drinking in the view and then he climbed back down the ladder and hurried into the house wearing the air of a bear with a job well done. All in all, it had been a good morning's work and he felt sure the Browns would be very pleased when they reached home and found how busy he'd been.

Pulling the brush back down the chimney proved to be a lot easier than pushing it up had been and it seemed only a matter of moments before he found himself reaching up behind the sheet for the last of the rods.

It was as he disentangled himself from the sheet that a startled expression suddenly came over Paddington's face, and he nearly fell over backwards with surprise as he stared at the rod in his paw. He rubbed his eyes in case he'd got some soot in them by mistake and then gazed at the end of the rod again. It was definitely the last one of the set, as he'd counted them all most carefully, but of the brush itself there was nothing to be seen.

After peering hopefully up the chimney several times Paddington sat down anxiously in the fireplace in order to consult the instructions on the box.

As he lifted the lid he suddenly caught sight of a large red label pasted to the bottom of the box. It had escaped his notice before and as he read it his eyes grew larger and larger. It said simply:

WARNING!

AFTER SWEEPING THE CHIMNEY, GREAT CARE

MUST BE TAKEN WHEN UNSCREWING RODS.

OTHERWISE THE BRUSH MAY BECOME DETACHED!

"My brush become detached?" exclaimed Paddington bitterly, addressing the world in general as he gazed at the rod in one paw and the box in the other.

Apart from leaving the warning about the brush becoming detached until it was far too late, the only advice the notice seemed to give for when things did go wrong was contained in the four words CONSULT YOUR NEAREST DEALER.

Paddington sat in the fireplace with a mournful expression on his face. He felt sure that Barkridges wouldn't be at all keen if he consulted them on the subject of Mr. Brown's brush being stuck up his chimney, and he was equally certain that Mr. Brown himself would be even less happy when he heard the news.

In fact, after giving the matter a great deal of thought, the only way he could see to soften the blow at all was to clear up some of the mess and hope that while he did so he might get an idea on the subject.

If, earlier in the day, the Browns' dining room had given the impression of having been in the path of a hurricane, it now looked as if a belt of thick smog had passed through as well. Despite the dust sheet, everything seemed to be covered in a thin layer of soot, and looking round the room Paddington decided that in more ways than one he'd never seen things looking quite so black.

◆◆◆

Mr. Brown took his head out of the chimney and looked round at the others. "I can't understand it," he exclaimed. "That's the third time I've tried to light the fire. It keeps going out."

Mrs. Brown picked up a newspaper and began waving some of the smoke away. "There's obviously been another fall of soot," she said. "It's everywhere. If you ask me, the chimney's blocked. I told you it needed sweeping."

"How *could* I sweep it?" said Mr. Brown crossly. "The kit only arrived this morning."

The Browns grouped themselves unhappily round the fireplace and stared at the pile of used matches.

"And that's another thing," continued Mr. Brown. "I'm sending it straight back to Barkridges. It's filthy dirty and there isn't even a brush. You can't sweep a chimney without a brush."

"Perhaps Paddington's borrowed it for something," said Mrs. Brown vaguely. "I can't find him anywhere."

"Paddington?" echoed Mr. Brown. "What would he want with a brush?"

"There's no knowing," said Mrs. Bird ominously.

Mrs. Bird didn't like the signs of a hurried cleaning up she'd noticed in the dining room or the various sooty paw marks which she'd discovered during a quick glance round the rest of the house, but in view of the look on Mr. Brown's face she wisely kept her thoughts to herself.

"He hasn't touched his stew," said Mrs. Brown. "And that's most unusual."

"Forget Paddington's stew," replied Mr. Brown. "I'm more worried about the fire."

Mrs. Brown opened the French windows and looked into the garden. "Perhaps Mr. Briggs can help," she said. "He's just come back."

In answer to Mrs. Brown's call Mr. Briggs, the builder, came into the dining room and put his ear to the chimney with an experienced air. "Jackdaws!" he said, after a moment. "You've got a jackdaw's nest in yer pot. If you listen you can hear 'em coughing."

"Coughing?" exclaimed Mrs. Bird. "I didn't know jackdaws coughed."

"You'd cough, Mum," said Mr. Briggs, "if someone tried to light a fire under your nest. But don't you worry," he continued, opening up Mr. Brown's cleaning set. "I'll have it out in a jiffy."

The Browns stood back and watched while Mr. Briggs began pushing the rods up the chimney. "Good thing you had these," he went on. "Otherwise it might have been a rare old job."

Mr. Briggs's face became redder and redder as the rods got harder to push, but at long last he gave a final upward heave and there was a loud crashing noise as something heavy landed in the grate.

"There you are," he announced triumphantly. "What did I tell you?"

Mr. Brown adjusted his glasses and peered at the round black bristly object lying on the hearth. "It looks a funny sort of bird's nest to me," he said. "In fact, if you ask me it's more like the brush out of a chimney-sweeping outfit."

"You're quite right," said Mr. Briggs, scratching his head. "It's a brush all right."

Mr. Briggs began to look even more puzzled as he picked up the object and examined it more closely. "It seems to be in some sort of container," he exclaimed.

"That's not a container," said Mrs. Brown. "It's Paddington's hat."

"Good heavens! So it is," exclaimed Mr. Brown. "But what's it doing up the chimney—and with my brush inside it?"

"Mercy me!" interrupted Mrs. Bird, pointing towards the window. "Look!"

The others turned and followed the direction of her gaze. "I can't see anything," said Mr. Brown.

"Is anything the matter?" asked Mrs. Brown, looking at her housekeeper with some concern. "You've gone quite white."

"I thought I saw a chimney pot go past the window," exclaimed Mrs. Bird.

Mr. and Mrs. Brown exchanged glances. Normally Mrs. Bird was the sanest member of the family and it was most unusual for her to have hallucinations.

"I think you'd better sit down," said Mr. Brown, drawing up a chair. "Perhaps the excitement's been too much for you."

"It's all right, Mrs. Bird," came a familiar, if somewhat muffled, voice from the dining room doorway. "It's only me."

If Mrs. Bird had been taken by surprise a moment before, the others looked even more amazed as they turned and stared at the black object before them. In place of his usual headgear Paddington was wearing what appeared to be half a chimney pot which covered his ears and came down over his eyes like an oversize top hat.

"I'm afraid it broke off when Mr. Briggs poked his rods up," he explained, when the noise had died down.

"But what on earth were you doing up on the roof in the first place?" asked Mr. Brown.

"I was dusting the chimney," said Paddington sadly. "The brush got detached by mistake and I was trying to rescue it."

"Paddington?" echoed Mr. Briggs disbelievingly as he began levering the pot off. "Proper mess he's in."

Paddington looked most offended at Mr. Briggs's words as he sat on the floor rubbing his ears. It had been bad enough losing Mr. Brown's brush up the chimney in the first place, but then to get his head stuck inside the pot and be mistaken for a bird's nest into the bargain seemed the unkindest cut of all.

"I know one thing," said Mrs. Bird sternly. "You're going straight up to the bathroom. We must have the dirtiest bear within fifty miles!"

Mr. Briggs gave a sudden chuckle as he looked at the others. "I'll say this much," he remarked, pouring oil on troubled waters. "You may not have the cleanest bear within fifty miles but I'm willing to bet there isn't a cleaner chimney."

Paddington looked at Mr. Briggs gratefully and then hurried out of the room before any more questions could be asked. For once in his life he agreed with Mrs. Bird that a nice hot bath with plenty of soap was the best order of the day.

Apart from that, he had just remembered that he hadn't eaten his stew. Paddington was very keen on stew and he was anxious to make sure the cooker was turned on so that it would be all ready for him when he got downstairs again.

Chapter 8

Paddington in a Hole

Mrs. Brown turned away from the hall mirror and made a face as the sound of hammering rent the morning air.

"I suppose I mustn't grumble," she said. "Henry's been making enough noise himself these past few weeks. But I do wish Mr. Curry would hurry up and finish all his jobs. He does go on rather."

"I wouldn't mind," said Mrs. Bird, "if they were his own ideas in the first place, but he must always go copying other people. He's even talking now of putting a serving hatch in his kitchen wall!"

Mrs. Bird gave one of her "Mr. Curry snorts" as she put some finishing touches to her hat. The Browns' neighbor, apart from having a reputation in the district for his meanness, also had a habit of copying other people, and living next door to him, the Browns suffered more than most.

Recently Mr. Brown had carried out quite a number of jobs in and round their house. Apart from decorating several of the rooms, he'd also laid a concrete path in the back garden and installed a serving hatch between their kitchen and the dining room.

Mr. Curry had had a hard time keeping up with all the activity in number thirty-two Windsor Gardens, but only the day before he'd announced in a loud voice his intention of carrying out the last two tasks himself in the near future, and that very morning he'd arrived in his back garden dressed in old overalls in order to make preparations for the path.

"I must say," began Mrs. Brown, "there are times when I find taking the family all the way across London just to visit the dentist a bit of a nuisance, but I shan't be at all sorry today." She gave a sigh as another burst of hammering echoed between the two buildings. "Are you sure you don't want to come with us, Paddington?" she called.

Paddington hurried into the hall at the sound of his name. "No thank you, Mrs. Brown," he exclaimed when she repeated her question. Although he'd never actually been to a dentist he didn't like the sound of them at all, especially after listening to some of Jonathan's graphic descriptions of what went on.

"I think perhaps I'll stay at home and sit in the garden instead," he announced before anyone could try to change his mind for him.

Mrs. Brown eyed the retreating figure of Paddington as he disappeared into the dining room. "You know, it's an extraordinary thing," she remarked, "but I do believe he's turned over a new leaf. Do you realize we haven't had a single disaster for some time? Not one!"

Mrs. Bird hastily touched wood as she made for the front door. "Don't tempt fate," she warned. "That young bear doesn't need any encouragement."

Mrs. Bird wasn't at all happy about leaving Paddington alone in the house. She had decided views about his various activities and the fact that nothing untoward had happened for a while left her unmoved.

But even the Browns' housekeeper would have found it hard to fault Paddington's behavior, at least for the next few minutes or so, had she been there to see it.

Having finished breakfast he carefully wiped his whiskers on the napkin provided by a hopeful Mrs. Brown and then made his way through the French windows and out onto the terrace where he stood for a moment sniffing the morning air.

Paddington liked the summer, especially in Mr. Brown's garden, which for a London garden was unusually large and full of flowers and shrubs, each with its own special smell.

But the peace of Paddington's morning was short-lived, for just as he was making some last-minute adjustments to a deck chair so that he could sit down for a while and enjoy the morning sunshine, a familiar voice rang out over the fence.

"Good morning, bear," said the voice.

Paddington jumped up. "Good morning, Mr. Curry," he said doubtfully, raising his hat politely.

But for once the Browns' neighbor seemed to be in an unusually jovial mood, and if he didn't actually beam at Paddington at least his lips cracked in something approaching a smile as he looked over the fence.

Mr. Curry waved a large mallet in Paddington's direction. "I wonder if you'd care to lend a paw, bear," he said casually. "I'm putting in some stakes and it's a bit difficult with only one pair of hands."

His voice droned on about his various jobs that needed to be done as he helped Paddington through a hole in the fence.

"Now, I've marked the positions where I want them all," he continued as Paddington stood up. "There are one hundred and fifty altogether. I'll just show you what I want done and then you can carry on while I go out and do my shopping. I want to get some paint for my new serving hatch when it's in."

Mr. Curry paused for breath. "I don't suppose you'll get all the stakes in before I'm back, but if you do you can collect some rubble for me. It's for the foundations and I'm running a bit short. In fact, I might even pay you if you do.

"Mind you," he added, before Paddington had time to speak, "I shan't if it's not proper brick rubble. I don't want to come back home and find half my rockery missing.

"Now, come along, bear," he growled sternly as he handed Paddington the mallet. "Don't just stand there. I've got a lot of shopping to do and I want to get out this morning."

Mr. Curry picked up a stake from a nearby pile and then pushed it firmly into the ground with both hands. "Now," he said, "when I nod my head, you hit it."

For a moment Paddington looked at Mr. Curry as if he could hardly believe his ears and then, as the Browns' neighbor closed his eyes and began nodding his head vigorously to show that he was ready, he took a firm grasp of the mallet with both paws.

A moment later a yell of pain rang out round Windsor Gardens, echoing and re-echoing in and out of the buildings.

Paddington jumped back in alarm and the mallet fell unheeded from his paws as, to his surprise, instead of looking pleased, Mr. Curry let go of the stake, gave

another tremendous yell, and then began dancing up and down clutching his head with both hands.

"Bear!" he roared, as Paddington disappeared through the hole in the fence. "Bear! Where are you, bear? Come back, bear!"

But Paddington was nowhere to be seen. Only the faintest movement of the raspberry canes betrayed his whereabouts, and a few moments later even that stopped as Mr. Curry peered over the fence before staggering back up the garden towards his house.

For the next few minutes the distant sound of banging doors and the hiss of running water greeted Paddington's ears, but at long last a final and much louder bang from the front of Mr. Curry's house caused him to heave a sigh of relief as he stood up and brushed himself clean.

Paddington hesitated for a moment and then climbed back through the hole in the fence and stared gloomily at the beginnings of Mr. Curry's path.

The Browns' neighbor had a habit of twisting words so that his listeners were never quite certain what had actually been said, but he was almost sure he hadn't agreed to lend a paw with *one* of the stakes let alone do all one hundred and fifty by himself.

Now that he had time to examine it more carefully, the pile of stakes looked even bigger than it had at first sight. Not only that, but to add to his troubles Mr. Curry appeared to have taken the mallet away with him.

After making several attempts to knock in some stakes with the aid of half a brick, Paddington gave up in disgust and hurried up the path in the direction of Mr. Curry's house.

In his haste the Browns' neighbor had left his back door ajar and a few moments later Paddington let himself cautiously into the kitchen.

The curtains were drawn and as he blinked in order to accustom his eyes to the change of light Paddington suddenly stopped in his tracks and stared in astonishment, all thoughts of the missing mallet driven from his mind.

It was some while since he'd last set foot in Mr. Curry's kitchen, and from the little he could remember of it the decorations then had been mostly of a rather dirty brown color, certainly nothing like the ones which greeted him now.

In fact, all in all, apart from a bag of tools in one corner and one or two obviously unfinished patches it now looked not unlike something out of one of Mrs. Brown's glossy magazines, or even, for that matter, Mrs. Brown's own freshly decorated kitchen itself. The walls were gleaming white, the floor black and equally shiny, and even the stove and the refrigerator looked new.

It was as he stood taking it all in that a thoughtful expression gradually came over Paddington's face. Leaning against one of the walls was a wooden frame and a pair of doors, and seeing it reminded him of a remark passed by Mr. Curry as he'd helped him through the fence.

"I'm on the last lap in my kitchen, bear," he'd said. "There's only the serving hatch to put in and the job will be done."

Mr. Curry had gone on to grumble about the number of unfinished jobs he had on hand but at the time Paddington had been too busy worrying about the stakes to take much notice. However, the more he thought about the matter now, the more it seemed like a golden opportunity to make amends for the unfortunate accident earlier in the day.

A few minutes later the sound of hammering could be heard in Windsor Gardens. It was followed shortly afterwards by the dull thud of a falling brick, the first of many which gradually found their way from inside the kitchen to a large pile outside the back door.

Paddington felt sure from the little Mr. Curry had said about all his jobs that he couldn't fail to be pleased if he arrived home later that morning and found his serving hatch already installed. And even if the hatch itself wasn't in place he couldn't possibly find anything to grumble at in having a start made on the hole.

Apart from that, knocking down walls was much more enjoyable work than banging in stakes. Once a start had been made by removing the first brick, which had taken rather a lot of hammering with a chisel, it was more a matter of clouting everything in sight as hard as possible, and standing back every now and then to

avoid being hit by some of the larger lumps as they parted company with the rest.

Soon the air was so thick with dust it became almost impossible to see, but as the last brick fell to the floor Paddington surveyed the result of his labors as best he could through half-closed eyes and then measured the space carefully with his paws in order to make sure it was the right size.

After placing the frame gently into position and making it secure by jamming a couple of pieces of wood in either side, he slipped the doors into their grooves and then stood back, waiting for the dust to settle so that he could inspect his handiwork.

As the air gradually cleared Paddington began to look more and more pleased with himself. Admittedly the hatch wasn't perfectly level, and there were one or two rather unfortunate paw marks on the surrounding wall, but those two things apart he decided it was one of the best jobs he could ever remember doing, and he felt sure Mr. Curry would be equally pleased when he saw it.

Dipping his paw into a nearby jar of marmalade he idly pushed one of the doors to one side in order to make sure it slid properly on its runners.

As he did so the pleased expression suddenly drained from Paddington's face and he nearly toppled over backwards with surprise as he took in the view through the open hatch.

Since he'd lived with the Browns he'd examined number thirty-two Windsor Gardens from a good many different angles but never in his wildest dreams had he ever pictured seeing it through a serving hatch in Mr. Curry's kitchen wall, particularly when he'd expected to see a dining room instead.

For a moment Paddington stood where he was with his feet frozen to the ground, and then he hurried outside rubbing his eyes in order to make sure it wasn't all part of some terrible dream.

As he peered up at the outside wall, Paddington's worst fears were realized and gradually the truth of the matter dawned on him. In his hurry to complete the job he'd quite forgotten the fact that although Mr. Curry's house was exactly the same in most respects as the Browns', because it was next door everything was the other way round, so that what was the dining room wall in the Browns' house became the outside wall in Mr. Curry's.

Paddington's face grew longer and longer as he considered the matter. According to Mrs. Bird, Mr. Curry had been doing quite a few jobs in his house of late, but for the life of him Paddington couldn't think of a single good reason why he would possibly want a serving hatch in his outside wall.

There were still several pieces of brick lying on the ground where they had fallen, but after one or two attempts he soon gave up all hope of fitting them back into position.

How long he stayed lost in thought Paddington wasn't quite sure, but he was suddenly roused from his daydreams by the sound of Mr. Curry's side gate banging shut.

Hurrying round to the back of the house he was just in time to meet the Browns' neighbor coming round the other way. Apart from a bandage on the back of his head, Mr. Curry looked little the worse for his earlier encounter with Paddington. Nevertheless his face darkened as they bumped into each other.

"What are you up to now, bear?" he growled.

"What am I up to, Mr. Curry?" said Paddington, playing for time.

Mr. Curry looked suspiciously at the brick dust sticking to Paddington's fur and then, as he caught sight of the pile of brick rubble outside the kitchen door, his face suddenly cleared.

"Good work, bear," he said approvingly as he felt in his pocket. "I promised to pay you, and I must say you've earned it."

"Thank you very much, Mr. Curry," said Paddington doubtfully, as he took the coin. "I'll keep it for a while in case you want it back."

"What!" exclaimed Mr. Curry. "Nonsense! Of course I shan't want it back. This rubble's just what I need for my path."

"I don't think I should use it for your path, Mr. Curry," said Paddington anxiously. "You may want it for something else."

Mr. Curry gave a loud snort as he picked up his shovel. "Not use it," he repeated. "Give me one good reason why I shouldn't, bear."

Paddington looked on unhappily as Mr. Curry transferred the pile of rubble into a nearby trench and when, some while later, the Browns' neighbor poured a barrowload of wet cement over the top, he looked unhappier still.

"There!" said Mr. Curry, rubbing his hands together. "That won't come up again in a hurry once it's set." He turned, but for the second time that morning found himself addressing the empty air, for his audience, like the brick rubble, had completely disappeared from view.

Paddington felt sure he could give the Browns' neighbor not one, but several very good reasons why he shouldn't have used the bricks he'd found outside his kitchen door. On the other hand he was equally sure he would be much happier if Mr. Curry discovered the reasons for himself, preferably sometime in the dim and distant future, and certainly when the cause of it all was a long, long way away.

◆ ◆ ◆

Paddington sat up in bed holding a thermometer in his paw. "I think I must have caught the measles, Mrs. Bird," he announced weakly. "My temperature's over one hundred and twenty!"

"One hundred and twenty!" Mrs. Bird hurriedly examined the thermometer. "That's not a temperature," she exclaimed with relief. "That's a marmalade stain."

Mrs. Brown looked Paddington over carefully. "He's certainly got some red spots on him," she said. "It's a bit difficult to tell with fur, but I suppose it could be measles."

"*Hmm,*" said Mrs. Bird suspiciously. "That's as may be. But it's the first time I've ever known measles spots to come off on the sheets."

"Perhaps they've worked loose, Mrs. Bird," said Paddington hopefully. "I've been scratching them."

Mrs. Brown exchanged a glance with her housekeeper. "It looks more like brick dust to me," she said.

Mrs. Bird glanced out of the window towards the house next door. "Talking of brick dust," she said, "reminds me that Mr. Curry called to see you just now, Paddington."

"Oh dear," said Mrs. Brown as a loud groan came from the direction of Paddington's bed. "Is anything the matter?"

"I think I've had a bit of a relapse, Mrs. Brown," said a weak voice from under the sheet. "I don't think I ought to do any more talking."

"That's a pity," said Mrs. Bird. "He asked me to give you fifty pence."

"Fifty pence!" exclaimed Paddington, sitting up in bed suddenly. "But I've already *had* fifty pence."

"In that case," said Mrs. Bird, "you've got a pound."

"Apparently he's very pleased with his new delivery hatch," explained Mrs. Brown. "All sorts of people have been congratulating him. The milkman. The baker. The boy from the grocery shop. They all think it's a splendid idea. Mr. Curry's going to build a cupboard inside so that they can leave things and he won't have to answer the door."

"There'll be no holding him now he's got something no one else has thought of," said Mrs. Bird. "He'll be like a dog with two tails. You mark my words, we shall hear of nothing else from morning to night."

"It certainly is a good idea," said Mrs. Brown, as she paused at the door. "Mind you," she continued, "I can't help feeling it's a good job Judy managed to catch the milkman when she did."

"And that Jonathan had a chat with the baker," added Mrs. Bird.

"Otherwise," said Mrs. Brown, "I might not have thought to have a word with the grocery boy."

"And where," said her housekeeper, "would we have been then?"

Mrs. Bird looked towards Paddington's bed, but the only answer she received was a loud groan as its occupant appeared to have another sudden relapse.

All the same, although as groans went it was a long and rather blood-curdling one, there was something about the set of Paddington's whiskers as they poked out from beneath the sheets which somehow managed to suggest the possibility of a recovery in the not-too-distant future.

"I give it until teatime at the outside," said Mrs. Brown as she closed the door.

"If not before," agreed Mrs. Bird. "I'm baking a chocolate cake for tea."

"In that case," said Mrs. Brown, "definitely before. There's nothing like a few whiffs of chocolate cake up the stairs for curing even the worst attack of a young bear's measles!"

Chapter 9

Pantomime Time

The Browns exchanged glances as they pushed their way through the crowds thronging the street outside the Alhambra Theater.

While Judy took a firm grip of Paddington's left paw, Mrs. Bird clasped her umbrella and took up station on his other side.

"Don't let go of my hand whatever you do," said Judy. "We don't want you to get lost."

"And watch your hat," warned Mrs. Bird. "If it gets knocked off and trampled underfoot you may never see it again."

Paddington needed no second bidding, and with his other paw he placed his suitcase firmly on top of his head.

It was the start of the pantomime season in London and as a special Christmas treat Mr. Brown had reserved seats for the opening night of *Dick Whittington*.

It was a long time since Paddington had been taken to a theater, and he'd certainly never ever been to a pantomime before, so he was very much looking forward to the occasion.

Mr. Gruber, who'd also been included in the party, brought up the rear, and as they made their way up the steps he tapped Paddington on the shoulder and motioned him to listen to an announcement coming through a loudspeaker. It was all about the dangers of buying souvenir programs from unauthorized sellers outside the theater, who were apparently charging no less than two pounds a time.

Paddington could hardly believe his ears and he gave one man, wearing an old raincoat, a very hard stare indeed from beneath his suitcase as a brightly colored booklet was thrust under his nose.

"*Two pounds* for a program!" he exclaimed.

"I've never heard of such a thing!" agreed Mrs. Bird, poking the man menacingly with her umbrella.

The man gave them a nasty look. "Just you wait," he said. "Some people don't know when they're well off."

"I wonder what he meant by that?" asked Mr. Brown, as they reached the entrance doors at long last.

Paddington didn't know either, but before he had time to consider the matter he found himself being addressed by a superior-looking official standing inside the foyer.

"Good for you," said the man approvingly. "I wish more of our patrons took such a firm line with these people. It's costing us a small fortune in lost sales. Allow me to offer you one of our official programs."

"Thank you very much," said Paddington gratefully. "I'll have seven, please."

"*Seven!*" The man looked even more impressed as he signaled to one of the ushers to join them.

"Seven of our special souvenir programs for the young bear gentleman, Mavis," he called.

"Thank you *very* much sir," said the girl as she counted out the programs and handed them to Paddington. "That'll be twenty-one pounds, please."

"*Twenty-one pounds!*" exclaimed Paddington, nearly falling over backwards in alarm. "That's *three* pounds each. I wish I'd bought some outside now!"

Mr. Gruber gave a cough. "I think perhaps we'd better have one for you to keep, Mr. Brown," he said, before anyone else had time to speak, "and seven ordinary ones for the rest of us."

"*Seven*, Mr. Gruber?" echoed Judy. "Don't you mean six?"

"I expect young Mr. Brown would like to send one to his Aunt Lucy when he next writes," said Mr. Gruber. And ignoring the protests from the others he handed over the money. "It's my pleasure," he said. "I don't know when I last went to a pantomime."

After thanking Mr. Gruber for his kind act, Paddington gave the staff in the lobby some very dark glances indeed as they went on their way. They suggested he was going to have a great deal to say on the subject of theaters when he next wrote to his aunt. In fact, it was going to take a very large postcard indeed to get it all in.

But as they took their seats in the front row of the orchestra section and he examined his program, Paddington began to cheer up again, for it was full of colored pictures with lots of reading as well, and despite the high cost the more he looked at it the better value it seemed.

"That's a picture of the Principal Boy," explained Judy, as she caught a puzzled look on his face. "It's being played by a girl."

"The Dame's played by a man," broke in Jonathan.

If they thought their explanations were going to help Paddington's understanding of pantomimes they were mistaken.

"Why don't they change over?" he asked. "Then everything would be all right."

"They can't," said Jonathan. "The Dame's *always* played by a man."

"And the Principal Boy is *always* a girl," agreed Judy. "It's traditional."

"I don't see why," insisted Paddington.

The others lapsed into silence. Now that Paddington mentioned it, they couldn't think of a very good reason either, but luckily the orchestra chose that moment to launch into the overture and so the subject was dropped for the time being.

Mrs. Brown glanced along the row. "Don't miss the opening scene, dear," she called. "You'll see Dick Whittington's marmalade cat."

Paddington licked his lips. "I shall enjoy that, Mrs. Brown," he announced.

The Browns looked at each other uneasily. "Well . . ." began Mr. Brown. "Don't be too disappointed. It isn't a *real* cat."

"I shouldn't think so," said Paddington. "Not if it's made of marmalade."

"It isn't actually *made* of marmalade either," said Judy.

"Besides, it's in two parts," remarked Jonathan.

"Dick Whittington's cat's in two parts!" exclaimed Paddington. He jumped up from his seat in order to consult his program. Once when he'd been taken to the theater there had been a small slip tucked inside saying that one of the actors was indisposed, but either words had failed the management on this occasion or they were keeping the matter very dark, for no matter how hard he shook his program, nothing fell out.

"I didn't mean the *cat* was in two parts," hissed Jonathan as the house lights dimmed. "I meant two people take turns to play it."

"It's hard work," said Judy. "It gets very hot inside the fur."

"I get very hot inside *my* fur sometimes," said Paddington severely, "but there's only one of me."

Judy gave a sigh. Paddington was inclined to take things literally and sometimes it was difficult explaining matters to him, but fortunately she was saved any further complications as the curtain rose to reveal the street outside the home of the famous London shipping merchant Alderman Fitzwarren.

The Browns settled back to enjoy the show, and as the cast went into the opening chorus even Paddington seemed to forget the problem.

He cheered loudly when Dick Whittington arrived on the scene with Sukie, the cat, and when both Dick and Sukie collapsed on the steps of Alderman Fitzwarren's house, faint with hunger, it was with difficulty that the Browns managed to restrain him from going up onstage.

"I don't think a marmalade sandwich would help, dear," whispered Mrs. Brown nervously, as Paddington began feeling inside his hat.

"It happens every night," hissed Mr. Brown.

"Twice nightly on Thursdays and Saturdays," agreed Jonathan.

Paddington fell back into his seat. He found it hard to picture anyone going without food at the best of times, let alone twice nightly on Thursdays and Saturdays, and having already removed the marmalade sandwich from under his hat he decided to make the most of it.

For the rest of the first act, apart from a few boos at appropriate moments, much to everyone's relief the only sound to be heard from Paddington's direction was that of a steady munching as he polished off the remains of his emergency supply.

During the intermission, while Mr. Brown went to fetch some ice cream, Mr. Gruber attempted to explain some of the plot to Paddington.

"You see, Mr. Brown," he said, "Dick Whittington came to London because he thought the streets were paved with gold, but like many others before him he soon found his mistake. Luckily, he was taken in by Alderman Fitzwarren—rather like Mr. and Mrs. Brown took you in when they found you on Paddington Station. Alderman Fitzwarren was so pleased at the way Sukie drove off all the rats in his house that when he sent one of his ships to the West Indies he let Dick and Sukie go along too."

"The second half is all about how they land on the Boko Islands and how Sukie saves the day there," said Judy.

"There's a magic act as well," broke in Jonathan, reading from his program. "He's called the Great Divide."

Paddington pricked up his ears as he finished the remains of his ice cream. He was keen on conjuring and, all in all, now that he'd got over his first confusion, he decided he liked pantomimes. There was a bit too much singing and dancing for his taste, but some of the scenery was very good indeed, and he applauded no end when Dick and Sukie arrived on the island and in the excitement of a quick change one of the stagehands got left onstage by mistake.

But he reserved his best claps for the moment when a black velvet cloth came down and in the glow of a single spotlight the majestic figure of the magician, resplendent in top hat and a flowing black cape, strode onto the stage.

After removing several rabbits and a goldfish bowl from his hat, and a seemingly endless string of flags of all nations from his left ear, the Great Divide came forward to address the audience, while behind him several girls in tights and gold costumes wheeled on an assortment of mysterious-looking boxes.

"And now," he said, silencing a drum roll with his hand, "I would like one volunteer from the audience."

"Oh dear, Henry," said Mrs. Brown, as there was a sudden flurry of movement from alongside them. "I knew it was a mistake to sit in the front row."

"Trust Paddington," agreed Jonathan.

"How was I to know this would happen?" said Mr. Brown unhappily.

The Browns watched anxiously as Paddington clambered onto the stage carrying his suitcase. But if the Great Divide was at all taken aback, he managed to hide his feelings remarkably well, and after some more chitchat he opened one of the boxes with a flourish and motioned Paddington to sit inside.

"I don't think I've ever sawed a bear in two before," he said, as he snapped the box shut.

"What!" exclaimed Paddington in alarm. "You're going to saw me in two!"

"They don't call me the Great Divide for nothing," chuckled the magician in an aside to the audience.

"You'd better watch the toggles on your duffle coat," he warned, as an assistant handed over one of the largest saws Paddington had ever seen and he pinged it with his finger to show it was genuine. "We don't want any trouble with splinters. I don't think there's a doctor on the island."

"Oh dear," said Mrs. Brown nervously. "I hope he *doesn't* damage Paddington's coat—we shall never hear the last of it if he does."

"It's not that bear's *coat* I'm worried about," said Mrs. Bird grimly.

The Browns watched in silent fascination as the Great Divide placed his saw in a groove and began moving it rapidly to and fro in time to the "Tritsch Tratsch Polka."

Although they knew nothing could possibly go wrong, the sound of metal going through wood seemed all too realistic. Their sighs of relief as the trick finally came to an end were matched only by Paddington's as he staggered round the stage feeling himself carefully in order to make sure he was still in one piece.

"And now"—once again the Great Divide raised his hand for silence—"as you have been such a good assistant, I'm going to make you disappear."

"Thank you very much," said Paddington gratefully.

He turned to leave, but before he had time to gather his wits about him he found himself being led into an even larger box. A moment later, as the doors slammed shut, he felt himself start to whirl round and round with ever-increasing speed as the magician began turning it on its wheels and the music rose to a crescendo.

A round of applause greeted the Great Divide as he brought the box to a stop and then opened up the doors in order to demonstrate how empty it was.

"Don't worry," said Mr. Gruber, as he caught sight of the look on Judy's face. "It's all done by mirrors. I'm sure young Mr. Brown will be all right."

As if to prove his statement, there came a loud knocking from somewhere on-stage. "Let me out!" cried a muffled voice. "It's all dark."

Almost immediately the Great Divide abandoned his intention of producing some more rabbits out of thin air. He gave his assistants a quick glance of warning and hastily closed the cabinet doors. After twirling it round several more times he brought it to a stop again and reopened the doors.

The applause as Paddington staggered out onto the stage was even louder than it had been for the first trick.

"There now," said the magician. "That wasn't so bad, was it? Tell everyone you are all right."

"I'm *not*," said Paddington, looking most upset. "I feel sick and I've lost my suitcase."

"You've lost your *what*?" repeated the Great Divide.

"My suitcase," said Paddington. "It's got all my important things inside it. I had it with me when I went inside your box—now it's disappeared."

The Great Divide's smile became even more fixed. For a moment or two he looked as if he was about to do a variation of his earlier trick, this time sawing Paddington not only in two, but into as many pieces as possible.

"Fancy taking a suitcase with you," he hissed as he closed the doors once again. "In all my years on the stage I've never had this happen to me before.

"We'd better make sure everything's still in there," he continued sarcastically, as he re-did the trick, and after removing Paddington's suitcase from the box, opened it up in order to show the audience.

But as the Great Divide shook the case and nothing fell out his face fell. "I thought you said it was full of things," he exclaimed.

"It is, Mr. Divide," said Paddington firmly. "I'll show you." And taking his suitcase from the magician he turned his back and began feeling in the secret compartment.

"That's a photograph of my Aunt Lucy," he announced, waving a postcard in the air. "And that's my passport. Then there's my savings. And that's a map of the

Portobello Road . . . and a photograph I took with my camera . . . and my opera glasses . . . and a marmalade chunk . . . and . . ."

The rest of Paddington's remarks were lost in the storm of applause which rang out from all directions as object after object landed at the feet of the Great Divide.

"Bravo!" shouted someone sitting near the Browns. "Best double act I've seen in years."

"Had me fooled," agreed someone else nearby. "I thought it was just someone ordinary from the audience."

"Ordinary!" Mrs. Bird turned and fixed her gaze on the speaker. "Whatever else he is, Paddington certainly isn't *ordinary*. That's the last thing he is.

"Mind you," she remarked, as she settled back in her seat again while Paddington and his belongings were helped off the stage, "I always knew he kept a lot of things in that case of his, but I never dreamed he had quite so much."

After Paddington's appearance the rest of the pantomime seemed almost tame by comparison, although it soon picked up again, and by the time Dick Whittington and Sukie arrived back in England, triumphant after their long voyage, Paddington was already safely in his seat and joining in the choruses. In fact, when Dick asked Alderman Fitzwarren for his daughter's hand in marriage and the news was given out that he would soon become Lord Mayor of London, he nearly lost his hat in the general excitement.

When the curtain finally came down, some envious glances were cast in the Browns' direction as they were ushered backstage in order to meet the cast. Several people stopped Paddington and asked for his autograph, and he added his special pawprint to show that it was genuine.

"I hope you'll be very happy, Miss Whittington," he said, as they had their photograph taken together.

"I don't know about Dick Whittington being happy," said the manager. "I certainly am. This picture is going straight into our souvenir program. It'll make it even a better value than ever, and it'll teach those rascals outside a thing or two."

Even the Great Divide came out of his dressing room to say goodbye, and to mark the occasion he presented Paddington with one of his magic saws.

It was a happy party of Browns who eventually climbed into the car for the journey home. To round things off Mr. Brown drove through the center of London so that they could see the Christmas lights, and then on to Westminster Abbey where Mr. Gruber pointed out a stained glass window which showed a picture of Dick Whittington's cat.

But as they turned for home Paddington grew more and more thoughtful.

"Is anything the matter?" asked Mrs. Brown.

Paddington hesitated. "I was wondering if anyone had a large wooden box they don't want," he said hopefully.

"A large wooden box?" repeated Mr. Brown. "Whatever do you want that for?"

"I think I can guess," said Mrs. Bird, with a wisdom born of long experience of reading Paddington's mind. "And the answer is no.

"I don't begrudge people their pleasures," she added as they turned a corner into Windsor Gardens and she picked up Paddington's present from the Great Divide. "But I am not having anyone sawed in two in our house, thank you very much. Least of all a certain bear."

"I quite agree," said Mr. Gruber. "After all, Mr. Brown," he added with a twinkle in his eye, "there's a lot of truth in the old saying 'Two's company, three's a crowd.' If there were two of you I might have trouble sharing out our elevenses in future, and I wouldn't want that to happen—not for all the cocoa in the world."

Chapter 10.

Paddington and the Cold Snap

Paddington stood on the front doorstep of number thirty-two Windsor Gardens and sniffed the morning air. He peered out through the gap between his duffle coat hood and a brightly colored scarf which was wound tightly about his neck.

On the little that could be seen of his face behind some unusually white-looking whiskers there was a mixture of surprise and excitement as he took in the sight which met his eyes.

Overnight a great change had come over the weather. Whereas the day before had been mild, almost springlike for early January, now everything was covered by a thick white blanket of snow which reached almost to the top of his Wellington boots.

Not a sound disturbed the morning air. Apart from the clatter of breakfast things in the kitchen, where Mrs. Brown and Mrs. Bird were busy washing up, the only sign that he wasn't alone in the world came from a row of milk-bottle tops poking through the snow on the step and a long trail of footprints where the post-man had been earlier that day.

Paddington liked snow, but as he gazed at the view in the street outside he almost agreed with Mrs. Bird, the Browns' housekeeper, that it was possible to have too much of a good thing. Since he'd been living with the Brown family there had been several of Mrs. Bird's "cold snaps," but he couldn't remember ever seeing one before in which the snow had settled quite so deep and crisp and evenly.

All the same, Paddington wasn't the sort of bear to waste a good opportunity and a moment or so later he closed the door behind him and made his way down the side of the house as quickly as he could in order to investigate the matter. Apart from the prospect of throwing snowballs, he was particularly anxious to test his new Wellington boots which had been standing in his bedroom waiting for just such a moment ever since Mrs. Brown had given them to him at Christmas.

After he reached Mr. Brown's cabbage patch Paddington busied himself scooping the snow up with his paws and rolling it into firm round balls which he threw at the clothesline. But after several of the larger ones narrowly missed hitting the next-door greenhouse instead, he hastily turned his attention to the more important task of building a snowman and gradually peace returned once again to Windsor Gardens.

It was some while later, just as he was adding the finishing touches to the snowman's head with some old lemonade bottle tops, that the quiet was suddenly shattered by the sound of a nearby window being flung open.

"Bear!" came a loud voice. "Is that you, bear?"

Paddington jumped in alarm as he lifted his duffle coat hood and caught sight of the Browns' next-door neighbor leaning out of his bedroom window. Mr. Curry was dressed in pajamas and a dressing gown, and half of his face seemed to be hidden behind a large white handkerchief.

"I've finished throwing snowballs, Mr. Curry," explained Paddington hastily. "I'm making a snowman instead."

To his surprise Mr. Curry looked unusually friendly as he lifted the handkerchief from his face. "That's all right, bear," he called in a mild tone of voice. "I wasn't grumbling. I just wondered if you would care to do me a small favor and earn yourself ten pence bun money into the bargain.

"I've caught a nasty cold in my dose," he continued, as Paddington climbed up on a box and peered over the fence.

"A cold in your *dose*, Mr. Curry," repeated Paddington, looking most surprised. He had never heard of anyone having a cold in their dose before and he stared up at the window with interest.

Mr. Curry took a deep breath. "Not *dose*," he said, swallowing hard and making a great effort. "*Dnose*. And as if that isn't enough, my system is frozen."

Paddington became more and more upset as he listened to Mr. Curry and he nearly fell off his box with alarm at the last piece of information. "Your system's frozen!" he exclaimed. "I'll ask Mrs. Bird to send for Doctor MacAndrew."

Mr. Curry snorted. "I don't want a doctor, bear," he said crossly. "I want a plumber. It's not my own pipes that are frozen. It's the water pipes. There isn't even enough left in the tank to fill my hot-water bottle."

Paddington looked slightly disappointed as a heavy object wrapped in a piece of paper landed at his feet.

"That's my front door key," explained Mr. Curry. "I want you to take it along to Mr. James the handyman. Tell him he's to come at once. I shall be in bed but he can let himself in. And tell him not to make too much noise—I may be asleep. And no hanging round the bun shop on the way—otherwise you won't get your ten pence."

With that Mr. Curry blew his nose violently several times and slammed his window shut.

Mr. Curry was well known in the neighborhood for his meanness. He had a habit of promising people a reward for running his errands, but somehow whenever the time for payment arrived he was never to be found. Paddington had a nasty feeling in the back of his mind that this was going to be one of those occasions and he stood staring up at the empty window for some moments before he turned and made his way slowly in the direction of Mr. James's house.

"Curry!" exclaimed Mr. James, as he stood in his doorway and stared down at Paddington. "Did you say Curry?"

"That's right, Mr. James," said Paddington, raising his duffle coat hood politely. "His system's frozen and he can't even fill his hot-water bottle."

"Hard luck," said the handyman unsympathetically. "I'm having enough trouble with me own pipes this morning, let alone that there Mr. Curry's. Besides, I know him and his little jobs. He hasn't paid me yet for the last one I did—and that was six months ago. Tell him from me, I want to see the color of his money before I do anything else, and even then I'll have to think twice."

Paddington looked most disappointed as he listened to Mr. James. From the little he could remember of Mr. Curry's money it was usually a very dirty color, as if it had been kept under lock and key for a long time, and he felt sure Mr. James would be even less keen on doing any jobs if he saw it.

"Tell you what," said the handyman, relenting slightly as he caught sight of the expression on Paddington's face. "Hang on. Seeing you've come a long way in the snow, I'll see what I can do to oblige."

Mr. James disappeared from view only to return a moment later carrying a large brown paper parcel. "I'm lending Mr. Curry a blowtorch," he explained. "And I've slipped in a book on plumbing as well. He might find a few tips in it if he gets stuck."

"A blowtorch!" exclaimed Paddington, his eyes growing larger and larger. "I don't think he'll like that very much."

"You can take it or leave it," said Mr. James. "It's all the same to me. But if you want my advice, bear, you'll take it. This weather's going to get a lot worse before it gets any better."

So saying, Mr. James bade a final good morning and closed his door firmly, leaving Paddington standing on the step with a very worried expression on his face as he stared down at the parcel in his paws.

Mr. Curry didn't have a very good temper at the best of times and the thought of waking him in order to hand over a blowtorch or even a book on plumbing, especially when he had a bad cold, filled Paddington with alarm.

Paddington's face grew longer and longer the more he thought about it, but by the time he turned to make his way back to Windsor Gardens his whiskers were so well covered by flakes that only the closest passerby would have noticed anything amiss.

◆◆◆

Mrs. Brown paused in her housework as a small figure hurried past the kitchen window. "I suppose," she said with a sigh, "we can look forward to pawprints all over the house for the next few days."

"If this weather keeps up, that bear'll have to watch more than his paws," said Mrs. Bird as she joined her. "He'll have to mind his p's and q's as well."

The Browns' housekeeper held very strict views on the subject of dirty floors, particularly when they were the result of bears' "goings-on" in the snow, and she followed Paddington's progress into Mr. Brown's garage with a disapproving look.

"I think he must be helping out next door," said Mrs. Brown as Paddington came into view again clutching something beneath his duffle coat. "It sounds as if Mr. Curry's having trouble with his pipes."

"I hope that's all he's having trouble with," said Mrs. Bird. "There's been far too much hurrying about this morning for my liking."

Mrs. Bird was never very happy when Paddington helped out, and several times she'd caught sight of him going past the kitchen window with what looked suspiciously like pieces of old piping sticking out of his duffle coat.

Even as she spoke a renewed burst of hammering came from the direction of Mr. Curry's bathroom and echoed round the space between the two houses. First there were one or two bangs, then a whole series which grew louder and louder, finally ending in a loud crash and a period of silence broken only by the steady hiss of a blowtorch.

"If it sounds like that in here," said Mrs. Brown, "goodness only knows what it must be like next door."

"It isn't what it sounds like," replied Mrs. Bird grimly, "it's what it looks like that worries me."

The Browns' housekeeper left the window and began busying herself at the stove. Mrs. Bird was a great believer in letting people get on with their own work, and the activities of Mr. Curry's plumber were no concern of hers. All the same, had she waited a moment longer she might have changed her views on the matter, for at that moment the window of Mr. Curry's bathroom opened and a familiar-looking hat followed by some equally familiar whiskers came into view.

From the expression on his face as he leaned over the sill and peered at the ground far below it looked very much as if Paddington would have been the first to agree with Mrs. Bird's remarks on the subject.

Paddington was an optimistic bear at heart but as he clambered back down from the window and viewed Mr. Curry's bathroom even he had to admit to himself that things were in a bit of a mess. In fact, taking things all around he was beginning to wish he'd never started on the job in the first place.

Apart from Mr. James's blowtorch and a large number of tools from Mr. Brown's garage, the floor was strewn with odd lengths of pipe, pieces of solder and several saucepans, not to mention a length of hosepipe which he'd brought up from the garden in case of an emergency.

But it wasn't so much the general clutter that caused Paddington's gloomy expression as the amount of water which lay everywhere. In fact, considering that the pipes had been completely frozen when he'd started, he found it hard to understand where it had all come from. The only place in the whole of the bathroom where there wasn't some kind of pool was in a corner by the washbasin where he'd placed one of his Wellington boots beneath a leaking pipe in the hope of getting enough water to fill Mr. Curry's hot-water bottle.

Paddington was particularly anxious to fill the bottle before Mr. Curry took it into his head to get up. Already there had been several signs of stirring from the direction of his bedroom and twice a loud voice had called out demanding to know what was going on. Both times Paddington had done his best to make a deep grunting noise like a plumber hard at work and each time Mr. Curry's voice had grown more suspicious.

Paddington hastily began scooping water off the floor with his paw in order to help matters along, but as fast as he scooped the water up it soaked into his fur and ran back up his arm. Hopefully squeezing a few drops from his elbow into the Wellington boot Paddington gave a deep sigh and turned his attention to the book Mr. James had lent him.

The book was called *The Plumber's Aide* by Bert Stilson, and although Paddington felt sure it was very good for anyone who wanted to fit pipes in their house for the first time, there didn't seem to be a great deal on what to do once they were in and frozen hard. Mr. Stilson seemed to be unusually lucky with the weather whenever he did a job, for in nearly all the photographs it was possible to see the sun shining through the open windows.

There was only one chapter on frozen pipes and in the picture that went with it Mr. Stilson was shown wrapping them in towels soaked in boiling water. With no water to boil Paddington had tried holding Mr. Curry's one and only towel near the blowtorch in order to warm it, but after several rather nasty brown patches suddenly appeared he'd hastily given it up as a bad job.

Another picture showed Mr. Stilson playing the flame of a blowtorch along a pipe as he dealt with a particularly difficult job and Paddington had found this method much more successful. The only trouble was that as soon as the ice inside the pipe began to melt, a leak appeared near one of the joints.

Paddington tried stopping the leak with his paw while he read to the end of the chapter, but on the subject of leaking pipes Mr. Stilson was even less helpful than he had been on frozen ones. In a note about lead pipes he mentioned hitting them with a hammer in order to close the gap, but whenever Paddington hit one of Mr. Curry's gaps at least one other leak appeared farther along the pipe, so that instead of the one he'd started with there were now five and he'd run out of paws.

For some while the quiet of the bathroom was broken only by the hiss of the blowtorch and the steady drip, drip, drip of water as Paddington sat lost in thought.

Suddenly, as he turned over a page near the end of the book, his face brightened. Right at the end of the very last chapter Mr. Stilson had drawn a chart which he'd labeled "Likely Trouble Spots." Hurriedly unfolding the paper, Paddington spread it over the bathroom stool and began studying it with interest.

According to Mr. Stilson most things to do with plumbing caused trouble at some time or another, but if there was one place which was more troublesome than all the others put together it was where there was a bend in the pipe. At the bottom of the chart Mr. Stilson explained that bends shaped like the letter U always had water inside them and so they were the very first places to freeze when the cold weather came.

Looking round Mr. Curry's bathroom Paddington was surprised to see how many U bends there were. In fact, wherever he looked there appeared to be a bend of one kind or another.

Holding Mr. Stilson's book in one paw Paddington picked up the blowtorch in the other and settled himself underneath the washbasin where one of the pipes made itself into a particularly large U shape before it entered the cold tap.

As he played the flame along the pipe, sitting well back in case he accidentally singed his whiskers, Paddington was pleased to hear several small crackling noises coming from somewhere inside. In a matter of moments the crackles were replaced by bangs, and his opinion of Mr. Stilson went up by leaps and bounds as almost immediately afterwards a loud gurgling sound came from the basin over his head and the water began to flow.

To make doubly sure of matters, Paddington stood up and ran the blowtorch flame along the length of the pipe with one final sweep of his paw. It was as he did so that the pleased expression on his face suddenly froze, almost as solidly as the

water in Mr. Curry's pipes had been frozen just a second before.

Everything happened so quickly it all seemed to be over in the blink of an eyelid, but one moment he was standing under the basin with the blowtorch, and the next moment there was a hiss and a loud plop and before his astonished gaze Mr. Curry's U bend disappeared into thin air. Paddington just had time to take in the pool of molten lead on the bathroom floor before a gush of cold water hit him on the chin, nearly bowling him over.

Acting with great presence of mind he knocked the hot flexible remains of the pipe and turned it back into Mr. Curry's bath, leaving the water to hiss and gurgle as he turned to consult Mr. Stilson's book once more. There was a note somewhere near the back telling what to do in cases of emergency which he was particularly anxious to read.

A few seconds later he hurried downstairs as fast as his legs would carry him, slamming the front door in his haste. Almost at the same moment as it banged shut there came the sound of a window being opened somewhere overhead and Mr. Curry's voice rang out. "Bear!" he roared. "What's going on, bear?"

"You're having trouble with your U bends, Mr. Curry!" cried Paddington.

"Round the bend!" spluttered Mr. Curry. "Did I hear you say I'm round the bend?"

Mr. Curry took a deep breath as he prepared to let forth on the subject of bears in general and Paddington in particular, but as he did so a strange look came over his face and before Paddington's astonished gaze he began dancing up and down, waving his arms in the air.

"Where's all this water coming from, bear?" he roared. "I've got ice-cold water all over my feet. Where's it all coming from?"

But if Mr. Curry was expecting an answer to his question he was unlucky, for a second later the sound of another front door being slammed punctuated his remarks, only this time it was the one belonging to number thirty-two.

Paddington had been thinking for some while that he'd had enough of plumbing for one day and the expression on Mr. Curry's face quite decided him in the matter.

◆ ◆ ◆

Mr. Brown looked up from his morning paper as a burst of hammering shook the dining room. "I shall be glad when they've finished next door," he said. "They've been at it for days now. What on earth's going on?"

"I don't know," said Mrs. Brown, as she poured out the coffee. "Mr. Curry's got the builders in. I think it's something to do with his bathroom. He's been acting strangely all week. He came round specially the other evening to give Paddington ten pence."

"Mr. Curry gave Paddington *ten pence*?" echoed Mr. Brown, lowering his paper.

"I think he had a nasty accident during the cold weather," said Mrs. Bird. "He's having a complete new bathroom paid for by the insurance company."

"Trust Mr. Curry to get it done for nothing," said Mr. Brown. "Whenever I try to claim anything from my insurance company there's always a clause in small print at the bottom telling me I can't."

"Oh," said Mrs. Bird. "I have a feeling this was more of a *paws* than a *clause*. It's what Mr. Curry calls an 'act of bear.'"

"An act of bear?" repeated Mr. Brown. "I've never heard of that one before."

"It's very rare," said Mrs. Bird. "Very rare indeed. In fact, it's so rare I don't think we shall hear of it again, do you, Paddington?"

The Browns turned towards Paddington, or what little could be seen of him from behind a large jar of his special marmalade from the cut-price grocer in the market. But the only sound to greet them was that of crunching toast as he busied himself with his breakfast.

Paddington could be very hard of hearing when he chose. All the same, there was a look about him suggesting that Mrs. Bird was right and that as far as one member of the household was concerned bathrooms were safe from "acts of bear" for many winters to come.

◆ ◆ ◆

· Chapter 11 ·

Paddington and "Do It Yourself"

"I've brought you your breakfast in bed," Mrs. Brown said to Paddington, "because Mrs. Bird and I have to go out this morning. We're taking Jonathan and Judy to the dentist and we thought perhaps you wouldn't mind being left on your own. Unless," she added, "you'd like to come too?"

"Oh, no," said Paddington hastily. "I don't think I should like to go to the dentist, thank you very much. I'd much rather stay at home."

Mrs. Brown paused in the doorway. "We shan't be any longer than we can help. You're sure you'll be all right?"

"I expect I shall find *something* to do," said Paddington vaguely.

Mrs. Brown hesitated before shutting the door. She would have liked to have asked Paddington a few more questions. He had a faraway look in his eyes that she didn't like the look of at all. But she was already late for the appointment, and conversation with Paddington, particularly in the early morning, was liable to become complicated.

When Mrs. Bird heard about Paddington's strange behavior she hurried upstairs to see what was going on, but she arrived back a few moments later with the news that he was sitting up in bed eating his breakfast and reading a catalogue.

"Oh, well," said Mrs. Brown, looking most relieved. "He can't come to much harm doing that."

In recent weeks Paddington had begun to collect catalogues and whenever he saw an interesting one advertised in the newspapers he usually sent away for it. In fact, hardly a day went by without the postman calling at least once with a letter addressed to "P. Brown, Esq."

Some of the catalogues were very good value indeed, full of pictures and drawings, and with quite a lot to read considering that they were free and that Mrs. Bird usually paid for the stamp.

Paddington kept them all in a cupboard beside his bed. There were a number on foreign travel—with pictures of exotic places in several colors, two or three on food, and one or two from some big London stores.

But the one which interested Paddington at the moment, and which was his favorite, showed a workbench on the front cover and was headed DO IT YOURSELF. He became so absorbed in the booklet, which was a thick one full of diagrams, that he suddenly found to his surprise that he had put the pepper and salt into his cup of tea and the sugar into his boiled egg. But it made quite an interesting taste so he didn't really mind and he concentrated on reading the catalogue over his toast and marmalade.

There was a particularly interesting section which caught his eye. It was headed DELIGHT YOUR FAMILY AND SURPRISE YOUR FRIENDS, and it was all about making a newspaper and magazine rack. "All you need," it said, "is a sheet of plywood, some nails, and a kitchen table."

Paddington wasn't at all sure about using Mrs. Bird's kitchen table, but the night before Mr. Brown had rashly promised him a sheet of plywood that was standing in the shed, as well as some old nails in a jam jar. And Mr. Brown was always grumbling about not being able to find his newspapers; Paddington felt sure he would be very pleased if he had a rack for them.

He examined the drawings and pictures carefully and consulted the instructions several times. It didn't say anything about bears in particular doing it themselves, but it did say it was suitable for anyone with a set of carpentry tools.

Paddington came to a decision. He hastily bundled the remains of his breakfast in a handkerchief in case the sawing made him hungry. Then, having marked the chapter on magazine racks in his catalogue with a piece of marmalade peel, he hurried along to the bathroom for a quick wash.

Paddington wasn't the sort of bear who believed in doing things unnecessarily and it wasn't worth having a proper wash if he was going to get dirty again. After passing the washcloth over his whiskers a couple of times he made his way downstairs and went out into the garden.

A box of carpenter's tools was standing in the middle of Mr. Brown's shed, and Paddington spent several minutes investigating it. Although all the tools seemed rather large for a bear he soon decided he was very pleased with them. There was a hammer, a plane, three chisels, a large saw and a number of other things which he didn't immediately recognize but which looked very interesting. The box was heavy and it took him some while to drag it outside into the garden. He had even more trouble with Mr. Brown's plywood, for it was a large sheet and there was a wind blowing. Each time he picked it up a gust of wind caught it and carried him farther and farther down the garden.

It was while he was trying to drag it back up again with the aid of a piece of rope that he heard a familiar voice calling his name. He looked round and saw Mr. Curry watching him over the fence. Mr. Curry didn't approve of bears and he usually viewed Paddington's "goings-on" with suspicion.

"What are you doing, bear?" he growled.

"Do It Yourself, Mr. Curry," said Paddington, peering out from behind the sheet of wood.

"What?" bellowed Mr. Curry. "Don't be impertinent, bear!"

"Oh, no," said Paddington hastily, nearly dropping the sheet of plywood in his fright at the expression on Mr. Curry's face. "I didn't mean you were to do it *yourself*, Mr. Curry. I meant I'm going to do it *myself*. I'm making a magazine rack for Mr. Brown."

"A magazine rack?" repeated Mr. Curry.

"Yes," said Paddington importantly, and he began explaining to Mr. Curry all about his new carpentry set.

As he listened to Paddington the expression on Mr. Curry's face gradually changed. Mr. Curry had a reputation in the neighborhood for being a skinflint and he was always on the lookout in the hope of getting something for nothing. He was very keen on doing things himself too, in order to save money, and he cast several envious glances at Paddington's tool set.

"*Hmm,*" he said when Paddington had finished. "And where are you going to make this magazine rack, bear? On the lawn?"

"Well," said Paddington doubtfully, "it's a bit difficult. It says in the instructions I'm supposed to have a kitchen table and Mrs. Bird's is full."

"*Hmm,*" said Mr. Curry once again. "If I let you make me a magazine rack, bear, you can use *my* kitchen table."

"Thank you very much, Mr. Curry," said Paddington. But he wasn't sure whether it was a good idea or not and he looked at Mr. Curry rather doubtfully. "That's most kind of you."

"I have to go out this morning," said Mr. Curry. "So you can have it ready for me when I get back.

"Mind you," he added, as he reached over the fence to give Paddington a hand with the plywood, "I'm not having any sawdust over the kitchen floor. And be careful you don't scratch anything."

The more he listened, the longer Paddington's face grew and he was glad when at last Mr. Curry left to do his shopping.

But as Paddington set to work he soon forgot all about Mr. Curry's lists of "don'ts," for there were a number of important things to be done. First of all he took a pencil and ruler and carefully marked out the shape of the magazine rack on the sheet of plywood. Then he placed this on top of the kitchen table, ready to be sawed in two.

Paddington had never actually sawed anything before, but he'd often watched Mr. Brown cutting up logs for the fire. From a safe distance it had always looked easy—but Paddington soon found it wasn't easy at all. To start with, the plywood was bigger than the top of Mr. Curry's table. Being small, Paddington had to climb on top of it and several times it nearly tipped over when he stood too near the edge. Then he found that the saw, although it was nice and sharp, was so large he had to use both paws, which made things even more difficult. For the first few strokes it went through the wood like a knife through butter, but for some reason or other it gradually became harder and harder to use.

After sitting down for a short rest Paddington decided to try starting from the other end. But once again, for some strange reason, he found it much easier at the beginning. However, as he made the last saw cut and scrambled clear he was pleased to see the two saw cuts met in the middle, dividing the sheet of plywood neatly in half.

It was then, as he reached up to take the newly sawed pieces of plywood down, that Paddington had his first shock of the morning.

There was a loud splintering noise, and he dodged back just in time to avoid being hit by Mr. Curry's table as it suddenly parted in the middle and fell with a crash to the floor.

Paddington sat in the middle of the kitchen floor with a mournful expression on his face for quite some time, surveying the wreckage and trying to think of a good reason why Mr. Curry would like two small tables with only two legs each instead of one big one with four legs.

He consulted the instructions in his catalogue hopefully several times, but there didn't seem to be anything about mending tables which had accidentally been sawed in half. In all the pictures the people seemed to be happy and smiling and their kitchens were as shiny as a new pin. Whereas, looking unhappily round Mr. Curry's kitchen, even Paddington had to admit it was in a bit of a mess.

He tried propping the two pieces of table up on some old cardboard boxes, but there was still a nasty sag in the middle, and even with the curtains drawn and the light out it was obvious something was wrong.

Paddington was a hopeful bear in many ways and he suddenly remembered seeing a large tube of glue in his toolbox. If he spread some of the glue along the two edges and nailed them together for good measure, perhaps even Mr. Curry might not notice anything was wrong. He worked hard for some minutes and by the time he had finished he felt quite pleased with himself. Admittedly the table had a funny tilt to one side and seemed a trifle wobbly, but it was definitely in one piece again. He spread some flour over the join and then stood back to admire his handiwork.

Having carefully examined it from all angles, he decided he might be able to improve matters still further by sawing a piece off one of the legs. But when he had done that the table seemed to lean the opposite way—which meant he had to saw a piece off one of the other legs as well. Then, when he had done that, he discovered the table was leaning the other way again.

Paddington gave a deep sigh. Carpentry was much more difficult than it looked. He was sure the man in the catalogue didn't have so much trouble.

It was after he had been at work for some time that he stood up and received his second shock of the morning.

When he had first started sawing the legs, Mr. Curry's table had been as tall as he was. Now he found he was looking down at it. In fact, he didn't remember ever having seen such a short table before and his eyes nearly popped out with astonishment.

He sat down on the pile of sawed-off table legs and consulted his catalogue once again.

"Delight your family and surprise your friends!" he said bitterly, to the world in general. He was quite sure Mr. Curry would be surprised when he saw his kitchen table, but as for anyone being delighted by their magazine racks—he hadn't even started work on those yet.

◆◆◆

Mrs. Brown looked anxiously at the dining room clock. "I wonder where on earth Paddington can have got to," she said. "It's almost lunchtime and it's most unlike him to be late for a meal."

"Perhaps he's doing a job somewhere," said Jonathan. "I looked in the shed just now and the toolbox has disappeared."

"*And* that sheet of plywood Daddy gave him," said Judy.

"Oh dear," said Mrs. Brown. "I do hope he hasn't built himself in anywhere and can't get out. You know what he's like."

"I don't know about Paddington building himself in," exclaimed Mrs. Bird as she entered carrying a tray of plates. "I think Mr. Curry must be having his house pulled down. I've never heard so much noise. Banging and sawing coming from the kitchen. It's been going on ever since we got back and it's only just this minute stopped."

Jonathan and Judy exchanged glances. Now that Mrs. Bird mentioned it, there had been a lot of noise coming from Mr. Curry's house.

"I wonder . . ." said Judy.

Jonathan opened his mouth, but before he had time to say anything the door burst open and Paddington entered dragging something large and heavy behind him.

"Well," said Mrs. Bird, voicing all their thoughts. "And what have you been up to now?"

"What have I been *up* to, Mrs. Bird?" exclaimed Paddington, looking most offended. "I've been making Mr. Brown a magazine rack."

"A magazine rack?" said Mrs. Brown, as Paddington stepped to one side. "What a lovely idea."

"It was meant to be a surprise," said Paddington modestly. "I made it all with my own paws."

"Gosh! It's super," said Jonathan, as the Browns all crowded round to admire Paddington's handiwork. "Fancy you doing it all by yourself."

"I should be careful," warned Paddington. "I've only just varnished it and it's still a bit sticky. I think some of it has come off on my paws already."

"Most sensible," said Mrs. Bird approvingly. "Mentioning no names, it's about time some people in this house had a place for their newspapers. Now perhaps they won't keep losing them."

"But you've made two," said Judy. "Whose is the other one?"

A guilty expression came over Paddington's face. "It's really for Mr. Curry," he said. "But I thought perhaps I'd better leave it on his doorstep after dark—just in case."

Mrs. Bird looked at Paddington suspiciously. Her ears had caught the sound of violent banging coming from the house next door, and she had a nasty feeling in the back of her mind that it had something to do with Paddington.

"Just in case?" she repeated. "What do you mean?"

But before Paddington had time to explain exactly what he did mean, Mrs. Brown pointed to the window in astonishment.

"Good gracious," she cried. "*There* is Mr. Curry. Whatever's the matter with him? He's running round the garden waving a kitchen table in the air." She peered through the glass. "And it doesn't seem to have any legs, either. How very odd!"

"Gosh!" cried Jonathan excitedly. "Now it's broken in two!"

The Browns stared through the window at the strange sight of Mr. Curry dancing round his pond waving the two halves of a table. "Bear!" he shouted. "Where are you, bear?"

"Oh dear," said Paddington, as everyone turned away from the window and

looked at him accusingly. "I'm in trouble again."

"Well, if you ask me," said Mrs. Bird, after he had explained everything to them, "the best thing you can do is offer Mr. Curry your toolbox as a present. Then perhaps he'll forget all about his kitchen table. And if he doesn't, just you tell him to come and see me."

Mrs. Bird held very strong views about people who tried to take advantage of others and she usually took Paddington's side in anything to do with Mr. Curry.

"Anyway," she concluded, in a voice which left no room for argument, "I'm certainly not having the lunch spoiled by Mr. Curry or anyone else, so just you all sit down while I fetch it."

With that argument the Browns had to agree and they meekly arranged themselves round the table.

Paddington in particular thought it was a very good idea. He was a bit fed up with carpentry. Sawing was hard work, especially for a small bear, and even more so when it was sawing through a kitchen table. Besides, he was hungry after his morning's work and he didn't want to offend Mrs. Bird by not eating her lunch down to the very last mouthful.

◆◆◆

Part Three

A Very Good
Bargain Indeed

Chapter 12

Paddington and the "Finishing Touch"

Mr. Gruber leaned on his shovel and mopped his brow with a large spotted handkerchief. "If anyone had told me three weeks ago, Mr. Brown," he said, "that one day I'd have my own patio in the Portobello Road I wouldn't have believed them.

"In fact," he continued, dusting himself down as he warmed to his subject, "if you hadn't come across that article I might *never* have had one. Now look at it!"

At the sound of Mr. Gruber's voice Paddington rose into view from behind a pile of stones. Lumps of cement clung to his fur like miniature stalactites, his hat was covered in a thin film of gray dust, and his paws—never his strongest point— looked for all the world as if they had been dipped not once but many times into a mixture made up of earth, brick dust and concrete.

All the same, there was a pleased expression on his face as he put down his trowel and hurried across to join his friend near the back door of the shop so that they could inspect the result of their labors. For in the space of a little over two weeks, a great and most remarkable change had come over Mr. Gruber's back yard.

It had all started when Paddington had come across an article in one of Mrs. Brown's old housekeeping magazines. The article in question had been about the amount of wasted space there was in a big city like London and how, with some thought and a lot of hard work, even the worst garbage dump could be turned into a place of beauty.

The article had contained a number of photographs showing what could be done, and Paddington had been so impressed by these that he'd taken the magazine along to show to his friend.

Mr. Gruber kept an antique shop in the Portobello Road and although his back yard wasn't exactly a dumping ground, over the years he had certainly collected a vast amount of trash, and he'd decided to make a clean sweep of the whole area.

For several days there had been a continual stream of junk dealers, and soon afterwards builders' trucks became a familiar sight behind the shop as they began to arrive carrying loads of broken paving stones, sand, gravel, cement, rocks and other items of building material too numerous to be mentioned.

Taking time off each afternoon, Mr. Gruber had set about the task of laying the stones for a patio, while Paddington acted as foreman in charge of cement-mixing and filling the gaps between the stones—a job which he enjoyed no end.

At the far end of the yard Mr. Gruber erected a fence against which he planted some climbing roses and in front of this they built a rock garden, which was soon filled with various kinds of creeping plants.

In the middle of the patio, space had been left for a small pond containing some goldfish and a miniature fountain, while at the house end there now stood a carved wooden seat with room enough for two.

It was on this seat that Paddington and Mr. Gruber relaxed after their exertions each day and finished off any buns which had been left over from their morning elevenses.

"I must say we've been very lucky with the weather," said Mr. Gruber, as Paddington joined him and they took stock of the situation. "It's been a real Indian summer. Though without your help I should never have got it all done before the winter."

Paddington began to look more and more pleased as he sat down on the seat and listened to his friend, for although Mr. Gruber was a polite man, he wasn't in the habit of paying idle compliments.

Mr. Gruber gave a sigh. "If you half close your eyes and listen to the fountain, Mr. Brown," he said, "and then watch all the twinkling lights come on as it begins to get dark, you might be anywhere in the world.

"There's only one thing missing," he continued, after a moment's pause.

Paddington, who'd almost nodded off in order to enjoy a dream in which it was a hot summer's night and he and Mr. Gruber were sipping cocoa under the stars, sat up in surprise.

"What's that, Mr. Gruber?" he asked anxiously, in case he'd left out something important by mistake.

"I don't know," said Mr. Gruber dreamily. "But there's something missing. What the whole thing needs is some kind of finishing touch. A statue or a piece of stonework. I can't think what it can be."

Mr. Gruber gave a shiver as he rose from his seat, for once the sun disappeared over the rooftops a chill came into the air. "We shall just have to put our thinking caps on, Mr. Brown," he said, "and not take them off again until we come up with something."

◆◆◆

"'Adrian Crisp—Garden Ornaments,'" exclaimed Mrs. Bird. "What's that bear up to now?" She held up a small piece of paper. "I found this under Paddingon's bed this morning. It looks as if it's been cut from a magazine. *And* my best shopping bag is missing!"

Mrs. Brown glanced up from her sewing. "I expect it's got something to do with Mr. Gruber's patio," she replied. "Paddington *was* rather quiet when he came in last night. He said he had his thinking cap on and I noticed him poking about looking for my scissors."

Mrs. Bird gave a snort. "That bear's bad enough when he *doesn't* think of things," she said grimly. "There's just no knowing what's likely to happen when he really puts his mind to it. Where is he, anyway?"

"I think he went out," said Mrs. Brown vaguely. She took a look at the scrap of paper Mrs. Bird had brought downstairs. "'Works of art in stone bought and sold. No item too small or too large.'"

"I don't like the sound of that last bit," broke in Mrs. Bird. "I can see Mr. Gruber ending up with a statue of the Duke of Wellington in his back garden."

"I hope not," said Mrs. Brown. "I can't picture even Paddington trying to get a statue onto a London bus. At least," she added uneasily, "I don't think I can."

Unaware of the detective work going on at number thirty-two Windsor Gardens, Paddington peered round with a confused look on his face. Altogether he was in a bit of a daze. In fact, he had to admit that he'd never ever seen anything quite like Mr. Crisp's establishment before.

It occupied a large wilderness of a garden behind a ramshackle old house some distance away from the Browns', and as far as the eye could see every available square inch of ground was covered by statues, seats, pillars, balustrades, posts, stone animals—the list was endless. Even Adrian Crisp himself, as he followed Paddington in and out of the maze of pathways, seemed to have only a very vague idea of what was actually there.

"Pray take your time, my dear chap," he exclaimed, dabbing his face with a silk handkerchief as they reached their starting point for the third time. "Some of these items are hundreds of years old and I think they'll last a while yet. There's no hurry at all."

Paddington thanked Mr. Crisp and then peered thoughtfully at a pair of small stone lions standing nearby. They were among the first things he'd seen on entering the garden and all in all they seemed to fit most closely with what he had in mind.

"I think I like the look of those, Mr. Crisp," he exclaimed, bending down in order to undo the secret compartment in his suitcase.

Adrian Crisp followed the direction of Paddington's gaze and then lifted a label attached to one of the lion's ears. "Er . . . I'm not sure if you'll be able to manage it," he said doubtfully. "The pair are two hundred and fifty pounds."

Paddington remained silent for a moment as he tried to picture the combined weight of two hundred and fifty jars of marmalade. "I quite often bring all Mrs. Bird's shopping home from the market," he said at last.

Adrian Crisp allowed himself a laugh. "Oh, dear me," he said. "I'm afraid we're talking at cross purposes. That isn't the weight. That's how much they cost."

"Two hundred and fifty pounds!" exclaimed Paddington, nearly falling over backwards with surprise.

Mr. Crisp adjusted his bow tie and gave a slight cough as he caught sight of the expression on Paddington's face. "I might be able to let you have a small faun for fifty pounds," he said reluctantly. "I'm afraid the tail's fallen off but it's quite a bargain. If I were to tell you where it came from originally you'd have quite a surprise."

Paddington, who looked as if nothing would surprise him ever again, sat down on his suitcase and stared mournfully at Mr. Crisp.

"I can see you won't be tempted, my dear fellow," said Mr. Crisp, trying to strike a more cheerful note. "Er . . . how much did you actually think of paying?"

"I was *thinking* of fifty pence," said Paddington hopefully.

"Fifty pence!" If Paddington had been taken by surprise a moment before, Adrian Crisp looked positively devastated.

"I could go up to one pound if I break into my bun money, Mr. Crisp," said Paddington hastily.

"Don't strain your resources too much, bear," said Mr. Crisp, delicately removing a lump of leaf mold from his suede shoes. "This isn't a charitable institution, you know," he continued, eyeing Paddington with disfavor. "It's been a lifetime's work collecting these items and I can't let them go for a song."

"I'm afraid I've only got one pound," said Paddington firmly.

Adrian Crisp took a deep breath. "I suppose I might be able to find you one or two bricks," he said sarcastically. "You'll have to arrange your own transport, of course, but . . ." He broke off as he caught Paddington's eye. Paddington had a very hard stare when he liked, and his present one was certainly one of the most powerful he'd ever managed.

"Er . . ." Mr. Crisp glanced round unhappily, and then his face suddenly lit up as he caught sight of something just behind Paddington. "The very thing!" he exclaimed. "I could certainly let you have *that* for one pound."

Paddington turned and looked over his shoulder. "Thank you very much, Mr. Crisp," he said doubtfully. "What is it?"

"*What is it?*" Mr. Crisp looked slightly embarrassed. "I think it fell off something a long time ago," he said hastily. "I'm not sure what. Anyway, my dear fellow, for one pound you don't ask what it is. You should be thankful for small mercies."

Paddington didn't like to say anything but from where he was standing Mr. Crisp's object seemed rather a large mercy. It was big and round and it looked for all the world like a giant stone football. However, he carefully counted out his one pound and handed the money over before the owner had time to change his mind.

"Thank you, I'm sure," said Mr. Crisp, reluctantly taking possession of a sticky collection of small coins. He paused as Paddington turned his attention to the piece of stone. "I shouldn't do that if I were you," he began.

But it was too late. Almost before the words were out of his mouth there came the sound of tearing paper. Paddington stood looking at the two string handles in his paw and then at the sodden remains of brown paper underneath the stone. "That was one of Mrs. Bird's best shopping bags," he exclaimed hotly.

"I did try to warn you, bear," said Mr. Crisp. "You've got a bargain there. That stone's worth two pounds of anybody's money just for the weight alone. If you'd like to hang on a moment I'll roll it outside for you."

Paddington gave Mr. Crisp a hard stare. "You'll roll it outside for me," he repeated, hardly able to believe his ears. "But I've got to get it all the way back to the Portobello Road."

Mr. Crisp took a deep breath. "I might be able to find you a cardboard box," he said sarcastically, "but I'm afraid we expect you to bring your own string for anything under two pounds."

Mr. Crisp looked as if he'd had enough dealings with bear customers for one day and when, a few minutes later, he ushered Paddington out through the gates he bade him a hasty farewell and slammed the bolts shut on the other side with an air of finality.

Taking a deep breath Paddington placed his suitcase carefully on top of the box, and then clasping the whole lot firmly with both paws, he began staggering up the road in the general direction of Windsor Gardens and the Portobello Road.

If the stone object had seemed large among all the other odds and ends in Mr. Crisp's garden, now that he actually had it outside it seemed enormous. Several times he had to stop in order to rest his paws and once, when he accidentally stepped on a grating outside a row of shops, he nearly overbalanced and fell through a window.

Altogether he was thankful when at long last he peered round the side of his load and caught sight of a small line standing beside a familiar-looking London Transport sign not far ahead.

He was only just in time, for as he reached the end of the line a bus swept to a halt beside the stop and a voice from somewhere upstairs told everyone to "hurry along."

"Quick," said a man, coming to his rescue, "there's an empty seat up front."

Before Paddington knew what was happening he found himself being bundled on to the bus while several other willing hands in the crowd took charge of the cardboard box for him and placed it in the aisle behind the driver's compartment.

He barely had time to raise his hat in order to thank everyone for their trouble before there was a sudden jerk and the bus set off again on its journey.

Paddington fell back into the seat mopping his brow and as he did so he looked out of the window in some surprise. Although, as far as he could remember it was a fine day outside, he'd distinctly heard what sounded like the ominous rumble of thunder.

It had seemed quite close for a second or two and he peered anxiously up at the sky in case there was any lightning about, but as far as he could tell there wasn't a cloud anywhere in sight.

At that moment there came a clattering of heavy feet on the stairs as the conductor descended to the bottom deck.

"'Ullo, 'ullo," said a disbelieving voice a second later. "What's all this 'ere?"

Paddington glanced round to see what was going on, and as he did so his eyes nearly fell out of their sockets.

The cardboard box, which a moment before had stood neatly and innocently

beside him, now had a gaping hole in its side. Worse still, the cause of the hole was now resting at the other end of the aisle!

"Is this yours?" asked the conductor, pointing an accusing finger first at the stone by his feet and then at Paddington.

"I think it must be," said Paddington vaguely.

"I'm not 'aving no bear's boulders on my bus," said the conductor. He indicated a notice just above his head. "It says 'ere plain enough—'Parcels may be left under the staircase by permission of the conductor'—and I ain't given me permission. Nor likely to neither. Landed on me best corn it did."

"It isn't a bear's boulder," exclaimed Paddington hotly. "It's Mr. Gruber's 'finishing touch.'"

The conductor reached up and rang the bell. "It'll be your finishing touch and all if I have any more nonsense," he said crossly. "Come on—off with you."

The conductor looked as though he'd been about to say a great deal more on the subject of bear passengers in general and Paddington and his piece of stonework in particular when he suddenly broke off. For as the bus ground to a halt the stone suddenly began trundling back up the aisle, ending its journey with a loud bang against the wall at the driver's end.

A rather cross-looking face appeared for a moment at the window just above it. Then the bus surged forward again and before anyone had time to stop it the stone began rolling back down the aisle, landing once more at the conductor's feet.

"I've 'ad just about enough of this!" he exclaimed, hopping up and down as he reached for the bell.

The words were hardly out of his mouth when a by now familiar thundering noise followed by an equally familiar thump drowned the excited conversation from the other passengers in the bus.

For a moment or two the bus seemed to hover shaking in midair as if one half wanted to go on and the other half wanted to stay. Then, with a screech of brakes, it pulled in to the side of the road, and as it came to a halt the driver jumped out and came hurrying round to the back.

"Why don't you make up your mind?" he cried, addressing the conductor. "First you rings the bell to say you want to stop. Then you bangs on me panel to say go on. Then you rings the bell again. Then it's bang on me panel. I don't know whether I'm on me head or me heels, let alone driving a bus."

"I like that!" exclaimed the conductor. "*I* banged on your panel. It was that blessed bear with 'is boulder what done it."

"A bear with a boulder?" repeated the driver disbelievingly. "Where? I can't see him."

The conductor looked up the aisle and then his face turned white. "He *was* there," he said. "And he had this boulder what kept rolling up and down the aisle. There he is!" he exclaimed triumphantly. "I told you so!"

He pointed down the road to where in the distance a small brown figure could be seen hurrying after a round gray object as it zigzagged down the road. "It must have fallen off the last time you stopped."

"Well, I hope he catches it before it gets to the Portobello Road," said the driver. "If it gets in among all them market stalls there's no knowing what'll happen."

"Bears!" exclaimed the conductor bitterly as a sudden thought struck him. "He didn't even pay for 'is fare let alone extra for 'is boulder."

Paddington and Mr. Gruber settled themselves comfortably on the patio seat. After all his exertions in the early part of the day Paddington was glad of a rest, and the sight of a tray laden with two mugs, a jug of cocoa and a plate of buns into the bargain was doubly welcome.

Mr. Gruber had been quite overwhelmed when Paddington presented him with the piece of stone.

"I don't know when I've had such a nice present, Mr. Brown," he said. "Or such an unexpected one. How you managed to get it all the way here by yourself I really don't know."

"It was rather heavy, Mr. Gruber," admitted Paddington. "I nearly strained my resources."

"Fancy that conductor calling it a boulder," continued Mr. Gruber, looking at the stone with a thoughtful expression on his face.

"Even Mr. Crisp didn't seem to know quite what it was," said Paddington. "But he said it was a very good bargain."

"I'm sure he was right," agreed Mr. Gruber. He examined the top of the stone carefully and ran his fingers over the top, which appeared to have a flatter surface than the rest and was surrounded by a rim, not unlike a small tray. "Do you know what I think it is, Mr. Brown?"

Paddington shook his head.

"I think it's an old Roman cocoa stand," said Mr. Gruber.

"A Roman cocoa stand," repeated Paddington excitedly.

"Well, perhaps it isn't exactly Roman," replied Mr. Gruber truthfully. "But it's certainly very old and I can't think of a better use for it."

He reached over for the jug, filled both mugs to the brim with steaming liquid and then carefully placed them on top of the stone. To Paddington's surprise they fitted exactly.

"There," said Mr. Gruber with obvious pleasure. "I don't think anyone could find a better finishing touch for their patio than that, Mr. Brown. Not if they tried for a thousand years."

Chapter 13

Paddington and the Christmas Shopping

"I suppose I shouldn't say it," remarked Mrs. Bird, "but I shall be glad when Christmas is over."

The few weeks before Christmas were usually busy ones for Mrs. Bird. There were so many mince pies, puddings, and cakes to be made that much of her time was spent in the kitchen. This year matters hadn't been helped by the fact that Paddington was at home for most of the day "convalescing" after having had the flu. Paddington was very interested in mince pies, and if he had opened the oven door once to see how they were getting on, he'd done it a dozen times.

Paddington's convalescence had been a difficult time for the Browns. While he had remained in bed it had been bad enough, because he kept getting grape seeds all over the sheets. But if anything, matters had got worse once he was up and about. He wasn't very good at doing nothing, and it had become a full-time occupation keeping him amused and out of trouble. He had even had several goes at knitting something—no one ever quite knew what—but he'd got in such a tangle with the wool, and it had become so sticky with marmalade, that in the end they had to throw it away. Even the garbage man had said some very nasty things about it when he came to collect the trash.

"He seems very quiet at the moment," said Mrs. Brown. "I think he's busy with his Christmas list."

"You're not *really* taking him shopping with you this afternoon, are you?" asked Mrs. Bird. "You know what happened last time."

Mrs. Brown sighed. She had vivid memories of the last time she had taken Paddington shopping. "I can't *not* take him," she said. "I did promise and he's been looking forward to it so much."

Paddington liked shopping. He always enjoyed looking in the store windows, and since he had read in the paper about all the Christmas decorations, he had thought of very little else. Besides, he had a special reason for wanting to go shopping this time. Although he hadn't told anyone, Paddington had been saving hard for some time in order to buy the Browns and his other friends some presents.

He had already bought a frame for his picture and sent it, together with a large jar of honey, to his Aunt Lucy in Peru, because presents for overseas had to be mailed early.

He had several lists marked SEACRET, which were locked away in his case, and he had been keeping his ears open for some time, listening to conversations in the hope of finding something they all needed.

"Anyway," said Mrs. Brown, "it's so nice having him round again, and he's been so good lately, I think he ought to have a treat. Besides," she added, "I'm not taking him to Barkridges this time—I'm taking him to Crumbold and Ferns."

Mrs. Bird put down her baking tray. "Are you sure you're doing the right thing taking him there?" she exclaimed. "You know what they're like."

Crumbold and Ferns was a very old established shop where everyone spoke in whispers and all the assistants wore frock coats. Only the best people went to Crumbold and Ferns.

"It's Christmas," said Mrs. Brown recklessly. "It'll be a nice treat for him."

And when Paddington set off with Mrs. Brown after lunch, even Mrs. Bird had to admit he looked smart enough to go anywhere. His duffle coat, which had just come back from the cleaners, was spotlessly clean, and even his old hat, which Paddington always insisted on wearing when he went on shopping expeditions, looked unusually neat.

All the same, as Paddington waved his paw at the corner and Mrs. Bird turned to go back indoors, she couldn't help feeling glad she was staying at home.

Paddington enjoyed the journey to Crumbold and Ferns. They went by bus and he managed to get a front seat downstairs. By standing on the seat he could just see through the little hole in the screen behind the driver's back. Paddington tapped on the glass several times and waved his paw at the man behind the wheel, but the driver was much too busy with the traffic to look round—in fact, they drove a long way without stopping at all.

The conductor was cross when he saw what Paddington was doing. "Oi!" he shouted. "Stop that there tapping! It's bears like you what get buses a bad name. We've gone past three stops already."

But he was a kindly man, and when Paddington said he was sorry, he explained to him all about the signals for making buses stop or go on, and he gave him the end of a roll of tickets as a present. When he had collected all the fares, he came back again and pointed out some buildings of interest to Paddington as they passed them. He even presented him with a large piece of hard candy—the kind Paddington knew had a soft and chewy center—that he found in his money bag. Paddington liked seeing new places, and he was sorry when the journey came to an end and he had to say goodbye to the conductor.

There was another slight upset when they reached Crumbold and Ferns. Paddington had an accident with the revolving door. It wasn't really his fault, but he tried to follow Mrs. Brown into the store just as a very distinguished-looking gentleman with a beard came out the other side. The man was in a great hurry, and when he pushed the revolving door it started going round at great speed, taking Paddington with it. He went round several times until he found to his astonishment that he was outside on the pavement once more.

He had a brief glimpse of the man with the beard waving to him from the back of a large car as it drove away. The man also appeared to be shouting something, but Paddington never knew what it was, for at that very moment he stepped on something sharp and fell over backwards again.

He sat in the middle of the pavement examining his foot and found to his surprise that it had a tie pin sticking in it. Paddington knew it was a tie pin because Mr. Brown had one very like it, except that his was quite ordinary, whereas this one had something big and shiny fixed to the middle of it. Paddington pinned it to the front of his duffle coat for safety and then suddenly became aware that someone was speaking to him.

"Are you all right, sir?" It was the doorkeeper—a very dignified man in a smart uniform with lots of medals.

"I think so, thank you," said Paddington as he stood up and dusted himself, "but I've lost my candy somewhere."

"Your candy?" said the man. "Dear me!" If he felt surprised he showed no signs of it. Doorkeepers at Crumbold and Ferns were always very well trained. All the same, he couldn't help wondering about Paddington. When he noticed the tie pin with the enormous diamond in the middle, he realized at once that he was dealing with someone very important. "Probably one of these society bears," he thought to himself. But when he caught sight of Paddington's old hat he wasn't quite so sure. "Perhaps he's a huntin', shootin' and fishin' bear up from the country for the day," he decided. "Or even a society bear that's seen better days."

So he held up the passersby with a stern wave of the hand while they searched the pavement until they found it. As he guided Paddington back through the revolving door to Mrs. Brown, who was waiting anxiously on the other side, he tried hard to look as if helping a young bear of quality find his candy was an everyday event at Crumbold and Ferns.

Paddington returned his salute with a wave of the paw and then looked round. The inside of the shop was most impressive. Everywhere they went, tall men in frock coats bowed low and wished them good afternoon. Paddington's paw was quite tired by the time they reached the household department.

As they both had some secret shopping to do, Mrs. Brown left Paddington with the sales assistant and arranged to meet him outside the entrance to the shop in a quarter of an hour.

The man assured Mrs. Brown that Paddington would be quite safe. "Although I don't recall any actual bears," he said, when she explained that Paddington came from Darkest Peru, "we have a number of very distinguished foreign gentlemen among our clients. Many of them do all their Christmas shopping here."

He turned and looked down at Paddington as Mrs. Brown left, brushing an imaginary speck of dust from his frock coat.

Secretly Paddington was feeling rather overawed by Crumbold and Ferns, and not wishing to disgrace Mrs. Brown by doing the wrong thing, he gave his own coat a passing tap with his paw. The assistant watched with fascination as a small cloud of dust rose into the air and then slowly settled on his nice, clean counter.

Paddington followed the man's gaze. "I expect it came off the pavement," he said, by way of explanation. "I had an accident in the revolving door."

The man coughed. "Oh dear," he said. "How very unfortunate." He gave Paddington a sickly smile and decided to ignore the whole matter. "And what can we do for you, sir?" he asked brightly.

Paddington looked round carefully to make sure Mrs. Brown was nowhere in sight. "I want a clothesline," he announced.

"A *what*?" exclaimed the assistant.

Paddington hurriedly moved the candy to the other side of his mouth. "A clothesline," he repeated in a muffled voice. "It's for Mrs. Bird. Her old one broke the other day."

The assistant swallowed hard. He found it impossible to understand what this extraordinary young bear was saying.

"Perhaps," he suggested, for a Crumbold and Ferns assistant rarely bent down, "you wouldn't mind standing on the counter?"

Paddington sighed. It was most difficult trying to explain things sometimes. Climbing up onto the counter he unlocked his suitcase and withdrew an advertisement which he'd cut from Mr. Brown's newspaper several days before.

"Ah!" The assistant's face cleared. "You mean one of our special *expanding* clotheslines, sir." He reached up to a shelf and picked out a small green box. "A very suitable choice, if I may say so, sir. As befits a young bear of taste. I can thoroughly recommend it."

The man pulled a piece of rope through a hole in the side of the box and handed it to Paddington. "This type of expanding clothesline is used by some of the best families in the country."

Paddington looked suitably impressed as he climbed down, holding on to the rope with his paw.

"You see," continued the man, bending over the counter, "it is all quite simple. The clothesline is all contained inside this box. As you walk away with the rope, it unwinds itself. Then, when you have finished with it, you simply turn this handle and . . ." A puzzled note came into his voice.

"You simply turn this handle," he repeated, trying again. Really, it was all most annoying. Instead of the clothesline going back into the box as it was supposed to, more was actually coming out.

"I'm extremely sorry, sir," he began, looking up from the counter. "Something seems to have jammed . . ." His voice trailed away and a worried look came into his eyes, for Paddington was nowhere in sight.

"I say," he called to another assistant farther along the counter. "Have you seen a young bear gentleman go past, pulling on a clothesline?"

"He went that way," replied the other man briefly. He pointed towards the china department. "I think he got caught in the crowd."

"Oh dear," said Paddington's assistant as he picked up the green box and began pushing his way through the crowd of shoppers, following the trail of the clothesline. "Oh dear! Oh dear!"

As it happened, the assistant wasn't the only one to feel worried. At the other end of the clothesline Paddington was already in trouble. Crumbold and Ferns was filled with people doing their Christmas shopping, and none of them seemed to have time for a small bear. Several times he'd had to crawl under a table in order to avoid being stepped on.

It was a very good clothesline, and Paddington felt sure Mrs. Bird would like it. But he couldn't help wishing he'd chosen something else. There seemed to be no end to it, and he kept getting it tangled round people's legs.

He went on and on, round a table laden with cups and saucers, past a pillar, underneath another table, and still the clothesline trailed after him. All the time the crowd was getting thicker and thicker and Paddington had to push hard to make any headway at all. Once or twice he nearly lost his hat.

Just as he had almost given up hope of ever finding his way back to the household department again, he caught sight of the assistant. To Paddington's surprise, the man was sitting on the floor, looking very red in the face. His hair was all ruffled, and he appeared to be struggling with a table leg.

"Ah, there you are!" he gasped when he caught sight of Paddington. "I suppose you realize, young bear, I've been following you all around the china department. Now you've tied everything up in knots."

"Oh dear," said Paddington, looking at the rope. "Did *I* do that? I'm afraid I got lost. Bears aren't very good in crowds, you know. I must have gone under the same table twice."

"What have you done with the other end?" shouted the assistant.

He wasn't in the best of tempers. It was hot and noisy under the table, and people kept kicking him. Apart from that, it was most undignified.

"It's here," said Paddington, trying to find his end of the rope. "At least—it was a moment ago."

"Where?" shouted the assistant. He didn't know whether it was simply the noise of the crowd, but he still couldn't understand a word this young bear uttered. Whenever he did say anything it seemed to be accompanied by a strange crunching noise and a strong smell of candy.

"Speak up," he shouted, cupping a hand to his ear. "I can't hear a word you say."

Paddington looked at the man uneasily. He looked rather cross, and Paddington was beginning to wish he had left his candy on the pavement outside. It was very nice candy, but it made talking most difficult.

It was as he felt in his duffle coat pocket for a handkerchief that it happened.

The assistant jumped slightly, and the expression on his face froze and then gradually changed to one of disbelief.

"Excuse me," said Paddington, tapping him on the shoulder, "but I think my candy has fallen in your ear!"

"Your *candy*?" exclaimed the man in a horrified tone of voice. "Fallen in my ear?"

"Yes," said Paddington. "It was given to me by a bus conductor, and I'm afraid it's got a bit slippery where I've been sucking it."

The assistant crawled out from under the table and drew himself up to his full height. With a look of great distaste, he withdrew the remains of Paddington's candy from his ear. He held it for a moment between thumb and forefinger and then hurriedly placed it on a nearby counter. It was bad enough having to crawl round the floor untangling a clothesline, but to have a candy in his ear—such a thing had never been known before in Crumbold and Ferns.

He took a deep breath and pointed a trembling finger in Paddington's direction. But as he opened his mouth to speak he noticed that Paddington was no longer there. Neither, for that matter, was the clothesline. He was only just in time to grab the table as it rocked on its legs. As it was, several plates and a cup and saucer fell to the floor.

The assistant raised his eyes to the ceiling and made a mental note to avoid any young bears who came into the shop in the future.

There seemed to be a commotion going on in the direction of the entrance hall. He had his own ideas on the possible cause of it, but wisely he decided to keep his thoughts to himself. He had had quite enough to do with bear customers for one day.

Mrs. Brown pushed her way through the crowd which had formed on the pavement outside Crumbold and Ferns.

"Excuse me," she said, pulling on the doorkeeper's sleeve. "Excuse me. You haven't seen a young bear in a blue duffle coat, have you? We arranged to meet here, and there are so many people about that I'm really rather worried."

The doorkeeper touched his cap. "That wouldn't be the young gentleman in question, ma'am?" he asked, pointing through a gap in the crowd to where another man in uniform was struggling with the revolving door. "If it is, he's stuck! Good and proper. Can't get in and can't get out. Right in the middle he is, so to speak."

"Oh dear," said Mrs. Brown. "That certainly sounds as if it might be Paddington."

Standing on tiptoe, she peered over the shoulder of a bearded gentleman in front of her. The man was shouting words of encouragement as he tapped on the glass and she just caught a glimpse of a familiar paw as it waved back in acknowledgment.

"It *is* Paddington," she exclaimed. "Now how on earth did he get in there?"

"Ah," said the doorkeeper. "That's just what we're trying to find out. Something to do with his getting a clothesline wrapped round the hinges, so they say."

There was a ripple of excitement from the crowd as the door started to revolve once more.

Everyone made a rush for Paddington, but the distinguished man with the beard reached him first. To everyone's surprise, he took hold of his paw and began pumping it up and down.

"Thank you, bear," he kept saying. "Glad to know you, bear!"

"Glad to know *you*," repeated Paddington, looking as surprised as anyone.

"I say," exclaimed the doorkeeper respectfully, as he turned to Mrs. Brown. "I didn't know he was a friend of Sir Gresholm Gibbs."

"Neither did I," said Mrs. Brown. "And who might Sir Gresholm Gibbs be?"

"Sir Gresholm," repeated the doorkeeper in a hushed voice. "Why, he's a famous millionaire. He's one of Crumbold and Ferns's most important customers."

He pushed back the crowd of interested spectators to allow Paddington and the distinguished man a free passage.

"Dear lady," said Sir Gresholm, bowing low as he approached. "You must be Mrs. Brown. I've just been hearing all about you."

"Oh?" said Mrs. Brown, doubtfully.

"This young bear of yours found a most valuable diamond tie pin that I lost earlier this afternoon," said Sir Gresholm. "Not only that, but he's kept it in safe custody all this time."

"A diamond tie pin?" exclaimed Mrs. Brown, looking at Paddington. It was the first she had heard of any diamond tie pin.

"I found it when I lost my candy," said Paddington in a loud stage whisper.

"An example to us all," boomed Sir Gresholm as he turned to the crowd and pointed at Paddington.

Paddington waved a paw modestly in the air as one or two people applauded.

"And now, dear lady," continued Sir Gresholm, turning to Mrs. Brown. "I understand you intend to show this young bear some of the Christmas decorations."

"Well," said Mrs. Brown, "I was hoping to. He hasn't seen them before, and it's really his first trip out since he was ill."

"In that case," said Sir Gresholm, waving to a luxurious car that was parked by the side of the pavement, "my car is at your disposal."

"Ooh," said Paddington. "Is it really?" His eyes glistened. He'd never seen such an enormous car before, let alone ever dreamed of riding in one.

"Yes, indeed," said Sir Gresholm as he held the door open for them. "That is," he added, as he noticed a worried expression cross Paddington's face, "if you would do me the honor."

"Oh, yes," said Paddington politely. "I would like to do you the honor very much indeed." He hesitated. "But I've left my candy on one of the counters in Crumbold and Ferns."

"Oh dear," said the gentleman, as he helped Paddington and Mrs. Brown into the car. "Then there's only one thing we can do."

He tapped on the glass window behind the driver with his stick. "Drive on, James," he said. "And don't stop until we reach the nearest candy shop."

"One with chewy candies, please, Mr. James," called Paddington.

"Definitely one with chewy candies," repeated Sir Gresholm. "That's most important." He turned to Mrs. Brown with a twinkle in his eye. "You know," he said, "I'm looking forward to this."

"So am I," said Paddington earnestly as he gazed out of the window at all the lights.

As the huge car drew away from the curb, he stood on the seat and gave a final wave of his paw to the crowd of open-mouthed spectators, and then settled back, holding on to a long gold tassel with his other paw.

It wasn't every day a bear was able to ride round London in such a magnificent car and Paddington wanted to enjoy it to the full.

Chapter 14

◆ ◆ ◆

Paddington Makes a Bid

Mr. Gruber kept an antique shop in the Portobello Road near the Browns' house and Paddington usually called in when he was doing the morning shopping so that they could share a bun and a cup of cocoa for their elevenses. In his younger days Mr. Gruber had been to South America and so they were able to have long chats together about Darkest Peru while sitting in their deck chairs on the sidewalk. Paddington always looked forward to seeing Mr. Gruber and he often lent a paw round the shop.

Most of the shops in the Portobello Road were interesting, but Mr. Gruber's was the best of all. It was like going into Aladdin's cave. There were swords and old suits of armor hanging on the walls, gleaming copper and brass pots and pans stacked on the floor, pictures, china ornaments, pieces of furniture and pottery piled up to the ceiling; in fact, there was very little one way and another that Mr. Gruber didn't sell, and people came from far and wide to seek his advice.

Mr. Gruber also kept a huge library of secondhand books in the back of his shop which he let Paddington consult whenever any problems cropped up. Paddington found this most useful as the public library didn't have a bears' department and the librarians usually looked at him suspiciously when he peered through the window at them.

It was while he was sitting back in his deck chair drinking cocoa and admiring the view that Paddington noticed Mr. Gruber's shop window for the first time that morning. To his surprise it looked unusually empty.

"Ah," said Mr. Gruber, following his glance. "I had a very busy day yesterday, Mr. Brown. A big group of American visitors came round and they bought all kinds of things. As a matter of fact," he continued, "I did so well I have to go to an auction this afternoon to pick up some more antiques."

"An auction?" said Paddington, looking most interested. "What does it look like, Mr. Gruber?"

Mr. Gruber thought for a moment. "Well," he began, "it's a place where they sell things to the highest bidder, Mr. Brown. All kinds of things. But it's very difficult to explain without actually showing you."

Mr. Gruber rubbed his glasses and coughed. "Er . . . I suppose, Mr. Brown, it wouldn't be possible for you to come along with me this afternoon, would it? Then you could see for yourself."

"Oooh, yes, please, Mr. Gruber," exclaimed Paddington, his eyes gleaming with excitement at the thought. "I should like that very much indeed."

Although they met most days, Mr. Gruber was usually busy in his shop and they seldom had the opportunity of actually going out together.

At that moment a customer entered the shop and so, having arranged to meet Mr. Gruber after lunch, Paddington raised his hat and hurried back home to tell the others.

"*Hmm,*" said Mrs. Bird, when she heard all about it over lunch. "I pity the poor auctioneer who tries to sell anything when Paddington's there. That bear'll knock anyone down to half price."

"Oh, I'm not *buying* anything, Mrs. Bird," said Paddington, as he reached out a paw for a second helping of apple tart. "I'm only going to watch."

All the same, when he left the house after lunch, Mrs. Bird noticed that he was carrying his old leather suitcase in which he kept all his money.

"It's all right, Mrs. Bird," said Paddington, as he waved goodbye with his paw. "It's only in case of an emergency."

"Just so long as he doesn't come home with a suite of furniture," said Mrs. Bird as she closed the door. "If he does it'll have to go in the garden."

◆◆◆

Paddington felt very excited as he entered the auction rooms. Mr. Gruber had put on his best suit for the occasion and a number of people turned to stare at them as they came through the door.

Having bought two catalogues, Mr. Gruber pushed his way to the front so that Paddington would have a good view. On the way he introduced him to several of the other dealers as "Mr. Brown—a young bear friend of mine from Darkest Peru who's interested in antiques."

They all shook Paddington's paw and whispered that they were very pleased to meet him.

It was all very different from what Paddington had expected. It was really like a very big antique shop, with boxes and tables loaded with china and silver round the walls. There was a large crowd of people standing in the middle of the room facing a man on a platform who appeared to be waving a hammer in the air.

"That's the auctioneer," whispered Mr. Gruber. "He's the man you want to watch. He's most important."

Paddington raised his hat politely to the auctioneer and then settled down on his suitcase and carefully looked round.

After a moment he decided he liked auctions. Everyone seemed so friendly. In fact, he had hardly made himself comfortable before a man on the other side of the room waved his hand in their direction. Paddington stood up, raised his hat and waved a friendly paw back.

No sooner had he sat down than the man waved again. Being a polite bear, Paddington stood up and once more waved his paw.

To his surprise the man stopped waving almost immediately and glared at him instead. Paddington gave him a hard stare and then settled down to watch the man on the platform who appeared to be doing something with his hammer again.

"Going . . ." the man shouted, hitting his table. "Going . . . gone! Sold to the young bear gentleman in the hat for three pounds fifty!"

"Oh dear," said Mr. Gruber, looking most upset. "I'm afraid you've just bought a set of carpenter's tools, Mr. Brown."

"*What!*" said Paddington, nearly falling off his suitcase with surprise. "*I've bought a set of carpenter's tools?*"

"Come along," said the auctioneer sternly. "You're holding up the proceedings. Pay at the desk, please."

"A set of carpenter's tools," exclaimed Paddington, jumping up and waving his paws in the air. "But I didn't even say anything!"

Mr. Gruber looked most embarrassed. "I'm afraid it's all my fault, Mr. Brown," he said. "I should have explained auctions to you before we came in. I think perhaps *I'd* better pay for them as it wasn't really your fault.

"You see," he continued when he returned from the desk, "you have to be very careful at a sale, Mr. Brown."

Mr. Gruber went on to explain how the auctioneer offered each item for sale, and how, after one person had made a bid for something, it was up to anyone else who wanted it to make a better offer.

"If you nod your head, Mr. Brown," he said, "or even scratch your nose, they think it's a sign you want to buy something. I expect the auctioneer saw you raise your hat just now and thought you were bidding."

Paddington wasn't at all sure what Mr. Gruber meant, but having carefully made sure the auctioneer wasn't looking, he quickly nodded and then sat very still while he watched the proceedings.

Although he didn't say anything to Mr. Gruber, he was beginning to wish he hadn't come to the auction. The room was hot and crowded and he wanted to take his hat off. Apart from that he was sitting on the handle of his suitcase, which was most uncomfortable.

He closed his eyes and was just about to try and go to sleep when Mr. Gruber nudged his paw and pointed to the catalogue.

"I say, Mr. Brown," he said. "The next item is very interesting. It's an old pistol—the sort highwaymen used. They're quite popular just now. I think I shall try bidding for it."

Paddington sat up and watched excitedly as the auctioneer held the pistol in the air for everyone to see. "Lot thirty-four," he shouted. "What am I bid for this genuine antique pistol?"

"Twenty pounds," came a voice from the back of the room.

"Twenty pounds fifty," called Mr. Gruber, waving his catalogue.

"Twenty-two pounds," came another voice.

"Oh dear," said Mr. Gruber, making some calculations on the side of his catalogue. "Twenty-two pounds fifty pence."

"Twenty-three," came the same voice again.

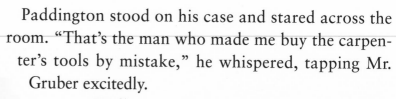

Paddington stood on his case and stared across the room. "That's the man who made me buy the carpenter's tools by mistake," he whispered, tapping Mr. Gruber excitedly.

"Well, we mustn't let *him* have it whatever we do," exclaimed Mr. Gruber. "Twenty-three pounds fifty!"

"Twenty-four pounds," cried Paddington wildly.

"Ahem," said Mr. Gruber tactfully, not wishing to offend Paddington. "I think we're bidding against each other, Mr. Brown."

"Any advance on twenty-four pounds?" shouted the auctioneer, looking most pleased.

As there was no reply he raised his hammer. "Going . . . going . . ." he called. "Gone!" He brought the hammer down with a loud crash. "Sold to the young bear gentleman in the front row for twenty-four pounds."

Mr. Gruber felt in his wallet for the money. Taking Paddington to an auction was becoming rather expensive.

"I'm sorry about that, Mr. Gruber," said Paddington guiltily, when he returned. "I'm afraid I got rather excited."

"That's all right," said Mr. Gruber. "It was still a very good bargain, Mr. Brown—and I did want it. I shall put it in my window tomorrow."

"I think perhaps I'd better not do any more bidding," said Paddington, looking very crestfallen. "I don't think bears are very good at it."

"Nonsense," said Mr. Gruber. "You've been doing very well for a first time."

All the same, Paddington decided to keep quiet for a while and watch Mr. Gruber. It was all very complicated and not a bit like shopping in the market, where he was allowed to test everything with his paws first before arguing over the price.

Mr. Gruber pointed out several items in the catalogue to Paddington and gave him a pencil so that he could mark off the ones he had bought and how much had been paid for them.

The list of items Mr. Gruber bought grew and grew until Paddington felt quite dizzy with writing down all the figures and he was pleased when at last Mr. Gruber announced that he had finished buying for the day.

"A very good day's work indeed, Mr. Brown," he said, as he checked Paddington's figures. "And thank you very much for all your help. I don't know what I would have done without you."

Paddington looked up from his own catalogue which he had been studying earnestly. "That's all right, Mr. Gruber," he said vaguely. "Excuse me, but what is a preserves stand?"

"A preserves stand?" said Mr. Gruber. "Well, it's a thing for holding jam or marmalade."

Paddington's eyes gleamed as he started to unlock his suitcase. "I think I shall bid for that, Mr. Gruber," he said excitedly, as he peered inside the secret compartment to see how much money he had. "It's the next item in the catalogue. I think I should like a preserves stand for my marmalade."

Mr. Gruber looked at him rather nervously. "I should be careful if I were you, Mr. Brown," he said. "It may be an antique one. If it is, it's probably worth a lot of money."

But before he had time to explain to Paddington just how much it might cost him the auctioneer rapped on his table for silence.

"Lot 99," he shouted, as he held up a piece of shining silver to the light. "A very unusual kind of preserves stand. What am I bid for this valuable piece of antique silver?"

"Five pence!" cried Paddington.

A hush fell over the room. "Five pence?" echoed the auctioneer, hardly able to believe his ears. "Did I hear someone say *five pence*?"

"I did," called Paddington, waving his catalogue in the air. "I want it to keep my marmalade in. Mrs. Bird's always grumbling because my jars get sticky."

"Your *jars* get sticky?" repeated the auctioneer, passing a hand over his forehead. It really was a most unusual day. Things hadn't gone at all according to plan. Some items had been sold for far more than he had ever expected. Others—like the preserves stand—were fetching nothing at all. He had a nasty feeling it had something to do with the young bear in the front row. He seemed to have a very powerful stare, and the auctioneer had done his best up to now to avoid catching Paddington's eye.

"Come, come," he said, giving a high-pitched laugh. "I'm sure we all enjoy a little joke. Let's start again. Now—what am I bid for this valuable item?"

"Six pence," said a voice at the back of the hall amid laughter.

"Ten pence," said Paddington firmly.

The laughter died down and there was silence. "If you ask me," whispered a

voice behind Paddington, "that bear knows something."

"It's probably a fake," whispered another voice. "After all, it's not the first thing he's bought this afternoon."

"He's with old Mr. Gruber, too," whispered the first voice. "And he said he was interested in antiques when he came in. I wouldn't touch it if I were you."

The auctioneer shuddered as he gazed at the preserves stand in his hand. "Any advance on ten pence?" he cried.

There was another long silence. "Going . . ." he shouted, raising his hammer and looking round hopefully. "Going . . ." Still no one spoke. "Gone!"

He brought his hammer down on the desk with a crash. "Sold to the young bear gentleman in the front row for ten pence."

"Thank you very much," said Paddington, as he hurried up to the table. "I hope you don't mind if I pay you in pennies but I've been saving up in case of an emergency."

"Pennies?" said the man. He mopped his brow with a spotted handkerchief. "I don't know," he said, turning to his assistant. "I must be getting old. Letting young bears get the better of me at my time of life."

"A very good bargain indeed," said Mr. Gruber admiringly, when they were outside the sale room. He turned Paddington's preserves stand over in his hands. "I should say it's worth every penny of fifty pounds."

"Fifty pounds?" exclaimed Paddington, staring at Mr. Gruber. "Fifty pounds for a marmalade stand?"

"At least that," said Mr. Gruber. "I'll put it in my window for you if you like, Mr. Brown."

Paddington thought hard for a moment. "I think I would like you to have it as a present, Mr. Gruber," he said at last. "I don't expect you'd have bought the carpenter's tools if I hadn't been at the auction."

Mr. Gruber looked most affected by Paddington's offer. "That's very kind of you, Mr. Brown," he said. "Very kind of you indeed. But I know how fond you are of marmalade and I'd much rather you had it. Besides," he added, "I've had a very good day and I think it was worth the price of the carpenter's tools just to see the expression on the auctioneer's face when you offered him five pence for the preserves stand."

Mr. Gruber chuckled at the thought. "I don't think he's had many dealings with young bears before," he said.

◆ ◆ ◆

"I've said it before," remarked Mrs. Bird, later that evening, "and I'll say it again. That bear's got an eye for a bargain."

The Browns were having a late supper before going to bed. Paddington's "antique" stood in the center of the table in a place of honor. He had spent most of the evening polishing it until he could see his whiskers in the side and Mrs. Bird had opened a new jar of his favorite marmalade especially for the occasion.

There was a blissful expression on Paddington's face—that part of it which could be seen behind bread and butter crumbs and smears of marmalade.

"I think," he announced, amid general agreement, "preserves taste even nicer when they come out of an antique.

"Especially," he added, as he dipped his paw into the marmalade, "a tenpenny one!"

Chapter 15

◆ ◆ ◆

Paddington Cleans Up

Paddington peered through the letter box at number thirty-two Windsor Gardens with a look of surprise on his face.

In point of fact he'd been watching out for the postman, but instead of the blue-gray uniform he'd hoped to see, Mr. Curry had loomed into view. Mr. Curry looked as if he was in a bad temper. He was never at his best in the morning, but even through the half-open flap it was plain to see he was in an even worse mood than usual. He was shaking a rug over the sidewalk, and from the cloud of dust surrounding him it looked as though he had been cleaning out his grate and had just had a nasty accident with the ashes.

The expression on his face boded ill for anyone who happened to come within his range of vision, and it was unfortunate that his gaze alighted on the Browns' front door at the very moment when Paddington opened the letter box.

"Bear!" he bellowed. "How dare you spy on me like that? I've a very good mind to report you!"

Paddington let go of the flap as if it had been resting in hot coals, and gazed at the closed door with a very disappointed air indeed. Apart from an occasional catalogue he didn't get many letters, but all the same he always looked forward to seeing the postman arrive, and he felt most aggrieved at being deprived of his morning's treat, especially as he'd been half expecting a postcard from his Aunt Lucy in Peru. Something she'd said when she'd last written had given him food for thought and he was anxiously awaiting the next installment.

All the same, he knew better than to get on the wrong side of Mr. Curry, so he decided to forget the matter and pay his daily visit to the nearby market in the Portobello Road instead.

A few minutes later, having taken his shopping basket on wheels from the cupboard under the stairs, he collected Mrs. Bird's shopping list, made sure the coast was clear, and set out on his journey.

Over the years Paddington's basket on wheels had become a familiar sight in the market and it was often much admired by passersby. Paddington took great care of it. He'd several times varnished the basketwork, and the wheels were kept so well oiled there was never a squeak. Earlier in the year Mr. Brown had bought him two new tires, so all in all it still looked as good as new.

After he'd completed Mrs. Bird's shopping, Paddington called in at the bakers for his morning supply of buns. Then he went on down the Portobello Road in order to visit the antique shop belonging to his friend Mr. Gruber.

Paddington liked visiting Mr. Gruber. Apart from selling antiques, Mr. Gruber possessed a large number of books, and although no one knew if he'd actually read

them all, it certainly seemed as though he must have, for he was a mine of information on almost every subject one could think of.

When he arrived he found Mr. Gruber sitting on the horsehair sofa just inside his shop clutching a particularly large volume.

"You'll never guess what today's book is about, Mr. Brown," he said, holding it up for Paddington to see. "It's called *Diseases of the Cocoa Bean*, and there are over seven hundred and fifty pages."

Paddington's face grew longer and longer as he listened to Mr. Gruber recite from the long list of things that could happen to a cocoa bean before it actually reached the shops. He always rounded off his morning excursions with a visit to his friend, and Mr. Gruber's contribution to the meeting was a never-ending supply of cocoa, which he kept at the ready on a small stove at the back of the shop. It didn't seem possible that this could ever come to an end.

"Perhaps we'd better get some more stocks in, Mr. Gruber," he exclaimed anxiously, when there was a gap in the conversation.

Mr. Gruber smiled. "I don't think there's any risk of our going short yet awhile, Mr. Brown," he replied, as he busied himself at the stove. "But I think it does go to show how we tend to take things for granted. We very rarely get something for nothing in this world."

Paddington looked slightly relieved at Mr. Gruber's reassuring words. All the same, it was noticeable that he sipped his cocoa even more slowly than usual, and when he'd finished he carefully wiped round his mug with the remains of a bun in order to make sure he wasn't letting any go to waste.

Even after he'd said goodbye to Mr. Gruber he still had a very thoughtful expression on his face. In fact, his mind was so far away it wasn't until he rounded a corner leading into Windsor Gardens that he suddenly came back to earth with a bump as he realized that while he'd been in the shop someone had pinned a note to his shopping basket.

It was short and to the point. It said:

> YOUR SHOPPING BASKET ON WHEELS IS IN SUCH GOOD CONDITION IT SHOWS YOU HAVE CHARACTER, DRIVE AND AMBITION. THIS MEANS YOU ARE JUST THE KIND OF PERSON WE ARE LOOKING FOR. YOU COULD EARN £100 PER WEEK WITH NO MORE EFFORT THAN IT TAKES TO VISIT THE GROCERS. I WILL BE IN TOUCH SOON WITH FURTHER DETAILS.

It was written in large capital letters and it was signed YOURS TRULY, A WELL-WISHER.

Paddington read the note several times. He could hardly believe his eyes. Only a moment before he'd been racking his brains to think up ways of earning some extra money so he could buy Mr. Gruber a tin or two of cocoa, and now, out of nowhere, came this strange offer. It couldn't have happened at a better moment, especially as he'd been tempted to break into the savings which he kept in the secret compartment of his suitcase, and which he held in reserve for important occasions, like birthdays and Christmas.

It was hard to believe he could earn so much money simply because he'd kept his shopping basket clean, but before he had a chance to consider the matter he saw a man in a tan raincoat approaching. The man was carrying a large cardboard box which seemed to contain something heavy, for as he drew near he rested it on Paddington's basket while he paused in order to mop his brow.

He looked Paddington up and down for a moment and then held out his hand. "Just as I thought!" he exclaimed. "It's nice when you have a picture of someone in your mind and they turn out exactly as you expected. I'm glad you got my note. If you don't mind my saying so, sir, you should go far."

Paddington held out his paw in return. "Thank you, Mr. Wisher," he replied. "But I don't think I shall go very far this morning. I'm on my way home." He gave the man a hard stare. Although he was much too polite to say so, he couldn't really return the man's compliments. From the tone of the letter he'd expected someone rather superior, whereas his new acquaintance looked more than a trifle seedy.

Catching sight of Paddington's glance, the man hastily pulled his coatsleeves down over his cuffs. "I must apologize for my appearance," he said. "But I've got rid of . . . er, I've obtained so many new clients for my vacuum cleaners this morning I don't know whether I'm coming or going. I haven't even had time to go home and change."

"Your *vacuum cleaners*!" exclaimed Paddington in surprise.

The man nodded. "I must say, sir," he continued, "it's your lucky day. It just so happens that you've caught me with my very last one. Until I take delivery of a new batch later on, of course," he added hastily.

Taking a quick glance over his shoulder, he produced a piece of cardboard, which he held up in front of Paddington's eyes for a fleeting moment before returning it to an inside pocket.

"My card," he announced. "Just to show that all's above board. You too could become a member of our happy band and make yourself a fortune. Every new member gets, free of charge, our latest model cleaner, *and* . . . for today only, a list of dos and don'ts for making your very first sale.

"Now"—he slapped the box to emphasize his point—"I'm not asking twenty pounds for this very rare privilege. I'm not asking fifteen. I'm not even asking ten. To you, because I like the look of your face, and because I think you're just the sort of bear we are looking for, *five* pounds!"

His voice took on a confidential tone. "If I was to tell you the names of some of the people I've sold cleaners to you probably wouldn't believe me. But I won't bore you with details like that. You're probably asking yourself what you have to do in order to earn all this money, right? Well, I'll tell you.

"You sell this cleaner for ten pounds, right? You then buy two more cleaners for five pounds each and sell *them* for twenty, making thirty pounds in all, right? Then you either keep the money or you buy six more cleaners and sell those. If you work hard you'll make a fortune so fast you won't even have time to get to the bank.

"Another thing you may be asking yourself," he continued, before Paddington had time to say anything, "is why anyone who already has a vacuum cleaner should buy one of ours?"

He gave the box another slap. "Never fear, it's all in here. Ask no questions, tell no lies. With our new cleaner you can suck up anything. Dirt, muck, ashes, soot . . . pile it all on, anything you like. A flick of the switch and whoosh, it'll disappear in a flash.

"But," he warned, "you'll have to hurry. I've a line of customers waiting round the next corner."

Paddington needed no second bidding. It wasn't every day such an offer came his way, and he felt sure he would be able to buy an awful lot of cocoa for thirty pounds. Hurrying behind a nearby car he bent down and opened his suitcase.

"Thank you very much," said the man, as Paddington counted out five pounds. "Sorry I can't stop, guv, but work calls . . ."

Paddington had been about to inquire where he could pick up his next lot of cleaners, but before he had a chance to open his mouth the man had disappeared.

For a moment he didn't know what to do. He felt very tempted to take the cleaner straight indoors in order to test it in his bedroom, but he wasn't at all sure Mrs. Bird would approve. In any case, number thirty-two Windsor Gardens was always kept so spotlessly clean there didn't seem much point.

And then, as he reached the end of the road, the matter was suddenly decided for him. Mr. Curry's front door shot open and the Browns' neighbor emerged once again carrying a dustpan and brush.

He glanced at Paddington. "Are you still spying on me, bear?" he growled. "I've told you about it once before this morning."

"Oh, no, Mr. Curry," said Paddington hastily. "I'm not spying on anyone. I've got a job. I'm selling a special new cleaner."

Mr. Curry looked at Paddington uncertainly. "Is this true, bear?" he demanded.

"Oh, yes," said Paddington. "It gets rid of anything. I can give you a free demonstration if you like."

A sly gleam entered Mr. Curry's eyes. "As a matter of fact," he said, "it does so happen that I'm having a spot of bother this morning. I'm not saying I'll buy anything mind, but if you care to clear up the mess I *might* consider it."

Paddington consulted the handwritten list of instructions which was pinned to the box. He could see that Mr. Curry was going to come under the heading of CUS-TOMERS—VERY DIFFICULT.

"I think," he announced, as the Browns' neighbor helped him up the step with his basket on wheels, "you're going to need what we call the 'full treatment.'"

Mr. Curry gave a snort. "It had better be good, bear," he said. "Otherwise I shall hold you personally responsible."

He led the way into his dining room and pointed to a large pile of black stuff in the grate. "I've had a bad fall of soot this morning. Probably to do with the noise that goes on next door," he added meaningfully.

"My cleaner's very good with soot, Mr. Curry," said Paddington eagerly. "Mr. Wisher mentioned it specially."

"Good," said Mr. Curry. "I'll just go and finish emptying my dustpan and then I'll be back to keep an eye on things."

As the Browns' neighbor disappeared from view Paddington hurriedly set to work. Remembering the advice he'd been given a short while before, he decided to make certain he gave Mr. Curry a very good demonstration indeed.

Grabbing hold of a broom which was standing nearby, he quickly brushed the soot into a large pile in the middle of the hearth. Then he poked the broom up the chimney and waved it round several times. His hopes were speedily realized. There was a rushing sound and a moment later an even bigger load of soot landed at his feet. Ignoring the black clouds which were beginning to fill the room, Paddington removed the cardboard box from his basket and examined Mrs. Bird's shopping. As he'd feared, some of it had suffered rather badly under the weight and he added the remains of some broken custard tarts, several squashed tomatoes, and a number of cracked eggs to the pile.

It was while he was stirring it all up with the handle of the broom that Mr. Curry came back into the room. For a moment he stood as if transfixed.

"Bear!" he bellowed. "Bear! What on earth do you think you're doing?"

Paddington stood up and gazed at his handiwork. Now that he was viewing it from a distance he had to admit it *was* rather worse than he had intended.

"It's all part of my demonstration, Mr. Curry," he explained, with more confidence than he felt.

"Now," Paddington said, putting on his best salesman's voice as he consulted the instructions again, "I'm sure you will agree that no ordinary cleaner would be any good with this mess."

For once in his life it seemed that Mr. Curry was in complete and utter accord with Paddington. "Have you taken leave of your senses, bear?" he spluttered.

Paddington gave the cardboard box a slap. "No, Mr. Curry," he exclaimed. "Never fear, it's all in here. Ask no questions, I'll tell no lies."

Mr. Curry looked as if there were a good many questions he was only too eager to ask, but instead he pointed a trembling finger at the box.

"'Never fear, it's all in here!'" he bellowed. "It had better all be in there! If it's not all in there within thirty seconds I shall—"

Mr. Curry paused for breath, suddenly at a loss for words.

Taking advantage of the moment, Paddington opened the lid of the box and withdrew a long piece of wire with a plug on the end.

He peered at the baseboard. "Can you tell me where your socket is, Mr. Curry?" he asked.

If Paddington had asked the Browns' neighbor for the loan of a million pounds he couldn't have had a more unfavorable reaction. Mr. Curry's face, which had been growing redder and redder with rage, suddenly went a deep shade of purple as he gazed at the object in Paddington's paw.

"My socket?" he roared. "*My socket?* I haven't any sockets, bear! I don't even have any electricity. I use gas!"

Paddington's jaw dropped, and the plug slipped from his paw and fell unheeded to the floor as he gazed at the Browns' neighbor. If Mr. Curry's face had gone a deep shade of purple, Paddington's—or the little that could be seen of it beneath his fur— was as white as a sheet.

He wasn't sure what happened next. He remembered Mr. Curry picking up the cardboard box as if he was about to hurl it through the window, but he didn't wait to see any more. He dashed out through the front door and back into number thirty- two Windsor Gardens as if his very life depended on it.

To his surprise the door was already open, but it wasn't until he cannoned into Mr. Gruber that he discovered the reason why. His friend was deep in conversation with the other members of the family.

For some reason they seemed even more pleased to see him than he was to see them.

"There you are!" exclaimed Mrs. Bird.

"Thank goodness," said Mrs. Brown thankfully.

"Are you all right?" chorused Jonathan and Judy.

"I think so," gasped Paddington, peering over his shoulder as he hastily closed the door behind him.

"No one's tried to sell you a vacuum cleaner?" asked Mrs. Bird.

Paddington stared at the Browns' housekeeper in amazement. It really was uncanny the way Mrs. Bird knew about things.

"There have been some goings-on down at the market this morning, Mr. Brown," broke in Mr. Gruber. "That's why I popped in. Someone's been selling dud vacuum cleaners and when I heard you'd been seen talking to him I began to get worried."

"When you were so late back we thought something might have happened to you," said Mrs. Brown.

"Well," said Paddington vaguely, "I think it has!"

Paddington launched into his explanations. It was a bit difficult, partly because he wasn't too sure how to put some of it into words, but also because there was a good deal of noise going on outside. Shouts and bangs, and the sound of a loud argument, followed a moment or so later by the roar of a car drawing away.

"Fancy trying to take advantage of someone like that," said Mrs. Bird grimly, when Paddington had finished.

"He seemed quite a nice man, Mrs. Bird," said Paddington.

"I didn't mean the vacuum cleaner salesman," said Mrs. Bird. "At least he gave you *something* for your money, even if it didn't work. I meant Mr. Curry. He's always after something for nothing."

"He's too mean to get his chimney swept for a start," said Judy.

"And I bet he's still waiting to see if electricity catches on before he changes over," agreed Jonathan.

They broke off as the telephone started to ring and Mrs. Bird hurried across the hall to answer it.

"Yes," she said after a moment. "Really? Yes, of course. Well, we'll do our best," she added after a while, "but it may not be for some time. Probably later on this morning."

The others grew more and more mystified as they listened to their end of the conversation.

"What on earth was all that about?" asked Mrs. Brown as her housekeeper replaced the receiver.

"It seems," said Mrs. Bird gravely, "that the police think they may have caught the man who's been selling the dud vacuum cleaners. They want someone to go down and identify him."

"Oh dear," said Mrs. Brown. "I don't really like the idea of Paddington being involved in things like that."

"Who said anything about Paddington?" asked Mrs. Bird innocently. "Anyway, I suggest we all have a nice hot drink before we do anything else. There's no point in rushing things."

The others exchanged glances as they followed Mrs. Bird into the kitchen. She could be very infuriating at times. But the Browns' housekeeper refused to be drawn, and it wasn't until they were all settled round the kitchen table with their second lot of elevenses that she brought the matter up again.

"It seems," she mused, "that the man they arrested was caught right outside our house. He was carrying a cleaner at the time. He said his name was Murray, or Hurry or something like that . . . Anyway, he insists we know him."

"Crumbs!" exclaimed Jonathan as light began to dawn. "Don't say they picked on Mr. Curry by mistake!"

"I bet that's what all the noise was about just now," said Judy. "I bet he was coming round here to complain!"

"Which is why," said Mrs. Bird, when all the excitement had died down, "I really think it might be better if Paddington doesn't go down to the police station. It might be rubbing salt into the wound."

"I quite agree," said Mr. Gruber. "In fact, while you're gone perhaps young Mr. Brown and I can go next door and clear up some of the mess."

"We'll help too," said Jonathan and Judy eagerly.

All eyes turned to Paddington, who was savoring his drink with even more relish than usual. What with Mr. Gruber's book on diseases and the disastrous events in Mr. Curry's house he'd almost begun to wonder if he would ever have any elevenses again.

"I think," he announced, as he clasped the mug firmly between his paws, "I shall never take my cocoa for granted again!"

◆ ◆ ◆

Part Four

A Case of
Mistaken Identity

Chapter 16.

Paddington at the Wheel

Paddington gave the man facing him one of his hardest stares ever. "I've won a bookmark!" he exclaimed hotly. "But I thought it was going to be a Rolls-Royce."

The man fingered his collar nervously. "There must be some mistake," he replied. "The lucky winner of the car has already been presented with it. And the second prize, a weekend for two in Paris, has gone to a senior citizen in Edinburgh. If you've had a letter from us, then you must be one of the ten thousand runners-up who merely receive bookmarks. I can't think why one wasn't enclosed."

"I'm one of *ten thousand runners-up?*" repeated Paddington, hardly able to believe his ears.

"I'm afraid so." Regaining his confidence, the man began rummaging in one of his desk drawers. "The trouble is," he said meaningfully, "so many entrants to competitions don't bother to read the small print. If you care to take another look at our entry form you'll see what I mean."

Paddington took the leaflet and focused his gaze on a picture of a large, sleek, silver-gray car. A chauffeur, standing beside one of the open doors, was flicking an imaginary speck of dust from the upholstery with one of his gloves, while across the hood, in large red letters, were the words ALL THIS COULD BE YOURS!

Having slept with an identical picture under his pillow at number thirty-two

Windsor Gardens for several weeks, Paddington felt he knew it all by heart. He turned it over and on the back were the self-same instructions for entering the competition, together with an entry form.

"Now look inside," suggested the man.

Paddington did as he was bidden, and as he did so his face fell. He'd been so excited by the picture of the Rolls-Royce he hadn't bothered to look any further, but as he pulled the pages apart he found it opened out into a larger sheet. On the left-hand side there was a picture of a French gendarme pointing towards a distant

view of the Eiffel Tower, and on the right, under the heading TEN THOUSAND CONSOLATION PRIZES TO BE WON, there was a picture of a bookmark, followed by a lot of writing.

By the end of the page some of the print was so small Paddington began to wish he'd brought his opera glasses with him, but there was no escaping the fact that the bookmark had an all-too-familiar look about it. One exactly like it had arrived that very morning in the envelope containing news of his success.

"I don't think a bookmark is much consolation for not winning a Rolls-Royce!" he exclaimed. "I put *mine* down the waste disposal. I didn't think it was a *prize*."

"Oh dear!" The man gave a sympathetic cluck as he riffled through a pile of papers on his desk to show that the interview was at an end. "How very unfortunate. Still, at least you've had the benefit of eating some of our sun-kissed currants." He opened one of his desk drawers again and took out a packet. "Have some more as a present," he said.

"But I don't even like currants!" exclaimed Paddington bitterly. "And I ate fifteen boxes of them!"

"*Fifteen?*" The man gazed at Paddington with new respect. "May I ask what your slogan was?"

"A currant a day," said Paddington hopefully, "keeps the doctor away."

"In that case," said the man, permitting himself a smile, "you shouldn't require any medical attention for quite a . . ." His voice trailed away as he caught sight of the look Paddington was giving him.

It had taken Paddington a long time to get through fifteen boxes of currants, not to mention think up a suitable slogan into the bargain. And, if the expression on his face was anything to go by, the whole thing had left him in need of *more* medical attention rather than less.

In fact, as he made his way back down the stairs Paddington began to look more and more gloomy. The news that he wasn't after all the proud possessor of a gleaming new car was a bitter blow, one made all the worse because he hadn't even wanted it for himself—it had really been intended as a surprise for Mr. Brown.

Mr. Brown's present car was a bit of a sore point in the Brown household. The general feeling at number thirty-two Windsor Gardens was that it ought to have been sold years ago. But Mr. Brown had held on to it because it was hard to find anything large enough to convey the whole family, not to mention Paddington and all his belongings, when they went on their outings.

Apart from its age it had a number of drawbacks, one of which was that instead of flashing lights, it relied on illuminated arms to indicate intended changes of direction. It was the failure of one of these arms when Mr. Brown had been turning into a main road one day that had attracted the attention of a passing policeman, who'd taken his number.

Paddington had been most upset at the time because he'd been sitting alongside Mr. Brown, ready to help out with paw signals when necessary.

The judge had had one or two pointed things to say about drivers who relied on bears for their signals, and much to Mr. Brown's disgust he'd been ordered to retake his driving test.

It was shortly after this disastrous event that Paddington had come across a leaflet in the local supermarket announcing a competition in which the first prize was a car. And it was not just any old car, but a Rolls-Royce. Paddington felt sure that with a car as grand as a Rolls, Mr. Brown couldn't possibly fail his coming test, let alone have any driving problems ever again.

The competition was sponsored by a well-known brand of currants, and the lady in the supermarket assured Paddington that there had been nothing like it in the dried-fruit world before. When he consulted the leaflet, with the aid of his flashlight under the bedclothes that night, he could quite see what she meant, for it couldn't have been simpler. All that was required was a suitable slogan to do with currants, together with three packet tops to show that the entry was genuine.

But the thing that really clinched matters for Paddington was the discovery that not only was the result of the competition being announced on the same day that Mr. Brown was due to take his test, but the firm who were running it occupied a building in the very same street as the Test Center.

Paddington was a great believer in coincidences; some of his best adventures had come about in just such a way—almost as if they had been meant to happen—and after buying some extra packets of currants in order to make doubly sure of success, he lost no time in sending off his entry.

The fact that in the end it had all come to nought was most disappointing, and as he left the building he paused in order to direct a few more hard stares in the direction of the upper floors. Then he collected his shopping basket on wheels from the car park outside and made his way slowly along the road towards the Test Center.

He was much earlier than he had expected to be and so he wasn't too surprised to find Mr. Brown's car still standing where it had been parked earlier that morning. Neither Mr. Brown nor Mrs. Brown was anywhere in sight, and being the sort of bear who didn't believe in wasting time, Paddington parked his shopping basket on wheels alongside it. Then he climbed into the driver's seat and switched on the radio while he awaited developments.

Like the car itself, Mr. Brown's radio had seen better days. It somehow managed to make everything sound the same, rather like an old-fashioned record player, and in no time at all Paddington found himself starting to nod off. His eyelids got heavier and heavier, and soon the sound of gentle snoring added itself to the music.

Paddington had no idea how long he slept, but he was just in the middle of a very vivid dream in which he was driving down a long road, battling against a storm of currants as big as hailstones, when he woke with a start and found to his surprise that two men were standing outside the car peering through the window at

him. One of them was carrying a large clipboard to which was attached a sheaf of very important-looking papers, and he was tapping on the glass in no uncertain manner.

Paddington hastily removed his paws from the steering wheel and opened the driver's door.

"Is your name Brown?" demanded the man with the clipboard, trying to make himself heard above the radio. "From number thirty-two Windsor Gardens?"

"That's right," said Paddington, looking most surprised.

"*Hmm.*" The man gave him an odd look and then consulted the papers on his board. "Er . . . I take it you *are* a British subject?" he asked.

Paddington considered the matter for a moment. "Well," he said, "yes and no . . . "

"Yes and no?" repeated the man sharply. "You can't be yes *and* no. You must be one thing or the other."

"I *live* at number thirty-two Windsor Gardens," said Paddington firmly, "but I *come* from Darkest Peru."

"Darkest Peru? Oh!" The man began to look as if he rather wished he hadn't brought the matter up. Hastily changing the subject, he motioned with his free hand towards his companion. "I take it you won't mind if we're accompanied?" he asked. Then, lowering his voice, he gave Paddington a knowing wink. "We instructors have to be tested every now and again as well, you know. It's my turn today."

"I didn't know," said Paddington with interest. "Perhaps I could ask you some questions on the Highway Code. I've been testing the others at breakfast all this week."

The examiner glared at him. "No you can't!" he snorted, above the sound of martial music from the radio. He looked as if he would have liked to say a good deal more, but instead he recovered himself and opened the rear door of the car for his superior to enter.

"Colonel Bogey," said the other man briefly, nodding towards the front of the car as he settled himself in the back seat.

Paddington raised his hat politely as the examiner made his way round the front of the car and climbed into the passenger seat. "Good morning, Mr. Bogey," he said.

The man clucked impatiently. He was about to explain that his superior had only been giving the name of the tune on the radio, not an introduction, but he thought better of it. Instead he reached forward for the switch. "I think we'll have the radio off for a start," he said severely. "I can't concentrate properly with that racket on, and I'm sure you can't eith—" He broke off and a strange look came over his face as he felt the seat. "I'm sitting on something," he cried. "Something wet and sticky!"

"Oh dear," said Paddington, looking most upset. "I expect that's my marmalade sandwiches. I put them there for my elevenses."

"Your *marmalade sandwiches*?" repeated the man as if in a dream. "They're all over my new trousers."

"Don't worry," said Paddington. He lifted up his hat and withdrew a small package. "I've got some more. I always keep some under my hat in case of an emergency."

The examiner's face seemed to go a funny color. But before he had a chance to open his mouth the man in the back reached over and tapped him on the shoulder. "Don't you think we ought to get cracking?" he said. "Time's getting on and we've a lot to get through."

The examiner took a deep breath as he gathered himself together. "I take it," he said, between his teeth, "you hold a current license?"

"A *currant* license?" It was Paddington's turn to look taken aback. He'd never heard of anyone needing a license just to eat currants before. "I don't think Mrs. Bird would let me be without one," he said, giving the man a hard stare.

The examiner wilted visibly under Paddington's gaze. "Perhaps you would like to switch the engine on?" he said hastily. "We, of the Department of Transport," he continued, in an attempt to regain his normal icy calm, "do find it easier to conduct our tests actually driving along the road."

Anxious to make amends, Paddington reached forward and punched a nearby button with one of his paws. A grinding noise came from somewhere outside.

The man in the back seat gave a cough. "I think you'll find that's the windscreen wiper, Mr. Brown," he said. "Why don't you try the button next to it?

"Don't worry," he continued, raising his voice as Paddington did as he was bidden and the engine suddenly roared into life, "we all get a little nervous at times like these."

"Oh, I'm not nervous," said Paddington. "It's just that they all look the same without my opera glasses."

"Er, quite!" The examiner gave a high-pitched laugh as he tried to humor his superior by joining in the spirit of things. "Perhaps," he said, "before we actually set out we could have a few questions on the Highway Code. Especially," he added meaningfully, "as you say you've made such a study of it. What, for instance, do we look out for when we're driving at this time of the year?"

Paddington put on his thoughtful expression. "Strawberries?" he suggested, licking his lips.

"Strawberries?" repeated the examiner. "What do you mean, *strawberries?*"

"We often stop for strawberries at this time of the year," said Paddington firmly. "Mrs. Bird makes some special cream to go with them."

"I would hardly call strawberries a hazard," said the examiner petulantly.

"They are if you eat them while you're going along," said Paddington firmly. "It's a job to know what to do with the stalks—especially if the ashtray's full."

"Good point," said the man in the back approvingly. "I must remember that one. So ought you," he added pointedly, addressing Paddington's companion.

The examiner took a deep breath. "I was thinking," he said slowly and carefully, "of sudden showers. If the weather has been dry for any length of time a sudden shower can make the road surface very slippery."

Removing a sheet of paper covered with drawings from his clipboard, he decided to have another try. "If you were going along the highway," he said, pointing to one of the drawings, "and you saw this sign, what would it mean?"

Paddington peered at the drawing. "It looks like someone trying to open an umbrella," he replied.

The examiner drew in his breath sharply. "That sign," he said, "happens to mean there is construction ahead."

"Perhaps they're expecting one of your showers?" suggested Paddington helpfully. He gave the man another stare. For an examiner he didn't seem to know very much.

The man returned his gaze as if in a dream. In fact, if looks could have killed, the expression on his face suggested that Paddington's name would have been added to the list of road casualties with very little bother indeed. However, once again he was saved by an impatient movement from the back of the car.

"Perhaps we should move off now?" said a voice. "We seem to be getting nowhere very fast."

"Very good." Taking a firm grip of himself, the examiner settled back in his seat. "Go straight up this road about two hundred yards," he commanded, "then when you see a sign marked BEAR LEFT—"

"A *bear's been left*?" Paddington suddenly sat bolt upright. He wasn't at all sure what was going on and he'd been trying to decide whether to obey his next set of instructions or wait for Mr. Brown to arrive back. The latest piece of information caused him to make up his mind very quickly indeed.

"I'm afraid I shall have to stand up to drive," he announced, as he clambered to his feet. "I can't see out properly if I'm sitting down, but I'll get there as quickly as I can."

"Now, look here," cried the examiner, a note of panic in his voice. "I didn't mean there was a *real* bear lying in the road. I only meant you're supposed to . . ." He broke off and stared at Paddington with disbelieving eyes. "What are you doing now?" he gasped, as Paddington bent down and disappeared beneath the dashboard.

"I'm putting the car into gear," said Paddington as he took hold of the lever firmly with both paws. "I'm afraid it's a bit difficult with paws."

"But you can't change gear with your head under the dashboard," shrieked the examiner. "No one does that."

"Bears do," said Paddington firmly. And he gave the lever another hard tug just to show what he meant.

"Don't do it!" shouted the examiner. "Don't do it!"

"Let the clutch out!" came a voice from the back seat. "Let the clutch out!"

But if either of the men expected their cries to have any effect they were doomed to disappointment. Once Paddington got an idea firmly fixed in his mind it was very difficult to get him to change course, let alone gear, and apart from hurriedly opening the car door to let out the clutch he concentrated all his energies on the task in hand.

In the past he had often watched Mr. Brown change gear. It was something Mr. Brown prided himself on being able to do very smoothly indeed, so that really it

was quite hard to know when it had actually taken place. But if Paddington hoped to emulate his example he failed miserably. As he gave the lever one final, desperate shove there was a loud grinding noise followed almost immediately by an enormous jerk as the car leaped into the air like a frustrated stallion. The force of the movement caused Paddington to fall over on his back and, in his excitement, he grabbed hold of the nearest thing to hand.

"Look out!" shrieked the examiner.

But he was too late. As Paddington tightened his grip on the gas pedal the car shot forward with a roar like an express train. For a second or two it seemed to hover in midair, and then, with a crash which made the silence that followed all the more ominous, it came to a halt again.

Paddington clambered unsteadily to his feet and peered out through the windscreen. "Oh dear," he said, gazing round at the others. "I think we've hit a car in front."

The examiner closed his eyes. His lips were moving as if he was offering up a silent prayer.

"No," he said, slowly and distinctly, "you haven't got it quite right. *We* haven't hit anything, *you* have. And it isn't just *a* car, it's . . ."

The examiner broke off and gazed up at the rearview mirror in mute despair as his eyes caught the reflection of those belonging to his superior in the back seat.

"It happens to be mine," said a grim voice from behind.

Paddington sank back into his seat as the full horror of the situation came home to him.

"Oh dear, Mr. Bogey," he said unhappily. "I do hope that doesn't mean you've failed your test!"

◆◆◆

As with Mr. Brown's encounter with the police, Paddington's disaster at the Test Center was a topic of conversation in the Brown household for many days afterwards. Opinions as to the possible outcome were sharply divided. There were those who thought he would be bound to hear something more, and others who thought the whole thing was so complicated nothing would be done about it, but none of them quite foresaw what would happen.

One evening, just as they were sitting down to their evening meal, there was an unexpected ring at the front-door bell. Mrs. Bird hurried off to answer it, and when she returned she was accompanied, to everyone's surprise, by Paddington's examiner.

"Please don't get up," he exclaimed, as Paddington jumped to his feet in alarm and hurried round to the far side of the table for safety.

He removed a large brown envelope from his briefcase and placed it on the table in front of Paddington's plate. "I . . . er . . . I happened to be passing so I thought I would drop this in for young Mr. Brown."

"Oh dear," said Mrs. Brown nervously. "It looks very official. I do hope it isn't bad news."

The man permitted himself a smile. "Nothing like that," he said. "Congratulations on passing your test," he continued, turning to Mr. Brown. "I was glad to hear you were able to take it again so quickly. All's well that ends well, and I'm sure you'll be pleased to know that now my superior officer has had his bumper straightened you'd hardly know anything had happened."

He mopped his brow with a handkerchief as the memory of it came flooding back. "It all sounded much worse than it actually was. As you know, I was being examined myself at the time, so I was under a certain amount of strain. As a matter of fact, I came through with flying colors. The chief examiner thought that in the circumstances I did extremely well. He's even recommended me for promotion."

"But whatever is it?" cried Judy, as Paddington opened the envelope and withdrew a sheet of paper with an inscription on it.

The examiner gave a cough. "It's a special test certificate," he said. "It enables the owner to drive vehicles in group S."

"Trust Paddington!" said Jonathan. "I bet he's the only one who's ever driven into the back of an examiner's car *and* still passed his test into the bargain."

Mr. Brown gave the examiner a puzzled look. "Group *S*?" he repeated. "I didn't know there was such a thing."

"It's very rare." The examiner permitted himself another smile. "In fact, there probably isn't another one like it in the whole world. It's for shopping baskets on wheels. I noticed young Mr. Brown had one with him at the time of our . . . er . . . meeting."

"Gosh, Paddington." Judy gazed at him in relief. "What are you going to do with it?"

Paddington considered the matter for a moment. He really felt quite overwhelmed by his latest piece of good fortune. "I think," he announced at last, "I shall fix it to the front of my basket. Then if I ever have trouble at the supermarket cash desk I shall be able to show it."

"What a good idea," said the examiner, looking very pleased at the reception his gift had met. "And you'll be pleased to see it's made out for life. That means," he added, gently but firmly, "that you need never, ever, *ever* come and see us to take your test again!"

Chapter 17

Goings-On at Number Thirty-two

Paddington woke with a start and then sat up in bed rubbing his eyes. For a moment or two he wasn't quite sure where he was, but gradually, as a number of familiar objects swam into view, he realized with surprise that he was in his own room.

The afternoon sun was streaming in through the window, and after blinking several times he lay back again with his paws behind his head and a thoughtful expression on his face.

Although he wasn't quite sure what had disturbed him, he felt very glad he'd woken when he did, for he had been in the middle of a particularly nasty dream about a large jar of his special marmalade from the cut-price grocer in the market.

In the dream something had gone wrong with the lid, and no matter how much he'd tried, nothing would budge it. Mrs. Bird's best tin opener had broken off at the handle, and when he'd tried squeezing it in a doorjamb the door had fallen off. Even Mr. Brown's hammer and chisel had made no impression at all, and after several bangs the head had flown off the hammer and broken the dining room window. In fact, if he hadn't woken at that moment, there was no knowing what other awful things might have happened.

Paddington heaved a sigh of relief, and after dipping a paw into an open jar of marmalade by his bed in order to make sure everything really was all right, he closed his eyes again.

The Brown household was unusually quiet and peaceful that afternoon, for Paddington had the house to himself. In the morning the postman had brought Jonathan and Judy a surprise invitation to a tea party, and by the same delivery a letter had arrived asking Mrs. Brown and Mrs. Bird to visit an old aunt who lived on the other side of London.

Even Paddington should have been out, for Mr. Brown had given him several books to take back to the public library, together with a long list of things he wanted him to look up in the reference department.

It was Mr. Brown's list that had proved to be Paddington's undoing, for he had taken it upstairs to his room after lunch in order to study it, and before he knew where he was he had nodded off.

Thinking the matter over, Paddington wasn't quite sure whether it was the result of an extra large lunch, with two helpings of apple pie and ice cream, or the hot afternoon sun, or even a mixture of both, but whatever the reason, he must have been asleep for over an hour, for in the distance he could hear a clock striking three.

It was as the last of the chimes died away that Paddington suddenly sat bolt upright in his bed and stared with wide-open eyes at the ceiling. Unless he was dreaming again, there was a strange scraping noise coming from somewhere directly overhead. It began by the door, then passed across the room in the direction of the window and paused for a moment before coming all the way back again.

Paddington's eyes got larger and larger as he listened to the sound, and they nearly popped out altogether a few moments later when a noise remarkably like that of a hammer and chisel broke the silence that followed the scraping.

After pinching himself several times to make sure it had nothing to do with his dream, Paddington jumped out of bed and hurried across the room in order to investigate the matter.

As he flung open the window, an even stranger thing happened, and he jumped back into the room as if he had been shot, for just as he peered outside a long black snakelike object came into view and hung there twisting and turning for several seconds before it finally disappeared from view below the ledge.

Paddington backed across the room and, after making a grab for his hat and suitcase, rushed out onto the landing, banging the door behind him.

Although after the dream and the strange events that had followed he was prepared for almost anything, Paddington certainly wasn't expecting the sight that met his eyes on the landing, and he almost wished he'd stayed in his room.

Only a few yards away, between his door and the top of the stairs, was a ladder that definitely hadn't been there after lunch. It was leaning against the trap door in the ceiling, and worse still, the trap door itself was wide open.

Paddington was a brave bear at heart, but even so it took him several moments to pluck up his courage again. After pulling his hat well down over his head and carefully placing his suitcase at the top of the stairs in case of an emergency, he began climbing slowly up the ladder.

It was when he reached the top rung and peered over the edge into the loft that Paddington's worst suspicions were realized. For there, tiptoeing across the rafters with a flashlight in one hand and what looked like a long knife in the other, was a man in a cap and blue overalls.

Holding his breath, Paddington considered the matter for several seconds before coming to a decision. As quietly as possible, he stretched his paw into the darkness until he felt the edge of the trap door, and then he flung it back into place and pushed the bolt home as hard as he could before scrambling down the ladder onto the landing and safety.

All at once there was a commotion in the roof as someone started to shout and several bumps were followed by the sound of banging on the other side of the trap door. But by that time Paddington was much too far away to hear what was going on. The sound of the Browns' front door slamming had added itself to the general hubbub, and he was halfway down Windsor Gardens, hurrying along the pavement with a very determined expression on his face indeed. All in all, he decided that bad though his dream had been, things had been even worse since he'd woken up, and it was definitely time to call for help.

After rounding several corners Paddington at last reached the place he had been looking for. It was a large, old-fashioned stone building that stood slightly apart from the rest on a corner site. Most of the windows had bars across them, and at the top of some steps leading up to the entrance there was a blue lamp with the word POLICE written across it in white letters.

Paddington hurried up the steps and then paused at the entrance. Leading from the hall were a number of doors, and it was difficult to decide which was the best one. In the end he picked on a large brown door on his right. It looked more important than any of the others, and Paddington was a firm believer in going to the top whenever he had an emergency.

After knocking several times, he waited with his ear against the keyhole until he heard a gruff voice call out, "Come in," and then he pushed the door open with his paw.

The only person in the room was a man sitting behind a desk near the window, and he looked rather cross when he saw Paddington. "You've come to the wrong place," he said. "Undesirables are supposed to report round the back."

"*Undesirables!*" exclaimed Paddington hotly, giving the man a hard stare. "I'm not an undesirable. I'm a bear!"

The man jumped up from behind his desk. "I beg your pardon," he said. "The light's none too good, and I thought for a moment you were Hairy Harry."

"*Hairy Harry?*" repeated Paddington, hardly able to believe his ears.

"He's what we call the Portobello Prowler," the man added confidentially, "and he's been giving us a lot of trouble lately. He's only small and he slips in through pantry windows when no one's looking."

His voice trailed away as Paddington's stare got harder and harder. "Er . . . what can we do for you?" he asked.

"I'd like to see Sid, please," said Paddington, putting down his suitcase.

"Sid?" repeated the man, looking most surprised. "I don't think we have any Sids here. We've several Alfs and a Bert, but I don't recall any Sids offhand."

"It says on the notice outside you've got one," said Paddington firmly. "It's written on the door."

The man looked puzzled for a moment, and then his face cleared. "You don't mean *Sid*—you mean CID. That's quite a different matter," he explained. "CID stands for Criminal Investigation Department."

"Well, there's a criminal in Mr. Brown's roof," said Paddington, not to be outdone. "And I think he needs investigating."

"A criminal in Mr. Brown's roof?" repeated the man, taking out a notepad and pencil as he listened while Paddington went on to explain all that had taken place.

"Good work, bear," he exclaimed when Paddington had finished talking. "We don't often catch anyone red-handed. I'll send out an alert at once."

With that he pressed a button on the side of his desk, and in a matter of seconds the police station became a hive of activity. In fact, Paddington hardly had time to adjust his hat and pick up his suitcase before he found himself being led by several policemen into a yard at the back of the building, where he was bundled into the back seat of a large black car.

Paddington felt most important as the car shot down the road in the direction

of Windsor Gardens. He had never been inside a police car before, and it was all very interesting. He didn't remember ever having traveled quite so fast either, and he was most impressed when a policeman on traffic duty held up all the other cars and waved them across some lights which were red.

"Right, bear," said the CID man as the car screeched to a halt outside the Browns' house, "lead the way. Only watch out—if he's got a knife he may be dangerous."

Paddington thought for a moment and then raised his hat. "After you," he said politely. Taking things all around, Paddington felt he'd had his share of adventures for one day, and apart from that he was anxious to make sure his store of marmalade was safe before anything else happened.

◆ ◆ ◆

"Do you mean to say," exclaimed the policeman as he looked down at the man in the blue overalls, "you were putting up a television aerial all the time?"

"That's right, officer," said the man. "And I've got a letter from Mr. Brown to prove it. Gave me the key to the house, he did. Said there would be no one here as he was getting rid of them for the day and I was to let myself in on account of it being a special surprise for the rest of the family and he didn't want them to know."

The man in the overalls paused for breath and then handed a card to the policeman. "Higgins is the name. Tip-Top Tellys. If you ever want a job done, just give me a ring."

"Tip-Top Tellys?" repeated the CID man, looking distastefully at the card. He turned to Paddington. "I thought you said he had a knife, bear?"

"That wasn't a knife," said Mr. Higgins. "That was my tweaker."

"Your *tweaker*!" exclaimed Paddington, looking most upset.

"That's right," said Mr. Higgins cheerfully as he held up a long screwdriver. "Always carry one of these on account of having to give the old tellys a tweak when they want adjusting.

"Tell you what," he added, waving his hand in the direction of a large cabinet that stood in one corner of the dining room, "I'm nearly ready to switch it on. Just got to connect the aerial. With this young bear's permission, I vote we take five minutes off and brew up a cup of tea. There's nothing like a nice cup of tea for cooling things down."

Mr. Higgins gave Paddington a broad wink. "If there's a detective play on, we might even pick up a few hints!"

As a spluttering noise came from one of the policemen, Paddington disappeared hurriedly in the direction of the kitchen. The CID man's face seemed to have gone a rather nasty shade of red, and he didn't like the look of it at all.

All the same, when he returned a few minutes later staggering under the weight of a tray full of cups and saucers and a large plate of buns, even the policemen began to look more cheerful, and in no time at all the living room began to echo with the sound of laughter as everyone recounted his part in the afternoon's adventure.

In between explaining all about the various knobs on the television and making some last-minute adjustments, Mr. Higgins kept them all amused with tales of other adventures he'd had in the trade. In fact, the time passed so quickly everyone seemed sorry when at last it was time to leave.

"I've just sold two more television sets," whispered Mr. Higgins, nodding towards the policemen as he paused at the door. "So if I can ever do you a favor, just let me know. One good turn deserves another."

"Thank you very much, Mr. Higgins," said Paddington gratefully.

Having waved goodbye to everyone, Paddington shut the front door and hurried back into the living room. Although he was pleased that the mystery of the bumps in the roof had been solved, he was anxious to test Mr. Brown's new television set before the others arrived home, and he quickly drew the curtains before settling himself comfortably in one of the armchairs.

In the past he had often watched television in a shop window in the Portobello Road, but the manager had several times come out to complain about his breathing heavily on the windows during the cowboy films, and Paddington was sure it would be much nicer to be able to sit at home and watch in comfort.

But when he had seen a cartoon, some football, two musical shows, and a program on bird-watching, Paddington's interest began to flag, and after helping himself to another bun he turned his attention to a small booklet that Mr. Higgins had left behind.

The book was called "How to Get the Best Out of Your Television," and it was full of pictures and diagrams—rather like maps of the Underground—showing the inside of the set. There was even a chapter showing how to adjust the various knobs in order to get the best picture, and Paddington spent some time sitting in front of the set turning the brightness up and down and making unusual patterns on the screen.

There were so many different knobs to turn and so many different things it was possible to do with the picture that he soon lost all account of the time, and he was most surprised when the living room clock suddenly struck six.

It was while he was hurriedly turning all the knobs back to where they'd been to start with that something very unexpected and alarming happened.

One moment a cowboy on a white horse was dashing across the screen in hot pursuit of a man with a black mustache and side whiskers; the next moment there was a click, and before Paddington's astonished gaze the picture shrank in size until there was nothing left but a small white dot.

He spent some moments peering hopefully at the screen through his opera glasses, but the longer he looked, the smaller the dot became, and even striking a match didn't help matters, for by the time he had been in the kitchen to fetch the box the spot had disappeared completely.

Paddington stood in front of the silent television set with a mournful expression on his face. Although Mr. Brown had gone to a lot of trouble in order to surprise the family, it was quite certain he wouldn't be at all pleased if they received that much of a surprise and arrived home to find it wasn't even working.

Paddington heaved a deep sigh. "Oh dear," he said as he addressed the world in general. "I'm in trouble again."

♦ ♦ ♦

"I can't understand it," said Mr. Brown as he came out of the living room. "Mr. Higgins promised faithfully it would be all ready by the time we got home."

"Never mind, Henry," said Mrs. Brown as the rest of the family crowded round the doorway. "It *was* a surprise, and I'm sure he'll be able to get it working soon."

"Wow!" exclaimed Jonathan. "He must have been having a lot of trouble. Look at all the pieces."

"Don't bother to draw the curtains. We'll eat in the kitchen," said Mrs. Brown as she took in the scene. There were bits and pieces everywhere, not to mention a large number of valves and a cathode ray tube on the settee.

Mrs. Bird looked puzzled. "I thought you said it wasn't working," she remarked.

"I don't see how it could be," replied Mr. Brown.

"Well, there's something there," said Mrs. Bird, pointing to the screen. "I saw it move."

The Brown family peered through the gloom at the television set. Although it didn't seem at all possible Mrs. Bird could be right, now that they looked, there was definitely some kind of movement on the glass.

"It looks rather furry," said Mrs. Brown. "Perhaps it's one of those animal programs. They do have a lot on television."

Jonathan was nearest to the screen, and he suddenly clutched Judy's arm. "Crumbs!" he whispered as his eyes grew accustomed to the dark and he caught sight of a familiar-looking nose pressed against the glass. "It isn't a program. It's Paddington. He must be stuck inside!"

"This is most interesting," said Mr. Brown, taking out his glasses. "Switch on the light, someone. I'd like a closer look."

As a muffled exclamation came from somewhere inside the television, Jonathan and Judy hurriedly placed themselves between Mr. Brown and the screen.

"Don't you think you ought to ring Mr. Higgins, Dad?" asked Judy. "He'll know what to do."

"We'll go down and fetch him if you like," said Jonathan eagerly. "It won't take a minute."

"Yes, come along, Henry," said Mrs. Brown. "I should leave things just as they are. There's no knowing what might happen if you touch them."

Rather reluctantly, Mr. Brown allowed himself to be shepherded out of the room, closely followed by Jonathan and Judy.

Mrs. Bird was the last one to leave, and before she closed the door she took one last look round the room. "There are some rather nasty marmalade stains on that television cabinet," she said in a loud voice. "If I were a young bear, I'd make sure they're wiped off by the time Mr. Higgins gets here . . . otherwise certain people may put two and two together."

Although Mrs. Bird kept a firm hand on goings-on in the Brown household, she was a great believer in the proverb "Least said, soonest mended," especially when it had to do with anything as complicated as television.

If Mr. Higgins was surprised at having to repay Paddington's good turn so soon, he didn't show it by so much as the flicker of an eyelid. All the same, after Mrs.

Bird had spoken to him, he took Paddington to one side and they had a long chat together while he explained how dangerous it was to take the back off a television set if you didn't know what you were doing.

"It's a good thing bears' paws are well insulated, Mr. Brown," he said as he bade goodbye to Paddington. "Otherwise you might not be here to tell the tale.

"That's all right," he said cheerfully as Paddington thanked him for all his trouble. "Got a bit of marmalade on my tweaker, but otherwise there's no harm done. And I daresay it'll wash off."

"It usually does," said Mrs. Bird with the voice of experience, as she showed him to the door.

As the Browns trooped into the living room for their first evening's viewing, it was noticeable that one member of the family settled himself as far away from the screen as possible. Although Mr. Higgins had screwed the back on the television as tightly as his tweaker would allow, Paddington wasn't taking any more chances than he could help.

"Mind you," said Mr. Brown later that evening, when Mrs. Bird came in with the bedtime snack, "I still can't understand what it was we saw on the screen. It was very strange."

"It was probably some kind of interference," said Mrs. Bird gravely. "I don't suppose it'll happen again, do you, Paddington?"

As she spoke, several pairs of eyes turned in Paddington's direction, but most of his face was carefully hidden behind a large mug, and very wisely he only nodded his agreement. Not that he was having to pretend he felt tired, for in fact it was only the cocoa steam that was keeping his eyelids open at all. Nevertheless, there was something about the way his whiskers were poking out on either side of the mug that suggested Mrs. Bird had hit the nail on the head. As far as the Brown family was concerned, there was one kind of interference they weren't likely to get on their television again in a hurry.

.Chapter 18.

Too Much Off the Top

Paddington and Mr. Gruber were having their elevenses one morning when Mr. Gruber began talking about the trouble he had been having. "If you don't get help, people just won't bother to wait. And if you get the wrong sort of help it frightens the customers away. Summer is our busy season too. Especially with all the American tourists over here for their holidays."

Mr. Gruber went on to explain that English antiques of almost any shape or form were very popular in the United States and that apart from the tourists, some dealers came over simply to buy up as many as possible.

He waved his hand at all the gleaming copper pots and pans, vases, books, ornaments and other bric-a-brac which lined the walls of his shop and overflowed out onto the pavement.

"I must say I've missed your help, Mr. Brown," he said. "Apart from the pleasure of our little chats, one young bear with a knowledge of antiques and an eye for a bargain is worth his weight in gold."

Mr. Gruber disappeared into his shop for a moment and when he returned he was carrying an old vase. "What would you say this is, Mr. Brown?" he asked casually, holding it up to the light.

Paddington looked most surprised at such a simple question. "That's an early Spode, Mr. Gruber," he replied promptly.

Mr. Gruber nodded his approval. "Exactly," he said. "But you'd be surprised how many people wouldn't realize it.

"Do you know, Mr. Brown, one young man I had working here while you were away on holiday actually called it a *jug* and he was going to let it go for fifty pence simply because it had this piece missing. I only just rescued it in time."

Mr. Gruber fell silent as he fitted the broken piece of china back into the vase and Paddington nearly fell off his deck chair with surprise at the thought of there being people in the world who didn't know about antique pottery and how valuable it could be. "Fifty pence for a Spode!" he exclaimed, hardly able to believe his ears.

"Mind you," said Mr. Gruber, "let's be fair. Not everyone has your advantage, Mr. Brown. After all, you've spent so much time in this shop I believe you know almost as much about it as I do. If you ever decide to go into business a lot of people will have to look to their laurels."

Paddington looked pleased at his friend's remarks. Mr. Gruber wasn't in the habit of paying idle compliments and praise from him was praise indeed.

"Perhaps I could help by repairing that vase for you, Mr. Gruber," he offered.

Mr. Gruber looked at him doubtfully over the top of his glasses. Although he had a high regard for Paddington and had meant every word he'd said, he also knew that accidents could happen in the best-regulated circles, especially bears' circles. However, he was a kindly man at heart and after a moment's thought he nodded his agreement.

"It's very kind of you, Mr. Brown," he said. "I know you'll take great care of it, but don't forget, there's many a slip 'twixt cup and lip."

"I won't, Mr. Gruber," said Paddington as he took the vase and its broken piece and laid them carefully among some cabbages in the bottom of his shopping basket on wheels.

After Mr. Gruber had sorted out some money for a tube of glue from a nearby store, Paddington waved goodbye and hurried off up the road with a thoughtful expression on his face.

Mr. Gruber's chance remark about going into business had suddenly reminded him of a notice that he'd seen in a shop window that very morning. At the time he hadn't given it a great deal of attention, but now, as he reached the shop and stood looking at it once again, he began to look more and more interested.

The shop, which was surmounted by a long striped pole, had the words S. SLOOP—GENTS HAIRDRESSING emblazoned across the door and the notice in the window said, quite simply, WILLING JUNIOR WANTED—URGENTLY.

Underneath, in rough capitals, Mr. Sloop had added the information that a good wage would be paid to any keen young lad willing to learn the trade.

Paddington stood for quite some time breathing heavily on the glass until he suddenly became aware of a face on the other side watching him with equal interest.

Taking his courage in both paws Paddington pushed open the door of the shop, dragging his shopping basket after him, and raised his hat as he bade the owner good morning.

"'Morning," replied Mr. Sloop breezily, reaching for a white cloth. "What can I do for you? Short back and sides, or would you like one of our specials? Haircut, shampoo and set—all for four pounds. Tell you what—seeing trade's a bit slack this morning, I'll give you special bear rates. You can have everything for two pounds."

Paddington stepped back hastily as Mr. Sloop waved a pair of clippers dangerously close to his head. "I haven't come for a haircut," he explained, placing his hat firmly back over his ears. "I've come about the job."

"You've *what*?" Mr. Sloop lost some of his breeziness as he stared at Paddington.

"It says in the window you want a willing junior," said Paddington hopefully.

"Blimey!" Mr. Sloop stood back and examined Paddington. "You wouldn't be a very good advertisement, I must say. This is a barbershop, not an art school. I'd have to whip all them whiskers off for a start."

"Whip my whiskers off!" exclaimed Paddington hotly. "But I've always had them."

Mr. Sloop considered the matter for a moment. "I suppose I could stand you in the window like one of them before-and-after advertisements," he said grudgingly. "Not that I'm saying yes, mind. But I don't mind admitting I've been let down badly by the Labor Exchange. Nobody wants to sweep up hairs these days."

"Bears are good at sweeping," said Paddington eagerly. "I don't think I've done any hairs before but I often help Mrs. Bird in the mornings."

"Errands," said Mr. Sloop. "There'll be lots of errands to run. And you'll have to look after things when I pop out for me morning coffee. Keep the customers happy till I get back. Then there's the shop to keep clean. It's not so bad in the week—it's Saturday mornings. The steam almost rises off me scissors on a Saturday morning."

Mr. Sloop mopped his brow at the thought as he gave Paddington a sidelong glance. "Some people might consider it a lot of work for . . . er . . . twenty-five pounds a week."

"Twenty-five pounds!" exclaimed Paddington, nearly falling over backwards at the thought of so much money. "*Every* week. That's over a hundred buns!"

"Done, then," said Mr. Sloop, hurriedly coming to a decision before Paddington could change his mind.

"Mind you," he added, "it's only a trial. And no reading comics on the sly when me back's turned. But if you watch carefully and don't get up to any tricks, I might even let you have a go with the clippers in a week or so."

"Thank you very much, Mr. Sloop," said Paddington gratefully. In the past he had often peered through the barbershop window and watched Mr. Sloop run his clippers round the necks of his customers and the thought of actually being allowed to have a go filled him with excitement.

Mr. Sloop clapped his hands together briskly and licked his lips. "No time like the present," he said. "I could do with a coffee right now. May as well take advantage of the lull, as you might say. You'll find a broom in that closet over there. When you've done the floor you can give the basins a going-over—only mind them razors—don't go nicking yer paws. I don't want no bear's blood all over the place—it'll give the shop a bad name."

Having finished his instructions Mr. Sloop added that he wouldn't be long and then disappeared out of the door, leaving Paddington standing in the middle of the shop with a slightly bemused expression on his face.

Cutting hair seemed much more complicated than it looked at first sight, and Mr. Sloop's shop, though it was only small, appeared to have almost as many things inside it as a supermarket.

Along one wall was a row of several benches for customers, together with a pile of newspapers for them to read while they were waiting, and pinned to the wall behind them were a number of pictures cut from magazines showing the various styles it was possible to have.

The back of the shop was given over to a large closet and a number of notices. Mr. Sloop didn't appear to have a great deal of trust in his fellow human beings, for most of them were to do with payment and the fact that under no circumstances would any checks be cashed or credit given.

But it was the business side of the room, where the chair itself stood, that aroused Paddington's immediate interest. Almost the whole wall was taken up by a long mirror and on a shelf in front of the mirror stood row upon row of bottles. There were bottles of hair oil, shampoo, mousse, hair restorer, cream—the list was endless, and Paddington spent several minutes unscrewing caps in order to sniff the contents of the various bottles.

It wasn't until he was having a practice snip with a pair of scissors and narrowly missed cutting off one of his own whiskers that Paddington suddenly came back to earth with a bump and realized that he hadn't even started work. He hurried across to the closet and opened the door, only to be met by a positive deluge of old brooms and brushes, not to mention white coats, towels and various other items.

As far as he could see, Mr. Sloop must have been without any help in his shop

for some while, for most of the things were so tangled together it took him all his time to find out which handle belonged to which broom, let alone decide on the one to use.

It was when the confusion was at its height that Paddington vaguely heard a bell ringing, and from his position in the back of the closet he suddenly realized that someone in the shop was carrying on a conversation.

"Say, do I get any service in this place?" called a voice with a strong American accent from the direction of Mr. Sloop's chair.

Paddington scrambled out of the closet and peered across the room to where the owner of the voice sat waiting with his arms folded and eyes closed.

"I'd like a trim, please," announced the man as he heard the commotion going on behind him. "Not too little—not too much—and don't touch the top. Make it snappy. I have a plane to catch later on and I have a lot of packing to do.

"Look," continued the voice impatiently, as Paddington hurried across the shop and peered hopefully out through the open door in search of Mr. Sloop, "this *is* a barbershop, isn't it? Do I get my hair cut or don't I? All I want is to get back to my hotel so as I can make up on some sleep before I catch my plane. I'm real tired. I've been on my feet for a week now . . ."

The man's voice trailed away into a loud yawn and to Paddington's astonishment, as he turned back into the shop he was greeted, not by a string of further complaints as he'd expected, but by a long, gentle snore.

Paddington had seen some people go to sleep quickly before—Mr. Brown in particular on a Sunday afternoon was often very quick—but he'd never seen it happen quite so suddenly. He stood in the middle of the shop for a moment looking anxiously at the figure in Mr. Sloop's chair and then gradually the expression on his face was replaced by one of interest.

Although the man in the chair had obviously dozed off for the moment, he'd certainly been in a great hurry. In fact, he'd definitely said to make it snappy. And although Mr. Sloop hadn't actually said Paddington could cut anyone's hair that very day, he had mentioned something about having a go at a later date and he'd also said that one of Paddington's first jobs would be to keep the customers happy.

As far as Paddington could see, about the only thing that would make Mr. Sloop's present customer happy would be if he were to wake up and find that his hair had been cut while he'd been asleep.

After giving the matter several moments' more thought, Paddington came to a decision. Taking care not to disturb the sleeping figure, he draped a white cloth round the man's shoulders and then picked up Mr. Sloop's electric clippers which were hanging from a nearby hook.

After giving a few practice waves through the air in order to get used to the tickling sensation they made when they were switched on, Paddington applied the business end carefully to the back of the man's neck, making a wide sweeping movement with his paw as he'd often seen Mr. Sloop do in the past.

The first stroke was rather disappointing. It went much deeper than he had intended and left a long white path up the back of the neck. The second stroke, on the other hand, didn't go nearly as deep so that he had to spend several minutes trying to match the two, and he cast some anxious glances over his shoulder in case Mr. Sloop returned before he could repair the damage.

In fact, for the next minute or so, Paddington spent almost as much time looking out of the window as he did looking at the job in front of him. When he did finally give his undivided attention to the figure in the chair, his eyes nearly popped out of their sockets with astonishment.

The clippers dropped from his paw and he stood rooted to the spot as he stared at the top of the man's head. Before he'd started work it had been covered by a mass of thick black hair, whereas now, apart from a fringe round the ears and neck, it was almost completely bald.

The strange thing was it must all have happened in the blink of an eyelid, for quite definitely the hair had been there when he'd looked a second before.

It was all most mysterious and Paddington sat down on his suitcase with a mournful expression on his face while he considered the matter. He was beginning to regret not having asked for his wages in advance, for the more he thought about things the more difficult it became to picture Mr. Sloop paying for one day's work, let alone a week's.

It was while he was sitting on his suitcase that he suddenly caught sight of a bottle on a shelf above his head. It was a large bottle and it had a picture on the outside which showed a group of men, all with a luxuriant growth of jet-black hair. But it wasn't so much the picture that caught his eye as the words underneath, which said, in large red letters: DR. SPOONER'S QUICK-ACTING MAGIC HAIR RESTORER.

Paddington was a hopeful bear in many ways but after using up several spoons of the thick yellow liquid even he began to admit to himself that he might be asking a little too much of Dr. Spooner's tonic. Looking through his binoculars didn't help matters either, for the top of the man's head remained as shiny and hairless as ever.

He was just toying desperately with the idea of buying some quick-drying black paint from a nearby hardware store in order to cover up the worst of the damage when his eye alighted on his shopping basket on wheels which was standing in a corner of the shop and an excited gleam came into his eyes.

Carefully lifting out Mr. Gruber's vase, which he placed on a shelf in front of the chair for safety, Paddington rummaged round in the basket until he found what he was looking for.

Although Mr. Gruber had asked him to buy the glue for the express purpose of mending the vase, Paddington felt sure he wouldn't mind if it was used for something else in an emergency, and as far as he could see this was definitely one of the worst emergencies he had ever encountered.

For the next few minutes Paddington was very busy. Having squeezed drops of Mr. Gruber's glue all over the man's head, he then rummaged round on the floor in search of some hair to fill in the vacant spot. Fortunately, being short of an assistant, Mr. Sloop hadn't bothered to sweep up that morning and so there was quite a selection to choose from.

At long last Paddington stood back and examined his handiwork with interest. All in all, he felt quite pleased with himself. Admittedly the top of the man's head had undergone a somewhat drastic change since he'd first sat in the chair—for one thing there were now quite a number of ginger curls, not to mention blond streaks, in the long straight black bits, and several of them were sticking out at a rather odd angle—but at least it was all covered and he heaved a sigh of relief as he wiped his paws on the cloth in front of him.

It was as he was pushing a particularly springy ginger curl into place with his paw as a final touch that to his alarm the figure in the chair began to stir.

Paddington hurried round the other side of the chair and stood between Mr. Sloop's customer and the mirror.

"That'll be four pounds, please," he said, holding out his paw hopefully in a businesslike manner as he consulted the price list on the wall.

If the man looked surprised at the sight of Paddington's paw under his nose, it was nothing compared with the expression which came over his face a moment later as he caught sight of his reflection in the mirror.

Jumping out of the chair, he pushed Paddington to one side and stood for a moment staring at the sight which met his eyes. For a second or two he seemed speechless and then he let out a roar of rage as he made a grab for the nearest object.

Paddington's own look of alarm changed to one of horror as the man picked up the vase from the shelf and made as if to throw it to the ground.

"Look out!" he cried anxiously. "That's Mr. Gruber's Spode."

To Paddington's surprise his words had a far greater effect than he'd expected, for the man suddenly froze in midair, lowered his arms and then stared at the object in front of him with a look of disbelief.

"Thank you very much," said Paddington gratefully, as he withdrew the vase from the man's hands and placed it carefully in his shopping basket on wheels. "It's got a piece missing already, and I don't think Mr. Gruber would like it very much if the rest was broken.

"Perhaps you'd like to break one of Mr. Sloop's bottles instead," he added generously. "He's got some old ones in the cupboard."

The man took a deep breath, looked at himself once again in the mirror, passed a trembling hand over his brow and then turned back to Paddington.

"Now see here, bear," he said. "I don't know what's been going on. Maybe it's all part of a bad dream, maybe I'm gonna wake up in a minute, but this Mr. Gruber—he's a friend of yours?"

"He's my special friend," said Paddington importantly. "We have buns and cocoa together every morning."

"And this is his Spode?" asked the man.

"Yes," said Paddington in surprise. "He's got lots. He keeps an antique shop and—"

"Lead me to him, bear," said the man warmly. "Just lead me to him."

◆◆◆

Mr. Gruber took one last look out of his door to make sure everything was in for the night and then turned back to Paddington.

"You know, Mr. Brown," he said, as they settled themselves on the horsehair sofa at the back of the shop, "I still can't believe it. I really can't."

Paddington, nodding from behind a cloud of cocoa steam, looked very much as if he agreed with every word.

"If anyone mentions the word 'coincidence' to me again," continued Mr. Gruber, "I shall always tell them the story of the day you got a job as a barber and knocked the toupee off an American antique dealer's head."

"I thought I'd cut all his hair off by mistake, Mr. Gruber," admitted Paddington.

Mr. Gruber chuckled at the thought. "I shouldn't like to have been in your paws if you really had, Mr. Brown.

"Imagine," he continued, "if you hadn't knocked his toupee off and put all that glue on his head he wouldn't have got cross. And if you hadn't put my Spode on the shelf he wouldn't have heard about my shop. And if he hadn't heard about my shop he would have gone back to America tonight without half the things he came over to buy. It's what they call a chain of events, Mr. Brown, and a very good day's work

into the bargain. I can see I shall have to go to a few more sales to make up for all the empty spaces on my shelves."

Paddington looked out through the window and then sniffed the warm air from the stove. Most of the other shops in the Portobello Road already had their shutters up and even those that were still open showed signs of closing for the night as one by one their lights went out.

"And if all those things hadn't happened, Mr. Gruber," he said, as he reached across for the earthenware jug, "we shouldn't be sitting here now."

Paddington always enjoyed his cups of cocoa with Mr. Gruber, but it was most unusual to have one together so late in the day, and he was anxious to make the most of it.

Mr. Gruber nodded his head in agreement. "And that, if I may say so, Mr. Brown," he said warmly, "is the nicest link of all."

Chapter 19.

◆ ◆ ◆

A Visit to the Bank

"Paddington looks unusually smart this morning," said Mrs. Bird.

"Oh dear," said Mrs. Brown. "Does he? I hope he's not up to anything."

She joined Mrs. Bird at the window and followed the direction of her gaze up the road to where a small figure in a blue duffle coat was hurrying along the pavement.

Now that Mrs. Bird mentioned it Paddington did seem to have an air about him. Even from a distance his fur looked remarkably neat and freshly combed, and his old hat, instead of being pulled down over his ears, was set at a very rakish angle with the brim turned up, which was most unusual. Even his old suitcase looked as if it had had some kind of polish on it.

"He's not even going in his usual direction," said Mrs. Brown as Paddington, having reached the end of the road, looked carefully over his shoulder and then turned right and disappeared from view. "He *always* turns left."

"If you ask me," said Mrs. Bird, "that young bear's got something on his mind. He was acting strangely at breakfast this morning. He didn't even have a second helping and he kept peering over Mr. Brown's shoulder at the paper with a very odd look on his face."

"I'm not surprised he had an odd look if it was Henry's paper," said Mrs. Brown. "I can never make head nor tail of it myself."

Mr. Brown worked in the City of London and he always read a very important newspaper over breakfast, full of news about stocks and shares and other money matters, which the rest of the Browns found very dull.

"All the same," she continued, as she led the way into the kitchen, "it's very strange. I do hope he hasn't got one of his ideas coming on. He spent most of yesterday evening doing his accounts and that's often a bad sign."

Mrs. Brown and Mrs. Bird were hard at work preparing for the coming holiday, and with only a few days left there were a thousand and one things to be done. If they hadn't been quite so busy they might well have put two and two together, but as it was, the matter of Paddington's strange behavior was soon forgotten in the rush to get everything ready.

Unaware of the interest he had caused, Paddington made his way along a road not far from the Portobello market until he reached an imposing building which stood slightly apart from the rest. It had tall bronze doors which were tightly shut, and over the entrance, in large gold letters, were the words FLOYDS BANK LIMITED.

After carefully making sure that no one was watching, Paddington withdrew a small cardboard-covered book from under his hat and then sat down on his suitcase outside the bank while he waited for the doors to open.

Like the building, the book had the words FLOYDS BANK printed on the outside, and just inside the front cover it had P. BROWN ESQ. written in ink.

With the exception of the Browns and Mr. Gruber, not many people knew about Paddington's bank account, as it was a closely kept secret. It had all started some months before when Paddington came across an advertisement in one of Mr. Brown's old newspapers which he cut out and saved. In it a very fatherly-looking man smoking a pipe, who said he was a Mr. Floyd, explained how any money left with him would earn what he called "interest," and that the longer he kept it, the more it would be worth.

Paddington had an eye for a bargain and having his money increase simply by leaving it somewhere had sounded like a very good bargain indeed.

The Browns had been so pleased at the idea that Mr. Brown had given him fifty pence to add to his Christmas and birthday money, and after a great deal of thought Paddington had himself added another ten pence which he'd carefully saved from his weekly bun allowance. When all these sums were added together they made a grand total of five pounds and twenty-five pence, and one day Mrs. Bird had taken him along to the bank in order to open an account.

For several days afterwards Paddington had hung about in a shop doorway opposite casting suspicious glances at anyone who went in or out. But after having been moved on by a passing policeman he'd had to let matters rest.

Since then, although he had carefully checked the amount in his book several times, Paddington had never actually been inside the bank. Secretly he was rather overawed by all the marble and thick polished wood, so he was pleased when at long last ten o'clock began to strike on a nearby church clock and he was still the only one outside.

As the last of the chimes died away there came the sound of bolts being drawn on the other side of the door, and Paddington hurried forward to peer eagerly through the letter box.

"'Ere, 'ere," exclaimed the porter as he caught sight of Paddington's hat through the slit. "No loiterers here, young feller. This is a bank, not a workhouse. We don't want no layabouts hanging round here."

"Layabouts?" repeated Paddington, letting go of the letter-box flap in his surprise.

"That's what I said," grumbled the porter as he opened the door. "Breathing all over me knockers. I 'as to polish that brass, yer know."

"I'm not a layabout," exclaimed Paddington, looking most offended as he waved his bankbook in the air. "I'm a bear and I've come to see Mr. Floyd about my savings."

"Ho, dear," said the porter, taking a closer look at Paddington. "Beggin' yer pardon, sir. When I saw your whiskers poking through me letter box I mistook you for one of them bearded gentlemen of the road."

"That's all right," said Paddington sadly. "I often get mistaken." And as the man held the door open for him he raised his hat politely and hurried into the bank.

On several occasions in the past, Mrs. Bird had impressed upon Paddington how wise it was to have money in the bank in case of a rainy day, and also how he might be glad to have it there one day for a special occasion. Thinking things over in bed the night before, Paddington had decided that going abroad for a holiday was certainly very much a special occasion, and after studying the advertisement once again he had thought up a very good idea for having the best of both worlds. But like many ideas he had had before at night under the bedclothes, it didn't seem quite such a good one in the cold light of day.

Now that he was actually inside the bank, Paddington began to feel rather guilty

and he wished he'd consulted Mr. Gruber on the matter, for he wasn't at all sure that Mrs. Bird would approve of his taking any money out without first asking her.

Hurrying across to one of the tellers at the counter, Paddington climbed up on his suitcase and peered over the edge. The man on the other side looked rather startled when Paddington's hat appeared over the top, and he reached nervously for a nearby alarm bell.

"I'd like to take out all my savings for a special occasion, please," said Paddington importantly, as he handed the man his book.

Looking rather relieved, the man took Paddington's book from him and then raised one eyebrow as he held it up to the light. There were a number of calculations in red ink all over the cover, not to mention blots and one or two rather messy-looking marmalade stains.

"I'm afraid I had an accident with one of my jars under the bedclothes last night," explained Paddington hastily as he caught the man's eye.

"One of your *jars*?" repeated the man. "Under the *bedclothes*?"

"That's right," said Paddington. "I was working out my interest and I stepped back into it by mistake. It's a bit difficult under the bedclothes."

"It must be," said the man distastefully. "Marmalade stains indeed! And on a Floyds bankbook!"

He hadn't been with the branch for very long, and although the manager had told him they sometimes had some very odd customers to deal with, nothing had been mentioned about bears' bank accounts.

"What would you like me to do with it?" he asked doubtfully.

"I'd like to leave all my interest in, please," explained Paddington. "In case it rains."

"Well," said the man in a superior tone of voice as he made some calculations on a piece of paper. "I'm afraid you won't keep very dry on this. It only comes to ten pence."

"*What!*" exclaimed Paddington, hardly able to believe his ears. "*Ten pence!* I don't think that's very interesting."

"Interest isn't the same thing as interesting," said the man. "Not the same thing at all."

He tried hard to think of some way of explaining matters, for he wasn't used to dealing with bears and he had a feeling that Paddington was going to be one of his more difficult customers.

"It's . . . it's something we give you for letting us borrow your money," he said. "The longer you leave it in the more you get."

"Well, my money's been in since just after Christmas," explained Paddington. "That's nearly six months."

"Ten pence," said the man firmly.

Paddington watched in a daze as the man made an entry in his book and then pushed a five pound note and some silver across the counter. "There you are," he said briskly. "Five pounds and twenty-five pence."

Paddington looked suspiciously at the note and then consulted a piece of paper he held in his paw. His eyes grew larger and larger as he compared the two.

"I think you must have made a mistake," he exclaimed. "This isn't my note."

"A mistake?" said the man stiffly. "We of Floyds never make mistakes."

"But it's got a different number," said Paddington hotly.

"A *different number*?" repeated the man.

"Yes," said Paddington. "And it said on mine that you promised to pay bear five pounds on demand."

"Not *bear*," said the teller. "Bear*er*. It says that on all notes. Besides," he continued, "you don't get the same note back that you put in. I expect yours is miles away by now if it's anywhere at all. It might even have been burned, if it was an old one. They often burn old notes when they're worn out."

"Burned?" repeated Paddington in a dazed voice. *"You've burned my note?"*

"I didn't say it *had* been," said the man, looking more and more confused. "I only said it might have been."

Paddington took a deep breath and gave the teller a hard stare. It was one of the extra special hard ones which his Aunt Lucy had taught him and which he kept for emergencies.

"I think I should like to see Mr. Floyd," he exclaimed.

"Mr. Floyd?" repeated the teller. He mopped his brow nervously as he looked anxiously over Paddington's shoulder at the line that was already beginning to form. There were some nasty murmurings going on at the back which he didn't like the sound of at all. "I'm afraid there isn't a Mr. Floyd," he said.

"We have a Mr. Trimble," he added hastily, as Paddington gave him an even harder stare. "He's the manager. I think perhaps I'd better fetch him—he'll know what to do."

Paddington stared indignantly after the retreating figure of the teller as he made his way towards a door marked MANAGER. The more he saw of things the less he liked the look of them. Not only did his note have a different number but he had just caught sight of the dates on the coins and they were quite different from those on the ones he had left. Apart from that his own coins had been highly polished, whereas these were old and very dull.

Paddington climbed down off his suitcase and pushed his way through the crowd with a determined expression on his face. Although he was only small, Paddington was a bear with a strong sense of right and wrong, especially when it came to money matters, and he felt it was high time he took matters into his own paws.

After he had made his way out of the bank Paddington hurried down the road in the direction of a red phone booth. Locked away in the secret compartment of his suitcase there was a note with some special instructions Mrs. Bird had written out for him in case of an emergency, together with ten pence. Thinking things over as he went along, Paddington decided it was very much a matter of an emergency— in fact, he had a job to remember when he'd had a bigger one—and he was glad when at long last the telephone booth came into view and he saw it was empty.

◆◆◆

"I don't know what's going on at the bank this morning," said Mrs. Brown as she closed the front door. "There was an enormous crowd outside when I came past."

"Perhaps there's been a robbery," said Mrs. Bird. "You read of such nasty goings-on these days."

"I don't think it was a robbery," said Mrs. Brown vaguely. "It was more like an emergency of some kind. The police were there and an ambulance *and* the fire brigade."

"*Hmm!*" said Mrs. Bird. "Well, I hope for all our sakes it isn't anything serious. Paddington's got all his money there and if there has been a raid we shall never hear the last of it."

Mrs. Bird paused as she was speaking and a thoughtful expression came over her face. "Talking of Paddington, have you seen him since he went out?" she asked.

"No," said Mrs. Brown. "Good heavens!" she exclaimed. "You don't think..."

"I'll get my hat," said Mrs. Bird. "And if Paddington's not somewhere at the bottom of it all I'll eat it on the way home!"

It took Mrs. Brown and Mrs. Bird some time to force their way through the crowd into the bank, and when they at last got inside their worst suspicions were realized, for there, sitting on his suitcase in the middle of a large crowd of officials, was the small figure of Paddington.

"What on earth's going on?" cried Mrs. Brown, as they pushed their way through to the front.

Paddington looked very thankful to see the others. Things had been going from bad to worse since he'd got back to the bank.

"I think my numbers have got mixed up by mistake, Mrs. Brown," he explained.

"Trying to do a young bear out of his life's savings, that's what's going on," cried someone at the back.

"Set fire to his money, they did," cried someone else.

"'Undreds of pounds gone up in smoke, so they say," called out a street trader who knew Paddington by sight and had come into the bank to see what all the fuss was about.

"Oh dear," said Mrs. Brown nervously. "I'm sure there must be some mistake. I don't think Floyds would ever do a thing like that on purpose."

"Indeed not, madam," exclaimed the manager as he stepped forward. "My name's Trimble," he continued. "Can you vouch for this young bear?"

"Vouch for him?" said Mrs. Bird. "Why, I brought him here myself in the first place. He's a most respectable member of the family and very law-abiding."

"Respectable he may be," said a large policeman, as he licked his pencil, "but I don't know so much about being law-abiding. Dialing the emergency number he was without proper cause. Calling out the police, not to mention the fire brigade and an ambulance. It'll all have to be gone into in the proper manner."

Everyone stopped talking and looked down at Paddington.

"I was only trying to call Mrs. Bird," said Paddington.

"Trying to call Mrs. Bird?" repeated the policeman slowly, as he wrote it down in his notebook.

"That's right," explained Paddington. "I'm afraid it's a bit difficult with paws to do one number at a time, so I just kept pressing and hoping for the best."

Mr. Trimble coughed. "I think perhaps we had better go into my office," he said. "It all sounds most complicated and it's much quieter in there."

With that everyone agreed wholeheartedly. And Paddington, as he picked up his suitcase and followed the others into the manager's office, agreed most of all. Having a bank account was quite the most complicated thing he had ever come across.

It was some time before Paddington finally got through his explanations, but when he had finished everyone looked most relieved that the matter wasn't more serious. Even the policeman seemed quite pleased.

"It's a pity there aren't more public-spirited bears about," he said, shaking Paddington by the paw. "If everyone called for help when they saw anything suspicious we'd have a lot less work to do in the long run."

After everyone else had left, Mr. Trimble took Mrs. Brown, Mrs. Bird and Paddington on a tour of the vault to show them where all the money was kept, and he even gave Paddington a book of instructions so that he would know exactly what to do the next time he paid the bank a visit.

"I do hope you *won't* close your account, Mr. Brown," he said. "We of Floyds never like to feel we're losing a valued customer. If you like to leave your twenty-five pence with us for safekeeping, I'll let you have a brand-new five pound note to take away for your holidays."

Paddington thanked Mr. Trimble very much for all his trouble and then considered the matter. "If you don't mind," he said at last, "I think I'd like a used one instead."

Paddington wasn't the sort of bear who believed in taking any chances, and although the crisp new note in the manager's hand looked very tempting he decided he would much prefer to have one that had been properly tested.

Chapter 20

Everything Comes
to Those Who Wait

Mrs. Bird gave a groan as the sound of several voices raised in song, followed almost immediately by a sharp rat-tat-tat on the front door, echoed down the hall.

"Not again," she said, putting down her sewing. "That's the fifth lot of carol-singers in half an hour. I shall be glad when Christmas is here."

"I'll go," said Mr. Brown grimly.

"I should be careful what you say, Henry," warned Mrs. Brown. "Don't forget Paddington's out doing the same thing."

Mr. Brown paused at the lounge door. "What!" he exclaimed. "Paddington's out *carol-singing*? You don't mean to say you let him go!"

"He seemed very keen on the idea," replied Mrs. Brown. "Jonathan and Judy are with him so he should be all right."

"I think they're collecting for some kind of party," broke in Mrs. Bird, coming to her rescue. "It's all rather secret."

"Well, I hope whoever they are they're not relying on Paddington's efforts for their Christmas entertainment," said Mr. Brown, feeling in his pocket. "Otherwise they're in for a pretty bleak time. Have you ever heard him sing?"

"He went out by himself the other evening before Jonathan and Judy came home for the school holidays," said Mrs. Brown. "And he did quite well considering."

"Two bananas, a button and some French francs," replied Mr. Brown. "And the bananas looked as if they'd seen better days."

"I wouldn't say singing was exactly his strong point," agreed Mrs. Brown reluctantly, "but he's been practicing quite hard up in his bedroom just lately."

"There's no need to tell me *that*," remarked Mr. Brown feelingly. "He had me out of bed twice last night. I thought it was the blessed cats!" He turned to go as once again the familiar strains of "Good King Wenceslaus" filled the air, and then his face brightened as a sudden thought struck him. "I suppose," he said, "it is *one* way of getting our own back!"

Had they been able to overhear the last remark not only Paddington, but both Jonathan and Judy would have been most upset, but fortunately for the sake of peace in the Browns' household they were much too far away at that moment, and in any case they had other more important problems to occupy their minds.

In particular there was the matter of the amount they had been able to collect from their evening's work.

"Eighty-two pence," said Jonathan bitterly, as he shone his flashlight into the cardboard box which they'd been using for the takings. "A measly eighty-two pence."

"It's not too bad," said Judy, "considering that only six people have answered the door."

"They can't have *all* been out," said Jonathan. "I wish we'd started our school holidays earlier. The trouble is everyone's getting fed up by now. I reckon we've left it a bit late."

"Perhaps we could say we're collecting for *next* Christmas," said Paddington hopefully.

It had been Paddington's idea to collect some money for the annual children's party at the hospital and he was beginning to feel a bit guilty about the whole affair, especially as they'd set themselves a target of ten pounds.

Judy squeezed his paw. "I don't think they'd be very pleased if we said that," she confided. "Never mind. We'll think of something. We mustn't give up now."

"Suppose we all separate," said Jonathan thoughtfully. "If we do that we ought to collect three times as much.

"We needn't go far away," he added, reading Judy's thoughts. "In fact, we needn't really lose sight of each other. Paddington can have the flashlight—then he can signal if he wants anything."

"All right," said Judy reluctantly. She glanced at the surrounding houses. "I'll take that one on the corner."

"I'll have a go at the one over there with the Christmas tree in the window," exclaimed Jonathan. "Which one are you going to do, Paddington?"

Paddington considered the matter for a moment as he peered round at all the houses. "I think I'd like to try that one over there," he announced, pointing towards an imposing-looking house standing slightly apart from the rest, from which there came the distinct sounds of a party in full swing.

"Come on, then," exclaimed Jonathan impatiently. "We shan't get anywhere if we don't make a start. We'll meet back here in half an hour."

"Don't forget," called Judy. "If you get into any trouble signal with the flashlight."

"Send an S.O.S.," shouted Jonathan. "Three short flashes, then three long ones and three short ones to follow."

After testing his flashlight carefully in order to make sure it was working, Paddington hurried up the path towards the front door of the house he'd chosen, cleared his throat several times, and then knocked loudly on the front door. He wasn't the sort of bear who believed in taking too many chances and with so much noise going on inside the house, he didn't want to knock *after* he'd sung his carol and then find that no one had heard him.

He opened his mouth and was about to launch into "Hark, the Herald Angels Sing" when to his surprise the door suddenly opened and a lady stood framed in the light from the hall.

"Thank goodness you've come," she exclaimed. "I was beginning to get quite worried.

"I'm Mrs. Smith-Cholmley," she added, as she opened the door wider and motioned Paddington to enter.

Paddington raised his hat politely as he stepped into the hall. "Thank you very much," he exclaimed. "I'm Paddington Brown."

For some reason the welcoming expression on Mrs. Smith-Cholmley's face began to fade. "Have you done much waiting?" she asked.

"Oh, no," said Paddington, looking round with interest. "I've only just got here."

"I mean have you had any previous experience of waiting?" said Mrs. Smith-Cholmley impatiently.

Paddington considered the matter for a moment. "I had to wait for a bus the other day when Mrs. Bird took me out shopping," he said thoughtfully.

Mrs. Smith-Cholmley gave a rather high-pitched laugh. "Mr. Bridges at the agency said waiters were a bit short this year," she remarked, looking down at Paddington, "but I didn't think he meant . . . I mean . . . I thought he meant they were hard to find . . . that is . . ." Her voice trailed away.

"Oh, well, at least they've sent *someone*," she continued brightly, avoiding Paddington's gaze. "We're having a little dinner party and it's long past time to serve the first course. You'd better go straight to the kitchen and see Vladimir. He's beside himself."

"Vladimir's beside himself!" exclaimed Paddington, looking most surprised.

"He's the chef," explained Mrs. Smith-Cholmley. "And if he doesn't get some help soon I'm sure he'll do something nasty with his chopper. He was looking very gloomy the last time I saw him." She glanced down at Paddington's paw. "Let me take your flashlight. I'm sure you won't want that."

"I think I'll keep it if you don't mind," said Paddington firmly. "I may want to send some signals."

"Just as you wish," said Mrs. Smith-Cholmley, giving him a strange look. She led the way down a long corridor and then paused before a door at the end as she opened her handbag. "Here's your ten pounds."

"My ten pounds!" Paddington's eyes nearly popped out of his head as he stared at the crisp new note in his paw.

"That's what I usually pay," said Mrs. Smith-Cholmley. "But I'd like you to start right away."

"Thank you very much," said Paddington, still hardly able to believe his good fortune. Ten pounds seemed a great deal of money to pay for a carol even if it was nearly Christmas and he hastily put the note into the secret compartment of his suitcase in case Mrs. Smith-Cholmley changed her mind when she discovered he only knew one verse.

As Paddington stood up, opened his mouth, and the first few notes of "Hark, the Herald Angels Sing" rang through the hall, the color seemed to drain from Mrs. Smith-Cholmley's face. "That's all I need," she cried, putting her hands to her ears. "A singing waiter!"

Paddington broke off in the middle of his opening chorus. "A singing waiter!" he repeated, looking most upset. "I'm not a singer—I'm a bear."

Mrs. Smith-Cholmley gave a shudder. "I can tell that," she said, opening the kitchen door. "And I shall certainly have something to say to Mr. Bridges about it in the morning. In the meantime you'd better start earning your money. Everyone's absolutely ravenous."

Without waiting for a reply she pushed Paddington through the door and hastily closed it behind him.

"Hah!"

Paddington jumped as a figure in white overalls and a tall white hat rose from behind a pile of saucepans and advanced towards him. "So! You have come at last. Quick . . . off viz your duffle coat and out viz your arms."

Paddington stood blinking in the strong white light of the kitchen, hardly able to believe his eyes let alone his ears. In fact, he was so taken aback at the sudden strange turn of events that before he knew what was happening he found that his duffle coat had been removed and he was standing with his arms outstretched while the man in white overalls balanced a row of bowls on each of them.

"Quick! Quick!" shouted Vladimir, snapping his fingers. "Get cracking viz your mulligatawnies."

"Get cracking with my mulligatawnies!" repeated Paddington carefully, finding his voice at last but hardly daring to breathe in case any of the bowls overbalanced.

"Zee soup," said Vladimir impatiently. "It's getting cold and on such short arms it is difficult to balance so much."

Paddington blinked several times to make sure he wasn't dreaming and then closed his eyes in order to count up to ten, but before he had time to reach even two he found himself being bundled back out of the kitchen and when he opened them again he was standing outside yet another door behind which could be heard the chatter of voices.

"Quick," hissed Vladimir, giving Paddington a firm push. "In here."

A buzz of excitement broke out in the room as Paddington entered, and several of the guests applauded.

"What a delightful idea, Mabel," said one lady. "Having a bear for a waiter.

Trust you to think up something unusual."

Mrs. Smith-Cholmley gave a sickly smile. "Oh, it wasn't really my idea," she said truthfully. "It just happened. But it makes a nice change."

She eyed Paddington warily as he arrived at the table with his load of bowls, but to her relief, apart from the fact that he was breathing rather heavily down the neck of one of her guests who happened to be in the way, there was little she could find fault with.

"I think we'd better give you a hand," she said hastily, when nothing happened. "We don't want any nasty accidents."

"Thank you very much," said Paddington gratefully as one by one the various diners relieved him of his burden. "It's a bit difficult with paws."

"Talking of paws," said the man Paddington had been standing behind, "you've got one of yours in my soup."

"Oh, that's all right," said Paddington politely. "It isn't very hot."

The man eyed the bowl distastefully. "May I give you a tip?" he asked.

"Oh, yes please," said Paddington eagerly. Now that he was getting used to the idea of being a waiter he was beginning to enjoy himself, and after giving his paw a hasty lick in order to remove some soup which had accidentally overflowed, he held it out hopefully.

"Don't carry quite so much next time," said the man sternly, as he helped himself to a roll. "Then it won't happen."

Mrs. Smith-Cholmley gave a nervous giggle as she caught sight of the expression on Paddington's face. "I think I should see how Vladimir's getting on with the next course," she called out quickly.

Paddington gave the man with the roll one final, long hard stare and then, after collecting several empty soup dishes, he made his way towards the door. The carol-singing, not to mention the waiting, had made him feel more than usually hungry and Mrs. Smith-Cholmley's words reminded him of the fact that during his brief spell in the kitchen he'd noticed some very interesting smells coming from beneath the lids of Vladimir's saucepans.

Although he still wasn't entirely sure what was happening, Paddington didn't want to run the risk of it all coming to an end before he'd had time to investigate the matter. What with one thing and another serving the first course had taken rather longer than he'd expected and he hurried back down the corridor as fast as his legs would carry him.

To his surprise, when he got back to the kitchen Vladimir was no longer dressed in white. His chef's hat was lying in a crumpled ball in the middle of the floor and Vladimir himself was standing by the back door clad in a black overcoat and muffler.

"I may go back to Poland," he announced gloomily when he caught sight of Paddington.

"Oh dear," said Paddington. "I hope nothing's wrong."

"*Everything* is wrong," said Vladimir. He thumped his chest. "I, Vladimir, I who have cooked for ze crowned 'eads of Europe. I, who have 'ad princes wait while I add ze final touches to my creations. I, Vladimir, am reduced to zis. Waiting . . . all ze time I am kept waiting." He waved his hand disconsolately in the air. "My soup, she is cold. My entrecôtes, zey are cold . . ."

"Your entrecôtes are cold!" repeated Paddington, looking most upset.

Vladimir nodded. "My beautiful steak—ruined!" He pointed towards a grill laden with slowly congealing pieces of meat.

"I 'ad to take them from the stove or they would 'ave been burned to a cinder." He reached out and clasped Paddington's paw. "They are yours, my friend. In the saucepans you will find the vegetables. You may serve it as you think fit. I, Vladimir, no longer care. Goodbye, my friend . . . and good luck!"

Worn out by his long speech Vladimir paused by the back door, waved his hand dramatically in the air, and then disappeared from view, leaving Paddington rooted to the spot in astonishment.

But if Paddington was upset by the sight of Vladimir's sudden departure, Mrs. Smith-Cholmley looked even more upset when, some time later, she caught sight of her steak.

By the time he'd got round to serving all the various vegetables and carried all the plates into the dining room, things had gone from bad to worse. Even putting some of the pieces of steak in an electric toaster hadn't helped matters, particularly as several of them had popped out and fallen on the floor before he'd had a chance to catch them.

Looking at his offering Paddington had to admit that he didn't really fancy it much himself and he felt pleased he'd taken time off to have his own snack before serving the others.

"If there's anything wrong with the baked Alaska," hissed Mrs. Smith-Cholmley, endeavoring to glare at Paddington with one half of her face and smile at her guests with the other, "I shall insist on Vladimir giving me my money back.

"Baked Alaska," she repeated through her teeth as she saw the look of surprise on Paddington's face. "It's a special surprise for my guests and I want it to be absolutely perfect."

If Paddington's spirits sank as he made his way slowly back down the corridor towards the kitchen, they fell still more during the next few minutes as he peered hopefully at first one cookbook and then another.

Although Mrs. Smith-Cholmley had only spoken of asking the chef for his money back, he had a nasty feeling that when it came down to it and she found Vladimir had disappeared, his own ten pounds might not be too safe.

Mrs. Smith-Cholmley had a large collection of cookbooks from many different parts of the world, but not one of them so much as mentioned the dish he was looking for.

It was as he closed the last of the books that Paddington caught sight of a nearby low hanging shelf which he hadn't noticed before and as he did so he gave a sudden start. For there, right in front of his eyes, was a row of tins, one of which was labeled with the very words he'd been looking for.

Hardly daring to close his eyes in case the tin disappeared, Paddington spent the next few minutes hastily making his preparations. First he turned the knob over the oven to read "high," then he looked round for a suitable dish. After carefully checking the thermometer in order to make sure the oven was hot enough he emptied the contents of the tin into the dish and placed it inside the oven.

Normally the only thing Paddington had against cooking was the amount of time it took for anything to happen, but on this occasion he hadn't long to wait. In fact, he'd hardly had time to settle down on his suitcase and make himself comfortable before several whiffs of black smoke rose from the oven, and the pleased expression on his face was rapidly replaced by a look of alarm as a most unappetizing smell began to fill the kitchen.

Hurrying across the room he tore open the oven door only to stagger back as a cloud of thick, black smoke poured out.

Holding his nose with one paw he picked up his flashlight with the other and peered mournfully at the contents of the baking dish as it sizzled and bubbled inside the oven.

Paddington was a hopeful bear at heart, but although Mrs. Smith-Cholmley had definitely said she wanted to surprise her guests, he couldn't help feeling as he trundled a cart laden with portions of his dessert down the corridor some while later that his efforts might prove rather more than she'd bargained for.

Giving vent to a deep sigh he took a firm grip of his flashlight as he tapped on

the dining room door. Jonathan had told him to send out a distress signal if he was in trouble and he had a nasty idea in the back of his mind that the moment to take this advice was not too far away.

◆◆◆

Mr. Brown stared at Paddington as if he could hardly believe his eyes. "Do you mean to say," he exclaimed, "that you actually served this Mrs. Smith-Cholmley baked *elastic*?"

Paddington nodded unhappily. "I found some rubber bands in a tin, Mr. Brown," he explained.

"He didn't realize Mrs. Smith-Cholmley said 'baked *Alaska*,'" explained Judy. "That's a sort of ice cream dish cooked in the oven."

"It was just after that he sent out his S.O.S.," added Jonathan.

"I'm not surprised," exclaimed Mrs. Bird. "It's a wonder some of the guests didn't send one as well."

"They were jolly nice about it all," said Judy. "When the real waiter turned up and they discovered Paddington had really only come to sing a carol they made us all stay."

"He'd met Vladimir on the way too," added Jonathan.

"*Vladimir?*" echoed Mr. Brown. He was rapidly losing track of the conversation. "Who's Vladimir?"

"The chef," explained Judy. "When he discovered the mistake he came back after all and he made some real baked Alaska so everyone was happy."

"We sang some carols afterwards," said Jonathan. "And we collected over fifteen pounds. That means we've nearly reached our target."

Judy gave a sigh. "The baked Alaska was super," she said dreamily. "I could eat some more."

"So could I," agreed Jonathan.

Paddington licked his lips. "I expect I could make you some if you like, Mr. Brown," he exclaimed.

"Not in *my* kitchen," said Mrs. Bird sternly. "I'm not having any young bear's elastic baked in my oven!"

She paused at the door. "Mind you," she added casually, "as it happens, we were going to have some ice cream for supper . . ."

"I must say it sounds rather nice," said Mrs. Brown.

Mr. Brown stroked his mustache thoughtfully. "I could toy with some myself," he agreed. "How about you, Paddington?"

Paddington considered the matter for moment. If one thing stood out above all others in his mind from the evening's adventure it was the memory of Vladimir's baked Alaska and he felt sure that an Alaska baked by Mrs. Bird would be nicer still.

The Browns' housekeeper looked unusually pink about the ears as she raised her hands at the noisy approval which greeted Paddington as he gave voice to his thoughts.

"Compliments are always nice," she said. "Especially genuine ones.

"But if you ask me," she continued, pausing at the door, "bears' compliments are the nicest ones of all and they certainly deserve the biggest helpings!"

Chapter 21

Paddington Recommended

Mrs. Brown tore open the first of the morning's mail, withdrew a large piece of white cardboard, and then stared at it in amazement. "Good gracious!" she exclaimed. "Fancy that! Mrs. Smith-Cholmley is holding a Christmas ball in aid of the local children's hospital and we've all been invited."

Paddington peered across the table with a slice of toast and marmalade poised halfway to his mouth. "Mrs. Smith-Cholmley's holding a Christmas ball?" he repeated in great surprise. "I hope we get there before she drops it!"

"It isn't that sort of a ball, dear," said Mrs. Brown patiently.

"It means she's having a dance," explained Judy.

"Who's Mrs. Smith-Cholmley when she's at home?" asked Mr. Brown.

Mrs. Brown handed him the card. "Don't you remember, Henry? Paddington met her when he was out carol-singing. She's the one he cooked the baked elastic for by mistake."

"Gosh!" broke in Jonathan, as he read the invitation. "She's either left it a bit late or it's been delayed in the mail. It's tomorrow night!"

"And that's not all," added Mrs. Brown. "Have you seen what it says at the bottom?"

Paddington hurried round the table and peered over Mr. Brown's shoulder. "Ruzzvup!" he exclaimed.

"No, dear," said Mrs. Brown. "R.S.V.P. That simply means *Répondez, s'il vous plâit*. It's French for 'please reply.'"

"You mean the bit about evening dress?" Mr. Brown looked round at Paddington, who was waving his toast and marmalade dangerously near his left ear. "Well, that's put an end to it. I suppose we shall just have to say no."

There was a note of relief in Mr. Brown's voice. He wasn't too keen on dancing at the best of times and the thought of going to a ball run by Mrs. Smith-Cholmley filled him with gloom. But any hopes he'd entertained of using Paddington as an excuse were quickly dashed by the chorus of dismay which greeted his last remark.

"I think we ought to try and arrange *something*, Henry," said Mrs. Brown. "After all, it's in a very good cause. It's the same hospital Paddington collected for last year, and if it wasn't for him we shouldn't be invited anyway."

"We'll take him along to Heather and Sons and have him fitted out for the evening," said Mrs. Bird decidedly, as she bustled round clearing up the breakfast things. "They hire out evening clothes and it says in their advertisements they fit anyone while they wait."

Mr. Brown eyed Paddington's figure doubtfully. "We need it *tomorrow* night," he said. "Not next year."

Paddington looked most upset at this last remark. It was bad enough writing things in initials, let alone French ones, but having to wear special clothes simply in order to dance seemed most complicated.

However, he brightened considerably at the thought of going up to London to be fitted out. And when Mr. Brown, recognizing defeat at last, announced that he would meet them afterwards and take them all out to lunch as a special treat, Paddington joined in the general excitement.

Paddington liked visiting London and he couldn't wait to get started, especially when Mr. Brown brought out his copy of a guide to good restaurants and began searching for a likely eating place.

"They have a restaurant at Heather's now," said Mrs. Brown. "We could combine the two things. It'll save a lot of trouble."

Mr. Brown made a quick check. "It isn't a Duncan Hyde recommended," he said disappointedly. "He doesn't even mention it."

"It only opened last week," replied Mrs. Brown, "so it wouldn't be. But not many people know about it yet so at least it won't be crowded."

"All right," said Mr. Brown. "You win!" He snapped the book shut and handed it to Paddington. "Perhaps you can test a few of the dishes at lunchtime," he continued, as the others hurried upstairs. "If they're any good we'll send a recommendation to Mr. Hyde."

"Thank you very much, Mr. Brown," said Paddington gratefully. He'd spent many happy hours browsing through the pages of Mr. Hyde's book, and he put it away carefully in the secret compartment of his suitcase while he got ready to go out.

Duncan Hyde spent his time visiting restaurants all over the country, awarding them various shaped hats for their cooking, ranging from a very small beret for run-of-the-mill dishes to a giant-size bowler for the very best, and some of the dishes he described were mouth-watering indeed.

Although no one had ever met him, for he preferred to remain anonymous, it was widely agreed that he must be a person of great taste, and when they arrived at Heather and Sons later that morning Paddington peered through the restaurant window with interest in case there was anyone round carrying a hat.

As they trooped through the main entrance the Browns were greeted by a man in formal clothes.

"We'd like to fit this young bear out for a special occasion," said Mrs. Brown. "Can you direct us to the right department, please?"

"Certainly, Modom. Please step this way." With scarcely the flicker of an eyelid the supervisor turned and led the way towards a nearby elevator. "Is the young . . . er, gentleman, being presented at Court?" he asked, glancing down at Paddington as the doors slid shut. "Or is he simply coming out?"

"Neither," said Paddington, giving the man a hard stare. "I'm coming in!" After the warmth of the Underground, the air outside had struck particularly cold to his whiskers and he didn't want to be sent out again.

"He's going to a ball," explained Mrs. Brown hastily. "We want to hire some evening dress."

"A ball?" The man looked slightly relieved. "One of the spring functions, no doubt?" he remarked hopefully.

"No," said Mrs. Bird firmly. "One of the Christmas ones. It's for tomorrow night, so there's no time to be lost."

"It says in the advertisement you fit anyone," broke in Jonathan.

"While you wait," added Judy imploringly.

"Er . . . yes," said the supervisor unhappily. He looked down at Paddington again. "It's just that the young . . . er . . . gentleman's legs are a bit . . . ahem . . . and we may have to do some rather drastic alterations if it's to be from stock."

"My legs are a bit 'ahem'?" exclaimed Paddington hotly.

He began giving the supervisor some very hard stares indeed, but fortunately the elevator came to a stop before any more could be said. As the doors slid open and the man gave a discreet signal to an assistant hovering in the background, Mrs. Brown exchanged glances with the others.

"I was wondering," she said, "if it wouldn't be better for the rest of us to carry on with our Christmas shopping? We can all meet in the restaurant downstairs at one o'clock."

"A very good idea, Modom!" The supervisor sounded most relieved. "Rest assured," he continued, as he ushered Paddington from the lift, "we will use our best endeavors and leave no stone unturned. I'll get our Mr. Stanley to look after the young gentleman. He does all our difficult cases and there's nothing he likes better than a challenge."

"That's as may be," said Mrs. Bird ominously, as the gates slid shut again, "but I have a feeling he's going to have to turn over a good few stones before that bear's fitted out. You mark my words!"

The Browns' housekeeper didn't entirely approve of leaving Paddington to the tender mercies of Heather and Sons, impressive though their store was, but as it happened the supervisor's confidence in his staff was not misplaced, for no sooner had the Browns departed than everyone sprang into action.

"I'll put 'Thimbles' Martin on the job," announced Mr. Stanley, making notes as he circled Paddington with a tape measure. "He's the fastest man with a needle and thread in the business. He'll fix you up in no time at all."

Looking suitably impressed Paddington settled down to read his Duncan Hyde book while he waited, and indeed, it seemed only a very short while before Mr. Stanley reappeared proudly carrying an immaculately pressed set of evening clothes.

"You'll look dashing in these and no mistake, sir," he exclaimed enthusiastically, as he led Paddington into a changing room.

"Quite the young bear about town," agreed the supervisor. "Mind you," he continued, allowing himself a smile of satisfaction as he helped Paddington on with the jacket, "you'll have to watch your p's and q's. There's no knowing who you might not get mistaken for dressed like that. Will you be taking them with you, or shall we send them?"

Paddington examined his reflection in the mirror—or rather, since there were mirrors on all four walls, what seemed like a never-ending line of his reflections stretching away into the distance.

Although he felt very pleased to get his evening clothes so quickly, he was looking forward even more to the thought of carrying out Mr. Brown's suggestion and investigating some dishes for the guide.

"I think," he announced at last, "I'll wear them, thank you very much." And disregarding the anxious expressions behind him, he picked up his belongings and headed for the lift.

As Mrs. Brown had forecast, not many people knew about Heather's restaurant and what with that and the early hour, it was still practically empty when Paddington entered.

Just inside the door there was an enormous dessert cart, and his eyes nearly popped out with astonishment as he took in the various items. There were so many different shapes, sizes and colors he soon lost count, and it was while he was on his paws and knees examining the mounds of chocolate mousse and the oceans of fruit salads on the bottom shelf that he suddenly realized someone was talking to him.

"May I be of assistance?" asked one of the waiters.

Paddington stood up and raised his hat politely. "No, thank you very much," he said sadly. "I was only looking." Holding up the Duncan Hyde book he ran his eye over the cart again. "I was hoping I might be able to do some testing later on. I think some of your dishes might be worth a bowler."

To Paddington's surprise his words seemed to have a magical effect on the waiter. "Pardon me, sir," he exclaimed, jumping to attention. "I didn't realize who you were. If you care to wait just one moment, sir, I'll call the manager."

Bowing low as he backed away, the man disappeared from view, only to return a moment later accompanied by an imposing figure dressed in a black coat and striped trousers.

"I can't tell you," boomed the second man, rubbing his hands with invisible soap, "how delighted we are that you've decided to honor us with your presence. It's just what our restaurant needs." Taking in Paddington's dress suit, hat and whiskers, he gave a knowing wink at the book. "I see you've been hiding your light under a bushel!"

"I have?" exclaimed Paddington, looking more and more surprised at the turn the conversation was taking.

"We'll put you in the window, sir," announced the manager, leading the way across the floor. "We have some very special dishes today," he confided with another wink, as he helped Paddington into a chair. "I'm sure we can find something to titillate your palate."

"I expect you can," said Paddington, politely giving the man a wink in return. "But I'm not sure if I can afford them."

"My dear sir!" The man raised his hands in mock horror as he whisked the menu away. "We don't want to bother ourselves with mere money."

"Don't we?" exclaimed Paddington excitedly.

The manager shook his head. "You need only sign the bill," he explained. "Let's think about food first. That's much more important. We want you to feel perfectly at home."

"Oh, I do already," said Paddington, grasping his knife and fork. "When can I start?"

"That's what I like to see," replied the manager, beaming all over his face. "Well," he continued, rubbing his hands in anticipation, "I can certainly recommend our avocado filled with sea-fresh shrimps and cream sauce.

"After that," he said, "may I suggest either pot-fresh lobster, Dover-fresh sole, farm-fresh escalope of veal, or oven-fresh steak and kidney pudding?"

All the talk of food was beginning to make Paddington feel hungry and it didn't take him long to make up his mind. "I think I'd like to try some of each," he announced rashly.

If the manager was surprised he concealed his feelings remarkably well. In fact, a look of respect came over his face as he handed Paddington's order to a waiter who was hovering nearby. "I must say," he remarked, "you take your job very seriously, sir. There aren't many people in your position who would take the trouble to try *everything* on the menu. Would you care to test one of our rare old wines?"

Paddington thought for a moment. "I think I'd sooner test some of your tin-fresh cocoa," he said.

"Tin-fresh *cocoa*?" For one brief moment the manager's calm seemed to desert him, then he brightened. "I have a feeling you're trying to catch us out," he said, wagging his finger roguishly.

"Perhaps," he added, waving in the direction of the cart, "you would care to contemplate the desserts over the cheese."

Paddington gave him an odd look. "I'd sooner eat them," he said. "But I think I'd better leave a little bit of room. I'm having lunch with someone at one o'clock."

A look of renewed admiration came over the man's face. "Well," he said, bow-

ing his way out as the first of the dishes began to arrive, "I'll leave you to your task, but I do hope you'll see fit to mention us when the time comes."

"Oh, yes," replied Paddington earnestly. "I shall tell all my friends."

Paddington still wasn't sure why he was being treated in such a royal manner, but he wasn't the sort of bear to look a gift horse in the mouth and as everyone obviously wanted him to enjoy his meal he was only too willing to oblige.

Already quite a large crowd had gathered on the pavement outside Heather's. In fact, the window was black with faces and it was getting darker with every passing moment.

Paddington's every move was watched with increasing interest, and as he settled to his gargantuan meal the applause which greeted each new course was exceeded only by the one which followed.

But if the vast majority of the audience viewed the goings-on inside the restaurant with wonder and delight, there were five new members who stood watching with horror and dismay on their faces.

The Browns had arranged to meet outside the store, but like most of the other passersby they had been drawn to the crowd gathered round the window, and now, as they pushed their way through to the front, their worst fears were realized.

"Mercy me!" cried Mrs. Bird. "What on earth is that bear up to now?"

"I don't know what he's *up* to," said Mr. Brown gloomily, as a loud groan rose from the audience. "But whatever it is I think it's coming to an end."

A sudden change had indeed taken place on the other side of the glass, and the Browns watched with sinking hearts.

It all began when a waiter arrived bearing a large sheet of folded paper on a plate. Handing Paddington a pen, he stood over him with a deferential smile on his face while he signed his name. Then gradually the smile disappeared, only to be replaced by an expression which the Browns didn't like the look of at all.

"Come on," cried Judy, grabbing her mother's arm. "We'd better do some rescuing."

"Oh, Lord!" groaned Mr. Brown, as they pushed their way back through the crowd. "Here we go again."

Unaware that help was on its way, Paddington stared at the waiter as if he could hardly believe his eyes, let alone his ears. "Fifty-six pounds!" he exclaimed. "Just for a meal?"

"Not just for *a* meal," said the waiter, eyeing all the stains. "About ten meals if you ask me. We thought you were Duncan Hyde, the famous gourmet."

Paddington nearly fell backwards off his chair at the news. "Duncan Hyde, the famous gourmet?" he repeated. "I'm not Duncan Hyde. I'm Paddington Brown from Darkest Peru, and I'm a bear."

"In that case," said the waiter, handing back the bill, "I'm afraid it's cash. It includes the cover charge," he added meaningfully, "but not the tip."

"A *cover* charge?" exclaimed Paddington hotly. "But I didn't even have one. It was all open." He peered at the piece of paper in his paw. *"Nine pounds fifty for a bombe surprise!"*

"That's all part of the surprise," replied the waiter nastily.

"Well, I've got one for you," said Paddington. "I've only got ten pence!"

Paddington felt most upset about the whole affair, especially as he hadn't intended eating in the first place. Apart from putting his signature on the bill as he'd been asked, he'd even added his special pawprint to show it was genuine, and he looked very relieved when he caught sight of the Browns heading in his direction.

Since he'd arrived a great change had come over the restaurant and it was now full almost to overflowing. The Browns had to weave a tortuous path in and out of the other diners, and before they were able to reach Paddington's table they found their way barred by the manager.

"Does this young gentleman belong to you?" he asked, pointing in Paddington's direction.

"Er . . . why do you ask?" queried Mr. Brown, playing for time.

"Henry!" exclaimed Mrs. Brown. "How could you?"

"I've never seen you before either, Mr. Brown," called Paddington, entering into the spirit of things.

Mr. Brown heaved a deep sigh as he reached for his wallet. "Since you ask," he said, "I'm afraid he does."

"Afraid?" The manager stared at the Browns. "Did you say *afraid*?" He waved an all-embracing hand round the restaurant. "Why, this is the best thing that's happened to us since we opened. That young bear's attracted so many new customers we don't know whether we're coming or going. There's certainly no charge."

He turned back to Paddington. "I wish we could have you sit in the window every day of the week. You may not be Duncan Hyde, but you're certainly worth your weight in lobster soufflé . . ."

The manager broke off and looked at Paddington with concern. For some reason or other his words seemed to be having a strange effect.

"Are you all right, sir?" he asked. "Your whiskers seem to have gone a very funny color. Let me help you up. Perhaps you'd like to try some of our bean-fresh coffee with cream?"

Paddington gave another groan. If he'd had to make a list of his needs at that moment, getting up would have figured very low, while food and drink would have been lucky to get a mention at all.

Dropping his guidebook he sank back into the chair and felt for the buttons on his jacket. "I'd rather not do any more testing today, thank you very much," he gasped.

Apart from all his other troubles, Paddington had noticed a rather ominous tearing sound whenever he moved, and although he'd minded his peas during lunch he had a feeling that both Mr. Stanley and "Thimbles" Martin were in for a busy afternoon dealing with his q's.

All the same, he had to admit he'd never had *quite* such a meal in his life before.

"I think," he announced, "that if I was a food tester I would award Heather's one of my uncle's hats!"

Mr. Brown smacked his lips in anticipation. "It must be good then," he said, reaching for the menu. "I shall enjoy my lunch.

"After all," he continued, amid general agreement, "one of Paddington's hats must be worth a whole closet full of Duncan Hyde bowlers any day of the week!"

◆◆◆

Part Five

Paddington
on the Move

Chapter 22

The Last Dance

M r. Brown hung his dressing gown on the bedroom door and then sat on the
bed rubbing his eyes. "Three times I've been down to the front door," he
grumbled, "and all the time it was Paddington banging about in his room!"

"I expect he's practicing his dancing," said Mrs. Brown sleepily. "He said he
was having trouble with his turns last night."

"Well, I'm having trouble with my *sleep* this morning," said Mr. Brown crossly.
"I've put my foot down."

"I can see you have," replied Mrs. Brown, eyeing her husband's slippers as he
took them off. "Right in the middle of Paddington's rosin! I think you'd better
scrape it off. He'll be most upset if there's any missing. He bought it specially to
stop his paws slipping on the linoleum. He had several nasty falls yesterday."

Mr. Brown looked at his soles in disgust. "Only a bear," he said bitterly, "would
want to do the tango at half past six on a Saturday morning. I only hope they don't
have a 'bear's excuse me' at the ball tonight. Anyone who lands Paddington as a
partner is in for a pretty rough time."

"Perhaps he'll have improved by then," said Mrs. Brown hopefully. "It can't be
easy rehearsing with a pillow."

Mrs. Brown turned over and closed her eyes, though more in an effort to blot out the mental picture of events to come than with any hope of going back to sleep. For although one half of her was looking forward to Mrs. Smith-Cholmley's annual Christmas ball that evening, the other half was beginning to have grave doubts about the matter, and recent events only served to tip the scales still further on the side of the doubts.

But daylight lends enchantment to the gloomiest of views and some, at least, of Mrs. Brown's worst fears were relieved when Paddington arrived downstairs a little later that morning looking unusually spick-and-span despite his disturbed night.

"I must say you look very smart," she remarked, amid murmurs of approval from the others. "There can't be many bears who sit down to breakfast in formal attire."

"There'll be one less," said Mrs. Bird, striking a warning note, "if certain of them get any marmalade down their front!"

Mrs. Bird had suffered from "bumps in the night" as well, and with Christmas looming large on the horizon she didn't want her kitchen turned into a bear's ballroom.

Paddington considered the matter for a moment while he tackled his bacon and eggs. He was the sort of bear who believed in getting value for money, and having heard how much Mr. Brown was paying to rent his suit, he wanted to make the most of it. All the same, if the Browns were having second thoughts on the subject of dancing, he had to admit that he was having third and even fourth ones himself.

In the past he had often watched dancing programs on the television and wondered why people made so much fuss, for it all looked terribly easy—just a matter of jumping about the floor in time to some music. But when he'd tried to do it he soon found that even without a partner his legs got tangled up and he shuddered to think what it might be like when he had someone else's in the way as well.

In the end he'd tried doing it on his bed for safety, but that had been worse still—rather like running round in circles on a cotton-wool-covered trampoline.

All in all, he decided dancing was much more difficult than it looked at first sight, and to everyone's relief he announced that he was going out that morning in order to consult his friend, Mr. Gruber, on the subject.

Over the years Mr. Gruber had proved himself helpful on a variety of subjects, and Paddington felt sure he would be able to find something among the many books which lined the walls of his antique shop. Even so, he was still taken by surprise when he arrived at Mr. Gruber's and found his friend doing a kind of jig round his knick-knacks table to the tune from an old wind-up gramophone.

Mr. Gruber looked at Paddington sheepishly over the top of his glasses as he drew up a chair. "I have a feeling you won't be the only one with problems tonight, Mr. Brown," he said, panting a little after his exertions. "It's a long time since I last tripped the light fantastic."

As Paddington had no idea Mr. Gruber could dance, let alone do a light fantastic, the news that he was going to Mrs. Smith-Cholmley's ball came like a bolt from the blue, and he grew more and more excited when his friend drew his attention to a large poster in the window.

"Practically anyone who's anyone round here is going tonight, Mr. Brown," he said. "They've got Alf Weidersein's orchestra, and Norman and Hilda Church are bringing their Formation Dance Team."

Paddington looked most impressed as Mr. Gruber went on to explain that Norman Church was a very famous ballroom dancer indeed, and that apart from bringing his team, he would be judging the various competitions to be held during the course of the evening.

And when Mr. Gruber, with a twinkle in his eye, reached up to one of the shelves and took down a book on dancing written by Mr. Church himself, Paddington could hardly believe his good fortune. He felt sure if he studied a book written by the man who was actually going to act as judge he ought to do very well indeed.

For the rest of that day, apart from odd strains of the Tango and an occasional thump from Paddington's room, number thirty-two Windsor Gardens remained remarkably quiet as everyone got ready for the big event.

Paddington himself was waiting in the hall quite early in the evening, clutching Mr. Gruber's book in one paw and an alarm clock in the other, while he did some last-minute promenades by the front door.

Although Norman Church's book was lavishly illustrated with footprints showing the various steps, none of them seemed to go anywhere, and as some were marked "clockwise" and others "counterclockwise," he got very confused trying to work out which ones to follow and watch the hands on the clock at the same time.

The book was called *Learning to Hold Your Own on the Dance Floor in Twenty-five Easy Lessons*, and with only a matter of minutes to go Paddington rather wished Mr. Church had made do with five hard ones indeed, for he found it difficult enough getting through the title, let alone reading the instructions.

All the same, when they set off shortly afterwards he soon joined in the general gaiety, and as they drew near the ballroom he grew more and more excited.

But the journey itself was nothing compared to the atmosphere once they were inside and Paddington peered round with growing interest as he handed his duffle coat to an attendant.

Strains of music floated out through a pair of double doors at the top of some stairs leading down to the dance floor, and beyond the stairs he could see couples in evening dress gliding about, their faces lit by twinkling reflections from an enormous mirrored globe revolving high above them.

Mr. Brown cocked an ear to the music as they joined Mr. Gruber and a small queue of other new arrivals. "They're playing 'Goodbye Blues,'" he said. "That's one of my favorites."

"'Goodbye Blues'?" repeated Paddington, looking most upset. "But we've only just arrived!"

Mr. Gruber gave a tactful cough. "I think there'll be plenty more tunes before we leave, Mr. Brown."

Bending down, he drew Paddington to one side as the line moved forward. "I should put your best paw forward," he whispered. "I think you're about to be announced."

Mr. Gruber pointed towards a man in an imposing wig and costume standing at the head of the stairs, and Paddington's eyes nearly popped out as he heard Mr. and Mrs. Brown's names ring out round the ballroom.

"I don't think I've ever been announced before, Mr. Gruber," he replied, hastily stuffing as many of his belongings as possible underneath his jacket.

"Oh no!" Judy gave a startled gasp as she gave Paddington a quick last-minute check. "You've still got your bicycle clips on!"

Catching her daughter's words, Mrs. Brown looked anxiously over her shoulder. "Do take them off, dear," she warned. "You won't feel the benefit otherwise."

Mindful of Mrs. Bird's remarks about keeping his formal suit clean, Paddington hadn't wanted to take any risks with the trouser bottoms, which tended to slip down rather, and with a forecast of snow in the air he'd decided to make doubly sure. All the same, he did as he was bidden, and as he approached the man doing the announcements he bent down.

"Excuse me," he called in a muffled voice. "I'm Mr. Brown and I'm having trouble with my bicycle clips."

"Mr. Cyclops Brown," called the man, in sonorous tones.

"Cyclops Brown!" exclaimed Paddington hotly. He stood up clutching his clips, looking most upset that on the very first occasion of being announced his name should have been wrongly called. But by that time the man was already halfway

through announcing Mr. Gruber, and Paddington found himself face to face with Mrs. Smith-Cholmley, who was waiting to greet her guests at the foot of the stairs.

"I'm so sorry," said Mrs. Smith-Cholmley, trying to pass the whole thing off with a merry laugh as she took Paddington's paw. "I always thought Cyclops only had one eye . . ." She broke off as she followed Paddington's gaze towards the middle of the dance floor, for it was all too obvious that Paddington not only had *two* eyes but they were both working extremely well.

"That's Mr. Church," she explained, catching sight of a nattily dressed man posing beneath a spotlight. "He's about to lead off."

As the music started up again Mrs. Smith-Cholmley turned back to Paddington. "Er . . . I see you've been doing some homework," she continued, catching sight of Mr. Gruber's book in his other paw. "If Mr. Church has trouble with his steps he'll know where to come—" Once again Mrs. Smith-Cholmley broke off, and a look of alarm came over her face. "I didn't say he *has* got trouble," she called. "I only said *if*. It was a joke. I—"

But Paddington was already halfway across the floor. "Don't worry, Mr. Church!" he cried, waving his book. "I'm coming. I think it's all on page forty-five."

Paddington reached the center of the floor in time to meet the first wave of advancing dancers. Norman and Hilda Church's Formation Dance Team was just get-

ting into its stride, and if the smile on Mrs. Smith-Cholmley's face had begun to look a trifle fixed, the one Mr. Church presented to his public looked as if it had been indelibly etched for all time.

"Go away," he hissed, as Paddington tapped him on the shoulder. "You're upsetting my Alberts."

Norman Church looked as if he'd just thought up a few more choice items for his chapter on ballroom etiquette, but before he had time to put any of them into words a very strange thing happened.

As his team turned to make a sweeping movement back down the floor, a bell started to ring somewhere in their midst.

There was a note of urgency about it which caused the leaders to falter in their stride. In a moment all was confusion as those in the rear cannoned into the ones in front, and in less time than it takes to form up for a quadrille, the damage had been done.

A group who thought a fire had broken out behind the bandstand jostled with another group who were equally convinced the floor was about to give way, and they, in turn, ran foul of those who simply wanted to see what was going on.

In the middle of all the hubbub Paddington suddenly reached inside his jacket. "It's all right, Mr. Church," he called, holding up a large round brass object. "It's only my alarm clock!"

In the silence that followed Mr. Brown's voice sounded unusually loud. "Two minutes!" he groaned. "That's all the time we've been here. *Two minutes*—and look at it!"

There was no need to suggest looking at the scene on the dance floor, for the rest of the Browns were only too painfully aware of what it was like.

Even Paddington, as he made his way back through the dancers, was forced to admit that he rather wished the floor *had* collapsed, for it would have afforded a quick means of escape from the glances of those round him.

"Never mind," said Judy, going forward to meet him. "We know you meant well."

"Thank you very much," said Paddington gratefully. "But I don't think Mr. Church does."

Casting an anxious glance over his shoulder, he allowed himself to be led off the floor in the direction of some tables to one side of the hall.

"I think I'll sit this one out, thank you very much," he announced, after consulting his book.

Although the chapter on ballroom behavior didn't include any mention of what to do following the kind of disaster he'd just experienced, there were quite a number of phrases Mr. Church recommended for use when you didn't want to dance and Paddington felt it was a good moment to test one or two of them.

"Not that anyone's likely to ask him after what's just happened," said Mr. Brown, as he whirled past the table a little later on.

"It's a shame really," agreed Mrs. Brown, catching sight of Paddington deep in his book. "He's been practicing so hard. I don't like to think of him being a wallflower, and he's been sitting there for ages."

Mr. Brown gave a snort. "Anything less like a wallflower than Paddington would be difficult to imagine," he remarked.

Mr. Brown was about to add pessimistically that the evening wasn't over yet, but at that moment there was a roll of drums and all eyes turned in the direction of the bandstand as Norman Church climbed up and grasped the microphone in order to announce the start of the competitions.

Now that the dance was in full swing Mr. Church seemed to have recovered his good humor. "Now I want everyone, but everyone, to join in," he boomed. "There are lots of prizes to be won—lots of dances—and a special mammoth Christmas hamper for the best couple of the evening . . ."

Mr. Church's words had a livening effect on the ball, and during the events which followed he proved his worth as a master of ceremonies. He kept up such a steady flow of patter even Paddington began to get quite worked up, and a marmalade sandwich that he'd brought along to pass the time with lay untouched on the table beside him.

It was while the fun was at its height that Mrs. Smith-Cholmley suddenly caught sight of him peering through a gap in the crowd.

"Come along," she called. "You heard what Mr. Church said. Everyone has to join in."

Paddington gave a start. "Thank you very much, Mrs. Smith-Cholmley," he called excitedly. "I'd like to very much."

"Oh!" Mrs. Smith-Cholmley's face dropped. "I didn't mean . . . that is, I . . . er . . ." She looked at Paddington uneasily and then glanced down at her program. "It *is* the Latin American section next," she said. "I believe you come from that part of the world."

"Darkest Peru," agreed Paddington earnestly.

Mrs. Smith-Cholmley gave a nervous laugh. "I'm not sure if Mr. Weidersein

knows any Peruvian dances," she said, "especially dark ones, but we could try our hand at the rumba if you like."

"Yes, please," said Paddington gratefully. "I don't think I've done one of those before."

Paddington was very keen on anything new, and after slipping the bicycle clips over one of his sleeves for safety, he hastily thrust the marmalade sandwich behind his back, picked up his book, and rose from the table.

"I see you're with it," said Mrs. Smith-Cholmley, mistaking the sudden flurry of movement for a dance step.

Paddington clasped Mrs. Smith-Cholmley firmly with both paws. "I'm never without it," he replied.

Peering round his partner's waist, he consulted the etiquette section of Mr. Church's book again.

"Do you come here often?" he inquired politely.

Mrs. Smith-Cholmley looked down at her feet, both of which were submerged beneath Paddington's paws. "No," she replied, in a tone of voice which suggested she was rather regretting her present visit. "Haven't you got any dancing pumps?" she asked.

Paddington glanced at his bicycle clips. "I haven't even got a bike," he exclaimed, looking most surprised.

Mrs. Smith-Cholmley gave him a strange look. "You really ought to have pumps," she said, breathing heavily as she tried to lift her own and Paddington's feet in time to the music. "It would make things so much easier."

Paddington returned her look. He was beginning to get a bit fed up with the way the conversation was going. It wasn't at all like any of the examples in Mr. Church's book, most of which were to do with sitting out on balconies eating snacks. "I think Mr. Brown's got a spare wheel," he replied helpfully. "Have you got a puncture?"

"No," said Mrs. Smith-Cholmley through her teeth, "I haven't. But if you stand on my feet much longer I'm liable to have one!" Paddington's claws were rather sharp and they were digging deeper and deeper into her instep with every passing moment. "I'd be obliged if you would find somewhere else to put your paws."

Paddington relaxed his grasp on Mrs. Smith-Cholmley and tried jumping up and down experimentally a few times. "I don't think I can," he gasped at last. "I have a feeling they're caught in your straps."

To his surprise, when he looked up again Mrs. Smith-Cholmley's face seemed to have gone a very funny color indeed. And not only that, but she had begun to wriggle in a way which certainly wasn't included in any of Mr. Church's illustrations for the rumba.

"My back!" she shrieked. "My back! There's an awful creature crawling down my back!" Almost turning herself inside out, Mrs. Smith-Cholmley reached behind herself and withdrew something long, golden and glistening, which she gazed at with increasing horror. "It's all wet and sticky . . . ugh!"

Paddington peered at the object dangling between his partner's forefinger and thumb with interest. "I don't think that's a *creature*, Mrs. Smith-Cholmley," he exclaimed. "It's a chunk. I must have dropped my marmalade sandwich down the back of your dress by mistake!"

Unaware of the drama that was taking place behind their hostess's back, Mr. Brown gave his wife a nudge. "Good Lord, Mary," he said. "Look at those two. They're going great guns."

Mrs. Brown turned and glanced across the dance floor. "Well I never!" she exclaimed with pleasure. "Who would have thought it?"

But if Mr. and Mrs. Brown were astonished at the sight of the gyrations on the other side of the floor, the rest of the dancers were positively astounded.

One by one the other couples dropped out in order to take a closer look as Paddington and Mrs. Smith-Cholmley, seemingly moving as one, rocked and wriggled in time to the music.

At a signal from Mr. Church, the man in charge of the spotlight concentrated his beam on the two figures, and as Alf Weidersein began urging his orchestra to greater and greater efforts, the shouts of encouragement, the clapping, and the stamping of feet began to shake the very rafters of the hall.

Paddington himself became more and more confused as he clung to his partner, and far from needing an alarm clock to show him the way he found himself wishing he'd brought a compass, for he hadn't the least idea where he'd started from, let alone where he was going.

From the word go, the winners of the mammoth hamper for the best couple of the evening were never in doubt. Indeed, it would have taken a very brave man to have gone in the face of the cheers which rang out as the music came to an end at last.

For some reason, as soon as willing hands had disentangled Paddington's paws from her shoe straps, Mrs. Smith-Cholmley beat a hasty retreat, and when she did reappear at long last it was in a different dress, but in the excitement this went largely unnoticed.

"A lovely little mover," said Norman Church enthusiastically, turning to Paddington as he presented the prize. "Very fleet. I wouldn't mind using you and your lovely lady in my Formation Dance Team when we do our final demonstration."

Mrs. Smith-Cholmley gave a shudder. "I don't think Mr. Brown and I are open to engagements," she broke in hastily, as she caught a momentary gleam in Paddington's eye.

Paddington nodded his agreement. "I haven't brought any more marmalade sandwiches either, Mr. Church," he said.

"Er . . . yes." Mr. Church looked slightly taken aback. "Talking of marmalade sandwiches," he continued, recovering himself, "what are you going to do with all this food?"

Paddington contemplated the prize for a moment. It was a large hamper. An enormous one, in fact, and it was difficult to picture the many good things there must be inside it.

"I think," he announced, amid general applause, "I'd like to send my half to the Home for Retired Bears in Lima, if it can be got there in time for Christmas. I don't think they can always afford very much extra."

"It'll be done," said Mr. Church. "Even if I have to fly it myself and divide it when I get there."

"There's no need to divide it," said Mrs. Smith-Cholmley, amid renewed applause. "They can have my half as well. After all, there's no time to be lost, and it sounds a very good cause. Especially," she added with a wry smile at her partner, "if the Home's full of bears like Paddington. I wouldn't like to think of them going short of marmalade."

◆ ◆ ◆

"I wonder what Mrs. Smith-Cholmley meant by that last remark?" said Mr. Brown, as they drove home later that night, tired but happy. He glanced across the front seat. "Have you any idea, Paddington?"

Paddington rubbed the steam from the window with his paw and peered out into the night. "I think it was to do with my chunks, Mr. Brown," he replied vaguely.

Mrs. Brown gave a sigh. Life with a bear was full of unsolved mysteries. "I know one thing," she said. "There may be a lot of deserving cases in the Home—and none more so than Aunt Lucy, I'm sure—but I very much doubt if they have any other bears quite like Paddington."

"Impossible!" agreed Mrs. Bird firmly.

"Absolutely!" said Judy.

"With a capital I," added Jonathan.

But Paddington was oblivious to the conversation going on about him. The first snowflakes of winter were already falling and with the promise of more to come, not to mention the approach of Christmas itself, he was already looking forward to things in store.

"I think," he announced to the world in general, "I shall keep my bicycle clips on in bed tonight. I want to keep myself warm in case I have any more adventures!"

Paddington Takes to the Road

The Browns were spending their summer holiday in France for a change, and Paddington soon made lots of new friends in the village where they were staying. His favorite one of all was Monsieur Dupont, the baker.

Paddington went to see Monsieur Dupont every morning, and it was through him that he first learned about bicycle racing.

"Do you mean to say, Monsieur le Bear," he said one day, "that you have never before heard of *le cyclisme*? Everyone should see a real bicycle race—it is most exciting. And you are indeed fortunate, for the one which is passing through our village tomorrow is the greatest of them all."

Monsieur Dupont paused to let his words sink in. "It is called the Tour de France," he continued impressively. "It lasts for twenty days, and people come from all over the world to see it."

Paddington listened carefully as Monsieur Dupont went on to explain what an honor it was to take part in the race and how the racers would be going through the village not once, but several times. "Up the hill," said Monsieur Dupont, "round the houses and down the hill again. In that way everyone will have a chance to see it. Why," he went on, "there is even a prize for the champion rider down the hill into the village. Think of that, Monsieur le Bear!"

At that moment Monsieur Dupont had to serve a customer and so, after thanking him very much for all his trouble, Paddington left the baker's shop and hurried across the square to have another look at the poster that had aroused his interest.

It was a large poster pasted on the side of a shop and it showed a long, winding road crowded with men on bicycles. All the men wore brightly colored cycling outfits and had very earnest expressions on their faces as they bent low over their handlebars. They seemed to have traveled a long way for they all looked hot and tired, and one man was even eating a sandwich as he rode along.

Seeing the sandwich reminded Paddington that it was nearly time for his elevenses, but before he went back into the hotel for his marmalade jar he spent some minutes with Mr. Gruber's phrasebook working out the words in small print at the bottom of the poster.

Paddington was most interested in the idea of anyone being able to win a prize simply by being the fastest person to ride down a hill on a bicycle. Not for the first time since he'd been on holiday he began to wish Mr. Gruber was on hand to explain matters to him.

There was a thoughtful expression on his face as he made his way to where the Browns were sitting outside the hotel, and several times during the next quarter of an hour he absent-mindedly dipped his paw into the cocoa by mistake instead of into his jar of marmalade.

Paddington was late arriving down at the beach that morning, and the others had already been there for some time when he came hurrying across the sand brandishing his bucket and spade and with a look on his face of a job well done.

"What on earth have you been doing, Paddington?" asked Mrs. Brown. "We were getting quite worried."

"Oh," said Paddington, waving his paws vaguely in the direction of the village, "things in general, Mrs. Brown."

Mrs. Bird looked at him suspiciously. Now that he was nearby, she could see several dark patches on his fur which looked remarkably like old oil stains, but before she had time to examine them closely Paddington had gone off again in the direction of the sea.

"You'd better not be late tomorrow, Paddington," called Mr. Brown. "It's the big cycle race. You mustn't miss that."

To everyone's astonishment, Mr. Brown's words had a very strange effect on

Paddington, for he nearly fell over backwards with surprise and his face took on a guilty expression as he collected himself and hurried into the water as fast as he could go, casting some anxious glances over his shoulder.

Mrs. Brown sighed. "There are times," she said, "when I would give anything to be able to read Paddington's mind. I'm sure it would be most interesting."

"*Hmm!*" said Mrs. Bird darkly. "There are times when I'm sure it's much better not to. We should never have a moment's peace. He looked much too pleased with himself just now for my liking."

With that the Browns settled down to enjoy themselves in the sun. With their holiday fast drawing to an end they wanted to make the most of it, and soon Paddington's odd behavior was forgotten for the time being.

But Mrs. Brown was still worrying about the matter when they went to bed that evening. Paddington had disappeared upstairs unusually early, and now there were some strange bumps coming from his room which she didn't like the sound of at all.

After spending some moments with her ear to the wall, she beckoned her husband over. "I think he must be making some marmalade sandwiches, Henry," she said. "Listen."

"Making marmalade sandwiches?" repeated Mr. Brown. "I don't see how you can *hear* anyone make marmalade sandwiches."

"You can with Paddington," said Mrs. Brown. "You can hear the jars going. When he's eating it he just dips his paw in and you can hear the breathing, but when it's sandwiches he uses a spoon and you can hear the clinks as well."

"They must be big ones then," said Mr. Brown vaguely, as he stood up. "He's puffing away like anything. It sounds just like someone blowing up a bicycle tire."

Mr. Brown had a problem of his own at that moment without worrying about Paddington making marmalade sandwiches. He had just made the surprising discovery that his washcloth, which he'd left on the balcony outside the room to dry, had completely disappeared and in its place someone had left a very black and oily piece of rag. It was most strange and he couldn't for the life of him think how it could have come about.

◆ ◆ ◆

Unaware of all the interest he had been causing in the next room, Paddington sat down in the middle of his bedroom floor with a marmalade sandwich in one paw and a large wrench in the other.

On either side of him there were a number of cardboard boxes full of bits and pieces, not to mention a large oil can, a bicycle pump, and several important-looking tools.

In front of him, looking as clean as a new pin and shiny enough for him to see the reflection of his whiskers on the polished surface, stood a small three-wheeled cycle, and there was a blissful expression on Paddington's face as he took several large bites out of the sandwich and surveyed the result of his evening's work.

Paddington had first seen the tricycle some days before standing in a yard outside a garage at the other end of the village, but until Monsieur Dupont explained about the cycle race that morning he hadn't thought any more about the matter.

The man in the garage had been most surprised when Paddington paid him a visit, and at first he had been rather doubtful about renting it to a bear, especially as Paddington had no references apart from some old postcards from his Aunt Lucy.

But Paddington was good at bargaining, and after promising to clean the tricycle he had at last convinced him. The garage man had even lent him the oil can, which had proved most useful, as the tricycle had been standing outside for a number of years and was rather rusty.

Luckily he had found a piece of cloth on the balcony outside Mrs. Brown's room and so he'd been able to clean off the worst of the dirt before getting down to the important job of taking it to pieces and polishing it.

All the same, taking the tricycle to pieces had been a lot easier than assembling it again, and as Paddington finished off his sandwich he noticed to his surprise that he had one or two very odd-looking parts left over in the cardboard boxes.

After tying his Union Jack on the handlebars in preparation for the next day, Paddington put the remains of the marmalade sandwiches into the basket on the handlebars and then climbed onto the saddle with an excited gleam in his eyes.

He had been looking forward to testing the tricycle but as he moved off he soon decided that riding it was much more difficult than it looked, and he began to wish he had longer legs with knees, for it was very hard to pedal and sit on the saddle at the same time.

Apart from that, for some reason which he couldn't quite make out, the tricycle was most difficult to stop, no matter what he pulled. Several times he ran into the wardrobe by mistake, and by the time he had finished there were a number of nasty tire stains on the wallpaper as well. Once, when he rounded a corner at the foot of the bed, the chain came off, nearly throwing him over the handlebars.

After several more turns round the bedroom Paddington fell off and lay where he was for a few moments, mopping his brow with an old handkerchief. Riding tricycles was hot work, especially in such a small space as a hotel bedroom, and after peering at his reflection in the handlebars once or twice he reluctantly decided to call it a day.

All the same, tired though he was, Paddington found it difficult to get to sleep that night. Apart from the fact that he had to lie on his back with his paws in the air in case any oil came off on the sheets, he had a great many things to think about as well.

But there was a contented expression on his face when he did finally nod off. It had been a good evening's work and he was looking forward to the next day. Paddington felt sure that with such a bright and shiny tricycle he would stand a very good chance indeed of winning a prize in the Tour de France cycle race.

◆ ◆ ◆

The Browns were wakened earlier than usual the next morning by the comings and goings in the square outside the hotel. As if by magic, the village was full of important-looking men wearing armbands.

There was an air of great excitement and every few minutes a loudspeaker van passed by and addressed the crowd which had collected on the pavement round the square and at the side of the hill leading out of the village.

The Browns had arranged to meet on the balcony outside Paddington's room, where there was a fine view of the hill, but to their surprise when they gathered there Paddington himself was nowhere to be seen.

"I do hope he won't be long," said Mrs. Brown. "He'll be most upset if he misses any of it."

"I wonder where on earth he can have got to?" said Mr. Brown. "I haven't seen him since breakfast."

"*Hmm!*" said Mrs. Bird, as she looked round the room. "I have my suspicions."

Mrs. Bird's sharp eyes had already noticed the remains of some hastily cleaned tire tracks on the floor. They went round the room several times and then out through the door before finally disappearing in the direction of some stairs which led to the back door of the hotel.

Fortunately for Paddington, before Mrs. Bird had time to say any more there was a burst of clapping from the crowd on the pavement below, and so the subject was forgotten as the Browns looked over the balcony to see what was happening.

"How very odd," said Mrs. Brown, as the clapping grew louder and several people cheered. "They seem to be pointing at us."

The Browns became more and more mystified as they waved back at the crowd.

"I wonder what they mean by 'Vive le Bear'?" said Mr. Brown. "It can't be anything to do with Paddington—he isn't here."

"Goodness only knows," said Mrs. Brown. "I suppose we shall just have to wait and see."

Had they but known, the Browns weren't the only ones to wonder what was going on at that moment, but fortunately for their peace of mind there were several streets and a large number of houses between them and the cause of all the excitement.

At the other end of the village, Paddington was even more puzzled at the way things were going. In fact, the more he tried to think about the matter, the more confused he became. One moment he had been sitting quietly on his tricycle in a side street, peering round the corner every now and then and checking the marmalade sandwiches in the basket on his handlebars as he waited for the race to appear.

The next moment, as the first of the riders came into sight and he pedaled out to join them, everything seemed to go wrong at once.

Before he knew where he was Paddington found himself caught up in a whirlpool of bicycles and shouting people and policemen and bells.

He pedaled as hard as he could and raised his hat to several of the other cyclists, but the harder he pedaled and the more he raised his hat, the louder they shouted and waved back at him, and by then it was much too late to change his mind and turn back even if he'd tried.

Everywhere he looked there were bicycles and men in shorts and striped shirts. There were bicycles in front of him. There were bicycles to the left and bicycles to the right of him. Paddington was much too busy pedaling for dear life to look back, but he was sure there were bicycles behind him as well because he could hear heavy breathing and the sound of bells ringing.

In the excitement someone handed him a bottle of milk as he went past, and in trying to take the bottle with one paw and raise his hat with the other, Paddington had to let go of the handlebars. He went twice round a statue in the middle of the street before joining the stream of cyclists once more as they swept round a corner onto a road leading out of the village.

Luckily the road was uphill and most of the other cyclists were tired after their long ride, so that by standing on the pedals and jumping up and down as fast as he could he was able to keep up with them.

It was as they reached the top of the hill and rounded another corner leading back down into the village that things suddenly took a decided turn for the worse. Just as he was about to sit back on the saddle and have a rest while he got his second wind, Paddington found to his surprise that without even having to turn the pedals he was beginning to gather speed.

In fact, he hardly had time to wave to the crowd before he found himself starting to overtake the riders in front. He passed one, then another, and then a whole bunch. The cyclists looked quite startled as Paddington flashed by, and all the time the cheering from the spectators on the side of the road grew louder. Quite a number recognized him and they called out words of encouragement, but by then Paddington was much too worried to notice.

He tried pulling as hard as he could on the brake lever but nothing happened, in fact, if anything he seemed to go faster than ever, and he began to wish he hadn't used quite so much oil on the moving parts when he'd cleaned them.

By then the pedals were going round so fast that he sat back on the saddle and hurriedly lifted up his feet in case his legs fell off.

It was as he gave the brake lever an extra hard pull that he had his second big shock of the day, for it suddenly came away in his paw. Paddington rang his bell frantically and waved the lever as he overtook the last of the riders in front.

"Apply your brakes, Monsieur le Bear!" yelled a man in English as he recognized the Union Jack on Paddington's bike.

"I don't think I can," cried Paddington, looking most upset as he shot past. "My lever's come off in my paw by mistake and I think I've left some of the bits in my box at the hotel!"

Paddington clung to the handlebars of his tricycle as he hurtled on down the hill towards the village square. All the villagers were most excited when they saw who was in the lead and a great cheer went up as he came into view, but as he lifted the brim of his hat and peered out anxiously, all Paddington could make out was a sea of white faces and a blurred picture of some buildings looming up ahead which he didn't like the look of at all.

But if Paddington was worried the Browns were even more alarmed.

"Good heavens!" exclaimed Mr. Brown. "It's Paddington!"

"He's heading straight for Monsieur Dupont's shop," cried Mrs. Brown.

"I can't watch," said Mrs. Bird, closing her eyes.

"Why on earth doesn't he put his brakes on?" exclaimed Mr. Brown.

"He can't!" exclaimed Jonathan. "His brake lever's come off!"

It was Monsieur Dupont himself who saved Paddington. Right at the very last moment his voice rose above the roar of the crowd.

"This way, Monsieur le Bear," he cried, as he flung open the big double gates at the side of his shop. "This way!"

And before the astonished gaze of the onlookers Paddington shot through them and disappeared from view.

As the rest of the cyclists sped past unheeded, the crowd surged forward and gathered round Monsieur Dupont's shop. The Browns only just managed to force their way through to the front before a gasp went up from everyone as a small white figure came into view through the doors.

Even Paddington looked very worried when he saw his reflection in Monsieur Dupont's window and he pinched himself several times to make sure he was all right before raising his hat to the crowd, revealing a small round patch of brown fur.

"I'm not a ghost," he explained, when all the cheering had died down. "I think I must have landed on one of Mr. Dupont's sacks of flour!"

And as the crowd gathered round Paddington to shake him by the paw, Monsieur Dupont echoed the feelings of them all.

"We of St. Castille," he cried, "shall remember for many years to come the day the Tour de France passed through our village."

There was a great deal of celebrating in the village that evening and everyone applauded when the mayor announced that he was giving Paddington a special prize, with as many buns as he could manage into the bargain.

"Not for the fastest rider *through* the village," he said, amid cheers and laughter, "but certainly for the fastest down the hill! We are very proud that someone from our village should have won the prize."

Paddington felt very pleased with himself as he sat up in bed that night surrounded by buns. Apart from having one paw in a sling, he was beginning to feel stiff after all his pedaling, and there were still traces of flour left on his fur despite several baths.

But as the mayor had explained, it was the first time in history that he could remember a bear winning a prize in the Tour de France race, and it was something to be proud of.

The next morning the Browns were up early again for it was time to start their journey back to England. To their surprise everyone else in the village seemed to be up as well in order to send them on their way.

Monsieur Dupont was the last to say goodbye, and he looked very sad as the Browns got ready to leave. "It will seem quiet without you, Monsieur le Bear," he said, shaking Paddington by the paw. "But I hope we shall meet again one day."

"I hope so too, Mr. Dupont," said Paddington earnestly, as he waved goodbye and climbed into the car.

Although he was looking forward to being back home again and to telling Mr. Gruber all about his adventures abroad, Paddington felt very sorry at having to say goodbye to everyone, especially Monsieur Dupont.

"All good things come to an end sooner or later," said Mrs. Brown, as they drove away. "And the nicer it is the sooner it seems to end."

"But if they didn't end," said Mrs. Bird wisely, "we shouldn't have other things to look forward to."

Paddington nodded thoughtfully as he peered out of the car window. He had enjoyed his holiday in France no end, but it *was* nice knowing that each day brought something new.

"That's the best of being a bear," said Mrs. Bird. "Things happen to bears."

Chapter 24

◆ ◆ ◆

Paddington Steps Out

M rs. Brown looked out of the car window. "If you want my opinion," she said, lowering her voice so that the occupants of the back seat, and one occupant in particular, shouldn't hear, "bringing Paddington with us is asking for trouble. You know what happened when he went to Jonathan's school."

"That wasn't exactly a disaster," said Mr. Brown mildly. "If I remember rightly he saved the day. If it hadn't been for him, the alumni would never have won their cricket match."

"Playing in a cricket match isn't the same as watching ballet," replied Mrs. Brown. "He'll never sit quietly through a whole afternoon of it. Something's bound to happen."

She gave a sigh. Ever since Paddington had taken part in an epic cricket match at Jonathan's school, Judy had been clamoring for him to visit her school in turn, and Mrs. Brown knew that she was fighting a losing battle.

Having a bear in the family gave both Jonathan and Judy a certain amount of prestige among their fellow pupils and Judy was anxious to catch up on the lead at present held by her brother. All the same, as they drew nearer and nearer to Judy's school, Mrs. Brown began to look more and more worried.

"Good heavens!" exclaimed Mr. Brown suddenly as they turned a corner and passed through some wrought iron gates in a gray stone wall. He waved his hand towards a seething mass of girls in uniform as he brought the car to a halt. "What's this—some sort of reception committee?"

"What did I tell you?" said Mrs. Brown, as the familiar figure of Judy detached itself from the crowd and came forward to greet them. "It's started already."

"Nonsense!" said Mr. Brown. All the same he cast some anxious glances towards the paintwork on his car as he helped the others out and exchanged greetings with his daughter.

Paddington, as he clambered out of the back seat, looked even more surprised as he stood blinking in the strong sunlight listening to the cheers, and he raised his hat several times in response to the cries.

"Come along, Paddington," said Judy, grabbing his paw. "You've lots of people to meet *and* we've got to pay a visit to the cafeteria. I told Mrs. Beedle, the lady in charge, all about you and she's made some special marmalade sandwiches."

"Mrs. Beedle's made some marmalade sandwiches!" exclaimed Paddington, looking most impressed. However, before he had time to pursue the matter, the throng of girls closed in behind him and he felt himself being propelled gently but firmly in the direction of a small building which stood to one side of the quadrangle in front of the school.

As the milling crowd of figures disappeared through the door of the cafeteria, Mrs. Brown looked towards a large, brightly colored poster on a board near the main gate. "I thought this Russian dancer they're having down, Sergei Oblomov, was supposed to be the guest of honor," she remarked. "I don't think he'll like it if

he turns up and there's no one here. I'm sure all these girls were meant for him, not Paddington."

"Talk of the devil," said Mr. Brown, as a large, important-looking black car swept in through the gates and came to a halt a few yards away. "I have a feeling this *is* him."

Pretending to study the scenery, the Browns nevertheless watched with interest as the door of the car opened and a tall figure dressed in a black cloak alighted and stood for a moment with one hand in the air looking expectantly all around.

"Gosh!" said Jonathan a few moments later as the sound of a door being slammed echoed round the quadrangle and the car swept past them in a cloud of dust towards the school building. "He didn't look in a very good mood."

"Black as ink," agreed Mr. Brown. "It wasn't exactly what you might call a good entrance. Not so much as a pigeon cooed."

"I don't suppose you'd like it," said Mrs. Brown, "if you were a famous dancer and you had your thunder stolen by a bear. Especially one stuffing himself with marmalade sandwiches in a school cafeteria."

"He doesn't know it's a bear," reasoned Mr. Brown. "He's never even met Paddington."

"No," said Mrs. Brown decidedly, as they made their way towards the school buildings, "he hasn't. And if I have my way he's not going to either."

She cast some anxious glances in the direction of the cafeteria as they passed by. Several times the ominous sound of cheering had come from the open windows and one or two of them had been decidedly loud, rather as if things were getting out of control.

All the same, as they seated themselves in the school hall some time later, even Mrs. Brown found it hard to fault Paddington's appearance. Admittedly there were still one or two traces of marmalade on his whiskers and his fur had lost some of its smooth sheen, but all in all he looked unusually well behaved as he settled himself at the end of the row by the aisle and examined his program with interest.

"You know, I'm really looking forward to this," said Mrs. Bird with enthusiasm, as she made herself comfortable. "I like ballet dancing."

The others looked at their housekeeper in surprise as a faraway look came into her eyes. "I haven't seen any good dancing for I don't know how many years."

"I'm not sure you're going to now," whispered Mr. Brown, as the curtain rose to reveal a woodland glade and several small figures dressed as toadstools.

"It's the Juniors," whispered Judy. "They're doing their nature dance."

Paddington opened his suitcase, took out his opera glasses, and peered at the stage with interest.

"Are you enjoying it?" whispered Judy.

Paddington thought for a moment. "It's all right," he announced after some thought. "But I can't hear what they're saying."

"People don't *say* anything in ballet," hissed Judy. "They mime it all. You have to guess what they're doing by the dancing."

Paddington sank back into his seat. Although he didn't want to hurt Judy's feelings by saying so, he didn't think much of ballet at all. As far as he could see it was just a lot of people running after each other on the stage, and apart from not saying anything, which made it all rather difficult to follow, he began to wonder why they didn't get taller dancers in the first place as some of the older girls in particular seemed to spend most of the time standing on their toes. However, he was a polite bear and he applauded dutifully at the end of each item.

"I must say that swan took a long time to die," said Mr. Brown, as the lights went up at long last to herald the intermission. "I thought she was never going to get it over with."

"I liked the flying ballet," said Mrs. Brown, amid general agreement. "I thought that was very well done."

"I'd like to go up in the air on a wire like that," said Jonathan. "I bet it's super."

Judy handed Paddington her program. "It's the famous Russian dancer next," she said. "Look—there's his picture."

Paddington peered at the program with interest. "Surge Oblomov!" he exclaimed in surprise.

"It's not *Surge*," said Judy. "It's pronounced Surguy."

"Sir Guy Oblomov," repeated Paddington, looking most impressed as he studied the picture. "I don't think I've ever seen a lord doing a ballet dance before."

"He isn't a lord, he's a . . ." Judy gave a sigh as she sought for the right words. Sometimes explaining things to Paddington became complicated out of all proportion.

"Well, whatever he is," said Mrs. Bird, coming to her rescue, "I'm really looking forward to it. It's a great treat."

"Oh no!" exclaimed Judy suddenly, as a girl from the row behind whispered something in her ear. "I'm not sure if he's going to appear after all. They're having some trouble backstage."

"What!" exclaimed Paddington hotly. "Sir Guy Oblomov's not going to appear!"

"Oh dear," said Mrs. Bird. "How very disappointing."

Paddington stared at the drawn curtains on the stage, hardly able to believe his ears as everyone began talking at once. Judy's words had reached several other people nearby and soon a buzz of excitement went round the hall.

"It's something to do with no one being at the gates to meet him," explained the girl in the seat behind. "He's a bit temperamental and it rather upset him."

Mr. and Mrs. Brown exchanged glances. "I told you so, Henry," said Mrs. Brown. "I said if we brought Paddington something would happen."

"Well, you can't really blame poor old Paddington for this," replied Mr. Brown indignantly. "It's not his fault if everyone wanted to meet him instead of some blessed ballet dancer chap. After all—" Mr. Brown suddenly broke off in midsentence. "That's funny," he said, as he looked along the aisle. "Talking of Paddington, where's he got to?"

"He was here a second ago," said Judy, looking all around.

"Look!" cried Jonathan, pointing down the aisle. "There he is!"

The Browns followed the direction of Jonathan's arm and were just in time to see a small figure disappear through a door at the side of the stage. From where they were sitting it wasn't possible to see the expression on Paddington's face but there was a determined slant to his hat and a look about his duffle coat which seemed to bode ill for anyone who got in his way.

"Don't you think you'd better go after him, Judy?" said Mrs. Brown anxiously.

"Too late," groaned Judy. "Did you see who was behind the door? Miss Grimshaw!"

Judy sank lower and lower into her seat as she contemplated the awful prospect of Paddington coming face to face with her principal, although had she but known, Miss Grimshaw, weighed down by all the worries backstage, seemed almost glad to find someone from outside the school she could talk to.

"Are you Russian?" she asked hopefully, after Paddington had introduced himself.

"Well, I am in a bit of a hurry," admitted Paddington, raising his hat politely. "I've come to see Sir Guy."

Miss Grimshaw looked at him suspiciously. "I said Russian," she explained. "Not *rushing*. And I'm not at all sure Mr. Oblomov will see you. I was hoping you might be Russian so that you could talk to him in his own language and make him feel more at home, but if you're not, I'd rather you didn't."

"Mrs. Bird's very upset," replied Paddington.

"I'm sure she is," said Miss Grimshaw. "We're all upset. Mr. Oblomov's upset. Deirdre Shaw's upset."

"*Deirdre Shaw?*" echoed Paddington, looking most surprised.

"She was supposed to partner Mr. Oblomov in the *pas de deux*," explained Miss Grimshaw. "Then when Mr. Oblomov said he wouldn't dance, she ran off to the dormitory in tears and no one's seen her since."

While Miss Grimshaw was speaking, a nearby door opened and a tall, imposing figure in black tights emerged.

"I hov changed my mind," announced Mr. Oblomov, waving his hand imperiously as he did a series of knee-bending exercises. "I will not disappoint my public. First I will dance my famous solo from the *Swan Lake*. Then I will perform the *pas de deux*. I trust everything is ready, no?"

"No," exclaimed Miss Grimshaw. "I mean . . . that is to say . . . yes. I'm sure it will be."

Miss Grimshaw's usual icy calm seemed to have deserted her for once as Sergei Oblomov strode past heading for the stage.

"Oh dear," she exclaimed. "Now he's changed his mind *again*—and Deirdre Shaw's disappeared. What he's going to say when he finds he's without a partner in the second half I shudder to think."

As the school orchestra started up and the curtain rose to a tremendous round of applause, Miss Grimshaw rushed off wringing her hands, leaving Paddington staring, with a very thoughtful expression on his face indeed, in the direction of the open door leading to Sergei Oblomov's dressing room.

It was an expression that the Browns, had they been there, would have recognized immediately. But fortunately for their peace of mind, they, like practically everyone else in the school, had their attention riveted to the stage.

Even Mr. Brown sat up in his seat and clapped as loudly as anyone as Sergei Oblomov executed one perfect pirouette after another, spinning round and round so fast it left the audience breathless. And when he followed this with a series of breathtaking arabesques everyone gasped with admiration and the rafters of the hall fairly shook with the ovation which greeted the end of this display.

As the applause died away and Sergei Oblomov stood for a moment motionless in the beam from a single spotlight, Mrs. Bird gave a quick glance at her program. "It's the *pas de deux* now," she whispered.

"Golly, I hope they've found Deirdre Shaw," said Judy in a low voice as the music started up. "There's going to be an awful row if they haven't."

"It's all right," said Mr. Brown. "I think I can see someone lurking at the side of the stage."

Judy followed the direction of Mr. Brown's gaze and then jumped up from her seat in alarm.

"Uh-oh!" she exclaimed. "That's not Deirdre Shaw. That's . . ."

"Paddington!" exclaimed the rest of the family, joining her in a chorus as the shadowy figure moved onto the stage and into the light.

"Mercy me!" cried Mrs. Bird. "What on earth is that bear up to now?"

Her words were lost in the gasp of astonishment which went up all around them as Paddington advanced towards the centre of the stage, placed his suitcase carefully in front of the footlights, and then raised his hat politely to the several members of the audience in the front row who began halfheartedly to applaud.

"Oh dear, I wish he wouldn't wear that old hat," said Mrs. Brown.

"And what on earth's he got on his legs?" asked Mrs. Bird.

"Looks like some kind of sacking to me," said Mr. Brown.

"They're not sacks," said Judy. "They're tights."

"Tights?" echoed Mr. Brown. "They don't look very tight to me. They look as if they're going to come down any moment."

The Browns watched in horror as Paddington, having ventured one bow too many, hurriedly replaced his hat and grabbed hold of the roll of material which hung round his waist in large folds.

Now, for the first time since he'd decided to lend a paw with the ballet, he was beginning to wish he'd resisted the temptation to use the pair of tights which he'd found hanging on the back of Mr. Oblomov's dressing room door.

Bears' legs being rather short put him at a disadvantage to start with, but as far as he could make out, Sergei Oblomov's legs were twice as long as anyone else's so that an unusually large amount of surplus material had to be lost at the top.

Apart from tying a piece of string round his waist, Paddington had hopefully made use of several thumbtacks which he'd found on a notice board at the back of the stage, but most of these seemed to have fallen out, so he had to spend moments making last-minute adjustments to a large safety pin that he'd put on in case of an emergency.

It was at this moment that Sergei Oblomov, oblivious to all that had been going on, finished executing a particularly long and difficult pirouette near a pillar at the back of the stage and came hurrying down towards him. He stood for a moment poised on one foot, his eyes closed as he prepared himself for the big moment.

Paddington raised his hat politely once again and then took hold of one of Mr. Oblomov's outstretched hands and shook it warmly with his paw.

"Good afternoon, Sir Guy," he exclaimed. "I've come to do the *pas de deux*."

Sergei Oblomov seemed suddenly to freeze in his position. For a brief moment, in fact, he seemed almost to have turned into stone and Paddington looked at him rather anxiously, but then several things happened to him in quick succession.

First he opened his eyes, then he closed them and a shiver passed through his body, starting at his toes and traveling up to his head, almost as if he had been shot. Then he opened his eyes again and stared distastefully at his hand. It was warm under the lights and some kind of sticky substance seemed to have transferred itself from Paddington's paw.

"It's all right, Sir Guy," explained Paddington, wiping his paw hastily on one of the folds of his tights. "It's only marmalade. I forgot to wash it off when I came out of the cafeteria."

If Mr. Oblomov knew what marmalade was or, for that matter, if he'd ever heard of a cafeteria, he gave no sign. A shiver again seemed to pass through his body and as the music reached a crescendo he closed his eyes and with a supreme effort prepared himself once more for the *pas de deux*.

Feeling very pleased that things seemed to have turned out all right in the end,

Paddington took hold of Sergei Oblomov's outstretched hand and bent down to pick up his suitcase.

The next moment it felt as if he was in the center of an earthquake, a tornado and a barrage of thunderbolts all rolled into one.

First it seemed as if his arm had been torn out of its socket; then he felt himself spinning round and round like a top; finally he landed, still spinning, in a heap on the floor of the stage some distance away from Mr. Oblomov.

For a moment he lay where he was gasping for breath, and then he struggled to his feet just in time to see a vague figure in tights heading towards him through the glare of the footlights. As he focused on the scene Paddington noticed a nasty-looking gleam in Sergei Oblomov's eyes which he didn't like the look of at all and so he hurriedly sat down again.

Mr. Oblomov came to a halt and stared down at the figure on the floor. "I cannot go on," he exclaimed gloomily. "For one zing, you hov too much shortness, and for zee second thing, your *entrechats*, zey are not clean."

"My *entrechats* are not clean!" exclaimed Paddington hotly. "But I had a bath last night."

"I do not mean zey are dirty," hissed Mr. Oblomov. "I mean zey should be clean—snappy—like so!"

Without further ado he threw himself into the air, beat his legs together, crossed them in time to the music, and then uncrossed them again as he landed gracefully on one foot facing the audience.

Paddington looked rather doubtful as the applause rang through the hall. "It's a bit difficult when you've only got paws, Sir Guy," he exclaimed. "But I'll have a try."

Closing his eyes as he'd seen Mr. Oblomov do, Paddington jumped into the air, made a halfhearted attempt to cross his legs and then, as his tights began to slip, landed rather heavily on the stage. As he did so, to everyone's surprise he suddenly shot up into the air, his legs crossing and uncrossing, almost as if he'd been fired from a cannon.

"Good gracious!" exclaimed someone near the Browns, "that young bear's done a triple!"

"A sixer," contradicted an elderly gentleman knowledgeably, as Paddington landed and then shot up in the air again with a loud cry. "Bravo!" he called, trying to make himself heard above the applause.

Even Sergei Oblomov began to look impressed as Paddington executed several more *entrechats*, each one higher and more complicated than the one which came before. Then, to show he wasn't beaten, he himself gave a tremendous leap into the air, changed his legs over, beat them together, changed them back again, beat them together once more, and then, to a roar from the audience, crossed them once again before landing on the stage.

Paddington, who had been spending the last few seconds sitting on the stage peering at one of his paws, jumped up with a loud cry which echoed round the rafters as Sergei Oblomov landed heavily on his other paw.

If the applause for Sergei Oblomov's *entrechat* had been loud it was nothing compared to that which greeted Paddington as he shot up into the air once more, waving his paws wildly to and fro, crossing and uncrossing them and bringing them together before he landed and then catapulted up again almost out of sight.

This time Sergei Oblomov himself had to acknowledge he'd met his match and with a graceful bow which brought murmurs of approval from the audience he stood back and joined in the applause as the music finally came to an end, and with Paddington's leaps growing higher and wilder with every passing second the curtain came down.

"Well," said Mr. Brown as the applause finally subsided. "It may not have been the best ballet I've ever seen but it was certainly the most exciting."

"Haven't seen anything like it since the Cossacks," agreed the elderly gentleman nearby. "Five grand royales in a row!"

Thoroughly surprised by the events of the afternoon the Browns tried to make their way backstage, but what with the speeches and the crowds of girls who came up to Judy in order to congratulate her on Paddington's performance, it was some time before they were able to force their way through the door at the side of the stage. When they did finally break through, they were even more surprised to find that Paddington had been removed to the school sickroom for what was called "urgent first aid."

"Oh dear, I hope he hasn't broken anything," said Mrs. Brown anxiously as they hurried across the quadrangle. "Some of those jumps he did were very high."

"More likely to have slipped on a marmalade chunk," said Mrs. Bird darkly as they hurried into the sickroom. But even Mrs. Bird looked worried when she caught sight of Paddington lying on a bed with his two back paws sticking up in the air swathed in bandages.

"I can't understand it," said Miss Grimshaw, as she came forward to greet them. "Both his back paws are full of holes. I really must find the nurse and see what she's got to say."

"Holes?" echoed the Browns.

"Holes," said Miss Grimshaw. "Quite small ones. Almost as if he's got woodworm. Not that he could have of course," she added hastily as a groan came from the direction of the bed.

"Such a shame after the magnificent performance he gave. I doubt if we shall see the like again."

As Miss Grimshaw hurried off in search of the nurse, Mrs. Bird gave a snort.

Something about Paddington's leaps on the stage had aroused her suspicions and now her eagle eyes had spotted a number of small shiny objects under the bed that so far no one else had seen.

"Bears who try to pin their tights up with thumbtacks," she said sternly, "mustn't be surprised when they fall out. And," she added, "they mustn't be disappointed if they step on them into the bargain and have to stay in the hospital and miss the special marmalade dessert that's waiting for them at home."

Paddington sat up in bed. "I think perhaps they're getting better now," he said hastily.

Being an invalid with everyone fussing round was rather nice. On the other hand, marmalade dessert, particularly Mrs. Bird's marmalade dessert, was even nicer.

"But it's no good if you want to carry on dancing," warned Mrs. Bird, as he clambered out of bed and tested his paws on the floor. "It's much too rich and heavy. In fact, I'm not sure that you oughtn't to go on a diet."

But Mrs. Bird's words fell on empty air as Paddington disappeared through the door in the direction of the car with remarkable haste for one who'd only just risen from a sickbed.

"Perhaps it's as well," said Mr. Brown gravely, as the others followed. "I can't really picture Paddington embarking on a career as a ballet dancer."

"All those exercises," agreed Mrs. Brown with a shudder.

"And those tights," said Judy.

"And all that leaping about," added Mrs. Bird. "If you ask me it's much better to be simply a bear who likes his marmalade."

"Especially," said Jonathan, amid general agreement, "if you happen to be a bear called Paddington."

◆ ◆ ◆

Chapter 25

Paddington and the *Pardon*

The Browns were on holiday. They were staying in a French village, and in no time at all it seemed as if they had always lived there. The news that a young English bear gentleman was staying at the hotel quickly spread, and Paddington was soon a popular figure in the streets, especially in the early mornings when he did his shopping before going down to the beach.

He paid a visit to his new friend, Monsieur Dupont, most days. Monsieur Dupont spoke very good English and they had several chats together on the subject of buns. Monsieur Dupont not only showed Paddington round his ovens but he also promised to bake some special English buns for his elevenses into the bargain.

"After all," he explained, "it is not every day we have a bear staying in St. Castille." And he put a notice in his shop window saying that in future special buns made according to the recipe of a young English bear of quality would be on sale.

There were so many new and interesting things to see and do that Paddington had to sit up late in bed several nights running in order to write everything in his scrapbook while it was still fresh in his mind.

One morning he was wakened early by the sound of shouting and banging outside the hotel, and when he looked out of the window he discovered to his

◆ 253 ◆

astonishment that a great change had come over the village.

It was always busy, with people hurrying to and fro about their daily tasks, but on this particular morning it seemed to be twice as busy as usual. Even the people were dressed in quite a different way. Instead of their blue overalls and red jerseys, the fishermen all had on their best suits, and the women and girls were wearing dresses covered in stiff white lace with tall lace hats to match.

Nearly all the fruit and vegetable stalls had gone and their place had been taken by other stalls decorated with colored flags and striped awnings and laden with boxes of candy and row upon row of wax candles.

It was all most unusual, and after a quick wash Paddington hurried downstairs to investigate the matter.

Madame Penet, the owner of the hotel, was at her desk in the entrance hall when Paddington entered and she looked at him rather doubtfully when he consulted his phrasebook. Madame Penet's English was no better than Paddington's French and things always seemed to go wrong when they tried to talk to each other.

"It is," she began, in reply to his question, "how do you say? . . . a *pardon*."

"That's all right," said Paddington politely. "I only wondered what was happening. It looks very interesting."

Madame Penet nodded. "That is right," she said. "It is, how do you say? . . . a *pardon*."

Paddington gave Madame Penet a hard stare as he backed away. Although he was a polite bear, he was beginning to get a bit fed up with raising his hat and saying "pardon" in return, and so he hurried outside and across the square in order to consult Monsieur Dupont on the subject.

To his surprise, when he entered the shop he made an even more startling discovery, for in place of the white smock and hat that Monsieur Dupont usually wore, he had on a very smart dark blue uniform covered in gold braid.

Monsieur Dupont laughed when he saw the expression on Paddington's face. "It is all to do with the *pardon*, Monsieur le Bear," he said.

And he went on to explain that in France *pardon* was the name given to a very special festival, and that in Brittany in particular there were *pardons* for many different reasons. There were *pardons* for fishermen and farmers, and there was even a *pardon* for the birds, not to mention horses and cattle.

"In the morning," said Monsieur Dupont, "there is always a procession, when everyone goes to church, and afterwards there is much celebration.

"This year," he went on, "we have a fair and a fireworks display. Why, there is even a parade of the village band!"

Monsieur Dupont drew himself up to his full height. "That is why I am in uniform, Monsieur le Bear," he exclaimed proudly. "For I am the leader of the band!"

Paddington looked most impressed as he listened to Monsieur Dupont, and after thanking him for all his trouble, he hurried back to the hotel in order to tell the others.

Most days the Browns went down to the beach, but when they heard Paddington's news they quickly changed their plans. After a hurried breakfast they joined the rest of the villagers in going to church, and that afternoon, by popular vote, they made their way towards a field just outside the village where the fair was taking place.

Paddington stood in a trance as he gazed at the sight which met his eyes. It was the first time he had been to a fair and he didn't remember ever having seen or heard anything quite like it before.

There were huge wheels soaring up into the sky. There were gaily painted swings and slides. There were merry-go-rounds carrying dozens of shrieking, laughing people round and round as they clung to wooden horses painted all the colors of the rainbow. There were coconut-shies and sideshows. Everywhere there were colored lights flashing on and off, and in the center of it all there was a huge organ playing happy music as it let out clouds of steam. In fact, there were so many things crammed into such a small space that it was difficult to decide what to do first.

In the end, after testing the slides and swings a number of times, Paddington turned his attention to one of the merry-go-rounds, and when he discovered that bears under sixteen were allowed on for half price on *pardon* days, he had several more goes for good measure.

It was when he came off the merry-go-round for the last time and stood watching Mr. Brown, Jonathan and Judy while they had a go, that he suddenly spied a most interesting-looking small striped tent which stood slightly apart from the rest

of the fair. There were several notices pinned to the outside, most of them printed in foreign languages, but there was one written in English which caught his eye at once, and he read it carefully. It said:

MADAME ZAZA
International Fortuneteller
PALMS READ
CRYSTAL-GAZING
SATISFACTION GUARANTEED

Pasted across the bottom was a smaller notice which had the words ENGLISH SPOKEN printed in red.

Mrs. Brown followed Paddington's gaze as he lifted up the tent flap and peered inside. "It says she reads palms," she remarked doubtfully, "but I should be careful—paws might be more expensive."

Mrs. Brown wasn't at all sure it would be a good thing for Paddington to have his fortune told—he got into enough trouble as it was without looking into the future. But before she had time to make him change his mind the tent flap had closed behind him. Paddington had never before heard of anyone having their paw read and he was anxious to investigate the matter.

After the strong sunlight it was dark inside the tent, and as he groped his way forward he had to blink several times before he could make out a shadowy figure sitting behind a small, velvet-covered table.

Madame Zaza had her eyes closed and she was breathing heavily. After waiting impatiently for a few moments Paddington gave her a poke with his paw and then raised his hat.

"Please," he announced, "I've come to have my paw read."

Madame Zaza jumped. *"Comment!"* she exclaimed hoarsely.

"Come on?" said Paddington, looking puzzled. There was hardly space inside the tent for the two of them, let alone room to go anywhere, so he tried climbing on the table as he explained once again what he had come for.

"Mind my crystal ball," cried Madama Zaza, breaking into English as the table rocked. "They're very expensive.

"I didn't realize you were a foreigner," she continued. "Otherwise I would have spoken to you in your own language."

"A foreigner!" exclaimed Paddington hotly. "I'm not a foreigner. I've come from England!"

"You're a foreigner when you're in another country," said Madame Zaza sternly. "And '*comment*' doesn't mean you're supposed to climb all over my table!"

Paddington sighed as he climbed down off the table. He didn't think much of French as a language. Everything seemed to have the opposite meaning to the one he was used to.

"Anyway, I don't usually do bears," said Madame Zaza cautiously. "But as you're on vacation, if you like to cross my palm with silver I'll see what I can do to oblige."

Paddington undid his suitcase and taking out ten pence passed it over Madame Zaza's outstretched hand before quickly putting it away again. Having his paw read was much cheaper than he had expected.

Madame Zaza gave Paddington a startled look. "You're supposed to stop halfway and drop it in," she exclaimed.

Paddington gave Madame Zaza one of his special hard stares in return before he undid his suitcase once again and handed back the ten pence.

"I don't usually take foreign coins either," said Madame Zaza, biting the ten pence to make sure it was good, "but it seems to be all right. Let me see your paw. I'll read the lines on that first."

As Paddington held out his paw, Madame Zaza took it in her hand. After staring at it disbelievingly for a moment, she rubbed her eyes and then took a magnifying glass out of her pocket.

"You seem to have a very long life line," she said, "even for a bear. I've never seen such a thick one before, and it runs the whole length of your paw."

Paddington followed her gaze with interest. "I don't think it *is* a life line," he said. "I think it's an old marmalade chunk."

"*An old marmalade chunk?*" repeated Madame Zaza in a dazed voice.

"That's right," said Paddington. "It got stuck on at breakfast and I must have forgotten to wash it off."

Madame Zaza passed a trembling hand across her brow. It seemed to be getting very hot inside the tent. "Well," she said, "I certainly can't read your paw if it's covered in old marmalade peel. I'm afraid you'll have to pay extra and have the crystal ball."

Paddington looked at her suspiciously as he withdrew another ten pence from his case. He was beginning to wish he hadn't thought of having his fortune told.

Madame Zaza snatched the money from him and then drew the crystal ball towards her. "First you must tell me when your birthday is," she said.

"June and December," replied Paddington.

"June *and* December?" repeated Madame Zaza. "But you can't have *two* birthdays. Nobody has more than one."

"Bears do," said Paddington firmly. "Bears always have two birthdays."

"Then that makes it more difficult," said Madame Zaza. "And I certainly can't guarantee results."

She waved her hands through the air several times and then stared hard at the ball. "It says you are going on a journey," she began, in a strange, distant voice, "quite soon!" She looked up at Paddington and added hopefully, "I think you ought to start right away."

"I'm going on a journey?" exclaimed Paddington, looking most surprised. "But I've only just been on one. I've come all the way from Windsor Gardens! Does it say where I'm going?"

Madame Zaza consulted her glass once more, and as she did so a crafty look came over her face. "No," she said, "but wherever it is things will certainly go off with a bang!"

Madame Zaza had remembered the fireworks display that was due to take place that evening, and it seemed a very good answer to Paddington's question. But as she gazed at her crystal ball a puzzled look gradually came over her face. After breathing on the glass she gave it a polish with the end of her shawl. "I don't remember this ever happening before," she exclaimed excitedly. "I can see another bear!"

"I don't think it's another one," said Paddington, as he stood on his suitcase and peered over Madame Zaza's shoulder. "I think it's me. But I can't see anything else."

Madame Zaza hastily covered the crystal ball with her shawl. "It's fading," she said crossly. "I think my palm needs crossing again."

"*Again?*" said Paddington suspiciously. "But it's only just been crossed!"

"Again," said Madame Zaza firmly. "Ten pence doesn't last very long."

Paddington looked very disappointed as he backed away from Madame Zaza, and he hurriedly dropped the tent flap before she could ask for any more money.

The Browns were standing by the merry-go-round chatting with Monsieur Dupont when Paddington came out of the tent and they looked up inquiringly as he hurried across to join them.

"Well, dear?" asked Mrs. Brown. "How did you get on?"

"Not very well, Mrs. Brown," said Paddington sadly. "It wasn't very good value. I think my lines must have been crossed."

Monsieur Dupont raised his hands in sympathy. "Ah, Monsieur le Bear," he exclaimed. "If only our troubles could be solved by looking into a crystal ball life would be very simple. I, too, would like to see into the future!"

Monsieur Dupont had a very worried look on his face and he had just been explaining to the Browns all about a problem which had to do with the celebrations that evening.

"Once a year," he said, as he repeated the story for Paddington's benefit, "we have a parade of the village band and tonight, of all nights, the man who plays the big drum has been taken ill!"

"What a shame," said Mrs. Brown. "It must be very disappointing."

"Can't you find *anyone* else?" asked Mr. Brown.

Monsieur Dupont shook his head sadly. "They are all much too busy enjoying themselves at the fair," he said. "And already we are late for rehearsals."

As he listened to the others talking Paddington's eyes got larger and larger, and several times he looked over his shoulder at Madame Zaza's tent as if he could hardly believe his ears.

"Perhaps I could help, Mr. Dupont," he said excitedly when the baker had finished talking.

"*You*, Monsieur le Bear?" said Monsieur Dupont, looking most surprised. "But what could you do?"

Everyone listened with growing astonishment as Paddington explained about his fortune and how Madame Zaza had said he would be going on a journey and that everything would go off with a bang.

When he had finished, Monsieur Dupont stroked his chin thoughtfully. "It is certainly most strange," he said. "It is *extraordinaire*!"

Monsieur Dupont grew more and more enthusiastic as he considered the matter. "I have never before heard of a bear playing in a band," he said. "It would be a great attraction."

The Browns exchanged glances. "I'm sure it's a very great honor," said Mrs. Brown doubtfully. "But is it wise?"

"What is a band," cried Monsieur Dupont, waving his arms dramatically in the air, "without someone at the back who can go *boom, boom, boom*?"

The Browns were silent. There didn't seem to be any answer to Monsieur Dupont's question.

"Oh, well," said Mr. Brown. "It's your band!"

"In that case," said Monsieur Dupont briskly, "the matter is settled!"

The Browns watched anxiously as Monsieur Dupont and Paddington hurried off to start their rehearsals. The idea of Paddington becoming a member of the village band gave rise to thoughts of all sorts of awful possibilities.

But as the afternoon wore on, despite their first misgivings, they became quite excited at the idea and by the time night fell and they settled themselves on the hotel balcony in readiness for the grand parade even Mr. Brown kept repeating how much he was looking forward to it all.

In the distance they could hear the musicians tuning up their instruments, and several times there was a loud bang as Paddington tested his drum for the last time.

"I only hope he doesn't make a mistake and ruin everything," said Mrs. Brown. "He's not really very musical."

"If some of the banging that goes on at home is anything to go by," said Mrs. Bird, looking up from her knitting, "there's nothing to worry about!"

Suddenly, after a short pause, there was a great flurry of sound and a cheer went up from the waiting villagers as the band, led by Monsieur Dupont, entered the square to the tune of a rousing march.

Monsieur Dupont himself looked very impressive as he threw his stick in the air with a flourish and caught it with one hand as it came down, but the biggest cheer of all was reserved for Paddington as he came into view behind a very large drum. The news that the young English bear gentleman had stepped in at the last moment to save the day had quickly gone the rounds and a large crowd had turned out to witness the event.

Paddington felt most important when he heard the applause, and he waved his paws several times in acknowledgment in between hitting the drum, reserving a special wave for the Browns as he passed the hotel.

"Well," said Mrs. Bird proudly, as the band disappeared from view up the street, "that bear may only be bringing up the rear, but I thought he was better than all the rest put together!"

"I've managed to get some pictures," said Mr. Brown, lowering his camera, "but I'm afraid they're only back views."

"You'll be able to get some front ones in a minute, Dad," said Jonathan. "I think they're on their way back."

Mr. Brown hurriedly reloaded his camera as the sound of the music got louder again. Having finished off the first tune with a series of loud crashes, the band had broken into another march and was heading back towards the square.

"Paddington doesn't seem to be quite so loud now," said Mrs. Brown as they settled back in their seats. "I hope he isn't having trouble with his sticks."

"Perhaps his paws are getting tired," said Judy.

"Uh-oh!" exclaimed Jonathan, jumping up as the band came into view again. "He isn't with them anymore."

"What's that?" exclaimed Mr. Brown, lowering his camera. "Not there! But he must be."

The Browns peered anxiously over the edge of the balcony, and even Monsieur Dupont glanced over his shoulder several times before he brought the band to a halt in the middle of the square, but Paddington was nowhere to be seen.

"That's funny," said Mr. Brown, cupping a hand to his ear as the music stopped. "I can still hear something."

The others listened intently. The sound Mr. Brown had heard seemed to be com-

ing from the far side of the village. It was getting fainter and fainter all the time, but it was definitely that of a drum.

"Gosh! I bet that's Paddington," said Judy. "He must have carried straight on by mistake when the others turned back."

"We'd better go after him then," said Mr. Brown urgently. "There's no knowing where he might end up."

The Browns began to look worried as the full meaning of the situation sank in. Even Paddington himself, had he been in a position to see what was going on, would have agreed that things looked rather black, but as it was he plodded on his way blissfully unaware of the turn of events.

All in all, what with the fair and the band rehearsal he had spent a most enjoyable day, but now that the first excitement of the parade was over he was beginning to wish it would soon come to an end.

To start with, the drum was much too large and heavy for his liking, and having short legs made it difficult to keep in step. The drum was strapped to his front and during rehearsals he had been able to rest it on his suitcase, but now he was on the march it was much higher and he couldn't even begin to see over the top. Apart from having no idea where he was, it was getting very hot inside his duffle coat and the marching had made the hood fall over his ears so that he couldn't hear the other musicians.

Monsieur Dupont had taken great pains to explain how important an instrument the drum was and that even when the band stopped playing it still had to be banged so that the others could keep in step, but as far as Paddington could make out for the past five minutes it had been all drum and no band and he was beginning to get a bit fed up.

The farther along the road he went, the heavier it became and, to add to his troubles, as his knees began to sag under the weight, the duffle coat hood fell completely over his head and stayed there.

Just as he was trying to make up his mind whether or not to call out for help, matters were suddenly decided for him. One moment he was plodding along the road, the next moment his foot met nothing but air. In fact, he hardly had time to

let out a gasp of surprise before everything seemed to turn upside down, and before he knew where he was he found himself lying on his back with what seemed like a ton weight on top of him.

Paddington lay where he was for some moments gasping for breath before he cautiously pulled back his duffle coat hood and peered out. To his surprise, neither Monsieur Dupont nor the rest of the band was anywhere in sight. In fact, the only things he could see at all were the moon and the stars in the sky above him. Worse still, when he tried to get up again he found he couldn't, for the drum was resting on his stomach and try as he might he couldn't move it.

Paddington let out a deep sigh as he lay back on the road. "Oh dear!" he said, addressing the world in general. "I'm in trouble again!"

"What a good thing you kept on banging the drum," said Mrs. Brown thankfully. "You might have stayed there all night."

It was some time later and everyone had gathered in the hotel lounge in order to hear Paddington's explanations of the evening's events and how he had come to be rescued. Monsieur Dupont in particular was very relieved to see Paddington again for he felt responsible for the whole affair.

"I think I must have put my paw in a pothole by mistake, Mrs. Brown," said Paddington. "Then I couldn't get up again because the drum was on top of me."

Mrs. Brown wanted to ask Paddington why he hadn't tried undoing the straps, but she tactfully kept silent. As it was, far too many people were talking at once and quite a crowd had collected in order to congratulate Paddington and Monsieur Dupont on their parade.

In any case Paddington was much too busy with his own problems and from a distance he looked as if he was trying to turn himself inside out.

"It's all right, Mrs. Brown," he said hurriedly, when he saw her look of concern. "I was only testing the lines on my paw."

"Well, I hope you found something interesting after all that," said Mrs. Bird. "It looked most uncomfortable."

"I'm not sure," said Paddington hopefully, "but it looked like a firework!"

"*Hmm!*" said Mrs. Bird darkly as a sudden whoosh came from outside and the first rocket of the evening lit up the sky. "It sounds suspiciously like a bear's wishful thinking to me!"

But her words fell on deaf ears for Paddington had already disappeared outside, closely followed by Jonathan and Judy, with Mr. Brown and Monsieur Dupont bringing up the rear.

Paddington liked fireworks and now that he had recovered from his adventure with the drum he was looking forward to the evening display. Judging by the noise going on in the square outside the hotel, he had a feeling that French fireworks might be very good value indeed and he didn't want to miss a single moment of the fun.

Chapter 26

Riding High

Paddington reined in his horse and stared at the judge's stand as if he could hardly believe his ears.

"I've got four hundred and fifty-two faults?" he exclaimed hotly. "But I've only been round once!"

"There are twelve fences," said Guy Cheeseman, measuring his words with care, "and you went straight through all of them—that's forty-eight for a start. Plus another four for going back over the last one.

"*And,*" he added, bringing the subject firmly to a close as he glared down at the battered remains of what had once been a hat, "your horse trampled all over my best bowler—the one I intended wearing at the presentation this afternoon—that's another four hundred!"

Mr. Cheeseman wasn't in the best of moods. In fact, the look on his face as he made an entry alongside Paddington's signature on the clipboard he was carrying was decidedly gloomy. He gave the distinct impression that he wished he'd never heard of St. Christopher's School and its teachers and parents in general, not to mention Paddington in particular.

The occasion was the end-of-term celebration at Judy's school, and instead of the usual speechmaking, Miss Grimshaw, the principal, had decided to hold a horse show to raise money for a new swimming pool.

There were a number of events on the program, and the two main items at the beginning and end were open to all and sundry—including the parents, relations and friends of the pupils.

The competitors were given "sponsor sheets," and each had to collect as many signatures as possible from people who were prepared to pay a small sum for every successful jump.

The Browns arrived quite early in the day and Paddington, who had decided to enter both events, had been kept very busy hurrying round the grounds collecting names for his sheet.

He was already a familiar figure at Judy's school, and almost everyone in the upper grades had persuaded their nearest and dearest to sponsor him. In view of the number of signatures Paddington had managed to collect, the swimming pool fund stood to benefit by a tidy amount.

Guy Cheeseman, the famous Olympic rider, had very kindly agreed to judge the contests and act as commentator, and with the sun shining down from a cloudless sky, the sound of horses' hooves pounding the turf, the murmur of the large crowd which had gathered round the sports field, and the creaking of innumerable picnic baskets, it promised to be a memorable occasion.

The roar of excitement as Paddington mounted his horse was equaled only by the groan of disappointment that went up as he disappeared from view over the other side. And when he eventually reappeared facing the wrong way an ominous silence fell over the field—a silence broken only by the crash of falling fences and a cry of rage from Mr. Cheeseman as he watched his best hat being ground to pulp.

Paddington was more upset than anyone, for although he'd never actually been on a horse before, let alone a jumping one, Mr. Gruber had lent him several very good books on the subject and he'd spent the last few evenings sitting astride a footstool in the Browns' sitting room, practicing with a homemade whip and some stirrups.

It was all most disappointing. In fact, he rather wished now he'd chosen something else to practice on. To start with, the horse was very much taller and harder than he'd expected—more iron and steel than flesh and blood—and whereas by gripping the footstool between his knees he'd been able to hop round the house at quite a speed, it was nothing compared with Black Beauty once she got going. That apart—aside from when he'd unexpectedly bumped into Mrs. Bird in the hall—he'd never attempted any kind of jumps on the footstool, and no matter what he shouted to Black Beauty, she seemed to have it firmly fixed in her mind that the shortest distance between two points was a straight line, regardless of what happened to be in the way.

According to Mr. Gruber's book one of the first require-ments in horseback riding was complete confidence between rider and mount and Paddington would have been the first to ad-mit that as far as he was concerned, he was a non-starter in this respect. He completed the round clinging helplessly to Black Beauty's tail with his eyes tightly closed, and the trail of damage they left behind made the hockey field at St. Christopher's resem-ble the fields of Belgium immediately after the battle of Waterloo.

"Never mind, Paddington," said Judy, grabbing hold of the reins. "We all thought you did really well.

"Especially as it was your first time out," she added, amid a chorus of sympathetic agreement from the other girls. "Not many people would have dared to try."

"Th . . . th . . . thank you v . . . v . . . v-very m . . . m . . . much," stuttered Paddington. He was still feeling as if he'd been for a ride on a particularly powerful pneumatic drill and he gave Mr. Cheeseman a very hard stare indeed as he was helped down to the ground.

"It's a shame really," said Mrs. Brown, as they watched his progress back to the horse enclosure. "It would have made such a nice start to the day if he'd had a clear round."

"Perhaps he'll do better in the 'Chase Me Charley,'" said Jonathan hopefully. "He's signed up for that as well at the end."

"Four hundred and fifty-two faults indeed!" snorted Mrs. Bird, as the commen-tator's voice boomed through the loudspeakers. "It's a good thing Mr. Cheeseman didn't tread on *Paddington's* hat. He'd have lost a good deal more than that!"

Giving a final glare in the direction of the judge's stand, the Browns' house-keeper began busying herself with the picnic basket in a way which boded ill for Mr. Cheeseman's chances of a snack if he found he'd left his own sandwiches at home.

"That's a good idea," said Jonathan enthusiastically. "I'm so hungry I could eat a horse."

"Pity you didn't eat Paddington's," said Mr. Brown gloomily. "Especially after that last round."

"*Ssh*, Henry," whispered Mrs. Brown. "Here he comes. We don't want to upset him any more."

Mr. Brown hastily turned his attention to the important matter of lunch and as the fences were put back and the next event got under way he began setting up a table and chair in the shade of a nearby oak tree. Mr. Brown didn't believe in doing things by halves, especially where picnics were concerned, and he shared the French habit of turning such affairs into a full-scale family occasion.

Mrs. Bird had packed an enormous hamper with jars and plastic containers brimful with sliced tomatoes, cucumber, beets, ham, beef, liver sausage, and seemingly endless supplies of mixed salads. What with these and strawberries and cream to follow, not to mention two sorts of ice cream, lemonade, tea, coffee, various cakes and cookies, and a jar of Paddington's favorite marmalade into the bargain, the table was soon groaning under the weight.

Even Mr. Brown, who wasn't normally too keen on equestrian events, had to admit that he couldn't think of a more pleasant way of spending a summer afternoon. And as event followed event and the contents of the hamper grew less and less, the bad start to the day was soon forgotten.

Paddington himself had worked up quite an appetite, though for once he seemed more interested in Mr. Gruber's book on riding, which he'd brought with him in case of an emergency, than in the actual food itself. Several times he dipped his paw into the bowl of salad dressing in mistake for the marmalade as he studied a particularly interesting chapter on jumping which he hadn't read before, and apart from

suddenly rearing up into the air once or twice as he went through the motions, he remained remarkably quiet.

It wasn't until nearly the end of the meal when he absent-mindedly reached into the basket and helped himself to one of Mrs. Bird's meringues that he showed any signs of life at all.

"Aren't they delicious?" said Mrs. Brown. "I don't think I've ever tasted better."

"Don't you like them, Paddington?" asked Mrs. Bird, looking most concerned at the expression on his face.

"Er . . . yes, Mrs. Bird," said Paddington politely. "They're . . . er . . . they're very unusual. I think I'll put some marmalade on to take the taste . . . to, er . . . "

Paddington's voice trailed away. Although not wishing to say so, he didn't think much of Mrs. Bird's meringue at all and he was glad it was particularly small and dainty. It was really most unusual, for Mrs. Bird was an extremely good cook and her cookies normally melted in the mouth, whereas the present one not only showed no signs of melting but was positively stringy.

And it wasn't just the texture. Paddington couldn't make up his mind if it was because he'd followed the ice cream with another helping of Russian salad or whether Mr. Brown had accidently spilled some paraffin over it when he'd filled the camping stove, but whatever the reason, Mrs. Bird's meringue was very odd indeed and not even a liberal splotch of marmalade entirely took the taste away.

However, Paddington was a polite bear and he had no wish to offend anyone, least of all Mrs. Bird, so he manfully carried on. Fortunately he was saved any further embarrassment by Guy Cheeseman announcing that the final event on the program was about to take place and asking the competitors to come forward.

Hastily cramming the remains of the meringue into his mouth, Paddington gathered up his book and sponsor sheet and hurried off in the direction of the saddling enclosure, closely followed by Judy and several of her friends.

"I know one thing," said Mr. Brown, as he disappeared from view into the crowd, "if he manages to get over *one* fence, the swimming pool fund won't do too badly. He's got enough signatures now to float a battleship."

For various reasons Paddington's sponsor sheet had grown considerably during the course of the afternoon. Apart from a number of people who'd added their names a second time to show they hadn't lost faith, there was a considerable new element who had signed for quite a different reason—sensing that in backing Paddington they could show support without too great an expense, and his sheet was now jam-packed with signatures.

"It would serve some of them right if he did do well," said Mrs. Bird darkly. "It might teach them a lesson."

Mrs. Bird looked as if she'd been about to add a great deal more but at that moment a burst of applause heralded the first of the long line of competitors.

The "Chase Me Charley" event was one in which all the contestants formed a circle, their horses nose to tail, and took it in turns to jump a single pole. Only one fault was allowed and each time a round had been completed those with faults dropped out and the pole was raised another inch until the final winner emerged.

Practically everyone who could ride was taking part and the circle of horses stretched right round the field, so that it was some time before Paddington came into view on Black Beauty.

There was a nasty moment when he came past the Browns and tried to raise his hat, which he'd insisted on wearing on top of his compulsory riding one, but he soon righted himself and disappeared from view again, holding the reins with one paw and anxiously consulting Mr. Gruber's book which he still held in the other.

"Oh dear," said Mrs. Brown nervously, "I do hope he takes care. I didn't like to say so in his presence but it must be terribly difficult with short legs. No wonder his paws keep coming out of the stirrups."

"I shouldn't worry," said Mrs. Bird. "There's one thing about bears—they always fall on their feet no matter what happens."

Mrs. Bird did her best to sound cheerful but she looked as worried as anyone as they waited for Paddington to make his first jump. Judy arrived back just in the nick of time and in the excitement only Mrs. Bird's sharp eyes noticed that she, too, was now wearing a very odd expression on her face. An expression, moreover, which was almost identical to the one Paddington had worn a little earlier when he'd had trouble with his meringue. But before she had time to look into the matter, her attention was drawn back to the field as a great roar went up from the crowd.

The Browns watched in amazement as Paddington and Black Beauty literally sailed over the pole. One moment they'd been trotting gently towards it, then Paddington appeared to lean forward and whisper something in the horse's ear. The very next instant horse and rider leapt into the air and cleared the hurdle with several feet to spare. Admittedly the pole was at its lowest mark, but even so the performance drew a gasp of astonishment from the onlookers.

"Bravo!" cried someone near the Browns. "That bear's done it at last. And not even a sign of a refusal!"

"Heavens above!" exclaimed Mr. Brown, twirling his mustache with excitement, "if he carries on like that he'll be up among the leaders in no time. Did you see it? He went higher than anyone!"

Jonathan listened to his sister as she whispered in his ear. "*If* he does it again," he said gloomily.

"Well, even if he doesn't, he's certainly not last this time," said Mrs. Brown thankfully, as a following rider brought the pole down with a clatter.

And as it happened Jonathan's worst fears went unrealized, for seeming miracle began to follow miracle as Paddington and Black Beauty made one effortless clear round after another and one by one the other competitors began to drop out.

Each time they drew near to the jump Paddington leaned over and appeared to whisper something in Black Beauty's ear and each time it had a magical effect as she bounded into action and with a whinny which echoed round the field, cleared the hurdle with feet to spare.

Paddington was so excited he discarded Mr. Gruber's book in order to raise his hat in acknowledgment of the cheers, and even those who'd signed his sheet rather late in the day, although they'd worn long faces at first, began applauding with the rest.

And when it came to the final round, with Paddington pitted against Diana Ridgeway, the head girl, the excitement was intense. Even with loyalties so divided the cheer which rang out as Paddington emerged the victor practically shook the school to its foundations, and Diana Ridgeway herself set the seal on the occasion by dismounting and running over to offer her congratulations.

Guy Cheeseman so far forgot the unpleasantness earlier in the day that phrases like "superb horsemanship," "splendid display," and "supreme example of rider and mount being as one" floated round the grounds with scarcely a pause for breath.

For some reason or other Diana Ridgeway appeared to have second thoughts as Paddington leaned down to speak to her, but with an obvious effort she overcame them and in the general excitement the moment passed practically unnoticed.

"What an incredible business!" exclaimed Mr. Brown, mopping his brow as he settled down again. "I wonder what on earth Paddington kept whispering to Black Beauty? It must have been something pretty good to make her want to jump like that."

Jonathan and Judy exchanged glances, then Judy took a deep breath. "I'm not sure he *whispered* anything," she began, only to break off again as she suddenly caught sight of Paddington and the principal about to converge a short distance away.

"Uh-oh! That's done it," said Jonathan, as Miss Grimshaw began pumping Paddington's paw up and down.

"Stout effort!" she cried. "Allow me to shake you by the paw. You've given our swimming pool a tremendous fillip."

Paddington began to look more and more surprised as he listened to the principal. He had no idea they'd dug the hole even, let alone filled it up. "I hope I haven't filled it too full, Miss Grimshaw," he exclaimed politely.

Miss Grimshaw's smile seemed to become strangely fixed, then she paused and gave a sniff. "I really must get Birchwood to look at the drains," she said, eyeing Paddington even more doubtfully. "I . . . er . . . I hope we shall meet again at the presentation."

"Wow!" said Judy, as the principal hurried on her way. "The presentation! We'd better do something before then."

Dashing over to Paddington she grabbed hold of his paw and then turned to her brother. "Come on, Jonathan," she called. "We'll take him to see the nurse. She's just over there in the first aid tent. She may be able to give him something."

"The nurse?" echoed Mrs. Brown, as Judy began whispering in Paddington's ear. "What on earth are they talking about?"

"It's all right, Mrs. Brown," cried Paddington. "It's nothing serious. I'm afraid I'm having trouble with one of Mrs. Bird's meringues."

"Trouble with one of my *meringues*?" Mrs. Bird began to look thoughtful as Judy and Jonathan whisked Paddington away. "How many did the children have?" she asked, rummaging in the picnic basket.

"Three each, I think," replied Mrs. Brown. "I remember them talking about it. Jonathan wanted another but there weren't any left. I had two—the same as you." She turned to her husband. "How many did you have, Henry?"

"Er . . . four," said Mr. Brown. "They were a bit moreish."

"That makes fourteen altogether," said Mrs. Bird, as she began emptying the contents of the picnic basket. "And that's all I made," she added ominously. "So whatever that bear ate, it certainly wasn't a meringue!"

◆ ◆ ◆

Mr. Brown wound down the window of his car to its fullest extent and then glanced across at Paddington. "How anyone could mistake a bulb of garlic for a meringue I just don't know," he said.

"Especially one of Mrs. Bird's," said Judy. "The nurse couldn't believe her ears."

"Or her nose!" added Jonathan.

Paddington looked at them sheepishly. "I'm afraid I was busy reading about my cavallettis," he explained. "That's to do with jumping. I didn't notice I'd made a mistake until it was too late."

"But a whole bulb," said Mrs. Brown from behind her handkerchief. "I mean . . . a clove would have been bad enough, but a *whole bulb!*"

"No wonder Black Beauty was jumping so well," said Judy. "Every time you leaned over her she must have got the full force."

"It's a wonder she didn't go into orbit," agreed Jonathan.

The Browns were making all possible speed in the direction of Windsor Gardens, but even with all the windows open there was a decided "air" about the car.

Paddington had been standing on the front seat with his head poking out of the sun roof for most of the way, and every time they stopped they got some very funny looks indeed from any passersby who happened to be downwind.

"I'll say one thing," remarked Mr. Brown, as they drew to a halt alongside a policeman, who hastily waved them on again, "it soon clears the traffic. I don't think we've ever made better time."

"Perhaps I could eat some garlic when we go out again, Mr. Brown," said Paddington, anxious to make amends.

Mr. Brown gave a shudder. "No, thank you," he said. "Once is quite enough."

"Anyway," broke in Judy, "all's well that ends well. There were over two hundred signatures on Paddington's sheet and Miss Grimshaw reckons it must be worth at least as many pounds to the fund."

"Mr. Cheeseman said he'd never seen anything like it before," said Jonathan.

"Nor will he again if I have anything to do with it," said Mrs. Bird grimly. "That's the last time I make any meringues."

In the chorus of dismay which greeted this last remark Paddington's voice was loudest of all.

"Perhaps you could make them extra large, Mrs. Bird," he said hopefully. "Then they won't get mistaken."

The Browns' housekeeper remained silent for a moment. All in all, despite everything, it had been a most enjoyable day and she was the last person to want to spoil it. "Perhaps you're right," she said, relenting at last. "But you must promise not to go riding on the footstool when we get home."

Paddington didn't take long to make up his mind. Although he was much too polite to say so the events of the day were beginning to catch up with him and sitting down, even on the softest of footstools, was the last thing he had in mind.

"I think," he announced, amid general laughter as he clambered up on the seat again, "I shall go to sleep standing up tonight!"

Part Six

A Bite to Eat

·Chapter 27·

A Sticky Time

Mrs. Bird paused for a moment and sniffed the air as she and Mrs. Brown turned the corner into Windsor Gardens. "Can you smell something?" she asked.

Mrs. Brown stopped by her side. Now that Mrs. Bird mentioned it, there was a very peculiar odor coming from somewhere near at hand. It wasn't exactly unpleasant, but it was rather sweet and sickly, and it seemed to be made up of a number of things she couldn't quite place.

"Perhaps there's been a bonfire somewhere," she remarked as they picked up their shopping and continued along the road.

"Whatever it is," said Mrs. Bird darkly, "it seems to be getting worse. In fact," she added, as they neared number thirty-two, "it's much too close to home for my liking.

"I knew it!" she exclaimed as they made their way along the drive at the side of the house. "Just look at my kitchen windows!"

"Oh dear," said Mrs. Brown, following the direction of Mrs. Bird's gaze. "What on earth has that bear been up to now?"

Looking at Mrs. Bird's kitchen windows, it seemed just as if in some strange way someone had changed them for frosted glass while they had been out. Worse still, not only did the glass have a frosted appearance, but there were several tiny rivers of a rather nasty-looking brown liquid trickling down them as well, and from a small, partly open window at the top there came a steady cloud of escaping steam.

While Mrs. Bird examined the outside of her kitchen windows, Mrs. Brown hurried round to the back of the house. "I do hope Paddington's all right," she exclaimed when she returned. "I can't get in through the back door. It seems to be stuck."

"*Hmm*," said Mrs. Bird grimly. "If the windows look like this from the outside, heaven alone knows what we shall find when we get indoors."

Normally the windows at number thirty-two Windsor Gardens were kept spotlessly clean, with never a trace of a smear, but even Mrs. Bird began to look worried as she peered in vain for a gap in the mist through which she could see what was going on.

Had she but known, the chances of seeing anything at all through the haze were more unlikely than she imagined, for on the other side of the glass even Paddington was having to admit to himself that things were getting a bit out of hand.

In fact, as he groped his way across the kitchen in the direction of the stove, where several large saucepans stood bubbling and giving forth clouds of steam, he decided he didn't much like the look of the few things he could see.

Climbing up on a kitchen chair, he lifted the lid off one of the saucepans and peered hopefully inside as he poked at the contents with one of Mrs. Bird's tablespoons. The mixture was much stiffer than he had expected, and it was as much as he could manage to push the spoon in, let alone stir with it.

Paddington's whiskers began to droop in the steam as he worked the spoon back and forth, but it wasn't until he tried to take it out in order to test the result of his labors that a really worried expression came over his face, for to his surprise, however much he pulled and tugged, it wouldn't even budge.

The more he struggled, the hotter the spoon became, and after a moment or two he gave it up as a bad job and hurriedly let go of the handle as he climbed back down off the chair in order to consult a large magazine that was lying open on the floor.

Making toffee wasn't at all the easy thing the article in the magazine made it out to be, and it was all most disappointing, particularly as it was the first time he'd tried his paw at making candy.

The magazine in question was an old one of Mrs. Brown's, and he had first come across it earlier in the day when he'd been at a bit of a loose end. Normally Paddington didn't think much of Mrs. Brown's magazines. They were much too full of advertisements and items about how to keep clean and look smart for his liking, but this one had caught his eye because it was a special cooking issue.

On the cover there was a picture showing a golden brown roast chicken resting on a plate laden with bright green peas, gravy, and roast potatoes. Alongside the chicken was a huge sundae oozing with layer upon layer of fruit and ice cream, while beyond that was a large wooden board laden with so many different kinds of cheese that Paddington had soon lost count of the number as he lay on his bed licking his whiskers.

The inside of the magazine had been even more interesting, and it had taken him a while to get through the colored photographs alone.

But it was the last article of all that had really made him sit up and take notice. It was called "TEN EASY WAYS WITH TOFFEE," and it was written by a lady called Granny Green who lived in the country and seemed to spend all her time making candy.

Granny Green appeared in quite a number of the pictures, and whenever she did, it was always alongside a pile of freshly made olde-fashioned peppermints, a dish of chocolate fudge, or a mound of some other candy.

Paddington had read the article several times with a great deal of interest, for although in the past he'd tried his paw at cooking various kinds of dinners, he'd never before heard of anyone making candy at home, and it seemed a very good idea indeed.

All Granny Green's recipes looked nice, but it was the last one of all, for olde-fashioned butter toffee, that had really made Paddington's mouth water. Even Granny Green herself seemed to like it best, for in one picture she was actually caught helping herself to a piece behind her kitchen door when she thought no one was watching.

It not only looked very tempting, but Paddington decided it was very good value for money as well, for apart from using condensed milk and sugar, all that was needed was butter, corn syrup, and some stuff called vanilla extract, all of which Mrs. Bird kept in her cupboard.

After checking carefully through the recipe once more, Paddington took another look at the magazine in the hope of seeing where he'd gone wrong, but none of the photographs were any help at all. All Granny Green's saucepans were as bright as a new pin, with not a trace of anything sticky running down the sides, and even her spoons were laid out neat and shining on the kitchen table. There was certainly no mention of any of them getting stuck in the toffee.

In any case, her toffee was a light golden brown color, and it was cut into neat squares and laid out on a plate, whereas from what he'd been able to make out of his own through the steam, it had been more the color of dark brown shoe polish, and even if he had been able to get it out of the saucepans, he couldn't for the life of him think what he would cut it with.

Paddington rather wished he'd tried one of the other nine recipes instead. Heaving a deep sigh, he groped his way across the kitchen and, stretching up a paw, rubbed a hole in the steam on one of the windowpanes. As he did so he jumped back into the middle of the room with a gasp of alarm, for there on the other side of the glass was the familiar face of Mrs. Bird.

Mrs. Bird appeared to be saying something, and although he couldn't make out the actual words, he didn't like the look of some of them at all. Fortunately, before she was able to say very much the glass clouded over again, and Paddington sat down in the middle of the kitchen floor with a forlorn expression on his face as he awaited developments.

He hadn't long to wait, for a few moments later there came the sound of footsteps in the hall. "What on earth's been going on?" cried Mrs. Bird as she burst through the door.

"I've been trying my paw at toffee-making, Mrs. Bird," explained Paddington sadly.

"Toffee-making!" exclaimed Mrs. Brown, flinging open the window. "Why, you could cut the air with a knife."

"That's more than you can say for the toffee," said Mrs. Bird as she pulled at the end of the spoon Paddington had left in the saucepan. "It looks more like glue."

"I'm afraid it is a bit thick, Mrs. Bird," said Paddington. "I think I must have got my Granny Greens mixed up by mistake."

"I don't know about your Granny Greens," said Mrs. Bird grimly as she surveyed the scene. "It looks as if you've got the whole pantry mixed up. I only cleaned the kitchen this morning, and now look at it!"

Paddington half stood up and gazed round the room. Now that most of the steam had cleared, it looked in rather more of a mess than he had expected. There were several large pools of syrup on the floor and a long trail of sugar leading from the table to the stove, not to mention two or three half-open tins of condensed milk lying on their side where they had fallen off the drainboard.

"It's a job to know where to start," said Mrs. Brown as she stepped gingerly over one of the pools of syrup. "I've never seen such a mess."

"Well, we shan't get it cleared up if we stand looking at it, that's a certainty," said Mrs. Bird briskly as she bustled round sweeping everything in sight into the sink. "I suggest that a certain young bear had better get down on his paws and knees with a scrub brush and a bucket of water before he's very much older, otherwise we shall all get stuck to the floor."

Mrs. Bird paused. While she'd been talking a strange expression had come over Paddington's face, one that she didn't like the look of at all. "Is anything the matter?" she asked.

"I'm not sure, Mrs. Bird," said Paddington, making several attempts to stand up and then hurriedly sitting down again, holding his stomach with both paws. "I've got a bit of a pain."

"You haven't been *eating* this stuff, have you?" exclaimed Mrs. Brown, pointing to the saucepans.

"Well, I did test it once or twice, Mrs. Brown," said Paddington.

"Gracious me!" cried Mrs. Bird. "No wonder you've got a pain. It's probably set in a hard lump in your inside."

"Try standing up again," said Mrs. Brown anxiously.

"I don't think I can," gasped Paddington, as he lay back on the floor. "I think it's getting worse."

"That poor bear," cried Mrs. Bird, all thoughts of the mess in the kitchen banished from her mind as she hurried into the hall. "We must ring for Doctor MacAndrew at once."

Mrs. Bird was only gone a moment or so before the door burst open again. "The doctor's out on his rounds," she said. "They don't know when he'll be back and they can't even find his locum."

"They can't find his locum!" repeated Paddington, looking more worried than ever.

"That's his assistant," explained Mrs. Brown. "There's nothing to get upset about. We could try a strong dose of castor oil, I suppose," she continued, turning to Mrs. Bird.

"I've a feeling it'll need more than castor oil," said Mrs. Bird ominously as

Paddington jumped up hurriedly with a "feeling better" expression on his face and then gave a loud groan as he promptly sat down again. "I've sent for the ambulance."

"The ambulance!" cried Mrs. Brown, going quite pale. "Oh dear."

"We should never forgive ourselves," said Mrs. Bird wisely, "if anything happened to that bear."

So saying, she put her arms underneath Paddington and, lifting him gently, carried him into the living room and placed him on the sofa, where he lay with his legs sticking up in the air.

Leaving Paddington where he was, Mrs. Bird disappeared upstairs, and when she returned she was carrying a small leather suitcase. "I've packed all his washing things," she explained to Mrs. Brown. "And I've put in a jar of his special marmalade in case he needs it."

Mrs. Bird mentioned the last item in a loud voice in the hope that it would cheer Paddington up, but at the mention of the word *marmalade* a loud groan came from the direction of the sofa.

Mrs. Brown and Mrs. Bird exchanged glances. If the thought of marmalade made Paddington feel worse, then things must be very bad indeed.

"I'd better ring Henry at the office," said Mrs. Brown as she hurried out into the hall. "I'll get him to come home straight away."

Fortunately, as Mrs. Brown replaced the telephone receiver and before they had time to worry about the matter any more, there came the sound of a siren ringing outside, followed by a squeal of brakes and a bang on the front door.

"Ho dear," said the ambulance man as he entered the living room and saw Paddington lying on the sofa. "What's this? I was told it was an emergency. Nobody said anything about it's being a bear."

"Bears have emergencies the same as anyone else," said Mrs. Bird sternly. "Now just you bring your stretcher, and hurry up about it."

The ambulance man scratched his head. "I don't know what they're going to say back at the hospital," he said doubtfully. "They've got an out-patients and an in-patients department, but I've never come across a bear-patients department before."

"Well, they're going to have one now," said Mrs. Bird. "And if that bear isn't in it by the time five minutes is up, I shall want to know the reason why."

The ambulance man looked nervously at Mrs. Bird and then back at the sofa as Paddington gave another loud groan. "I must say he doesn't look too good," he remarked.

"He's all right when he's got his legs in the air," explained Mrs. Brown. "It's when he tries to put them down it hurts."

The ambulance man came to a decision. The combination of Mrs. Bird's glares and Paddington's groans was too much for him. "Bert," he called through the open door. "Fetch the number-one stretcher. And be quick. We've a young bear emergency in here and I don't much like the look of him."

Nobody spoke in the ambulance on the way to the hospital. Mrs. Bird, Mrs. Brown, and the man in charge traveled in the back with Paddington, and all the while his legs got higher and higher, until by the time the ambulance turned in through the hospital gates they were almost doubled back on themselves.

Even the ambulance man looked worried. "Never seen anything like it before," he said.

"I'll cover him over with a blanket, ma'am," he continued to Mrs. Bird as they came to a stop. "It'll save any explanations at the door. We don't want too many delays filling in forms."

Mrs. Brown and Mrs. Bird hurried in after the stretcher, but the ambulance man was as good as his word, and in no time at all Paddington was being whisked away from them down a long white corridor. In fact, he only had time to poke a paw out from under the blanket in order to wave goodbye before the doors at the end of the corridor closed behind him and all was quiet again.

"Oh dear," said Mrs. Brown, sinking down on a wooden bench. "I suppose we've done all we can now."

"We can only sit and wait," said Mrs. Bird gravely as she sat down beside her. "Wait and hope."

▶ ◆ ◀

The Browns and Mr. Gruber sat in a miserable group in the corridor as they watched the comings and goings of the nurses. Mr. Brown had arrived soon after the ambulance, bringing with him Jonathan and Judy, and shortly after that Mr. Gruber had turned up, carrying a bunch of flowers and a huge bag of grapes.

"They're from the traders in the market," he explained. "They all send their best wishes and hope he soon gets well."

"It won't be long now," said Mr. Brown as several nurses entered the room at the end of the corridor. "I think things are beginning to happen."

As Mr. Brown spoke, a tall, distinguished-looking man dressed from head to foot in green came hurrying down the corridor and with a nod in their direction disappeared through the same door.

"That must be Sir Mortimer Carroway," said Judy knowledgeably. "That ambulance man said he's the best surgeon they have."

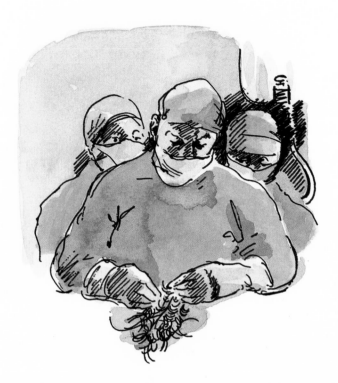

"Wow!" said Jonathan in a tone of awe. "Fancy Paddington having him!"

"Quite right too," said Mrs. Bird decidedly. "There's nothing like going to the top. People at the top are always more understanding."

"I feel so helpless," said Mrs. Brown, voicing the thoughts of them all as they sat and prepared themselves for a long wait. They were each of them busy with their own thoughts, and although not one of them would have admitted it to the others, even the knowledge that such a famous person as Sir Mortimer Carroway was in charge didn't help matters.

"Good heavens!" exclaimed Mr. Brown a few minutes later as the door at the end of the corridor opened once again and the figure of Sir Mortimer appeared. "That was quick."

Mrs. Brown clutched her husband's arm. "You don't think anything's gone wrong, do you, Henry?" she asked.

"We shall soon know," said Mr. Brown as Sir Mortimer caught sight of them and came hurrying along the corridor, holding a piece of fur in his hand.

"Are you that young bear's . . . er . . . next of kin?" he asked.

"Well, he lives with us," said Mrs. Brown.

"He *is* going to be all right?" exclaimed Judy, looking anxiously at the piece of fur.

"I should think," said Sir Mortimer in a grave voice, but with the suspicion of a twinkle in his eyes, "there's every chance he'll pull through."

"Gracious me!" exclaimed Mrs. Bird as there was a sudden commotion at the end of the corridor. "There *is* Paddington. Don't tell me he's up already."

"A bad case of galloping toffee drips," said Sir Mortimer. "Most unusual. On the stomach too. Worst possible place."

"Galloping toffee drips?" repeated Mr. Brown.

"I think I must have spilled some on my fur when I was testing it, Mr. Brown," explained Paddington as he joined them.

"It probably set when he was sitting down," said Sir Mortimer. "No wonder he couldn't get up again."

Sir Mortimer chuckled at the look on everyone's face. "I'm afraid he'll have a bare patch for a week or so, but I don't doubt if you keep him on a diet of marmalade for a while, it'll start to grow again. It should be all right by Christmas.

"If you don't mind, bear," he said as he made to leave, "I'd like to keep this piece of fur as a souvenir. I've done a good few operations in my time, but I've never had a bear's emergency before."

"What a good thing Sir Mortimer had a sense of humor," said Mrs. Brown as they all drove home in Mr. Brown's car. "I can't imagine what some surgeons would have said."

"Fancy keeping Paddington's fur as a souvenir," said Judy. "I wonder if he'll have it framed."

Looking out from behind Mr. Gruber's bunch of grapes, Paddington gave the rest of the carload one of his injured expressions. He felt very upset that everyone was taking his operation so lightly now that it had turned out all right, especially as he had a cold spot in the middle of his stomach where Sir Mortimer had removed the fur.

"Perhaps," said Mr. Gruber, as they turned into Windsor Gardens, "he just likes bears. After all, Mr. Brown," he added, turning to Paddington, "joking aside, it might have been serious, and it's nice to know there *are* people like that in the world to whom you can turn in times of trouble."

And to that remark even Paddington had to nod his wholehearted agreement.

Chapter 28.

A Visit to the Dentist

Paddington stared at Mrs. Brown as if he could hardly believe his ears. "You've dropped my tooth down the garbage disposal!" he exclaimed. "I shan't even be able to put it under my pillow now!"

Mrs. Brown peered helplessly into the gaping hole at the bottom of her kitchen sink. "I'm awfully sorry, dear," she replied. "It must have been in the leftovers when I cleared up after breakfast. I think you'll have to leave a note explaining what happened."

It was a tradition in the Browns' household that anyone who lost a tooth and left it under their pillow that night would find it replaced by a fifty-pence piece the next morning and Paddington looked most upset at being deprived of this experience.

"Perhaps we could try looking under the cover outside," suggested Judy hopefully. "It might still be in the drain."

"I shouldn't think so," said Jonathan. "Those garbage disposals are very good. They grind up anything. It even managed that everlasting toffee Paddington gave me yesterday.

"It was a super one," he added hastily, as he caught Paddington's eye. "I wish I could make one half as nice. It was a bit big, though. I couldn't quite finish it."

"Well," said Mr. Brown, returning to the vexed question of Paddington's tooth, "at least it didn't jam the machine."

But if Mr. Brown was trying to strike a cheerful note he failed miserably, for Paddington gave him a very hard stare indeed.

"I've had my tooth ever since I was born," he said. "And it was my best one. I don't know what Aunt Lucy's going to say when I write and tell her."

And with that parting shot he hurried out of the kitchen and disappeared upstairs in the direction of his room leaving behind a very unhappy group of Browns indeed.

"I don't see how anyone can have a *best* tooth," said Mr. Brown, as he got ready to leave for the office.

"Well," said Mrs. Bird, "best or not I must say I don't blame that bear. I don't think I'd be too happy at the thought of one of my teeth going down a garbage disposal, even if it was an accident."

"It would have to be Paddington's," said Judy. "You know how he hates losing anything. Especially when it's something he's cleaned twice a day."

"We shall never hear the last of it," agreed Mrs. Brown. She looked round the kitchen at the remains of the breakfast things. "I do hate Mondays. I don't know why, but there always seems to be more dried egg on the plates than any other day."

The others fell silent. It was one of those mornings at number thirty-two Windsor Gardens. Things had started badly when Paddington announced that he'd found a bone in his boiled egg. The Browns had pooh-poohed the idea at first and it wasn't until a little later on when he'd gone upstairs to do his Monday morning accounts that the trouble had really begun.

A sudden cry of alarm had brought the rest of the family racing to the scene, only to find Paddington on his bed with a pencil stuck in a large gap where one of his back teeth should have been.

Immediately the whole house had been in an uproar. The bed was stripped, carpets were turned back, the vacuum cleaner was emptied, pockets were turned out; Paddington even tried standing on his head in case he'd swallowed the lost half by mistake, but all to no avail—it was nowhere to be seen.

It wasn't until Mrs. Bird remembered the episode with the boiled egg that they suddenly put two and two together and went scurrying back downstairs again as fast as their legs would carry them.

But they were too late. Before they were halfway down they heard a loud grinding noise coming from the kitchen and they arrived there just in time to see Mrs. Brown switch the machine off.

The garbage disposal was still a new toy in the household. Everything from used matchsticks to old bones was fed into its ever-open mouth, but never in her wildest moments would Mrs. Brown have dreamed of disposing of one of Paddington's teeth, and she was as upset as anyone when she realized what had happened.

"I can't see them taking him at the dentist," she said. "Perhaps he'd better go to the vet."

"Certainly not," said Mrs. Bird decidedly. "He'll have to go as a private patient. I'll ring Dr. Leach straight away."

Although the Browns' housekeeper kept a firm hand on Paddington's "goings-on," she was always quick to come to his aid in time of trouble and she bustled out of the room in a very determined manner.

All the same, the others awaited her return with some anxiety, for although Dr. Leach had looked after the family's teeth for more years than they cared to remember, he'd never actually been asked to deal with one of Paddington's before. They weren't at all sure how he would view the matter, and their spirits rose when Mrs. Bird reappeared wearing her coat and hat.

"Dr. Leach will see him as soon as we can get there," she announced. "He keeps a free period for emergencies."

Mrs. Brown heaved a sigh of relief. "How nice," she said. "It's not as if we've ever taken Paddington to him."

"Who said anything about Paddington?" replied Mrs. Bird innocently. "I simply said we have an emergency in the house." She glanced up at the ceiling as a loud groan came from somewhere overhead. "And if you ask me there's no one who'll deny the truth of that! I'd better order a taxi."

While Mrs. Bird got busy on the phone again, the others hurried upstairs to see how Paddington was getting on. They found him sitting on the side of his bed wearing a very woebegone expression on his face indeed. Or rather, the little of his face that could be seen, for most of it was concealed behind a large bath towel. Every so often a low groan issued from somewhere deep inside the folds, and if the news of his forthcoming visit to the dentist did little to raise his spirits, they received a further setback a few minutes later when he was ushered into the back of a waiting taxi.

"'Aving trouble with yer choppers, mate?" asked the driver, catching sight of the towel.

"My *choppers*?" exclaimed Paddington.

Mrs. Brown hastily closed the window between the two compartments. "Don't

take any notice, dear," she said. "I'm sure you're doing the right thing. Dr. Leach is very good. He's been practicing for years."

"Dr. Leach has been *practicing*?" repeated Paddington with growing alarm. "I think I'd sooner pay extra and have someone who knows what he's doing."

The Browns exchanged glances. It was sometimes very difficult explaining things to Paddington, especially when he had his mind firmly fixed on something else, and they completed the rest of the journey in silence.

However, if Paddington himself was beginning to have mixed feelings on the subject of his tooth, Dr. Leach had no such problems when they reached his office a short while later.

"I'm afraid I shall have to charge extra," he said, as the situation was explained to him. "Bears have forty-two teeth."

"I've only got forty-one," said Paddington. "One of mine's been disposed of."

"That's still nine more than I normally deal with," said Dr. Leach firmly, ushering Paddington into his surgery. "None of my charts cover it for a start. I shall have to get my nurse to draw up a completely new one."

"I do hope we *are* doing the right thing," said Mrs. Brown anxiously, as the door closed behind them. "I feel it's all my fault."

Mrs. Bird gave a snort. "More likely that bear's everlasting toffees," she said grimly. "They're well named. It's almost impossible to get rid of them. It's no wonder he's lost a tooth. He was testing them all day yesterday. I had to throw the saucepan away and there were toffees all over the kitchen floor. I nearly twisted my ankle twice."

Paddington's homemade toffees were a sore subject in the Brown household. It wasn't so much that they had set hard. In fact, if they had, there might have been fewer complaints, but they'd ended up as a pile of large glutinous balls which stuck to everything they came in contact with, and Mrs. Bird spent the next few minutes holding forth on what she would like to do with them.

However, it was noticeable that all the while she was talking the Browns' housekeeper kept her gaze firmly fixed on the door leading to the surgery, rather as if she wished she had X-ray eyes.

But as it happened for once Mrs. Bird's worst fears weren't being realized, for Paddington was beginning to have second thoughts about dentists.

Looking round Dr. Leach's surgery he decided it was all very much nicer than he'd expected. Everything was gleaming white and spotlessly clean, with not a marmalade stain to be seen anywhere. And although it wasn't what Mrs. Bird would have called "overfurnished," the chair that Dr. Leach did possess more than made up for the fact.

Paddington had never come across anything quite like it before. It was like a long couch which rose into the air and took on all kinds of shapes simply at the press of a button. It seemed very good value indeed and Paddington was most impressed.

Above his head there was a nice, warm lamp and just beside his left paw there was a glass of pinkish liquid and a basin, while on the other side, next to Dr. Leach, there was a table fixed to an arm on which a number of instruments were laid.

Paddington hastily averted his gaze from these as he settled back in the chair, but he liked anything new, and despite his aching tooth he dutifully opened his mouth and eyed Dr. Leach with interest as the latter picked up a small rodlike object and what looked like a mirror on the end of a stick.

Dr. Leach gave several grunts of approval as he peered into Paddington's mouth, tapping the teeth one by one with the end of the rod, and several times he broke into song as he delved deeper and deeper.

"We've got a good one there, bear," he said, standing up at last. "I'm glad you came along."

Paddington sat up looking most relieved. "Thank you very much, Dr. Leach," he exclaimed. "That didn't hurt a bit."

Dr. Leach looked slightly taken aback. "I haven't done anything yet," he said. "That was only an inspection—just to see what's what. We've a long way to go yet. I'm afraid you have a fractured cusp."

"What!" exclaimed Paddington hotly. "My cusp's fractured!" He peered at the rod in Mr. Leach's hand. "It was all right when I came in," he added meaningfully. "I think it must have happened when you tapped it."

"A fractured cusp," said Dr. Leach stiffly, as he busied himself with the tray of instruments, "merely means you have a broken tooth." He wagged his finger roguishly. "I have a feeling we've been eating something we shouldn't."

Paddington sank back in his chair and looked at the dentist with renewed interest. "Have you been making toffee too, Dr. Leach?" he exclaimed.

Dr. Leach gave Paddington a strange look. "You have quite a large piece of double tooth missing," he said, slowly and carefully, "and I shall have to make you a new top to replace it."

Looking most upset at this piece of news, Paddington reached out a paw for the nearby glass of pink liquid. "I think I'll have my orangeade now, Dr. Leach, if you don't mind," he exclaimed.

"That," said Dr. Leach sternly, "is *not* orangeade. It's not even for drinking. It's put there so that you can swill your mouth out and get rid of the bits and pieces after I've finished drilling. If I kept every young bear who came in here supplied with free drinks, I'd soon be out of business."

He looked distastefully at Paddington's front where the fur had already become rather soggy from the drips, and then signaled to his nurse to tie a plastic bib round Paddington's neck. "Would we like an injection?" he asked. "It may hurt otherwise."

"Yes, please," said Paddington promptly. "I'll have two if you like."

"I think one will be sufficient," replied Dr. Leach, holding a syringe up to the light. "Now, open your mouth wide, please," he continued. "And don't forget, this is going to hurt me more than it hurts you."

Paddington dutifully obeyed Dr. Leach's instructions and, in fact, apart from a slight prick, it was much less painful than he had expected.

"Shall I do yours now, Dr. Leach?" he asked.

Dr. Leach gave him a strange look. "Mine?" he repeated. "*I* don't have an injection."

Paddington gave Dr. Leach an equally strange look in return. "You said *we* were going to have one," he persisted. "*And* you said yours would hurt more than mine."

Dr. Leach stared at Paddington for a moment as if he could hardly believe his ears and then turned to his nurse. "I think," he said, breathing heavily, "we'll try putting a wedge in his mouth. It may make things easier.

"Now," he continued, turning back to Paddington as the nurse handed him a piece of plastic-looking material, "I want you to open your mouth again, say 'Ah,' and when I've put this in take a good, hard bite."

Paddington opened his mouth and let out a loud "Aaaaah."

"Good," said Dr. Leach approvingly, as he reached into the opening. "Now, one more 'Aah' like that and then a good, hard bite. And whatever happens from now on, don't let go."

"Aaaaah," said Paddington.

Dr. Leach's face seemed to change color suddenly. "Ooooooooh," he cried.

"Ooooooooooooh," repeated Paddington, biting harder than ever.

"Owwwwwwwwwwwwww," shouted Dr. Leach, as he began dancing up and down.

"Owwwwwwwwwwwwwwwww," called Paddington, nearly falling out of the chair in his excitement. "Owwwwwwwwwwww!"

"Ouch!" shrieked Dr. Leach. "Owwwwwwww! Ooooooooooo! Aaaaaaaaaah!"

Outside in the waiting room the Browns looked anxiously at one another. "Poor old Paddington," said Jonathan. "It sounds as if he's going through it."

"I do hope it doesn't take much longer," said Mrs. Brown. "I don't know about Paddington, but I'm not sure if I can stand a lot more."

As it happened Mrs. Brown's prayers were answered almost before the words were out of her mouth, for at that moment the door burst open and a white-faced nurse appeared in the opening.

"Can you come quickly?" she cried.

Mrs. Brown clutched at her throat. "Paddington!" she cried. "He's not . . ."

"No," said the nurse "he's not! We haven't even started on *him* yet. It's Dr. Leach we're having trouble with."

Mrs. Bird hurried into the office clutching her umbrella. "Whatever's going on?" she demanded.

"Aaaaaaaaaaaaah," replied Paddington.

"Ooooooooooh!" shrieked Dr. Leach. "Ooooh! Ouch! Aaaaaaaah!"

"Uh-oh!" exclaimed Jonathan, as he and Judy dashed towards the chair where Paddington and Dr. Leach appeared to be inextricably locked together.

"You grab Dr. Leach," cried Judy. "I'll pull Paddington."

A moment later Dr. Leach staggered back across the room. "My thumb," he said, slowly and distinctly as he glared at the occupant of the chair, "my thumb—or what's left of it—was caught under your wedge, bear!"

Paddington put on his injured expression. "You said bite hard and not let go whatever happened, Dr. Leach," he explained.

Mrs. Brown gazed anxiously at the dentist as he stood in the middle of the office nursing his injury. "Would you like us to come back another day?" she asked doubtfully.

Dr. Leach appeared for a moment to be undergoing some kind of deep internal struggle and then he got a grip on himself. "No," he said at last. "No! When I became a dentist I knew there would be days when things wouldn't always go right." He looked at Paddington and then reached for his drill. "I've had twenty most enjoyable years. I suppose it had to come to an end sometime, and I'm certainly not letting a bear's cusp get the better of me now!"

It was some time before Paddington emerged from Dr. Leach's office, and although all had remained quiet, the Browns were relieved to see him looking none the worse for his experience. Indeed, as he hurried into the waiting room holding his mouth open for all to see, he looked positively excited.

"Dr. Leach is going to give me a new gold tooth," he announced importantly. "My cusp's so large he doesn't think an ordinary one would stand the strain."

Dr. Leach permitted himself a smile as he hovered in the doorway nursing a bandaged thumb. "I think we're winning at long last," he said. "I'd like to see young Mr. Brown again next week for a final fitting."

"Thank you very much, Dr. Leach," said Paddington gratefully. Bending down he undid his suitcase, withdrew a large paper bag, and held it out. "Perhaps you'd like to try one of these?"

Dr. Leach hesitated. "I . . . er . . . I don't normally indulge," he said, peering into the bag. "It doesn't set a very good example. But I must say they look tempting. It's very kind of you. I . . . er . . ."

As he placed one of Paddington's everlasting toffees into his mouth Dr. Leach's voice trailed away and for the second time that morning his face took on a glazed expression.

"Grrrrrr," he gurgled, pointing to his mouth. "Glug!"

Paddington peered at him with interest. "I hope you haven't fractured one of *your* cusps now, Dr. Leach," he said anxiously.

Dr. Leach glared at him for a moment and then staggered back into his office, clutching his jaw. Far from being fractured his cusps gave the impression that they were cemented together for all time and the look on his face as he slammed the door boded ill for the next patient on his list that morning.

Paddington looked most upset. "I only thought he would like one to be going on with," he exclaimed.

"Going on with is right," said Mrs. Bird grimly, as a series of muffled exclamations reached their ears. "By the sound of things it'll be going on until this time next week."

She held out her hand. "I know something else that's due to be disposed of just as soon as we get home. We've had quite enough bear's everlasting toffee for one day."

Judy squeezed Paddington's paw as they climbed into a taxi to take them home. "Never mind," she whispered. "There can't be many bears who are able to say they're having a gold tooth made for them."

"I'll tell you something else," said Mrs. Brown. "It'll make you even more valuable than you are at the moment. While you have a gold tooth in your head, you'll never be poor, whatever else happens."

Paddington digested this latest piece of information for a moment or two as he settled back in his seat. So much had happened that morning he felt he'd have a hard time remembering it all, let alone putting it down on a postcard when he wrote next to his Aunt Lucy in Peru. But all in all he was beginning to feel rather pleased at the way things had turned out and he felt sure she would be equally delighted by the news.

Mrs. Bird glanced across at him with the suspicion of a twinkle in her eye. "If this morning's events are anything to go by," she said, "it strikes me that a tooth in the sink is worth two under the pillow any day of the week."

Paddington nodded his agreement. "I think," he announced at last, amid sighs of relief, "I'll always have my old teeth disposed of in future."

Chapter 29.

◆ ◆ ◆

Christmas

Paddington found that Christmas took a long time to come. Each morning when he hurried downstairs he crossed the date off the calendar, but the more days he crossed off, the further away it seemed.

However, there was plenty to occupy his mind. For one thing, the postman started arriving later and later in the morning, and when he did finally reach the Browns' house, there were so many letters to deliver he had a job to push them all through the mailbox. Often there were mysterious-looking parcels as well, which Mrs. Bird promptly hid before Paddington had time to squeeze them.

A surprising number of the envelopes were addressed to Paddington himself, and he carefully made a list of all those who had sent him Christmas cards so that he could be sure of thanking them.

"You may be only a small bear," said Mrs. Bird as she helped him arrange the cards on the mantelpiece, "but you certainly leave your mark."

Paddington wasn't sure how to take this, especially as Mrs. Bird had just polished the hall floor, but when he examined his paws they were quite clean.

Paddington had made his own Christmas cards. Some he had drawn himself, decorating the edges with holly and mistletoe; others had been made out of pictures cut from Mrs. Brown's magazines. But each one had the words A MERRY CHRISTMAS AND A HAPPY NEW YEAR printed on the front, and they were signed PADINGTUN BROWN on the inside, together with his special pawmark to show that they were genuine.

Paddington wasn't sure about the spelling of A MERRY CHRISTMAS. It didn't look at all right. But Mrs. Bird checked all the words in a dictionary for him to make certain.

"I don't suppose many people get Christmas cards from a bear," she explained. "They'll probably want to keep them, so you ought to make sure they are right."

One evening Mr. Brown arrived home with a huge Christmas tree tied to the roof of his car. It was placed in a position of honor by the dining room window, and both Paddington and Mr. Brown spent a long time decorating it with colored lights and silver tinsel.

Apart from the Christmas tree, there were paper chains and holly to be put up, and large colored bells made of crinkly paper. Paddington enjoyed doing the paper chains. He managed to persuade Mr. Brown that bears were very good at putting up decorations, and together they did most of the house, with Paddington standing on Mr. Brown's shoulders while Mr. Brown handed up the thumbtacks. It came to an unhappy end one evening when Paddington accidentally put his paw on a thumbtack that he'd left on top of Mr. Brown's head. When Mrs. Bird rushed into the dining room to see what all the fuss was about, and to inquire why all the lights had suddenly gone out, she found Paddington hanging by his paws from the chandelier and Mr. Brown dancing round the room rubbing his head.

But by then the decorations were almost finished and the house had taken on quite a festive air. The sideboard was groaning under the weight of nuts and oranges, dates and figs, none of which Paddington was allowed to touch.

The excitement in the Browns' house mounted until it reached fever pitch a few days before Christmas, when Jonathan and Judy began their school holidays.

But if the days leading up to Christmas were busy and exciting, they were nothing compared with Christmas Day itself.

The Browns were up early on Christmas morning, much earlier than they had intended. It all started when Paddington woke to find a large pillowcase at the bottom of his bed. His eyes nearly popped out with astonishment when he switched his flashlight on, for it was bulging with parcels, and it certainly hadn't been there when he'd gone to bed on Christmas Eve.

Paddington's eyes grew larger and larger as he unwrapped the brightly colored paper round each present. A few days before, on Mrs. Bird's instructions, he had made a list of all the things he hoped to have given him and had hidden it up one of the chimneys. It was a strange thing, but everything on that list seemed to be in the pillowcase.

There was a large chemistry set from Mr. Brown, full of jars and bottles and test tubes, which looked very interesting. And there was a miniature xylophone from Mrs. Brown, which pleased him no end. Paddington was fond of music—especially the loud sort, which was good for conducting—and he had always wanted something he could actually play.

Mrs. Bird's parcel was even more exciting, for it contained a checked cap, which he'd especially asked for and had underlined on his list. Paddington stood on the end of his bed, admiring the effect in the mirror for quite a while.

Jonathan and Judy had each given him a travel book. Paddington was very interested in geography, being a much-traveled bear, and he was pleased to see there were plenty of maps and colored pictures inside.

The noise from Paddington's room was soon sufficient to waken both Jonathan and Judy, and in no time at all the whole house was in an uproar, with wrapping paper and bits of string everywhere.

"I'm as patriotic as the next man," grumbled Mr. Brown. "But I draw the line when bears start playing the national anthem at six o'clock in the morning, especially on a xylophone."

As always, it was left to Mrs. Bird to restore order. "No more presents until after lunch," she said firmly. She had just tripped over Paddington on the upstairs landing, where he was investigating his new chemistry set, and something strange had gone into one of her slippers.

"It's all right, Mrs. Bird," said Paddington, consulting his instruction book, "it's only some iron filings. I don't think they're dangerous."

"Dangerous or not," said Mrs. Bird, "I've a big dinner to cook—not to mention your birthday cake to finish decorating."

Being a bear, Paddington had two birthdays each year, one in the summer and one at Christmas, and the Browns were holding a party in his honor, to which Mr. Gruber had been invited.

After they'd had breakfast and been to church, the morning passed quickly, and Paddington spent most of his time trying to decide what to do next. With so many things from which to choose, it was most difficult. He read some chapters in his books and made several interesting smells and a small explosion with his chemistry set.

Mr. Brown was already in trouble for having given it to him, especially when Paddington found a chapter in the instruction book headed "Indoor Fireworks." He made himself a "never-ending snake," which wouldn't stop growing and frightened Mrs. Bird to death when she met it coming down the stairs.

"If we don't watch out," she confided to Mrs. Brown, "we won't last through Christmas. We shall either be blown to smithereens or poisoned. He was testing my gravy with some litmus paper just now."

Mrs. Brown sighed. "It's a good thing Christmas only comes once a year," she said as she helped Mrs. Bird with the potatoes.

"It isn't over yet," warned Mrs. Bird.

Fortunately, Mr. Gruber arrived at that moment, and some measure of order was established before they all sat down to dinner.

Paddington's eyes glistened as he surveyed the table. He didn't agree with Mr. Brown when he said it all looked too good to eat. All the same, even Paddington got noticeably slower towards the end, when Mrs. Bird brought in the Christmas pudding.

"Well," said Mr. Gruber a few minutes later, as he sat back and surveyed his empty plate, "I must say that's the best Christmas dinner I've had for many a day. Thank you very much indeed!"

"Hear! Hear!" agreed Mr. Brown. "What do you say, Paddington?"

"It was very nice," said Paddington, licking some cream from his whiskers. "Except I had a bone in my Christmas pudding."

"You *what*?" exclaimed Mrs. Brown. "Don't be silly—there are no bones in Christmas pudding."

"I had one," said Paddington firmly. "It was all hard, and it stuck in my throat."

"Good gracious!" exclaimed Mrs. Bird. "The five pence! I always put a silver coin in the Christmas pudding."

"What!" said Paddington, nearly falling off his chair. "A five pence? I've never heard of a five pence pudding before."

"Quick!" shouted Mr. Brown, rising to the emergency. "Turn him upside down."

Before Paddington could reply, he found himself hanging head down while Mr. Brown and Mr. Gruber took it in turns to shake him. The rest of the family stood round watching the floor.

"It's no good," said Mr. Brown after a while. "It must have gone too far." He helped Mr. Gruber lift Paddington into an armchair, where he lay gasping for breath.

"I've got a magnet upstairs," said Jonathan. "We could try lowering it down his throat on a piece of string."

"I don't think so, dear," said Mrs. Brown in a worried tone of voice. "He might swallow that, and then we should be even worse off." She bent over the chair. "How do you feel, Paddington?"

"Sick," said Paddington in an aggrieved tone of voice.

"Of course you do, dear," said Mrs. Brown. "It's only to be expected. There's only one thing to do—we shall have to send for the doctor."

"Thank goodness I scrubbed it first," said Mrs. Bird. "It might have been covered with germs."

"But I *didn't* swallow it," gasped Paddington. "I only nearly did. Then I put it on the side of my plate. I didn't know it was a coin because it was all covered with Christmas pudding."

Paddington felt very fed up. He'd just eaten one of the best dinners he could ever remember and now he'd been turned upside down and shaken without even being given time to explain.

Everyone exchanged glances and then crept quietly away, leaving Paddington to recover by himself. There didn't seem to be much they *could* say.

But after the dinner things had been cleared away, and by the time Mrs. Bird had made some strong coffee, Paddington was almost himself again. He was sitting up in the chair helping himself to some dates when they trooped back into the room. It took a lot to make Paddington ill for very long.

When they had finished their coffee and were sitting round the blazing fire feeling warm and comfortable, Mr. Brown rubbed his hands. "Now, Paddington," he said, "it's not only Christmas, it's your birthday as well. What would you like to do?"

A mysterious expression came over Paddington's face. "If you all go in the other room," he announced, "I've a special surprise for you."

"Oh dear, *must* we, Paddington?" said Mrs. Brown. "There isn't a fire."

"I won't be long," said Paddington firmly. "But it's a special surprise and it has to be prepared." He held the door open, and the Browns, Mrs. Bird, and Mr. Gruber filed obediently into the other room.

"Now close your eyes," said Paddington when they were all settled, "and I'll let you know when I'm ready."

Mrs. Brown shivered. "I hope you won't be too long," she called. But the only reply was the sound of the door clicking shut.

They waited for several minutes without speaking, and then Mr. Gruber cleared his throat. "Do you think young Mr. Brown's forgotten about us?" he asked.

"I don't know," said Mrs. Brown. "But I'm not waiting much longer.

"Henry!" she exclaimed, as she opened her eyes. "Have you gone to sleep?"

"Er, wassat?" snorted Mr. Brown. He had eaten such a large dinner he was finding it difficult to keep awake. "What's happening? Have I missed anything?"

"Nothing's happening," said Mrs. Brown. "Henry, you'd better go and see what Paddington's up to."

Several more minutes went by before Mr. Brown returned to announce that he couldn't find Paddington anywhere.

"Well, he must be *somewhere*," said Mrs. Brown. "Bears don't disappear into thin air."

"Wait!" exclaimed Jonathan, as a thought suddenly struck him. "You don't think he's playing Father Christmas, do you? He was asking all about it the other day when he put his list up the chimney. I bet that's why he wanted us to come in here—because this chimney connects with the one upstairs, and there isn't a fire."

"Father Christmas?" said Mr. Brown. "I'll give him Father Christmas!" He stuck his head up the chimney and called Paddington's name several times. "I can't see anything," he said, striking a match. As if in answer, a large lump of soot descended and burst on top of his head.

"Now look what you've done, Henry," said Mrs. Brown. "Shouting so—you've disturbed the soot. All over your clean shirt!"

"If it *is* young Mr. Brown, perhaps he's stuck somewhere," suggested Mr. Gruber. "He did have rather a large dinner. I remember wondering at the time where he put it all."

Mr. Gruber's suggestion had an immediate effect on the party, and everyone began to look serious.

"Why, he might suffocate with the fumes," exclaimed Mrs. Bird as she hurried outside to the broom closet.

When she returned, armed with a mop, everyone took it in turns to poke it up the chimney, but even though they strained their ears, they couldn't hear a sound.

It was while the excitement was at its height that Paddington came into the room. He looked most surprised when he saw Mr. Brown with his head up the chimney.

"You can come into the dining room now," he announced, looking round the room. "I've finished wrapping my presents and they're all on the Christmas tree."

"You don't mean to say," spluttered Mr. Brown as he sat in the fireplace rubbing his face with a handkerchief, "you've been in the other room all the time?"

"Yes," said Paddington innocently. "I hope I didn't keep you waiting too long."

Mrs. Brown looked at her husband. "I thought you said you'd looked every-

where," she exclaimed.

"Well, we'd just come from the dining room," said Mr. Brown, looking very sheepish. "I didn't think he'd be *there*."

"It only goes to show," said Mrs. Bird hastily, as she caught sight of the expression on Mr. Brown's face, "how easy it is to give a bear a bad name."

Paddington looked most interested when they explained to him what all the fuss was about.

"I never thought of coming down the chimney," he said, staring at the fireplace.

"Well, you're not thinking about it now, either," replied Mr. Brown sternly.

But even Mr. Brown's expression changed as he followed Paddington into the dining room and saw the surprise that had been prepared for them.

In addition to the presents that had already been placed on the tree, there were now six newly wrapped ones tied to the lower branches. If the Browns recognized the wrapping paper they had used for Paddington's presents earlier in the day, they were much too polite to say anything.

"I'm afraid I had to use old paper," said Paddington apologetically as he waved a paw at the tree. "I hadn't any money left. That's why you had to go in the other room while I wrapped them."

"Really, Paddington," said Mrs. Brown. "I'm very cross with you—spending all your money on presents for us."

"I'm afraid they're rather ordinary," said Paddington as he settled back in a chair to watch the others. "But I hope you like them. They're all labeled so that you know which is which."

"Ordinary?" exclaimed Mr. Brown as he opened his parcel. "I don't call a pipe rack ordinary. And there's an ounce of my favorite tobacco tied to the back as well!"

"Gosh! A new stamp album!" cried Jonathan. "And it's got some stamps inside already."

"They're Peruvian ones from Aunt Lucy's postcards," said Paddington. "I've been saving them for you."

"And I've got a box of paints," exclaimed Judy. "Thank you very much, Paddington. It's just what I wanted."

"We all seem to be lucky," said Mrs. Brown as she unwrapped a parcel containing a bottle of her favorite lavender water. "How *did* you guess? I finished my last bottle only a week ago."

"I'm sorry about your parcel, Mrs. Bird," said Paddington, looking across the room. "I had a hard time with the knots."

"It must be something special," said Mr. Brown. "It seems all string and no parcel."

"That's because it's really a clothesline," explained Paddington, "not string. I rescued it when I got stuck in the revolving door at Crumbold and Ferns."

"That makes two presents in one," said Mrs. Bird, as she freed the last of the knots and began unwinding yards and yards of paper. "How exciting. I can't think what it can be.

"Why," she exclaimed, "I do believe it's a brooch! And it's shaped like a bear—how lovely!" Mrs. Bird looked most touched as she handed the present round for everyone to see. "I shall keep it in a safe place," she added, "and only wear it on special occasions, when I want to impress people."

"I don't know what mine is," said Mr. Gruber as they all turned to him. He squeezed the parcel. "It's such a funny shape. . . . It's a drinking mug!" he exclaimed, his face lighting up with pleasure. "And it even has my name painted on the side!"

"It's for your cocoa, Mr. Gruber," said Paddington. "I noticed your old one was getting rather chipped."

"I'm sure it will make my cocoa taste better than it ever has before," said Mr. Gruber.

He stood up and cleared his throat. "I think I would like to offer a vote of thanks to young Mr. Brown," he said, "for all his nice presents. I'm sure he must have given them a great deal of thought."

"Hear! Hear!" echoed Mr. Brown, as he filled his pipe.

Mr. Gruber felt under his chair. "And while I think of it, Mr. Brown, I have a small present for you."

Everyone stood round and watched while Paddington struggled with his parcel, eager to see what Mr. Gruber had bought him. A gasp of surprise went up as he tore the paper to one side, for it was a beautifully bound leather scrapbook, with "Paddington Brown" printed in gold leaf on the cover.

Paddington didn't know what to say, but Mr. Gruber waved his thanks to one side. "I know how you enjoy writing about your adventures, Mr. Brown," he said. "And you have so many I'm sure your present scrapbook must be almost full."

"It is," said Paddington earnestly. "And I'm sure I shall have lots more. Things happen to me, you know. But I shall only put my best ones in here!"

When he made his way up to bed later that evening, his mind was in such a whirl and he was so full of good things that he could hardly climb the stairs, let alone think about anything. He wasn't quite sure which he had enjoyed most, the presents, the Christmas dinner, the games, or the tea—with the special marmalade-layer birthday cake Mrs. Bird had made in his honor. Pausing on the corner halfway up, he decided he had enjoyed giving his own presents best of all.

"Paddington! Whatever have you got there?" He jumped and hastily hid his paw behind his back as he heard Mrs. Bird calling from the bottom of the stairs.

"It's only some Christmas pudding, Mrs. Bird," he called, looking over the banister guiltily. "I thought I might get hungry during the night, and I didn't want to take any chances."

"Honestly!" Mrs. Bird exclaimed as she was joined by the others. "What *does* that bear look like? A paper hat about ten sizes too big on his head, Mr. Gruber's scrapbook in one paw, and a plate of Christmas pudding in the other!"

"I don't care what he looks like," said Mrs. Brown, "so long as he stays that way. The place wouldn't be the same without him."

But Paddington was too far away to hear what was being said. He was already sitting up in bed, busily writing in his scrapbook.

First of all, there was a very important notice to go on the front page. It said:

PADINGTUN BROWN,

32 WINDSOR GARDENS,

LUNDUN,

ENGLAND,

YUROPE,

THE WORLD.

Then, on the next page he added, in large capital letters, MY ADDVENTURES. CHAPTER WUN.

Paddington chewed his pen thoughtfully for a moment and then carefully replaced the top on the bottle of ink before it had a chance to fall over on the sheets. He felt much too sleepy to write any more. But he didn't really mind. Tomorrow was another day, and he felt quite sure he *would* have some more adventures, even if he didn't know what they were going to be as yet.

Paddington lay back and pulled the blankets up round his whiskers. It was warm and comfortable, and he sighed contentedly as he closed his eyes. It was nice being a bear. Especially a bear called Paddington.

◢ ◢ ◾

Chapter 30

Something Nasty in the Kitchen

"Two days!" exclaimed Mrs. Brown, staring at Dr. MacAndrew in horror. "Do you mean to say we have to stay in bed for two whole days?"

"Aye," said Dr. MacAndrew. "There's a nasty wee bug going the rounds and if ye don't I'll no' be responsible for the consequences."

"But Mrs. Bird's away until tomorrow," said Mrs. Brown. "And so are Jonathan and Judy . . . and . . . and that only leaves Paddington."

"Two days," repeated Dr. MacAndrew as he snapped his bag shut. "And not a moment less. The house'll no' fall down in that time.

"There's one thing," he added, as he paused at the door and stared at Mr. and Mrs. Brown with a twinkle in his eye. "Whatever else happens you'll no' die of starvation. Yon wee bear's verra fond of his inside!"

With that he went downstairs to tell Paddington the news.

"Oh dear," groaned Mr. Brown, as the door closed behind the doctor. "I think I feel worse already."

◆ ◆ ◆

Paddington felt most important as he listened to what Dr. MacAndrew had to say and he carefully wrote down all the instructions. After he had shown him to the door and waved goodbye, he hurried back into the kitchen to collect his shopping basket on wheels.

Usually with Paddington shopping in the market was a very leisurely affair. He liked to stop and have a chat with the various traders in the Portobello Road, where he was a well-known figure. To have Paddington's business was considered to be something of an honor as he had a very good eye for a bargain. But on this particular morning he hardly had time even to call in at the baker's for his morning supply of buns.

It was early and Mr. Gruber hadn't yet opened his shutters, so Paddington wrapped one of the hot buns in a piece of paper, wrote a message on the outside saying who it was from and explaining that he wouldn't be along for "elevenses" that morning, and then pushed it through the mailbox.

Having finished the shopping and been to the pharmacy with Dr. MacAndrew's prescription, Paddington made his way quickly back to number thirty-two Windsor Gardens.

It wasn't often Paddington had a chance to lend a paw round the house, let alone cook the dinner, and he was looking forward to it. In particular, there was a new feather duster of Mrs. Bird's he'd had his eye on for several days and which he was anxious to test.

"I must say Paddington looks very professional in that old apron of Mrs. Bird's," said Mrs. Brown later that morning. She sat up in bed holding a cup and saucer. "And it was kind of him to bring us up a cup of coffee."

"Very kind," agreed Mr. Brown. "But I rather wish he hadn't brought all these sandwiches as well."

"They *are* rather thick," agreed Mrs. Brown, looking at one doubtfully. "He said they were emergency ones. I'm not quite sure what he meant by that. I do hope nothing's wrong."

"I don't like the sound of it," said Mr. Brown. "There've been several nasty silences this morning—as if something were going on." He sniffed. "And there seems to be a strong smell of burned feathers coming from somewhere."

"Well, you'd better eat them, Henry," warned Mrs. Brown. "He's used some of his special marmalade from the cut-price grocer and I'm sure they're meant to be a treat. You'll never hear the last of it if you leave any."

"Yes, but *six!*" grumbled Mr. Brown. "I'm not even very keen on marmalade.

And at eleven o'clock in the morning! I shan't want any lunch." He looked thoughtfully at the window and then at the plate of sandwiches again.

"No, Henry," said Mrs. Brown, reading his thoughts. "You're not giving any to the birds. I don't suppose they like marmalade.

"Anyway," she added, "Paddington did say something about lunch being late, so you may be glad of them."

She looked wistfully at the door. "All the same, I wish I could see what's going on. It's not knowing that's the worst part. He had flour all over his whiskers when he came up just now."

"If you ask me," said Mr. Brown, "you're probably much better off being in the dark." He took a long drink from his cup and then jumped up in bed, spluttering.

"Henry, dear," exclaimed Mrs. Brown. "*Do* be careful. You'll have coffee all over the sheets."

"Coffee!" yelled Mr. Brown. "Did you say this was coffee?"

"*I* didn't, dear," said Mrs. Brown mildly. "Paddington did." She took a sip from her own cup and then made a wry face. "It *has* got rather an unusual taste."

"Unusual!" exclaimed Mr. Brown. "It tastes like nothing on earth." He glared at his cup and then poked at it gingerly with a spoon. "It's got some funny green things floating in it too!" he exclaimed.

"Have a marmalade sandwich," said Mrs. Brown. "It'll help take the taste away."

Mr. Brown gave his wife an expressive look. "Two days!" he said, sinking back into the bed. "Two whole days!"

Downstairs, Paddington was in a bit of a mess. So, for that matter, were the kitchen, the hall, the dining room and the stairs.

Things hadn't really gone right since he'd lifted up a corner of the dining room carpet in order to sweep some dust underneath and discovered a number of very interesting old newspapers. Paddington sighed. Perhaps if he hadn't spent so much time reading the newspapers he might not have hurried quite so much over the rest of the dusting. Then he might have been more careful when he shook Mrs. Bird's feather duster over the fireplace.

And if he hadn't set fire to Mrs. Bird's feather duster, he might have been able to take more time over the coffee.

Paddington felt very guilty about the coffee and he rather wished he had tested it before taking it upstairs to Mr. and Mrs. Brown. He was very glad he'd decided to make cocoa for himself instead.

Quite early in the morning Paddington had run out of saucepans. It was the first big meal he had ever cooked and he wanted it to be something special. Having carefully consulted Mrs. Bird's cookbook, he'd drawn out a special menu in red ink with a bit of everything in it.

But by the time he had put the stew to boil in one big saucepan, the potatoes in another saucepan, the peas in a third, the brussels sprouts in yet another, and used at least four more for mixing operations, there was really only the electric kettle left in which to put the cabbage. Unfortunately, in his haste to make the coffee, Paddington had completely forgotten to take the cabbage out again.

Now he was having trouble with the dumplings!

Paddington was very keen on stew, especially when it was served with dumplings, but he was beginning to wish he had decided to cook something else for lunch.

Even now he wasn't quite sure what had gone wrong. He'd looked up the chapter on dumplings in Mrs. Bird's cookbook and followed the instructions most carefully; putting two parts of flour to one of suet and then adding milk before stirring the whole lot together. But somehow, instead of the mixture turning into neat balls as it showed in the colored picture, it had all gone runny. Then, when he'd added more flour and suet, it had gone lumpy instead and stuck to his fur, so that he'd had to add more milk and then more flour and suet, until he had a huge mountain of dumpling mixture in the middle of the kitchen table.

All in all, he decided, it just wasn't his day. He wiped his paws carefully on Mrs. Bird's apron and, after looking round in vain for a large enough bowl, he scraped the dumpling mixture into his hat.

It was a lot heavier than he had expected and he had a hard time lifting it up onto the stove. It was even more difficult putting the mixture into the stew as it kept sticking to his paws, and as fast as he got it off one paw it stuck to the other. In the end he had to sit on the drainboard and use the broom handle.

Paddington wasn't very impressed with Mrs. Bird's cookbook. The instructions seemed all wrong. Not only had the dumplings been difficult to make, but the ones they showed in the picture were much too small. They weren't a bit like the ones Mrs. Bird usually served. Even Paddington rarely managed more than two of Mrs. Bird's dumplings.

Having scraped the last of the mixture off his paws, Paddington pushed the saucepan lid down hard and scrambled clear. The steam from the saucepan had made his fur go soggy and he sat in the middle of the floor for several minutes getting his breath back and mopping his brow with an old dishcloth.

It was while he was sitting there, scraping the remains of the dumplings out of his hat and licking the spoon, that he felt something move behind him. Not only that, but out of the corner of his eye he could see a shadow on the floor which definitely hadn't been there a moment before.

Paddington sat very still, holding his breath and listening. It wasn't so much a noise as a feeling, and it seemed to be creeping nearer and nearer, making a soft

swishing noise as it came. Paddington felt his fur begin to stand on end as there came the sound of a slow *plop . . . plop . . . plop* across the kitchen floor. And then, just as he was summoning up enough courage to look over his shoulder, there was a loud crash from the direction of the stove. Without waiting to see what it was Paddington pulled his hat down over his head and ran, slamming the door behind him.

He arrived in the hall just as there was a loud knock on the front door. To his relief he heard a familiar voice call his name through the mailbox.

"I got your message, Mr. Brown, about not being able to come for elevenses this morning," began Mr. Gruber, as Paddington opened the door, "and I just thought I would call round to see if there was anything I could do . . ." His voice trailed away as he stared at Paddington.

"Why, Mr. Brown," he exclaimed, "you're all white! Is anything the matter?"

"Don't worry, Mr. Gruber," cried Paddington, waving his paws in the air. "It's only some of Mrs. Bird's flour. I'm afraid I can't raise my hat because it's stuck down with dumpling mixture, but I'm very glad you've come because there's something nasty in the kitchen!"

"Something nasty in the kitchen?" echoed Mr. Gruber. "What sort of thing?"

"I don't know," said Paddington, struggling with his hat. "But it's got a shadow and it's making a funny noise."

Mr. Gruber looked round nervously for something to defend himself with. "We'll soon see about that," he said, taking an umbrella from the hall.

Paddington led the way back to the kitchen and then stood to one side by the door. "After you, Mr. Gruber," he said politely.

"Er . . . thank you, Mr. Brown," said Mr. Gruber doubtfully.

He grasped the umbrella firmly in both hands and then kicked open the door. "Come out!" he cried. "Whoever you are!"

"I don't think it's a *who*, Mr. Gruber," said Paddington, peering round the door. "It's a *what*!"

"Good heavens!" exclaimed Mr. Gruber, staring at the sight which met his eyes. "What *has* been going on?"

Over most of the kitchen there was a thin film of flour. There was flour on the table, in the sink, on the floor—in fact, over practically everything. But it wasn't the general state of the room which made Mr. Gruber cry out with surprise—it was the sight of something large and white hanging over the side of the stove.

He stared at it for a moment and then advanced cautiously across the kitchen and poked it with the umbrella. There was a loud squelching noise and Mr. Gruber jumped back as part of it broke away and fell with a plop to the floor.

"Good heavens!" he exclaimed again. "I do believe it's some kind of dumpling, Mr. Brown. I've never seen quite such a big one before," he went on as Paddington joined him. "It's grown right out of the saucepan and pushed the lid onto the floor. No wonder it made you jump."

Mr. Gruber mopped his brow and opened the window. It was very warm in the kitchen. "How ever did it get to be that size?"

"I don't really know, Mr. Gruber," said Paddington, looking puzzled. "It's one of mine, and it didn't start off that way. I think something must have gone wrong in the saucepan."

"I should think it has," said Mr. Gruber. "If I were you, Mr. Brown, I think I'd

turn the stove off before that dumpling catches fire and does any more damage. There's no knowing what might happen once it gets out of control.

"Perhaps, if you'll allow me," he continued tactfully, "I can give you a hand. It must be very difficult cooking for so many people."

"It is when you only have paws, Mr. Gruber," said Paddington gratefully.

Mr. Gruber sniffed. "I must say it all smells very nice. If we make some more dumplings quickly, everything else should be just about ready."

As he handed Paddington the flour and suet Mr. Gruber explained how dumplings became very much larger when they were cooked and that it really needed only a small amount of mixture to make quite large ones.

"No wonder yours were so big, Mr. Brown," he said, as he lifted Paddington's old dumpling into the dishwashing bowl. "You must have used almost a bag of flour."

"Two bags," said Paddington, looking over his shoulder. "I don't know what Mrs. Bird will say when she hears about it."

"Perhaps if we buy her some more," said Mr. Gruber, as he staggered into the garden with the bowl, "she won't mind quite so much."

◆ ◆ ◆

"That's queer," said Mr. Brown as he stared out of the bedroom window. "A big white thing has suddenly appeared in the garden. Just behind the nasturtiums."

"Nonsense, Henry," said Mrs. Brown. "You must be seeing things."

"I'm not," said Mr. Brown, rubbing his glasses and taking another look. "It's all white and shapeless and it looks horrible. Mr. Curry's seen it too—he's peering over the fence at it now. Do *you* know what it is, Paddington?"

"A big white thing, Mr. Brown?" repeated Paddington vaguely, joining him at the window. "Perhaps it's a snowball."

"In summer?" said Mr. Brown suspiciously.

"Henry," said Mrs. Brown. "Do come away from there and decide what you're having for lunch. Paddington's gone to a lot of trouble writing out a menu for us."

Mr. Brown took a large sheet of drawing paper from his wife, and his face brightened as he studied it. It said:

MENUE

SOOP

•　　•　　•

FISH

OMMLETS

ROWST BEEF

Stew with Dumplings—Potatows—Brussle Sprowts
Pees—Cabbidge—Greyvy

•　　•　　•

MARMALADE AND CUSTERD

•　　•　　•

COFFEY

•　　•　　•

"How nice!" exclaimed Mr. Brown when he had finished reading it. "And what a good idea putting pieces of vegetable on the side as illustrations. I've never seen that done before."

"They're not really meant to be there, Mr. Brown," said Paddington. "I'm afraid they came off my paws."

"Oh," said Mr. Brown, brushing his mustache thoughtfully. "Mmm. Well, you know, I rather fancy some soup and fish myself."

"I'm afraid they're off," said Paddington hastily, remembering a time when he'd once been taken out to lunch and they had arrived late.

"Off?" said Mr. Brown. "But they can't be. No one's ordered anything yet."

Mrs. Brown drew him to one side. "I think we're meant to have the stew and dumplings, Henry," she whispered. "They're underlined."

"What's that, Mary?" asked Mr. Brown, who was a bit slow to grasp things at times. "Oh! Oh, I see . . . er . . . on second thought, Paddington, I think perhaps I'll have the stew."

"That's good," said Paddington, "because I've got it on a tray outside all ready."

"By Jove," said Mr. Brown, as Paddington staggered in breathing heavily and carrying first one plate and then another piled high with stew. "I must say I didn't expect anything like this."

"Did you cook it all by yourself, Paddington?" asked Mrs. Brown.

"Well . . . almost all," replied Paddington truthfully. "I had a bit of an accident with the dumplings and so Mr. Gruber helped me make some more."

"You're sure you have enough for your own lunch?" said Mrs. Brown anxiously.

"Oh, yes," said Paddington, trying hard not to picture the kitchen, "there's enough to last for days and days."

"Well, I think you should be congratulated," said Mr. Brown. "I'm enjoying it no end. I bet there aren't many bears who can say they've cooked a meal like this. It's fit for a queen."

Paddington's eyes lit up with pleasure as he listened to Mr. and Mrs. Brown. It had been a lot of hard work, but he was glad it had all been worthwhile—even if there was a lot of mess to clear up.

"You know, Henry," said Mrs. Brown, as Paddington hurried off downstairs to see Mr. Gruber, "we ought to think ourselves very lucky having a bear like Paddington about the house in an emergency."

Mr. Brown lay back on his pillow and surveyed the mountain of food on his plate. "Dr. MacAndrew was right about one thing," he said. "While Paddington's looking after us, whatever else happens we certainly shan't starve."

Paddington Dines Out

"I vote," said Mr. Brown, "that we celebrate Paddington's birthday by visiting a restaurant. All those in favor say aye."

Mr. Brown's suggestion had a mixed reception. Jonathan and Judy called out "aye" at once. Mrs. Brown looked rather doubtful and Mrs. Bird kept her eyes firmly on her knitting.

"Do you think it's wise, Henry?" said Mrs. Brown. "You know what Paddington's like when we take him out. Things happen."

"It *is* his birthday," replied Mr. Brown.

"And his anniversary," said Judy. "Sort of."

The Browns were holding a council of war. It was Paddington's summer birthday. Being a bear, Paddington had two birthdays every year, one at Christmas and the other in midsummer. That apart, he had now been with the Browns for a little over a year, and it had been decided to celebrate the two occasions at the same time.

"After all, we ought to do *something*," said Mr. Brown, playing his trump card. "If we hadn't seen him that day at Paddington Station, we might never have met him and goodness knows where he would have ended up."

The Browns were silent for a moment as they considered the awful possibility of never having met Paddington.

"I must say," remarked Mrs. Bird, in a voice which really decided the matter, "the house wouldn't be the same without him."

"That settles it," said Mr. Brown. "I'll ring the Porchester right away and reserve a table for tonight."

"Oh, Henry," exclaimed Mrs. Brown. "Not the *Porchester*. That's such an expensive place."

Mr. Brown waved his hand in the air. "Nothing but the best is good enough for Paddington," he said generously. "We'll invite Mr. Gruber as well and make a real party of it.

"By the way," he continued, "where *is* Paddington? I haven't seen him for ages."

"He was peering through the mailbox just now," said Mrs. Bird. "I think he was looking for the postman."

Paddington liked birthdays. He didn't get many letters—only his catalogues and an occasional postcard from his Aunt Lucy in Peru—but today the mantelpiece in the dining room was already filled to overflowing with cards and he was looking forward to some more arriving. There had been a card from each of the Browns, one from Mr. Gruber, and quite a surprising number from various people who lived in the neighborhood. There was even an old one from Mr. Curry, which Mrs. Bird recognized as one Paddington had sent him the year before, but she had wisely decided not to point this out.

Then there were all the parcels. Paddington was very keen on parcels, especially

when they were well wrapped up with plenty of paper and string. In fact, he had done extremely well for himself, and the news that they were all going out that evening too came as a great surprise.

"Mind you," said Mrs. Brown, "you'll have to have a bath first."

"A bath!" exclaimed Paddington. "On my birthday?"

Paddington looked most upset at the thought of having a bath on his birthday.

"The Porchester is a very famous restaurant," explained Mrs. Brown. "Only the best people go there."

And, despite his protests, he was sent upstairs that afternoon with a washcloth and some soap and strict instructions not to come down again until he was clean.

Excitement in the Browns' house mounted during the afternoon and by the time Mr. Gruber arrived, looking rather self-conscious in an evening-dress suit which he hadn't worn for many years, it had reached fever pitch.

"I don't think I've ever been to the Porchester before, Mr. Brown," he whispered to Paddington in the hall. "So that makes two of us. It'll be a nice change from cocoa and buns."

Paddington became more and more excited on the journey to the restaurant. He always enjoyed seeing the lights of London and even though it was summer, quite a few of them had already come on by the time they got there.

He followed Mr. Brown up the steps of the restaurant and in through some large doors, giving the man who held them open a friendly wave of his paw.

In the distance there was the sound of music and as they all gathered inside the entrance in order to leave their coats at the cloakroom, Paddington looked round

with interest at the chandeliers hanging from the ceiling and at the dozens of waiters gliding to and fro.

"Here comes the headwaiter," said Mr. Brown, as a tall, superior-looking man approached. "We've booked a table near the orchestra," he called. "In the name of Brown."

The headwaiter stared at Paddington. "Is the young . . . er . . . bear gentleman with you?" he asked, looking down his nose.

"With us?" said Mr. Brown. "We're with *him*. It's his party."

"Oh," said the man disapprovingly. "Then I'm afraid you can't come in."

"What!" exclaimed Paddington amid a chorus of dismay. "But I went without a second helping at lunch specially."

"I'm afraid the young gentlemen isn't wearing evening dress," explained the man. "Everyone at the Porchester has to wear evening dress."

Paddington could hardly believe his ears and he gave the man a hard stare.

"Bears don't have evening dress," said Judy, squeezing his paw. "They have evening fur—and Paddington's has been washed specially."

The headwaiter looked at Paddington doubtfully. Paddington had a very persistent stare when he liked, and some of the special ones his Aunt Lucy had taught him were very powerful indeed. The headwaiter coughed. "I dare say," he said, "we might make an exception—just this once."

He turned and led the way through the crowded restaurant, past tables covered with snowy white cloths and gleaming silver, towards a big round table near the orchestra. Paddington followed close behind, and by the time they reached it the man's neck had gone a funny shade of red.

When they were all seated, the headwaiter gave them each a huge card on which was printed a list of all the dishes. Paddington had to hold his with both paws and he stared at it in amazement.

"Well, Paddington," said Mr. Brown. "What would you like to start with? Soup? An hors d'oeuvre?"

Paddington looked at his menu in disgust. He didn't think much of it at all. "I don't know what I would like, Mr. Brown," he said. "My menu's full of mistakes and I can't read it."

"*Mistakes!*" The headwaiter raised one eyebrow to its full height and looked at Paddington severely. "There is never a mistake on a Porchester menu."

"These aren't mistakes, Paddington," whispered Judy, as she looked over his shoulder. "It's French."

"French!" exclaimed Paddington. "Fancy printing a menu in French!"

Mr. Brown hastily scanned his own menu. "Er . . . have you anything suitable for a young bear's treat?" he asked.

"A young bear's treat?" repeated the headwaiter haughtily. "We pride ourselves that there is nothing one cannot obtain at the Porchester."

"In that case," said Paddington, looking most relieved, "I think I'll have a marmalade sandwich."

Looking round, Paddington decided a place as important as the Porchester must serve very good marmalade sandwiches, and he was anxious to test one.

"I beg your pardon, sir?" exclaimed the waiter. "Did you say a marmalade sandwich?"

"Yes, please," said Paddington. "With custard."

"For dinner?" said the man.

"Yes," said Paddington firmly. "I'm very fond of marmalade and you said there was nothing you don't have."

The man swallowed hard. In all his years at the Porchester he'd never been asked for a marmalade sandwich before, particularly by a bear. He beckoned to another waiter standing nearby. "A marmalade sandwich for the young bear gentleman," he said. "With custard."

"A marmalade sandwich for the young bear gentleman—with custard," repeated the second waiter. He disappeared through a door leading to the kitchens as if in a dream and the Browns heard the order repeated several more times before it closed. They looked round uneasily while they gave another waiter their own orders.

There seemed to be some sort of commotion going on in the kitchen. Several times they heard raised voices, and once the door opened and a man in a chef's hat appeared round the corner and stared in their direction.

"Perhaps, sir," said yet another waiter, as he wheeled a huge cart laden with dishes towards the table, "you would care for some hors d'oeuvres while you wait?"

"That's a sort of salad," Mr. Brown explained to Paddington.

Paddington licked his whiskers. "It looks like a very good bargain," he said, staring at all the dishes. "I think perhaps I will."

"Oh dear," said Mr. Brown, as Paddington began helping himself. "You're not supposed to eat it *from* the cart, Paddington."

Paddington looked most disappointed as he watched the waiter serve the hors d'oeuvres. It wasn't really quite such good value as he'd thought. But by the time the man had finished piling his plate with vegetables and pickles, salad, and a pile

of interesting-looking little silver onions, he began to change his mind again. Perhaps, he decided, he couldn't have managed the whole cartful after all.

While Mr. Brown gave the rest of the orders—soup for the others, followed by fish and a special omelette for Mr. Gruber—Paddington sat back and prepared to enjoy himself.

"Would you like anything to drink, Paddington?" asked Mr. Brown.

"No, thank you, Mr. Brown," said Paddington. "I have a bowl of water."

"I don't think that's drinking water, Mr. Brown," said Mr. Gruber tactfully. "That's to dip your paws in when they get sticky. That's what's known as a paw bowl."

"A paw bowl?" exclaimed Paddington. "But I had a bath this afternoon."

"Never mind," said Mr. Brown hastily. "I'll send for the lemonade waiter—then you can have an orange squash or something."

Paddington was getting more and more confused. It was all most complicated and he'd never seen so many waiters before. He decided to concentrate on eating for a bit.

"Most enjoyable," said Mr. Gruber a few minutes later when he had finished his soup. "I shall look forward to my omelette now." He looked across the table at Paddington. "Are you enjoying your hors d'oeuvres, Mr. Brown?"

"It's very nice, Mr. Gruber," said Paddington, staring down at his plate with a puzzled expression on his face. "But I think I've lost one of my onions."

"You've what?" asked Mr. Brown. It was difficult to hear what Paddington was saying because of the noise the orchestra was making. It had been playing quite sweetly up until a moment ago, but suddenly it had started making a dreadful racket. It was something to do with one of the saxophone players in the front row. He kept shaking his instrument and then trying to blow it, and all the while the conductor was glaring at him.

"My onion!" exclaimed Paddington. "I had six just now and when I put my fork on one of them it suddenly disappeared. Now I've only got five."

Mrs. Brown began to look more and more embarrassed as Paddington got down off his seat and began peering under the tables. "I do hope he finds it soon," she said. Everyone in the restaurant seemed to be looking in their direction and if they weren't actually pointing, she knew they were talking about them.

"Gosh!" exclaimed Jonathan suddenly. He pointed towards the orchestra. "There is Paddington's onion!"

The Browns turned and looked at the orchestra. The saxophone player seemed to be having an argument with the conductor.

"How can I be expected to play properly," he said bitterly, "when I've got an onion in my instrument? And I've a good idea where it came from too!"

The conductor followed his gaze towards the Browns, who hurriedly looked the other way.

"For heaven's sake don't tell Paddington," said Mrs. Brown. "He'll only want it back."

"Never mind," said Mr. Gruber, as the door leading to the kitchen opened. "I think my omelette's just coming."

The Browns watched as a waiter entered bearing a silver chafing dish, which he placed near their table. Mr. Gruber had ordered an omelette "flambée," which meant it was set on fire just before it was served. "I don't know when I had one of those last," he said. "I'm looking forward to it."

"I must say it looks very nice," said Mr. Brown, twirling his mustache thoughtfully. "I rather wish I'd ordered one myself now.

"Come along, Paddington," he called, as the waiter set light to the pan. "Come and see Mr. Gruber's omelette. It's on fire."

"What!" cried Paddington, poking his head out from beneath the table. "Mr. Gruber's omelette's on fire?"

He stared in astonishment at the waiter as he bore the silver tray with its flaming omelette towards the table.

"It's all right, Mr. Gruber," he called, waving his paws in the air. "I'm coming!"

Before the Browns could stop him, Paddington had grabbed his paw bowl and had thrown the contents over the tray. There was a loud hissing noise, and before the astonished gaze of the waiter Mr. Gruber's omelette slowly collapsed into a soggy mess in the bottom of the dish.

Several people near the Browns applauded. "What an unusual idea," said one of them. "Having the cabaret act sit at one of the tables just like anyone else."

One old gentleman in particular who was sitting by himself at the next table laughed no end. He had been watching Paddington intently for some time and now he began slapping his knee at each new happening.

"Uh-oh!" said Jonathan. "We're in for it now." He pointed towards a party of very important-looking people, led by the headwaiter, who were approaching the Browns' table.

They stopped a few feet away and the headwaiter pointed at Paddington. "That's the one," he said. "The one with the whiskers!"

The most important-looking man stepped forward. "I am the manager," he announced. "And I'm afraid I must ask you to leave. Throwing water over a waiter. Putting onions in a saxophone. Ordering marmalade sandwiches. You'll give the Porchester a bad name."

Mr. and Mrs. Brown exchanged glances. "I've never heard of such a thing," said Mrs. Bird. "If that bear goes we all go."

"Hear! Hear!" echoed Mr. Gruber.

"And if you go I shall go too," came a loud voice from the next table.

Everyone looked round as the old gentleman who had been watching the proceedings rose and waved a finger at the manager. "May I ask why this young bear's being asked to leave?" he boomed.

The manager began to look even more worried, for the old gentleman was one of his best customers and he didn't want to offend him. "It annoys the other diners," he said.

"Nonsense!" boomed the old gentleman. "I'm one of the other diners and I'm not annoyed. Best thing that's happened in years. Don't know when I've enjoyed myself so much." He looked down at Paddington. "I should like to shake you by the paw, bear. It's about time this place was livened up a bit."

"Thank you very much," said Paddington, holding out his paw. He was a bit overawed by the old gentleman and he wasn't at all sure what it was all about anyway.

The old gentleman waved the waiters and the manager to one side and then turned to Mr. Brown. "I'd better introduce myself," he said. "I am Sir Huntley

Martin, the marmalade king. I've been in marmalade for fifty years," he boomed, "and been comin' here for thirty. Never heard anyone ask for a marmalade sandwich before. Does me old heart good."

Paddington looked most impressed. "Imagine being in marmalade for fifty years!" he exclaimed.

"I hope you'll allow me to join you," said Sir Huntley. "I've done a good many things in my life but I don't think I've ever been to a bear's birthday party before."

The old gentleman's presence seemed to have a magical effect on the manager of the Porchester, for he had a hurried conference with the headwaiter, and in no time at all a procession started from the kitchen headed by a waiter bearing a silver tray on which was another omelette for Mr. Gruber.

Even the headwaiter allowed himself a smile, and he gave Paddington a special autographed menu to take away as a souvenir and promised that in future there would always be a special section for marmalade sandwiches.

It was a hilarious party of Browns who finally got up to go. Paddington was so full of good things he had trouble getting up at all. He had a last lingering look at the remains of some ice cream on his plate but decided that enough was as good as a feast. He'd enjoyed himself no end and after a great deal of thought he left a penny under his plate for the waiter.

Sir Huntley Martin seemed very sad that it had all come to an end. "Most enjoyable," he kept booming as they left the table. "Most enjoyable. Perhaps," he added hopefully to Paddington, "you'll do me the honor of visiting my factory one of these days."

"Oh, yes, please," said Paddington. "I should like that very much."

As they left the restaurant he waved goodbye with his paw to all the other diners, several of whom applauded when the orchestra struck up "Happy Birthday to You."

Only Mrs. Bird seemed less surprised than the others, for she had seen Sir Huntley slip something into the conductor's hand.

It had become really dark outside while they had been eating their dinner and all the lights in the street were on. After they had said goodbye to Sir Huntley, and because it was a special occasion, Mr. Brown drove round Piccadilly Circus so that Paddington could see all the colored signs working.

Paddington peered out of the car window and his eyes grew larger and larger at the sight of all the red, green and blue lights flashing on and off and making patterns in the sky.

"Have you enjoyed yourself, Paddington?" asked Mr. Brown as they went round for the second time.

"Yes, thank you very much, Mr. Brown," exclaimed Paddington.

Altogether Paddington thought it had been a wonderful day and he was looking forward to writing a letter to his Aunt Lucy telling her everything about it.

After giving a final wave of his paw to some passersby, he raised his hat to a policeman who signaled them on and then settled back in his seat to enjoy the journey home with Mr. Gruber and the Browns.

"I think," he announced sleepily as he gave one final stare at the fast-disappearing lights, "I would like to have an anniversary every year!"

"And so say all of us, Mr. Brown," echoed Mr. Gruber from the back of the car. "And so say all of us!"

Part Seven

A Special Day Comes Undone

Chapter 32

A Birthday Treat

Paddington pressed his nose against the door of the Brightsea Imperial Theater and peered at a notice pinned to a board on the other side of the glass.

"I think we're in time, Mr. Brown!" he exclaimed excitedly. "It's called Bingo Tonight, and it's on for two weeks."

Mr. Brown joined Paddington at the door and looked in at the darkened interior of the foyer. "That's not a play," he said. "It's a game."

"It means they've closed the theater down," exclaimed Judy. "It's been turned into a bingo hall."

The Browns gazed at each other in dismay. It was Paddington's summer birthday, and as a treat they had decided to take him to see a show. The day had dawned bright and sunny, and on the spur of the moment they'd set off to visit Brightsea, a large town on the south coast, where plays were often tried out before being put on in London.

Paddington had talked of nothing else all the way down, and the news that he was to be done out of his treat was, to say the least, a bad start to the day.

"Perhaps you'd like to go and see the gnomes in Sunny Cove Gardens instead?" suggested Mrs. Brown hopefully. "I did hear they've all been repainted this year . . ." Her voice trailed away as she caught sight of the expression on Paddington's face.

Even the brightest of gnomes was hardly a substitute for a visit to the theater, especially when it was a birthday treat.

"We could go down to the beach while we think about it," said Judy.

Mr. Brown hesitated. "All right," he replied. "We'll get some ice cream on the way to keep us going."

Paddington brightened considerably at Mr. Brown's remarks, and after casting one more glance at the deserted theater, he turned and followed the others as they made their way along the road leading to the promenade.

Although he was disappointed about the play, Paddington wasn't the sort of bear to stay down in the dumps for long, and when they came to a halt alongside a van and Mr. Brown ordered six ice creams, including "a special large cone for a young bear who's just suffered a disappointment," he felt even better.

Clutching the ice cream in one paw and his suitcase in the other, Paddington followed the rest of the family as they trooped onto the beach. His suitcase was full of birthday cards, a good many of which he hadn't really had time to read properly, and he didn't want to let them out of his sight before he'd been able to go through them all again.

Mr. Brown put some deck chairs near the water's edge, and while Jonathan and Judy changed into their bathing suits, Paddington made some holes in the wet sand with his paws and then let the incoming waves smooth them over again. It was all very pleasant, for the sea was warm, and calm enough to paddle in without getting the rest of his fur soggy.

It was while he was in the middle of making a particularly deep hole that he happened to glance up hopefully in order to see if there were any more waves on the way, and as he did so he suddenly caught sight of a speedboat. His eyes nearly popped out of their sockets as it shot past. In fact, if his paws hadn't been firmly embedded in the sand he might well have fallen over backwards with surprise.

It wasn't the boat itself that caused his astonishment, for the sea was alive with boats of all shapes and sizes; it was the fact that just behind it there was a man skimming along the surface of the water on what seemed to be two large planks of wood. But before he had a chance to take it all in, both boat and man had disappeared from view behind the pier.

Paddington sat down on the beach in order to consider the matter. It looked just like the kind of thing for a birthday treat, and he wished he knew more about it. But Mr. Brown had settled down behind his newspaper for a pre-lunch nap, and Jonathan and Judy were having a swimming race and had already gone too far to ask. For a moment or two he toyed with the idea of mentioning his idea to Mrs. Brown, but she was busy helping Mrs. Bird with a knitting problem. In any case, he had a feeling in the back of his mind that she might not entirely approve,

so in the end he decided he would have to do his own investigations.

Mrs. Brown eyed him nervously as he stood up and announced his intention of taking a stroll along the promenade.

"Don't be too long," she warned. "We'll be having lunch soon. And you should take your duffle coat. It looks rather stormy."

Mrs. Bird nodded her agreement. Since they'd arrived in Brightsea a change had come over the weather, and the sky was now more than half covered by clouds, some of which looked very dark indeed.

"You'd better have my umbrella as well," she said. "You don't want to be taken unawares."

Mrs. Bird followed Paddington's progress up the beach. She was never very happy when he went off on his own, especially when he was wearing one of his far-away looks.

"Perhaps he wants to stretch his paws after the long car journey," said Mrs. Brown, with more conviction than she actually felt.

The Browns' housekeeper gave a snort. "He's much more likely to be looking for the ice cream van again," she remarked.

All the same, Mrs. Bird looked noticeably relieved when she turned and saw him peering at a row of posters on the promenade.

On the way down to the beach Paddington had spotted quite a number of advertisements, and although he hadn't actually read any of them he felt sure there must be at least one which would provide an answer to his question.

As he made his way along the front he stopped and examined several of them very carefully, but as far as he could make out, all they dealt with were things like band concerts and mystery coach tours. None of them so much as mentioned boats, let alone where he could buy any planks of wood.

Paddington had often noticed that whenever he went to the seaside all the really good events were due to happen the following week, and it wasn't until he was well past the pier that he suddenly came across the one he had been looking for.

It showed a man standing on the crest of a wave behind a large red speedboat. With one hand he was hanging on to the stern of the boat, and with the other he was pointing to a sign which said LINE UP HERE FOR SIGNOR ALBERTO'S INTERNATIONAL SCHOOL OF WATER SKIING.

There was some more writing underneath, most of which had to do with a special crash course for beginners, in which not only did Signor Alberto guarantee to get any of his pupils, regardless of age, out of the water and onto their skis in only one lesson, but he promised to present them with a special certificate afterwards to show their friends.

It all sounded very good value indeed, and Paddington was about to go down on the beach to where Signor Alberto's boat was moored when he caught sight of yet another notice hanging from a nearby post. It said, quite simply, GONE TO LUNCH—BACK SOON.

Feeling somewhat disappointed, Paddington turned to retrace his steps. As he did so he saw some figures waiting on a bench a little way along the promenade. The bench seemed to belong to the skiing school as well, for as one of the occupants shifted his position he caught a brief glimpse of Signor Alberto's name chiseled into the wooden backrest.

In his advertisement Signor Alberto had said that he would teach anyone, no matter what their age, but as far as Paddington could make out, some of his clients looked as if they would find it hard to make it to the boat, let alone climb inside. As he hurried along the front to join them he began to get more and more excited. He felt sure that if they were able to water-ski, he would have no trouble at all.

"May I join you?" he inquired, raising his hat politely.

The nearest man gave him an odd look. "I don't suppose it'll do any harm," he said grudgingly.

"The more the merrier," agreed the one sitting next to him as he shifted to make room. "It'll help keep us all warm."

Paddington thanked them both very much and then squeezed in at the end. He waited for a moment or two, but no one else spoke. Indeed one man at the other end of the bench looked as if he was in great danger of falling asleep at any moment.

"Do you come here often?" he asked loudly, in the hope of livening things up a bit.

The man next to him nodded. "I've been here every day for the last six years," he said. "Come rain or shine. Mind you," he added, "you 'as to wrap up a bit on days like today."

"Wouldn't do to catch a chill," agreed his friend.

"You mean I can keep my duffle coat on?" exclaimed Paddington.

"Bless you, yes," said the first man encouragingly. "It's a free world. You do as you like."

Paddington settled back again with a pleased expression on his face. He'd been wondering what he could do with his belongings.

"Does it take you very long to get up?" he asked.

The man gave him another funny look. "About ten minutes," he replied. "But once I'm up, I'm up. Mind you, that includes shaving."

"Shaving!" exclaimed Paddington, nearly falling off the bench with surprise. He looked at his acquaintance with new respect. He'd been most impressed by the picture on the poster of the man hanging on to a rope with only one hand, but shaving at the same time was quite a different matter.

"I hope we don't have long to wait!" he exclaimed excitedly.

"I've been here since nine o'clock this morning," said a third man gloomily. "I got here at nine o'clock and I've been here ever since."

Paddington's face fell. Four hours sounded a very long time to wait for a skiing lesson, and he was just trying to make up his mind whether to go back and tell the Browns where he was and risk losing his place or stay on for a little while longer in the hope that the line would begin to move, when he felt a dig in the ribs.

"Watch out!" warned his neighbor. "Here comes the man in charge."

Paddington stared at the approaching figure. From the drawing on the poster he'd expected Signor Alberto to be large and bronzed, whereas the person coming along the promenade seemed quite the reverse. In fact, he was rather like a walking advertisement for indigestion tablets, and from the look on his face as he caught sight of Paddington it seemed as though he was just about to have another bad attack of his complaint.

As he drew near he held out his hand. "Right," he said grumpily. "Where's your book?"

"My *book*?" repeated Paddington. "But I haven't got one."

"Hah!" said the man triumphantly. "I thought as much. I dare say that explains why you're here. You probably can't read either."

Paddington gave him a hard stare. "I do a lot of reading!" he exclaimed hotly. "I always read a story under the blankets at night before I go to sleep. Mr. Brown gave me a flashlight specially."

"I'm sorry," said the man sarcastically, "but we don't provide blankets here. I shall have to ask you to move on. Unless," he added, "you're over sixty-five?"

"Over *sixty-five*?" Paddington stared at the man as if he could hardly believe his ears. Although he had two birthdays a year, he felt sure his latest one hadn't caused him to look that much older.

Already several passersby had stopped to watch the proceedings and some of them started to join in.

"Fancy wanting blankets," said one. "Don't know what it'll come to next."

"Mollycoddling, I calls it," agreed another.

"Let him be," called a woman somewhere near the back. "We've all got to go that way sooner or later."

"Shame!" shouted someone else.

"That's all very well," said the man. "But I 'as my job to do. Suppose I let every Tom, Dick and Harry sit here, what then?"

"Tom, Dick and Harry?" repeated Paddington. He looked most upset. "I'm not one of those, Signor Alberto. I'm a Paddington."

"You're a Paddington?" echoed the man. Scratching his head, he turned to the crowd for sympathy. "What *is* he talking about?" he asked.

The man who'd been sitting next to Paddington rose to his feet as light began to dawn. "I think I know," he said.

He pointed to a notice on the back of the bench and then turned to Paddington. "This isn't a line for Signor Alberto," he explained. "This is a special bench for senior citizens. This gentleman's Alf, the beach captain."

"Alf, the beach captain!" exclaimed Paddington, as if in a dream. He gazed at the newcomer indignantly. "Do you mean to say I've been waiting all this time for nothing?"

"Not for nothing," said the man, taking a ticket machine triumphantly from his inside pocket. "For fifty pence. If you can't produce your old-age pension book on demand, you 'as to pay fifty pence an hour to sit here or else."

But he might just as well have saved his breath. Out of the corner of his eye Paddington had seen some activity round the ski boat, and taking advantage of the argument, he stuffed Mrs. Bird's umbrella inside his duffle coat and crawled through a gap in the crowd while the going was good.

He felt sure that if ever there was a time to take to the water this was it, and, hurrying down the beach towards the boat, he approached a sweater-clad figure bending over the outboard motor.

"Excuse me, Signor Alberto," he announced, tapping him urgently on the shoulder. "I should like to take one of your crash courses in skiing, please. Starting now, if I may!"

◆ ◆ ◆

The Browns gathered in a worried group on the promenade as they exchanged notes. There was so much noise going on—bursts of cheering alternating with loud groans—that it was difficult to make themselves heard; all the same it was obvious that in their search for Paddington they had drawn a blank.

"We've been to both ends of the promenade," said Jonathan.

"We've even tried the amusement arcade on the pier," added Judy. "There isn't a sign of him anywhere."

"I do hope he's not doing the undercliff walk," said Mrs. Brown anxiously. "There isn't a way up for miles and he'll be most upset if he misses lunch—especially today of all days."

"Perhaps we could try asking the beach captain?" suggested Judy. She pointed to a figure a little way along the front. "I bet he's good at remembering faces."

The beach captain was hovering on the edge of a crowd who were leaning on the railings watching something that was taking place far out at sea, and he didn't look best pleased at being interrupted.

"A bear?" he said. "Wearing a duffle coat and carrying an umbrella. I expect that'll be the one I moved on about half an hour ago."

"You moved him on!" exclaimed Mrs. Bird severely. "I'll have you know it's his birthday!"

"I dare say," said the man, wilting under her gaze, "but I never intended to move him on that far."

He pointed to a spot beyond the end of the pier, where a speedboat was bobbing up and down in the water. As the Browns turned to follow the direction of his arm, there was a roar from the engine and the boat moved off. Almost immediately a small but familiar figure rose up out of the water a little way behind. It hovered on the surface for a moment or two and then, to a groan of disappointment from the crowd, slowly disappeared into the sea again.

It was only a fleeting glimpse, but brief though it was, the Browns gasped with astonishment.

"Good gracious!" cried Mrs. Bird. "What on earth's that bear doing now?"

Mrs. Bird's question wasn't unreasonable in the circumstances, but it was one which even Paddington himself would have been very hard put to answer. In fact, he'd been asking himself the very same thing a number of times over the last half-hour. Although he had to admit that he'd enrolled for one of Signor Alberto's special crash courses, he hadn't expected there to be quite so many crashes. As far as he could make out, every time he tried to do anything at all it ended in disaster.

But if Paddington was taking a gloomy view of the proceedings, Signor Alberto looked even more down in the mouth. The change in the weather had brought about a big enough drop in his takings as it was, but with what seemed like the whole of Brightsea watching his attempts to teach Paddington to water-ski, he was beginning to think that trade might never pick up again. As he sat huddled in the back of the boat he looked as if he very much wished he was back on the sunny shores of his native Mediterranean again.

"Please," he called, making one last despairing effort, "we will try once more. For the very last time. Relax. You are toa da stiff. You ava to relax. You are like a stick in zee water."

Listening to Signor Alberto's instructions, Paddington suddenly realized that one of his problems was the fact that he still had Mrs. Bird's umbrella under his duffle coat, so while the other's back was turned he hastily withdrew it, made some last-minute adjustments to the tow rope and then lay back in the water again with the skis pointing upwards as he'd been shown.

Signor Alberto looked back over his shoulder, but if he felt any surprise at seeing Paddington's latest accessory, he showed no sign. In fact, he looked as if nothing would surprise him ever again.

"Now," he called. "When I open zee throttle and we begin to move, you 'ave to pull on zee rope and push with your legs into zee water. Remember, whatever you do . . . watch zee 'eels."

Paddington looked most surprised at this latest piece of advice. He'd never actually seen a real live eel before, and as the boat moved away from him and took up the slack he peered into the water with interest.

Slowly and inexorably the boat gathered speed as Signor Alberto pushed home the throttle. Suddenly the rope tightened, and for a second or two it seemed as if he was about to be cut in two. Then gradually he felt himself begin to rise out of the water.

He'd never experienced anything quite like it before, and grasping Mrs. Bird's umbrella he began to wave it at Signor Alberto for all he was worth.

"Help!" he shouted. "Help! Help!"

"Bravo!" cried Signor Alberto. "Bravo!"

But there was worse to follow, for no sooner had Paddington become accustomed to one motion than there was a click and a sudden tug, and to his alarm Mrs. Bird's umbrella suddenly shot open and he felt a completely new sensation as he rose higher and higher into the air.

The promenade loomed up and then disappeared as they turned at the very last moment and headed out to sea again. The cheers from the watching crowd almost drowned the noise of the engine, but Paddington hardly heard, for by that time there was only one thing uppermost in his mind—and that was to get safely back on to dry land again.

Mrs. Bird had said he might need her umbrella in case he got taken unawares, but as far as Paddington was concerned, he'd never been taken quite so unawares in the whole of his life, for as he glanced down he saw to his horror that the sea, which a moment before had been skimming past his knees, was now a very long way away indeed.

◆ ◆ ◆

Mrs. Bird opened and closed her umbrella several times. "They certainly knew how to make them in those days," she said with satisfaction.

"I bet they never thought it would be used for a bear's parachute skiing," said Judy.

"Perhaps Paddington could write a testimonial?" suggested Jonathan.

"I think we've had quite enough testimonials for one day," said Mrs. Bird.

The Browns were enjoying a late lunch in a restaurant overlooking Signor Alberto's skiing school.

Paddington in particular was eating for all he was worth. Although he was looking none the worse for his adventure, there had been a moment when he'd thought he might never live to enjoy another meal, and he was more than making up for lost time.

He had fully expected to be in trouble when he got back, but in the event the reverse had been true. The Browns had been so relieved to see him safe and sound they hadn't the heart to be cross, and Signor Alberto had been so pleased at the success of his lessons he'd not only refused any payment but he'd even presented Paddington with a special certificate into the bargain. It was the first time anyone in Brightsea had seen parachute skiing, and if the size of the line on the promenade was anything to go by, there would be no lack of customers at his school for some time to come. Even a man who ran an umbrella shop nearby had come along to offer his congratulations. Despite the fact that the sun had come out again, he was doing a roaring trade.

"What beats me," said Mr. Brown, "is how you managed to stand up on the skis at all. I didn't think you'd ever make it."

Paddington considered the matter for a moment. "I don't think I could really help myself, Mr. Brown," he said truthfully.

In point of fact, he'd wrapped the rope round himself several times just to make sure, but he'd had such a lecture from Signor Alberto afterwards about the dangers of doing such a thing ever again, he decided he'd better not say anything about it, and wisely the Browns didn't pursue the matter.

"Perhaps you'd like to round things off with a plate of jellied eels?" suggested Mr. Brown some time later, as they took a final stroll along the promenade.

Paddington gave a shudder. What with the ice cream, the water skiing, and an extra-large lunch into the bargain, he decided he'd had quite enough for one day, and eels were the last thing he wanted to be reminded of.

All in all, he felt he would much rather round off his birthday treat in as quiet a way as possible.

"I think," he announced, "I'd like to sit down for a while. Perhaps we could all go to Sunny Cove Gardens. Then you can watch the gnomes while I read my birthday cards."

Chapter 33

A Day to Remember

Mrs. Brown stared at Paddington in amazement. "Harold Price wants you to be an usher at his wedding?" she repeated. "Are you sure?"

Paddington nodded "I've just met him in the market, Mrs. Brown," he explained. "He said he was going to give you a ring as well."

Mrs. Brown exchanged glances with the rest of the family as they gathered round to hear Paddington's news.

Harold Price was a young man who served on the preserves counter at a large grocery store in the Portobello Road, and the events leading up to his forthcoming marriage to Miss Deirdre Flint, who worked on the adjacent bacon-and-eggs counter, had been watched with interest by the Browns, particularly as it was largely through Paddington that they had become engaged in the first place.

It had all come about some months previously when Paddington had lent a paw at a local drama festival in which Miss Flint had played the lead in one of Mr. Price's plays.

A great many things had gone wrong that evening, but Mr. Price always maintained afterwards that far from Paddington causing a parting of the ways, he and Miss Flint had been brought even closer together. In any event, shortly afterwards they had announced their engagement.

It was largely because of Paddington's part in the affair, and the numerous large orders for marmalade he'd placed with Mr. Price over the years, that all the Browns had been invited to the wedding that day, but never in their wildest dreams had it occurred to any of them that Paddington might be one of the wedding party.

During the silence that followed while everyone considered the matter, he held up a small bright metal object. "Mr. Price has given me the key to his flat," he announced importantly. "He wants me to pick up the list of guests on the way to the church."

"Well, I must say it's rather a nice idea," said Mrs. Brown, trying to sound more enthusiastic than she actually felt. "It's really a case of history repeating itself."

"Remembering what happened last time," murmured Mr. Brown, "I only hope it doesn't repeat itself too faithfully."

"Everything turned out all right in the end," Mrs. Brown broke in hastily, as Paddington gave one of his hard stares. "Harold's play *did* win first prize and he was very glad of Paddington's help when the sound effects man let him down."

"I think he's been let down again, Mrs. Brown," said Paddington earnestly. "He's got no one to keep quiet during the ceremony."

"No one to keep quiet?" echoed Jonathan. Paddington's thought processes were sometimes rather difficult to follow, and his present one was no exception.

"I've no doubt that bear will do as well as anyone if he sets his mind to it," said Mrs. Bird, the Browns' housekeeper, as Paddington, having startled everybody by announcing that he was going to have a special bath in honor of the occasion, disappeared upstairs in order to carry out his threat. "No doubt at all. After all, it's only a matter of lending a paw and showing people to their right places in the church."

"Knowing the usual state of Paddington's paws," replied Mr. Brown, "I think I'd sooner find my own way."

"He *is* having a bath, Daddy," reminded Judy. "He just said so."

"He may be having a bath," retorted Mr. Brown grimly. "But he's still got to get to the church. All sorts of things can happen before then."

"'Ush!" cried Jonathan suddenly. "I bet he thinks being an usher means he has to keep hush during the service."

"Oh dear," said Mrs. Brown, as Jonathan's words sank in. "I do hope he doesn't tell Deirdre to be quiet when she's making her responses. You know what a quick temper she's got, and I expect she'll be all on edge as it is."

Mrs. Brown began to look somewhat less happy about the whole affair as she

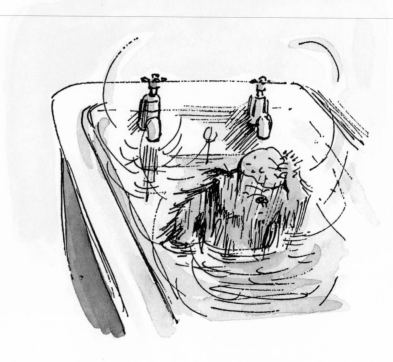

turned the matter over in her mind, but at that moment the shrill sound of the telephone broke into her thoughts.

"It's Harold Price," she hissed, putting her hand over the receiver. "He wants to know if it's all right. What *shall* I say?"

Mr. Brown looked up at the ceiling as the sound of running water came from somewhere overhead. "Whatever we say it had better not be no," he replied. "Not at this stage. We shall never hear the last of it if Paddington's had a bath for nothing. Especially one he's volunteered for.

"All the same," he continued, giving his suit a passing flick with the clothesbrush, "I can't help feeling it isn't the best of ways to start married life. I don't think I should have been very keen on having a bear as an usher at my wedding—even if I had been let down."

Mr. Brown wasn't overenthusiastic about weddings at the best of times, and the thought of attending one at which Paddington was lending a paw filled him with foreboding.

Nevertheless, even Mr. Brown's fears were gradually set at rest as the day wore on, for Paddington's behavior seemed beyond reproach.

When they arrived at the church he was busily engaged with a long and important-looking list of names which enabled him to check the invitations and sort out the friends of the bride from those of the groom, and as he led them down the aisle towards their allotted places they couldn't help noticing how spick and span he looked. His fur had a newly brushed, glistening appearance, and his whiskers were so shiny they made the large white carnation which he wore tied round his neck look almost dowdy by comparison.

If the Browns had any criticism at all it was that he was taking his job a little over seriously. Jonathan's earlier theory proved all too correct and as soon as anyone so much as parted their lips he hurried up to them with his paw raised and gave them a hard stare. Some of his stares, which had been handed down to him by his Aunt Lucy in Peru, were very powerful indeed and in no time at all it would have been possible to have heard the proverbial pin drop.

Even the vicar looked most impressed when he came into the church and saw the attentive state of his congregation.

"I don't see how we *can* explain now," hissed Mr. Brown. "It's a bit difficult when you're not allowed to say anything."

The others contented themselves with a nod of agreement, for at that moment Paddington, having carefully checked the list of guests for the last time to make certain everyone was present, settled himself down in a nearby pew in order to enjoy the forthcoming ceremony in comfort.

In any case, they soon had other matters to occupy their minds for a moment or so later Mr. Price and his best man arrived and took up their places near the front.

They both looked unusually agitated, even for such a nerve-racking occasion as a wedding, and Mr. Price in particular kept jumping up and down like a jack-in-the-box. He seemed to want to speak to Paddington, but each time he turned round and opened his mouth Paddington put a paw firmly to his lips.

"I don't remember Harold having that nervous twitch before," whispered Mrs. Brown uneasily.

"I think it's got something to do with the ring," whispered Judy, passing on what little bit of information she'd been able to glean from those in front. "They're going to have to make do with a brass one off Mr. Price's bedroom curtains. Apparently the real one's disappeared."

"Disappeared!" echoed Mrs. Brown. For a moment she quite forgot Paddington's presence in the nearby pew, but as it happened she needn't have worried, for Paddington seemed even more affected than anyone by this piece of news. His whiskers sagged, his face took on a sudden woebegone expression, and even the carnation round his neck seemed to wilt in sympathy.

"Deirdre's not going to be very pleased when she hears," murmured Mr. Brown. "I shouldn't like to be the person who's got it!"

"*Ssh!*" hissed Mrs. Brown. "Here she comes!"

The Browns fell silent as there was a rustle of silk behind them and Deirdre, resplendent in a snow-white wedding gown, sailed past on the arm of Mr. Flint.

Only Paddington failed to join in the general gasps of admiration that greeted her entrance. For some reason best known to himself, he appeared to be engaged in a kind of life-and-death struggle on the floor of the church. Several times he was lost to view completely, and each time he rose again he was breathing more and more heavily and his expression looked, if possible, unhappier than before.

However, unhappy though it was, it seemed almost joyful by comparison with the grim one which came over Miss Flint's face a moment or so later when she took in the whispered aside from her husband-to-be.

For one brief moment, indeed, it looked as if for two pins Miss Flint would have called the whole thing off, and when it came to the time for her to say "I do," there was quite a nasty pause before she managed to get the words out.

When the ceremony finally came to an end both she and Harold hurried towards the vestry in order to sign the register rather as if they had a bus to catch, and not a bit like two people who had just agreed to spend the rest of their lives together.

"I'm glad I'm not in Harold's shoes," said Mr. Brown, as the door closed behind them. "Deirdre looked as black as thunder."

"*Ssh!*" began Mrs. Brown. "We don't want Pad—"

She was about to say that one upset was enough and they didn't want to add to the confusion by having Paddington take up his 'ushing duties again, but as she looked round the church it was only to discover that Paddington was nowhere in sight.

"There he is!" cried Judy suddenly, as she looked back over her shoulder.

Turning round to follow her gaze, the rest of the Browns were just in time to catch a glimpse of a familiar figure hurrying up the aisle in the direction of the entrance doors.

"Perhaps he wants to be in the front of the photograph," said Mrs. Brown hopefully, as Paddington, after casting an anxious glance over his shoulder, picked up his suitcase and hat from behind a nearby pillar and disappeared from view. "He's always very keen on anything like that for his scrapbook, and he looks as if he's got something on his mind."

"*Hmm,*" said Mrs. Bird. "That's as may be. But if you ask me that young bear's mind is not the only thing he's got something on."

Mrs. Bird's sharp eyes had noticed a momentary gleam from one of Paddington's paws as he'd gone out into the sunshine. It was the second time within the space of a few minutes she'd spotted the strange phenomenon. The first occasion had been during the service itself, when the vicar had asked the assembly if anyone present knew of any good reason why Deirdre and Harold shouldn't get married. Paddington had half raised his paw and then, much to her relief, he'd changed his mind at the last moment.

Mrs. Bird was good at adding two and two together as far as Paddington was concerned, but wisely she kept the result of her calculations to herself for the time being.

In any case, before the others had time to question her on the subject, a rather worried-looking churchwarden hurried up the aisle and stopped at their pew in order to whisper something in Mr. Brown's ear.

Mr. Brown rose to his feet. "I think we're wanted in the vestry," he announced ominously. "It sounds rather urgent."

Mr. Brown was tempted to add that the churchwarden had also asked if Paddington could accompany them, but in the event he decided not to add to their worries.

All the same, as he led the way into the vestry he began to look more and more worried, and if he'd been able to see through the stone walls into the churchyard outside, the chances are that he would have felt even more so.

For Paddington was in trouble. Quite serious trouble. One way and another he was used to life having its ups and downs, but as he held his paw up to the light in order to examine it more closely, even he had to admit he couldn't remember a time when his fortunes had taken quite such a downward plunge.

Sucking it had made no difference at all; jamming it in the railings which surrounded the churchyard only seemed to have made matters worse; and even the application of a liberal smear of marmalade from an emergency jar which he kept in his suitcase had been to no avail.

As far as paws went, his own was looking unusually smart and well cared for. Apart from the remains of the marmalade it wouldn't have disgraced an advertisement for fur coats in one of Mrs. Brown's glossy magazines. Even the pad had an unusual glow about it, not unlike that of a newly polished shoe.

However, it wasn't the pad or its surroundings which caused Paddington's look of dismay, but the sight of a small gold wedding ring poking out from beneath his fur; and the longer he looked at it, the more unhappy he became.

He'd found the ring lying on the dressing table when he'd gone to Harold Price's room in order to pick up the wedding list, and at the time it had gone on one of his claws easily enough. But now it was well and truly stuck, and nothing he could do would make it budge one way or the other.

In the past he had always kept on very good terms with Mr. Price. Even so, he couldn't begin to imagine what his friend would have to say about the matter. Nor, when he considered it, could he picture Deirdre exactly laughing her head off when she heard the news that her wedding ring was stuck round a bend on a bear's paw. From past experience he knew that Deirdre had a very sharp tongue indeed when even quite minor things went wrong with her bacon-slicer, and he shuddered to think what she would have to say about the present situation.

As if to prove how right he was, his thoughts were broken into at that very moment, as the sound of Deirdre's voice raised in anger floated out through the open window above his head.

By climbing on top of his suitcase and standing on tiptoe Paddington was just able to see inside the vestry, and when he did so he nearly fell over backwards again in alarm, for not only was Deirdre there, laying down the law to a most unhappy-looking Mr. Price, but the best man, sundry relatives, the Browns and quite a number of other important-looking people were there as well.

Indeed, so great was the crowd and so loud the argument, it gave the impression that more people were attending the signing of the register than had been present at the actual ceremony.

Paddington was a hopeful bear at heart but the more he listened to Deirdre, the more his spirits dropped and the more he realized that the only thing they had in common was a wish that he'd never been invited to the wedding in the first place, let alone acted as an usher.

After a moment or two he clambered back down again, took a deep breath, picked up his suitcase and headed towards a large red booth just outside the churchyard.

It wasn't often that Paddington made a telephone call—for one thing he always found it a bit difficult with paws—but he did remember once reading a poster in a phone booth about what to do in times of an emergency and how it was possible to obtain help without paying.

It had seemed very good value at the time and as far as he could make out it would be difficult to think of a situation which was more of an emergency than his present one.

His brief appearance at the window didn't go entirely unnoticed, but fortunately the only person who saw him was Judy, and by the time she'd passed the message on to Jonathan he'd disappeared again.

"Perhaps it was a mirage," said Jonathan hopefully.

"It wasn't," said Judy. "It was Paddington's hat."

"Paddington!" echoed Deirdre, catching the end of Judy's reply. "Don't mention that name to me.

"Look!" she announced dramatically, holding up her wedding finger for what seemed to her audience like the hundredth time. "A curtain ring! A brass curtain ring!"

"I thought it would be better than nothing," said the best man, hastily cupping his hands under Deirdre's in case the object of her wrath fell off. "I was hoping you might have big fingers."

Deirdre gave the best man a withering glare and then turned her attention back to the unfortunate Harold. "Don't just stand there," she exclaimed. "*Do* something!"

"Look here," broke in Mr. Brown. "I still don't see why you're blaming Paddington."

"My room's on the fifth floor," said Mr. Price briefly. "And there are only two keys. Paddington had the other one."

"Fancy asking a bear to be an usher," said Deirdre scornfully. "You might have known *something* would happen. I shall never be able to show my face in the shop again. Practically all our best customers are here."

The new Mrs. Price broke off as quite clearly above her words there came the unmistakable sound of a siren, at first in the distance, and then gradually getting closer and closer.

The vicar glanced nervously out of his vestry window. Quite a crowd seemed to have collected outside the church and even as he watched, a large red fire engine, its siren wailing furiously, screamed to a halt and several men in blue uniforms jumped off, their hatchets at the ready.

"That's all I need," said Deirdre bitterly, as the vicar excused himself and hurried off to investigate the matter. "A fire! That'll round off the day nicely!"

The room fell silent as Mr. Price's bride, having exhausted the topic of the things she would like to do, embarked on a long list of the things she *wasn't* going to do under any circumstances until she got her wedding ring back, including signing the register, having her photograph taken, and going on her honeymoon.

It was just as she reached the last item and Mr. Price's face had fallen to its longest ever that the door burst open and the vicar hurried back into the room, closely followed by a man in fireman's uniform, and behind him, Paddington himself.

"*There* you are, Paddington," said Mrs. Brown thankfully. "*Where* have you been?"

"Having a bit of a sticky time of it, if you ask me, ma'am," began the fireman, "what with one thing and another."

"My ring!" broke in Deirdre, catching sight of a shiny object in Paddington's outstretched paw.

"I'm afraid it got stuck round a bend, Mrs. Price," explained Paddington.

"Stuck round a *bend*?" repeated Deirdre disbelievingly. "How on earth did that happen?"

Paddington took hold of the ring in his other paw in order to demonstrate exactly what had gone wrong. "I'm not sure," he admitted truthfully. "I just slipped it on for safety and when I tried to take it off again . . ."

The fireman gave a groan. "Don't say you've done it again!" he exclaimed. "I've only just got it off."

"Bears!" groaned Deirdre. "I'm not meant to get married."

"What I can't understand," said Mr. Price, "is why you put it on your paw in the first place, Mr. Brown."

"You said you were going to give Mrs. Brown a ring," said Paddington unhappily. "I thought I'd save you the bother."

"I said I was going to give Mrs. Brown a ring?" repeated Harold, hardly able to believe his ears.

"I think you did," said Mrs. Brown. "Paddington probably didn't realize you meant a ring on the telephone."

"Quite a natural mistake," said Mrs. Bird in the silence that followed. "Anyone might have made it in the circumstances."

"Never mind," said the fireman. "What goes on must come off—especially the second time.

"I tell you what," he continued, sizing up the situation as he got to work on Paddington's paw with a pair of pliers, "if the happy couple would like to sign the register while I do this, I'll get my crew to form a guard of honor outside the church."

"A guard of honor!" exclaimed Deirdre.

"With axes," said the fireman.

The new Mrs. Price began to look slightly more pleased. "Well, I don't know really . . ." she simpered, patting her hair.

"It's a bit irregular," whispered the fireman in Paddington's ear, "and we don't normally do it for people outside the service, but we've a big recruiting drive on at the moment and it'll be good publicity. Besides, it'll help calm things down a bit."

"Thank you very much," said Paddington gratefully. "I shall ask for you if ever I have a real fire."

"It'll make a lovely photograph," said Harold persuasively, taking Deirdre's hand and leading her across the room. "And it'll be something to show the girls back in the shop."

"If the ring won't come off, perhaps I could come on the honeymoon with you, Mrs. Price," said Paddington hopefully. "I've never been on one of those before."

Deirdre's back stiffened as she bent down to sign the register.

"I don't think that'll be necessary," said the fireman hastily, as he removed the ring at long last and handed it to Mr. Price for safekeeping.

"Tell you what, though," he added, seeing a look of disappointment cross Paddington's face. "As you can't go on the honeymoon, perhaps we'll give you a lift to the wedding breakfast on our way back to the station instead.

"After all," he continued, looking meaningfully at Mrs. Price, "if this young bear hadn't had the good sense to call us when he did, he might still be wearing the ring, and then where would you be?"

And to that remark not even Deirdre could find an answer.

"Gosh!" said Jonathan as the Browns made their way back up the aisle. "Imagine riding on the back of a fire engine!"

"I don't suppose there are many bears who can say they've done that," agreed Judy.

Paddington nodded. A lot of things seemed about to happen all at once, and he wasn't quite sure which he was looking forward to most. Apart from the promised ride, he'd never heard of anyone having their breakfast in the afternoon before, let alone a wedding one, but it sounded like a very good way of rounding things off.

"If you and Mrs. Price ever want to get married again," he announced, as Harold led Deirdre out of the church and paused for the photographers beneath an archway of raised fire axes, "I'll do some more 'ushing for you if you like."

Deirdre shuddered. "Never again," she said, taking a firm grip on Harold's arm. "Once is quite enough."

Mr. Price nodded his agreement. "It's as I said in the beginning," he remarked from beneath a shower of confetti. "Young Mr. Brown has a habit of bringing people closer together in the end, and this time it's for good!"

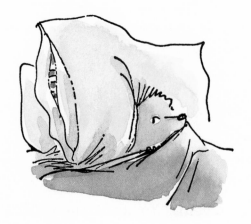

Mr. Curry Lets Off Steam

On the morning of Mr. Brown's birthday Paddington overslept, which was most unusual. When he did finally emerge from his slumbers it was to the sound of a strange knocking noise. At first he thought it was to do with a dream he'd been having, all about a woodpecker which had accidentally got trapped inside his hat. But his hat was still lying on the dressing table where he'd left it the night before, and when he felt his head it didn't show any signs of having been pecked.

In any case, having rubbed his eyes several times to make doubly sure he was properly awake, he discovered that the noise hadn't stopped. If anything it seemed to be getting worse, and it appeared to be coming from somewhere outside.

Paddington hurried to his bedroom window and peered out. As he did so he nearly fell over backwards with surprise, for while he'd been asleep a strange-looking wooden hut had appeared in the garden. It was standing in the middle of the snow-covered cabbage patch, and as far as he could make out it had no windows at all, although it made up for this by having a short chimney, out of which rose a thin column of steam.

The noise was being caused by two workmen who were busy putting some finishing touches to the flat roof, and as one of them paused in order to rest from his hammering he looked up and caught sight of Paddington.

"You wait till this 'eats up properly, mate," he called. "It'll take the cobwebs out of your whiskers and no mistake."

Paddington had never heard of a hut for removing cobwebs before, so he put on his duffle coat and, after a quick look at his own whiskers in the bathroom mirror, hurried downstairs in order to tell the others.

Mrs. Brown and Mrs. Bird exchanged uneasy glances as he burst into the dining room. Knowing how keen Paddington was on trying things out, they had been hoping to keep the whole matter a secret until the last possible moment.

"It's Daddy's birthday present," explained Judy. "It's what's known as a sauna."

"It's meant to be a surprise," added Jonathan. "That's why the workmen are in such a hurry. We want to get it ready and working by the time he gets home."

Paddington listened carefully while the others explained all about saunas and how they worked.

"You see," said Judy, "you have lots of large stones which you stand on a special place inside the hut. You heat them up and then pour cold water over them and it turns into steam. It's supposed to be very good for you. It opens up all the pores."

"In some parts of the world they even beat you with birch twigs afterwards," added Jonathan. "It gives you a nice glow. Dad keeps on talking about wanting to lose weight—that's why we've bought it for him."

Paddington considered the matter for a moment. He'd never heard of anyone having a bath as a birthday present before, and although he was quite sure Mr. Brown would be surprised by it all, being soaked in steam and then beaten by birch twigs didn't seem like a very good way of celebrating the occasion.

All the same, it definitely sounded worth investigating, even if he didn't actually test it out.

"Perhaps," he announced, "I'll just have a look through the keyhole, otherwise my whiskers might go soggy."

"Very wise," said Mrs. Bird. "Not that a sauna mightn't do certain of those among us some good," she added meaningfully as Paddington donned his Wellington boots. "Mr. Brown isn't the only one who could do with losing a few pounds."

Paddington looked most offended at this last remark, but as he hurried out into the garden he quickly forgot about it in his excitement.

By the time he reached the hut the workmen had already left, but they had obviously got the stones in a state of readiness for Mr. Brown's homecoming. Steam was billowing out through the chimney and from odd cracks in the woodwork. In fact, the whole thing looked rather like some primitive space rocket a few moments before launching.

Paddington approached it gingerly and was about to apply his eye to a knothole which was low down in the door and looked slightly less steamy than the rest when he heard a familiar voice bark out his name.

He jumped to his feet and as he turned round he saw to his dismay that Mr. Curry was gazing at him over the top of the fence.

"What's going on, bear?" demanded Mr. Curry. "Was that you making all that noise just now?"

"Oh, no, Mr. Curry," said Paddington hastily. "It woke *me* up. I was asleep too."

"Asleep!" exclaimed Mr. Curry. "I wasn't *asleep*. I never sleep." He gazed suspiciously across the fence. "What's that monstrosity? And what's all that smoke doing? It ought not to be allowed. I've a good mind to report it."

"Oh, that isn't *smoke*, Mr. Curry," said Paddington knowledgeably. "That's steam. It's a special birthday surprise for Mr. Brown. It's what's known as a sauna."

"A sauna, eh?" Mr. Curry took a closer look at the hut.

"It's supposed to be very good for you," said Paddington, warming to his subject as he went on to repeat all that he'd been told about the matter.

"Very interesting, bear," said Mr. Curry when he'd finished. "Very interesting indeed. You say it's all ready to use?"

Paddington nodded. "They've heated the stones especially," he explained. "*And* they've put some cold water on to make the steam. Look . . ." And he opened the door slightly to show the Browns' neighbor what he meant.

"Thank you very much, bear," said Mr. Curry unexpectedly. "That's very kind of you. I've always wanted to try one. I'll go in and change now."

Paddington's jaw dropped as the Browns' neighbor disappeared from view. He was used to Mr. Curry's habit of twisting other people's words to suit his own ends, but never in his wildest dreams had he meant to invite him over.

"The cheek of it!" exclaimed Mrs. Bird when she heard the news. "That's typical of Mr. Curry—always poking his nose in and wanting something for nothing."

"He'll get steam up his nose if he pokes it in there," said Jonathan, glancing out of the window.

"I hope he doesn't let it all out," said Judy. "Daddy *must* be the first one to try it. After all, it's *his* present."

A feeling of indignation ran round the Browns' dining room. They had gone to great lengths to keep Mr. Brown's present from him until it was ready, even to the extent of persuading him to go into work that morning instead of taking the whole day off as he usually did, and they had no wish to spoil his homecoming by indulging in an argument with Mr. Curry.

"We should have put a padlock on the door," said Mrs. Brown. "I don't know why I didn't think of it at the time."

While the others were talking a thoughtful expression gradually crept over Paddington's face. Opening up his suitcase he felt inside the secret compartment and withdrew a small parcel done up in brightly colored wrapping paper.

"Perhaps," he announced, "you could use *my* present to Mr. Brown?" And to everyone's astonishment he unwrapped the paper and held up a small silvery object.

"I *was* going to send a telegram as a surprise," he said, "but I had a bit of trouble, so I bought this instead. It was really meant for his toolshed, but I expect it will look much better on a sauna—especially a new one."

"Gosh!" said Jonathan enviously, as he examined Paddington's present. "It's a special combination lock. I bet Dad'll be pleased."

"Just so long as he doesn't forget the number," said Mrs. Brown nervously. "You know what he's like when it comes to things like that. It would be awful if he couldn't get the door open on the first day."

"It's all right, Mrs. Brown," said Paddington. He looked round carefully to make sure no one could overhear. "The man in the shop adjusted it specially so that it used my birthday date. He said that way we would never forget."

"A good idea," said Mrs. Bird approvingly. "And if you want my advice you'll put it on the door straight away. It'll stop Mr. Curry taking advantage."

Paddington needed no second bidding and a few seconds later he hurried back down the garden path as fast as his legs would carry him. There was already a hasp on the door and it was a moment's work to push the flap home and slip the padlock into place. As he squeezed the two halves together they met with a satisfying click. He twiddled the various sets of numbers several times with his paws, just as the man in the shop had shown him, and then stood back breathing heavily before testing it once more to make sure all was well.

It had been a race against time, but in the circumstances Paddington felt sure Mr. Brown would be more than pleased with his extra present. He could still hardly believe his good fortune at having chosen something which worked so well with the Browns' gift, for no matter how hard he pulled the padlock it showed no sign of coming apart again.

The heat from the sauna was slightly overpowering, and it was as he moved away in order to mop his brow that a puzzled expression came over Paddington's face. It was very strange, but it was almost as if he could hear a repetition of the knocking which had woken him earlier in the day.

Admittedly it was rather more muffled than it had been before, but it was getting louder with every passing moment, and it seemed to be coming from *inside* the hut. In fact, even as he watched, the door began to shake, just as if someone was rattling it from the other side.

He gave the door a couple of taps with his paw. "Excuse me," he called. "Is anyone there?"

Paddington wasn't quite sure what, if anything, he expected by way of a reply, but in the event he nearly jumped out of his skin with surprise.

"Yes, there is!" bellowed an all-too-familiar voice. "Is that you, bear? Let me out at once!"

Paddington gazed at the door in alarm. It hadn't occurred to him for one moment that Mr. Curry might have beaten him to it.

Recovering in double-quick time, he took hold of the padlock. "Coming, Mr. Curry," he called. "Don't worry. I've only got to set up my birthday date."

"Your *what*?" shouted Mr. Curry.

"My birthday date," called Paddington. "It's the twenty-fifth of June."

Paddington's words were the signal for a renewed burst of banging on the door. "But it's not the twenty-fifth of June," roared Mr. Curry. "That was months ago. And it's not *your* birthday. It's Mr. Brown's!"

But Paddington wasn't listening. Instead he gazed unhappily at the door. He couldn't remember ever having seen one quite so tightly shut before. Even allowing for the fact that Mr. Curry wasn't exactly helping matters by banging it, something seemed to have gone very wrong with the lock. No matter how hard he pulled, the two halves showed no sign whatsoever of coming apart.

"I shan't be long, Mr. Curry," he gasped, giving the lock one more tug. "It's a bit difficult with paws and the steam keeps going in my eyes . . ."

"The steam keeps going in *your* eyes!" bellowed Mr. Curry. "What do you think's happening to mine? I'm being boiled alive in here!"

Bending down, Paddington peered through the knothole he'd used earlier that morning. At first it was difficult to make out anything through the steam, but as his eyes grew accustomed to the gloom he gradually made out the shape of the Browns' neighbor. Even through the haze he could see what Mr. Curry meant. During the short space of time he'd been locked inside the hut, he'd taken on the appearance of an overboiled lobster. A lobster, moreover, which was jumping up and down and showing every sign of wanting to get its pincers on the person responsible for its present condition.

Paddington looked round for help, but there wasn't a soul in sight. In desperation he opened his suitcase to see if there were any instructions that went with the lock, but apart from several testimonials on the outside of the box—all saying how impossible it was to open once it had been set—there was nothing at all.

As he gazed mournfully at his own lock Paddington felt he could have written a very good testimonial himself at that moment, and given a tape recorder he could have provided some appropriate sound effects to go with it into the bargain.

He rummaged through the suitcase again. "Would you like an old marmalade sandwich to be going on with, Mr. Curry?" he called. "I expect I could push some bits through one of the holes."

Paddington was a hopeful bear at heart, but even he had to admit that if Mr. Curry's reply was anything to go by, the market for sandwiches was at a particularly low ebb at that moment.

It was as he was about to close the lid of his suitcase that his gaze alighted on an object lying in the bottom. Over the years Paddington had collected quite a number of souvenirs, and he usually carried a selection of the more important ones around with him. By a strange coincidence, the particular one which had just caught his eye had been given to him some years before when he'd visited Mr. Curry in the hospital.

It was a stethoscope, and seeing it reminded him of a film he'd recently seen on television, all about a famous safe-breaker called "Lobes" Lavone. In the film no lock had been too complicated for Mr. Lavone. A few moments on his own with a stethoscope and even the toughest of safe doors would swing open to reveal its secrets. It had been a most exciting program, and before he'd gone to bed that night Paddington had spent some time testing his own stethoscope on the Browns' front door. However, he'd never actually tried it out on a real combination lock before and this seemed like a very good opportunity.

Paddington donned the earpieces as fast as he could and then began twiddling the numbers while he applied the business end of the stethoscope to the lock. As he did so his face fell. Apart from the background music which always accompanied his escapades, Mr. Lavone insisted on working in complete silence. In fact, he got very cross if anyone so much as dared to breathe within earshot, whereas, heard through the earpieces, Mr. Curry's wheezing sounded not unlike a herd of elephants trying to get over a heavy cold. Far from being able to detect any telltale clicks, all Paddington could hear was the sound of banging and crashing as the Browns' neighbor stomped about inside the hut.

Taking advantage of a sudden lull, he was about to have one final go when his eardrums were nearly punctured by an unusually loud bellow from what seemed like two inches away.

"I can see you, bear!" roared Mr. Curry. "What are you doing now? Listening to the radio? How dare you at a time like this?"

Paddington dropped his stethoscope like a hot potato. "I wasn't listening to the radio, Mr. Curry," he called. "I was having trouble with my dial."

"Your *dial*?" The Browns' neighbor sounded as if he could hardly believe his ears. "What *dial*?"

Paddington looked round hopefully for inspiration. "Stay where you are, Mr. Curry," he called. "I'll think of something."

"Stay where I am!" spluttered Mr. Curry. "*Stay where I am!* I can't do anything else, thanks to you. It's disgraceful. I'm being boiled alive. Call the fire brigade. Ooh! Help!"

But Mr. Curry's cries fell on deaf ears, for Paddington was already halfway up the garden. Desperate situations demanded desperate measures, and something Mr. Curry said had triggered off an idea in his mind.

♦♦♦

Mrs. Brown glanced out into the garden and as she did so a puzzled look came over her face. "What on earth is that bear up to now?" she exclaimed.

As the others joined her at the dining room window, she pointed towards a small figure clad in a duffle coat and hat struggling to prop a ladder against the side of the sauna hut.

"And what's he doing with my best plastic bucket?" demanded Mrs. Bird.

If the Browns' housekeeper was expecting an answer from the others to her question, she was disappointed, for they were as mystified as she was. In any case they were saved the trouble, for almost before she had finished speaking Paddington had climbed up the ladder and was crawling across the roof of the hut as if his very life depended on it. Before their astonished gaze, he filled the bucket with snow and then removed the cowl from the top of the chimney and began pouring the contents down the open end.

As he did so the column of steam which rose from the hole surpassed anything that had gone before. For a moment or two Paddington completely disappeared from view. Then, as the mist gradually cleared, he once again came into view look-

ing, if anything, even more worried than he had before.

As a distant roar of rage followed by the sound of renewed banging came from somewhere inside the hut Jonathan and Judy looked at each other. The same thought was in both their minds.

"Come on," said Jonathan. "If you ask me, Paddington's in trouble!"

"And what," called Mrs. Bird, as she hurried down the garden path after the others, "do you think you're doing up there? You'll catch your death of cold in all that steam."

Paddington peered down unhappily from the roof of the sauna hut. "I think I've shut Mr. Curry inside by mistake, Mrs. Bird," he announced. "And I think something's gone wrong with my padlock."

"Uh-oh! Let me have a go at that." Jonathan took hold of the lock and began twiddling the dials as a sudden thought struck him. Almost at once there was a satisfying click and to everyone's surprise the two halves then parted. "Stand by for blasting!" he called, as he removed the lock from the hasp and the door swung open.

The others waited with bated breath to hear what Mr. Curry would have to say as he emerged from the hut. Far from losing weight he seemed to have gained several pounds as he swelled up in anger at the sight of the Browns. Then, just as he opened his mouth in order to let forth a yell, he gave a shiver and pulled his towel tightly round himself as a sudden draft of cold air caught him unawares. In the end all he could manage was a loud *"Brrrrrr!"*

"Perhaps I could beat you with twigs, Mr. Curry?" called Paddington hopefully. "I expect bears are good at that and it'll warm you up."

As he peered over the edge of the roof, a lump of snow detached itself from his hat and landed fairly and squarely on top of Mr. Curry's head.

"Bah!" The Browns' neighbor found his voice at last. "Come down here at once, bear. Wait until I get dressed. I'll . . . I'll . . ."

Mrs. Bird took a firm grip of her broom handle. "You'll *what*?" she asked.

Mr. Curry swelled up again and opened his mouth as if he was about to say something. Then he thought better of it and a moment later he stalked off and disappeared through the hole in the fence.

"Thank goodness for that!" said Mrs. Brown in tones of relief. "Anyway, at least we know Henry's present works."

"Even if Paddington's doesn't," said Judy. "Perhaps they'll change it for you if you take it back to the shop," she added, catching sight of the disappointed look on his face as he clambered back down the ladder.

"It's a bit difficult with paws," said Paddington sadly as he tested the lock. For some reason or other it seemed to have jammed shut again. He glanced hopefully at the sauna hut. "Perhaps my pores need opening?"

"Pores nothing!" broke in Jonathan. "What date did you say you used?"

"My birthday date," replied Paddington. "June the twenty-fifth."

"That's your summer one," said Jonathan. "You want to try the winter one next time. *December* the twenty-fifth." And to prove his point he took the lock from Paddington, twiddled the dials, and then opened and closed it several times in quick succession.

"I always knew there must be something against having two birthdays a year," said Mrs. Brown. "Now I know. Life must be very confusing sometimes—especially if you're a bear."

"Especially," agreed Paddington, "if you're a bear with a combination lock."

Chapter 35

An Unexpected Party

Paddington paused on the stairs of number thirty-two Windsor Gardens and sniffed the morning air. A few moments later, having consulted the Browns' calendar through the banisters, he hurried on his way with a puzzled expression on his face.

There was definitely something mysterious going on that morning and he couldn't for the life of him make out what it was. Unless Mrs. Bird had made a mistake when she'd changed the date, which would have been most unusual, and unless he'd also overslept by two or three days, which seemed even more unlikely, it should have been a Thursday—and yet all the signs were Sunday ones.

To start with there was a strong smell of freshly baked cake coming from the direction of the kitchen and although Mrs. Bird occasionally did her baking during the week she was much more inclined to do it on a Sunday. In any case she never made cakes quite so early in the morning.

Then there was the strange behavior of Mr. Brown. Mr. Brown worked in the City of London and in the mornings he followed a strict timetable. Breakfast was served punctually at half past eight and before that, come rain or shine, he always took a quick stroll round the garden in order to inspect the flowerbeds.

On this particular morning Paddington had nearly fallen over backwards with surprise when he'd drawn back his curtains and peered out of the window only to see a very unkempt-looking Mr. Brown pushing a wheelbarrow down the garden path.

"I was wondering when you were going to put in an appearance," said Mrs. Bird, as Paddington poked his head round the kitchen door with an inquiring look on his face. "I've never known such a bear for smelling out things."

Mrs. Bird hastily closed the oven door before Paddington could see inside and then began serving his breakfast. "Don't go eating too much," she warned. "We're having a party this afternoon and I've enough to feed a regiment of bears."

"A party!" exclaimed Paddington, looking more and more surprised. Paddington liked parties. Since he'd been with the Browns they'd had quite a number of Christmas and birthday ones, but it was most unusual to have a party in between times.

"Never you mind," said Mrs. Bird mysteriously, when he inquired what it was all about. "It's a party—that's all you need to know. And don't go getting egg all over your whiskers," she warned. "Mr. Gruber's been invited, *and* Mr. Curry—not to mention quite a few other people."

Paddington carried his plate of bacon and eggs into the dining room and settled himself at the table with a thoughtful expression on his face. The more he considered the matter, the more mysterious it seemed. The most surprising thing of all was that the Browns' next-door neighbor had received an invitation and Paddington decided it must be a very important occasion indeed. Mr. Curry often turned up at the Browns' parties, but almost always it was because he'd asked himself and very rarely because he'd actually been invited.

Jonathan and Judy were most unhelpful as well. They came into the dining room to say good morning while Paddington was having his breakfast, but as soon as he asked what was going on, they both hurried out of the room again.

"It's a special party, Paddington," said Judy, squeezing his paw as she left. "Just for you. But don't worry—you'll find out all about it later on."

Even Mr. Gruber quickly changed the subject when Paddington asked him about it later that morning.

"I think it's meant to be a bit of a surprise, Mr. Brown" was all he would say. "And a surprise wouldn't be a surprise if you knew what it was."

Before any more questions could be asked Mr. Gruber hastily broke a bun in two and gave half to Paddington before disappearing into the darkness at the back of his shop in order to make the morning cocoa.

When he returned he was carrying a large book on the cocoa tray. "I expect we shall be having fun and games this afternoon, Mr. Brown," he said, as he handed the book to Paddington. "I thought you might like to have a browse through this. It's a giant book of party tricks."

Paddington thanked Mr. Gruber, and after he had finished his cocoa he hurried back in the direction of Windsor Gardens. Mrs. Bird had warned him that with a party in the offing there would be a lot of work to do and he didn't want to be late home. Apart from that Mr. Gruber's book looked very interesting and he was anxious to test some of the tricks before lunch.

But as it happened all thoughts of party games passed completely out of his mind as soon as he reached home.

While he had been out everyone else had been busy and a great change had come over the dining room. An extra leaf had been put in the table and the snow-white cloth was barely visible beneath all the food. Paddington's eyes grew larger and larger as he took in the dishes of jello, fruit and cream, and the plates laden with sandwiches and cakes, not to mention mounds of biscuits and piles of jam and marmalade. In the middle of it all, in a place of honor, was a large iced cake. The cake had some foreign words written across the top, but before he had time to make out what they were, Mrs. Bird discovered him and drove him up to the bathroom.

"You'll have to be at the front door to welcome your guests," she warned. "You can collect as many marmalade stains as you like this afternoon but not before."

With that Paddington had to be content. But as the time for the party drew near he became more and more excited. The Browns had invited not only Mr. Gruber and Mr. Curry but a number of the traders from the Portobello Road as well. Despite his habit of driving a hard bargain Paddington was a popular bear in the market and by the time all the guests had arrived the Browns' dining room was full almost to overflowing.

When the last of the visitors had settled themselves comfortably Mr. Brown called for silence.

"As you all know," he began, "this is Paddington's party. I have an important announcement to make later on, but first of all I think Paddington himself wants to entertain you with a few special tricks he has up his paw."

Everyone applauded while Paddington took his place on the rug in front of the fireplace and consulted Mr. Gruber's giant book of party games. There was one chapter in particular which he'd had his eye on. It was called "One Hundred Different Ways of Tearing Paper," and he was looking forward to trying some of them out.

"I like paper-tearing tricks," said Mr. Curry, when Paddington explained what he was going to do. "I hope they're good ones, bear."

"I think the first one is, Mr. Curry," replied Paddington. "It's called 'THE MYSTERY OF THE DISAPPEARING TEN POUND NOTE!'"

"Oh dear," said Mrs. Brown nervously. "Must it be a ten pound note? Couldn't you use something else?"

Paddington peered at his book again. "It doesn't say you can," he replied doubtfully. "But I expect I could make do with a five pound one."

"I'm afraid I've left my wallet in my other jacket," said Mr. Brown hastily.

"And I've only got coins," said Mr. Gruber, taking the hint as all Paddington's other friends from the market hurriedly buttoned their jackets.

Everyone turned and looked towards Mr. Curry. "You did say you like paper-tearing tricks," said Mr. Brown meaningfully. "And it *is* Paddington's party."

Mr. Curry took a deep breath as he withdrew his wallet from an inside pocket and undid the clasp. "I hope you know what you're doing, bear," he growled, handing Paddington a five pound note.

"So do I!" whispered Jonathan as Paddington took the note and, after consulting his book once more, folded it in half and began tearing pieces out.

The Browns watched anxiously while Paddington folded the note yet again and Mr. Curry's face got blacker and blacker at the sight of all the pieces fluttering to the floor.

After a slight pause Paddington took another look at his book and as he did so his expression changed. Whereas a moment before he had seemed full of confidence, now his whiskers drooped and a worried look came over his face.

"What are you doing now, bear?" growled Mr. Curry as Paddington hurried over and began peering in his ear.

"I'm afraid something's gone wrong with my trick, Mr. Curry," said Paddington unhappily.

"What!" bellowed Mr. Curry, jumping to his feet. "What do you mean—*something's gone wrong with it?*"

"The note's supposed to turn up in your ear," explained Paddington, looking more and more unhappy.

"Perhaps it's in the other one, dear," said Mrs. Brown hopefully.

"I don't think so," replied Paddington. "I think I must have turned over two pages at once in my instructions. I've been doing the paper doily trick by mistake."

"The paper doily trick," repeated Mr. Curry bitterly, as Paddington unfolded the remains of his note and held it up for everyone to see. "My five pound note turned into a bear's doily!"

"Never mind," said Mrs. Bird, bending down to pick up the pieces. "If you stick them all together, perhaps they'll change it at the bank."

"It looks very pretty," said Judy.

Mr. Curry snorted several times as he helped himself to cake. "I've had enough of bears' paper-tearing tricks for one day," he exclaimed.

Mr. Gruber gave a slight cough. "Perhaps you could try one of the other chapters, Mr. Brown," he said. "I believe there's a very good one at the end of the book."

"Thank you very much, Mr. Gruber," said Paddington gratefully. Mr. Curry wasn't the only one who was tired of paper-tearing tricks. Tearing paper, especially banknotes when they were folded, was much more difficult than it sounded, and his paws were beginning to ache.

"There's a very good trick here," he announced after a short pause. "It's called 'Removing a Guest's Vest Without Taking Off His Jacket.'"

"It sounds rather a long trick," said Mrs. Brown doubtfully. "Isn't there anything shorter?"

"Nonsense!" said Mr. Curry from behind a plate of sandwiches. "It's a very good trick. I saw it done once years ago in the theater. I'd like to see it again."

Mr. Brown and Mr. Gruber exchanged glances. "I'm afraid it'll have to be your vest then," said Mr. Brown. "You're the only person who's wearing one."

Mr. Curry's jaw dropped. "What!" he exclaimed. "If you think that bear's going to remove my vest you're—"

Whatever else Mr. Curry had been about to say was drowned in a roar of protest from the others.

"You said you wanted to see it again," called out the man from the cut-price grocer's. "Now's your chance."

With very bad grace Mr. Curry got up from his chair and knelt on the rug in front of the fireplace with his arms raised while Paddington put his paws down behind his neck.

"I thought you said you were going to remove my vest, bear," he gurgled, "not choke me with it."

"Well, it's half off anyway," said Mr. Brown, as Paddington pulled the vest over Mr. Curry's head until it rested under his chin. "What happens now?"

Paddington put his paw up one of Mr. Curry's sleeves and began searching. "I'm not quite sure, Mr. Brown," he gasped. "I haven't practiced this trick before and I

can't see the book from where I am."

"Oh dear," said Mrs. Brown, as there came a loud tearing noise and Paddington pulled something out of Mr. Curry's sleeve. "That looks like a piece of lining."

"What!" bellowed Mr. Curry, struggling to see what was going on. "Did you say *lining*?"

Mr. Brown picked up the book of party games and adjusted his glasses. "Perhaps I'd better give you a hand, Paddington," he said.

After a moment he put the book down again and knelt on the rug. "You're quite right," he said, feeling up Mr. Curry's sleeve. "It definitely says you should pull the end of the vest down the sleeve, but it doesn't say how you do it. It's very odd."

Mr. Gruber joined the others on the rug. "Perhaps if we work backwards it might help," he suggested.

"I think you ought to do something quickly," said Mrs. Brown anxiously as Mr. Curry gave another loud gurgle.

Mr. Gruber studied Paddington's book carefully. "Oh dear," he exclaimed. "I hate to tell you this, Mr. Brown, but one of the pages appears to be missing."

Mr. Curry's eyes bulged and he gave a loud spluttering noise as he took in Mr. Gruber's words. "What's that?" he bellowed, jumping to his feet. "I've never heard of such a thing!"

"I don't think you should have done that," said Mr. Gruber reprovingly. "It sounded as though you split your jacket."

Mr. Curry danced up and down with rage as he examined the remains of his jacket. "*I* split it!" he cried. "I like that. And what was that bear doing at the time, I'd like to know?"

"He wasn't anywhere near," said Mrs. Bird.

"I was looking for my missing page, Mr. Curry," explained Paddington. "I think I must have used it by mistake when I was practicing one of my paper-tearing tricks."

Mr. Brown held up his hand for silence. Mr. Curry's face had changed from red to purple back to an even deeper shade of red again and it looked very much as if it was high time to call a halt to the proceedings. "I'm sure Mrs. Bird can mend it for you later on," he said. "But now I think we ought to get down to the business at hand."

"Hear! Hear!" echoed a voice in the audience.

Mr. Brown turned to Paddington. "Do you know how long you've been with us now?" he asked.

"I don't know, Mr. Brown," said Paddington, looking most surprised at the question. "It feels like always."

"Nearly three years," replied Mr. Brown. "Which is quite a long time, considering you only came to tea in the first place.

"Now," he continued when the laughter had died down, "we have a surprise for you. The other day we had a telegram all the way from the Home for Retired Bears in Lima. It seems that Aunt Lucy is celebrating her hundredth birthday very soon, and the warden thought it would be a nice idea if all her family could be there with her."

"Fancy being a hundred!" exclaimed Jonathan. "That's really old."

"Bears' years are different," said Mrs. Bird.

"They have two birthdays a year, for a start," said Judy.

"Anyway, Paddington," said Mr. Brown, "however many years it is, she's obviously very old and it's a big occasion, so we wondered if you would like to go."

"Speech!" cried someone at the back of the room.

Paddington thought for a moment. "Will I have to travel in a lifeboat and live on marmalade like I did when I came?" he asked.

"No," said Mr. Brown, amid more laughter. "I've been to see one of the big shipping companies and they've promised to give you a cabin all to yourself this time at special bear rates and a steward who knows all about these things to look after you."

Paddington sat down on his chair and considered the matter. Everything had come as such a surprise and his mind was in such a whirl he didn't know quite what to say apart from thanking everyone.

"I shouldn't say anything," said Mrs. Bird. "I should have a piece of cake instead. I've made one specially."

"It's got *bon voyage* written on it," explained Judy. "That means we all hope you have a good journey."

"Come on," said the man from the cut-price grocer's as Paddington began cutting the cake. "Let's have a chorus of 'For He's a Jolly Good Bear Cub.'"

For the next few minutes number thirty-two Windsor Gardens echoed and re-echoed to the sound of singing as Paddington handed round pieces of cake, and it was noticeable that even Mr. Curry sang "And so say all of us" as loudly as anyone.

"It'll seem quiet without you, bear," he said gruffly, when he paused at the front door some time later and shook Paddington's paw. "I don't know who'll do my odd jobs for me."

"Oh dear," sighed Mrs. Brown, as one by one the guests departed until only Mr. Gruber was left. "Everything feels so flat now. I do hope we've done the right thing."

"No more marmalade stains on the walls," said Mr. Brown, trying to sound a cheerful note, but failing miserably as Paddington hurried upstairs leaving the others to make their way back to the dining room.

"I shall leave them on," said Mrs. Bird decidedly. "I'm not having them washed off for anyone."

"Well, I think you're doing the right thing," said Mr. Gruber wisely. "After all, Paddington's Aunt Lucy did bring him up and if it hadn't been for her sending him out into the world, we should never have met him."

"I know what you're thinking, Mary," said Mr. Brown, taking his wife's arm. "But if Paddington does decide to stay in Peru we can't really stand in his way."

The Browns fell silent. When the telegram from Peru first arrived it had seemed like a splendid idea to let Paddington go back there for the celebrations, but now that things were finally settled an air of gloom descended over everyone.

In the few years he'd spent with them Paddington had become so much a part of things that it was almost impossible to picture life without him. The thought of perhaps never seeing him again caused their faces to grow longer and longer.

Their silence was suddenly broken by a familiar patter of feet on the stairs and a bump as the dining room door was pushed open and Paddington entered, carrying his leather suitcase.

"I've packed my things," he announced. "But I've left my washcloth out in case I want a bath before I go."

"Your things?" repeated Mrs. Bird. "But what about all the rest of the stuff in your room?"

"You'll need a trunk for all that," said Judy.

Paddington looked most surprised. "I'm only taking my important things," he explained. "I thought I'd leave the rest here for safety."

The Browns and Mr. Gruber exchanged glances. "Paddington," said Mrs. Brown, "come and sit down. You may not have made much of a speech at the party, but you couldn't have chosen anything nicer to say to us now. You'll never know what it means."

"I know one thing it does mean," said Mrs. Bird. "I can wash those marmalade stains off the walls now with a clear conscience.

"After all," she added, "we shall need plenty of room for fresh ones when Paddington gets back. That's most important."

In the general agreement which followed Mrs. Bird's remark Paddington's voice was the loudest of all.

There was a contented expression on his face as he settled back in his armchair. Although he was most excited at the thought of seeing Aunt Lucy again he was already looking forward to his return, and he felt sure that on a journey all the way to Peru and back he would be able to collect some very unusual stains indeed.

The End